M000119328

ONE IN A MILLION

"Paranormal fans should enjoy this strange brew of revelations and romance, saints and sinners, remembering the past and attempting to save the future."

Kirkus Reviews

"It is an edge of your seat ride that will keep you up at night and leave you unsettled until the last page of the last book."

Amazon Review - 5 stars

"Original, absorbing, exceptional, and a thoroughly entertaining read from beginning to end...that is highly recommended."

Midwest Book Review

A MILLION TO ONE

".. a psychopathic torturer and serial killer in the tradition of Hannibal Lecter."

Kirkus Reviews

"A second powerful work from Faggioli. Non-stop action and suspense on the way to the third book."

"Another thrilling creepy story that grabs you by the throat and takes you on a page turning heart pounding thrill ride! Vivid characters, great plot with twists and turns you can't imagine. Loved it."

ONE PLUS ONE

"If a movie should ever be made of this final installment in Faggioli's (One In A Million, 2016, etc.) trilogy, the Eagles' "Hotel California" might be a contender for the theme song. Like the tune's lyrics, book passages reference voices that call in the middle of the night, characters who are prisoners of their own device, and spirits that could be in heaven or could be in hell."

"One of the BEST stories on the battle between good and evil, as in heaven and hell, I've ever read, and I've recommended it over and over again."

"I was sorry to say goodbye to the characters in the Millionth Trilogy. This is one of the best supernatural thrillers I've ever read."

ANOTHER ONE

THE SNOW GLOBE

ONE GRAY DAY

Book 3 of The Parker Trilogy

TONY FAGGIOLI

Atticus Creative

For Ed, thanks for being such
a shining example of faith.

"When you start to live outside yourself, it's all dangerous."

— Ernest Hemingway

Prologue

THE OLD MAN walked unevenly down the side of the road, his grief like a bag over his shoulder throwing him off balance, his feet stirring up dirt clouds beneath the canopy of maple trees that stretched over the road between him and the cold Connecticut sky. He wanted to be alone, but her words would not leave him.

A flock of sparrows lit from a nearby tree and flew downward, towards the east, before reversing course entirely and swooping towards the west in a sharp curve upwards, as if they were dancing with the currents in the air. And this reminded him of her, too. How he hated to dance but she always managed to get him onto the dance floor and how, once there, she made him feel weightless and less awkward. Like his feet weren't made of stone. Like his heart was made of feathers.

A truck was approaching on the newly paved road. A Studebaker, maybe a few years old, it came by loaded with teenagers, the radio on too loud, playing that irritating new Buddy Holly song that was all over the place these days. The old man sighed. She had left him behind now and it felt like so had the world. Ike would be leaving office soon and God help everyone if that Kennedy kid won office.

Yeah. As if it mattered. As if anything mattered anymore. The sky could collapse like a curtain over the forest now, right before his eyes, and he couldn't have cared less. He knew he wasn't in his right mind, but that was because her words would not let his mind be. They kept floating there. A seven-word sentence rolling over and over behind his eyes, blinding his concentration.

The thing was, the old man knew, he *knew*, you weren't ever supposed to love someone this much. He'd known it all his life. Love was a dangerous thing. He'd seen it stroll in and out of his courtroom like a harlot, from divorce cases to crimes of passion, over twenty-five years on the bench. He told himself that the former didn't understand the weight of true love, and the latter had been crushed by the responsibility of it. All along, thinking that what he and her had was different. That what they had was special. And it was true, for the most part. Their love story had not resulted in divided property or a bloody murder.

But it had ended, all the same, hadn't it? And now the old man finally understood that wild, crazed look people would often have in his courtroom. Eyes full of both rage and desperation. Sometimes the men would have it, sometimes the women. It was the look you had when you had a broken heart with no idea how to fix it. When the realization was finally dawning on you that it would never be fixed. That it would just clunk along now, like a broken motor.

They'd never had any children together. She couldn't. It didn't matter. He loved her all the same. Even more, really, because he was then more the focus of her life. There was more time to read together, take walks together, travel together. They worked with the church for a while, as foster parents, until the goodbyes became too hard. After that, he volunteered with troubled youth in the area and she worked for a time at the orphanage in Waterbury, enjoying the kids like rays from the sun, knowing the warmth would pass each day and the night would come but there was always tomorrow.

He sighed and moved on, down the road, still walking away from home, knowing that eventually he would have to walk back, the day cool but feeling hot, both from his clothes and what he was sure was a rising fever in his body. Not born of sickness, no, but rather born of rage. Step by step he made his way, knowing full well that he'd left behind a house full of family and guests, all dressed in black. But not him. He'd worn his favorite gray suit for her because she said it brought out the blue in his eyes and he wanted to look good for her, one last time. But it had been too much. The wake. The funeral. Like rocks being poured over him in a quarry, he would never escape. The reception afterwards had been too much, too. How could they chat and eat and so blatantly display that life was just moving right along? So he'd fled his own home, the guests speaking in hushed whispers of concern, a few of them telling the others to let him be. To let him walk it off. As if grief were a cramp and not a permanent wound.

The light was beginning to wane and stretch lazily across the horizon, but he didn't have far to go. Just a little further and he'd be there, at her favorite meadow, where she liked to sneak off with hot tea in her *Peanuts* thermos and wait behind the same large oak tree, every time, for the deer to come out. As if the deer didn't know by now, hadn't told each other over the years in whichever way deer communicated, that she was there. That the slender woman with the soft brown hair and caramel colored eyes, that had both faded over the years, was one of the loving humans you could trust not to harm you.

When he arrived, he began to cry immediately, just like he knew he would. He let the tears come because he knew he had no hope in the world of stopping them. They burned his face and blurred his vision and did absolutely nothing to quench his rage that was boiling deep in his soul. He was a church-going man with a regular seat in the same pew every Sunday, and he knew full well that the rage in him now was not healthy. That it was so red hot that it might be from hell itself. He didn't care.

God, you see, had done this to him. God. And he had come to this meadow, like Jacob, to have it out with Him. There would be blood. He took off his suit jacket, folded it in half, laid it over one of the tree stumps nearby, and waded full speed into the tall grass, fists balled up, past wanting answers and only wanting revenge on the being who had done this to him. Who had taught him how to love and then taken that love away, despite a thousand prayers at the foot of her bed the past year, as the leukemia destroyed her one ruthless, gasping, rattling breath at a time.

God had done that to her. God. No need for explanations. That would be too respectful. No. Now it was time for open defiance. Confrontation. And his rage in him agreed, whole-heartedly, that this was a grand idea. That every Maker had to someday contend with what it made. People were not toy cars. They weren't ideas to just be thought up and then erased. No. No. No.

He was still crying as he rolled up his sleeves. When he noticed there were no deer present, he was not the least bit surprised. He had no doubt they knew she was dead and gone and that some-where in the depths of the woods they were mourning, too. And the thought of this brought too much pain to bear, so he looked up into the sky and screamed full bore. He screamed again and again and again, demanding an audience with Him. Cursing Him. Using foul words that he'd never used or allowed others to use in his presence in his entire life. Daring Him to come out.

Daring Him.

Instead, all he got were her words again, back in his mind, refusing to go away. So worried about him. She had been beyond concerned. As if she knew his faith, his soul, were not strong enough for what was coming. For her exit. She had loved him so much she had stayed way past when her pain was too much to try and protect him. But God had finally insisted, hadn't He? So, a day before she died, she uttered her final words to him. Calling him by name. Promising him that he'd be okay. Promising it. Then? Just seven words.

"A broken heart is an open heart," she whispered, her frail hands cupping his, her eyes imploring him to continue the journey of his life without her now. As if it were that easy. As if you could lose the love of your life and just pack up and push on. Like a vagabond. Like some damned nomad.

He was still screaming in the meadow—his voice going hoarse, his face strained, the memory like a vicious shard of glass slicing into his mind—when he noticed it swaying there in the grass all by itself: a lone marigold, determined to outlive the autumn.

It was nothing special but . . . there was something about it that took his rage away, just like that. Perplexed, he realized that his sorrow remained. But the flower kept looking at him and he at it, so he reached down and plucked it.

Night was approaching, and a cold wind came through the hills and across the meadow. But he no longer felt alone. He had the flower, and that was something. A little something. Something better than nothing.

"A broken heart is an open heart," she had said. But had she lied to him? Because the truth was, sometimes a broken heart was just a broken heart. Especially when you were too old to put it back together again. What was he going to do now? Who was he going to turn to? The answer was simple: the same being he'd come here to fight. He struggled mightily to get the words to the prayer out, but he finally did. "God. Please forgive me. Please help me."

Silence. He sighed, walked back to the tree stump, grabbed his suit jacket, and was just about to head back to the house when he felt the air crackle like lightning behind him and go white-hot. Something was there. Human instinct said to turn around and then not to.

For a tick of time, nothing happened, then someone spoke

his name in a voice that was deep, authoritative and came from somewhere to his right.

"William Chesterson?"

"Y-y-yes?" was all he managed in reply.

"You have sinned greatly by calling on the Living God with pride and blasphemy. But you have also prayed for forgiveness and help. And God has heard."

He was suddenly filled with fear. "What? Wait. I'm sorry. I didn't—"

"Don't apologize, my friend. Because with what now lies ahead of you?" The voice was sad. "You may regret that your prayer today was ever heard."

The old man gasped, and as the air around him crackled with energy, he was suddenly ripped from all the reality he ever knew.

But he did not drop the marigold.

Chapter One

THE CITY WAS STAINED with rain. Rain that wouldn't end. Rain that came sideways from the west one day and in flat, hard sheets straight down the next. In Seattle, two weeks of rain would've been nothing to notice, but in Los Angeles, the city built in a desert, it was unheard of. The streets became slick with oil and grease that leached up from the asphalt, making them hard to navigate and turning the freeways into treacherous strings of car accidents. The trash of the city clogged drains, causing the gutters to overflow, and the LA Reservoir reached its highest point since 1948. Hollywood Lake, man-made and hemmed in by the Hollywood Hills, became a spectacle, climbing so high that it began to drag down at the roots of trees along its bank. Landslides struck the Foothills, the Valley flooded and the beaches became frigid in the face of a churning ocean that would not relent. The news reported on it all as if it were the End Times, while the rest of the country, quite honestly, laughed. Angelenos were famous for wilting in the face of a two-day storm, but two weeks? Two weeks was unthinkable. Two weeks was outrageous. Two weeks had them readying for the apocalypse.

Detective Evan Parker sat at his desk, numb, and watched

the wetness outside his window at the LAPD's Hollenbeck Station and couldn't have cared less. He had only one thing on his mind: Güero Martinez, the drug dealer and human sex trafficker that had, nearly a week ago, tried to murder Parker's girlfriend, Trudy. The coward hadn't tried to do it himself, though. No. Instead, he'd called Parker to say it was going to happen and then sent his goons to do all the dirty work. Seven of them, to be exact. Four of whom Parker had sent to the hospital and three of whom Parker had sent to the morgue. It had to be done. If he had to do it all over again, he would, and in exactly the same way.

But that still didn't make what had just gone down, minutes ago, in his meeting with Captain Holland and the Feds, any easier to swallow.

"We're removing you from the case," the cap had said, barely even able to look at Parker.

You should've seen it coming, Parker told himself. The truth was, things had begun to go downhill fast once the press had caught on. Detective Evan Parker? Wasn't he the one who helped catch The Bread Man, that serial killer who had been murdering young women across San Bernardino County? Yes. But hadn't he done that while on suspension? Yes. But, wait. Wasn't he also the one who later saw his partner, Detective Napoleon Villa, get shot to death in Hollenbeck Park? Yeah. Then, waitaminute now, wasn't he *also* the one who just two weeks ago had been involved in a shootout at The Mayan nightclub downtown? The one where his newest partner, Eloy Campos, was shot and wounded? Yep. They'd put Parker on desk duty during the investigation of that most recent fiasco. And now this: an apartment complex in Pasadena turned into a scene from a movie – bodies everywhere, a man with a hunting knife through his hand – during Detective Evan Parker's bold rescue of his girlfriend.

The *LA Times* was in convulsions over the story. In a city and a country already on the brink with police brutality stories all over the news, valid or otherwise, it was trouble, and Parker was trouble. As a result, the department was backpedaling quickly on any notion of supporting him in the face of all the heat.

Anyone could see that it could break either way. But in politics it always only broke one way: the easy way. Parker knew his number was up when the chief had strolled in that morning with a lieutenant, both of them in full-dress code, marching with a purpose, a wake of anxiety spreading out before them.

It reminded Parker of when he was in the military. When the officers got involved, it would all turn into a big shit show, sooner rather than later. And sure enough, that's exactly what had happened the minute they all gathered in the conference room.

SWAT Sergeant Davenport had fought for Parker, and so had Detectives Murillo and Klink, the latter getting so upset that his face turned a beet red that spread up his forehead and over his balding scalp like a hot rash. But surprisingly it had been the Fed heading up the Güero Martinez case, FBI Special Agent Olivia Clopton, who had been most adamant that Parker stay on.

In the middle was Captain Holland, his face twisted with concern as he tried arguing that Parker be allowed to work the case from the station, in a research capacity only. But by then the DA had arrived, in his tight brown suit and fancy blue tie, and he was having none of it. "No way in the world he stays on," he said, waving his hand at Parker. "If he does? When we catch this guy, his defense attorney will be licking his chops. I can hear the arguments for police vendetta and evidence tampering already, and who knows what else."

The room grew silent as the cold rationale spread.

The DA continued, "It would totally jeopardize the entire case. Both ours locally and at the Federal level."

Clopton put her hands on her hips in frustration and nodded slowly.

Parker hated the DA for making complete sense.

Captain Holland sighed. "Fine. I'll transfer him to another case and we'll—"

"No," the lieutenant said, his blue eyes burning with frustration, as if the entire affair of doing his job was annoying. "Enough. Full suspension, pending the completion of *both* investigations into what happened at The Mayan and Arroyo Villas."

"What?" Parker said, stunned. "How long will that take?"

The cap looked at him sympathetically. "Three to six months. But it'll be with pay."

"That's bullshit," Parker spat.

"Would you rather it be without pay, detective?" the lieutenant shot back.

Klink looked at the table in dismay, then murmured to Parker, "Your union rep is right outside the door, man."

"Yeah, go ahead and call him in," the lieutenant snapped.

"Lieutenant . . ." the cap began. But he got no further.

"No, Captain Holland. I've had enough. Let's call it what it is; I think we've got ourselves a loose cannon on our hands here. Something's up with Detective Parker. Until this point, both you and your predecessor have been able to argue the good with the bad. But after what just happened at that apartment complex last week? Are you shitting me?"

"He went in—"

"In direct defiance of Sergeant Davenport's orders that he wait for her and the SWAT unit to arrive."

"Shots were fired. He had to go in," Davenport cut in meekly.

"Of course, he did. Does he ever not? Time and again, Detective Parker has charged in. Need I remind you that his last partner, Detective Villa, is dead? And that his latest partner, Detective Campos, is still laid up in the hospital with multiple gunshot wounds?"

It was the quiet ones you always had to worry about in life, and that was Murillo in a nutshell. Evidently, though, he'd had enough. "That's a low blow!" he shouted, startling the room.

Captain Holland had the look of a man watching a nuclear reactor melting down right before his eyes. First, Klink had mentioned the union rep, then Davenport had spoken out of turn, and now Murillo had just shouted at a superior.

The DA cleared his throat. "I think everyone needs to take a deep breath."

The lieutenant sighed heavily. "Fine." But he said it with a hint of contempt.

Parker seethed. "Screw that. You got something to say? You say it, Lieutenant."

"Yeah?"

"Detective . . . this is insubordination," the chief said firmly.

"No, Chief. Please. Let him be. You want me to say it straight, Detective Parker?" The lieutenant leaned over the table.

"I'd have it no other way," Parker replied, leaning to match him.

"I think you're an agent of chaos. Because wherever you go? Chaos follows. And worse still? People die."

The air left the room in a sickening rush, but what was worse for Parker was the silence that followed. He and the lieutenant both leaned back but continued staring at each other as the group moved on and ironed out a few other details about the case.

After the meeting was adjourned, Parker met with his union rep to hear all his options before telling him he needed some time to think. The rep had pressed, but Parker was having none of it. He. Needed. Time. To. Think.

And that's what he was doing now.

His head was pounding as he stared out at the storm. But he didn't see the storm. Instead, all he saw was Afghanistan.

Big sun. Massive desert. Small lives.

Beckoning to him. Again.

He fought it off. Trudy was being discharged from the hospital in an hour and he had to get there. And he would. After a few more minutes. He concentrated. Decisions in life were like decisions on the battlefield. You had to remember to still your mind.

You had to remember to focus, breathe and aim.

If he stayed on and fought this thing, it'd be a circus that would only get worse. One of the reporters for *The Times* was already asking questions about Parker's military history, and the term "PTSD" was being whispered around. If it all continued to gain momentum then it could drag his VA therapist and a whole host of innocent people – men and women he had served with, friends, even Trudy – into the quagmire.

No. He couldn't allow that. That was the honorable reason for what he was thinking. But the hardest person in the world to lie to was yourself, and Parker knew the real reason: because of something Agent Clopton had said during the meeting that had frozen Parker's attention.

Standing solemnly, he looked around the squad room. It was a good place. A warm place. He hadn't been there long, but between the chatter and ringing phones, it was a place where justice was mostly done. It once had a crooked cop, Detective Hopkins, who'd been working for Güero Martinez, but he'd been dragged out two days ago in handcuffs when the Feds decided they had enough on him to make an arrest. At the moment, it was a fairly quiet place.

But it was no longer his place.

He walked into the captain's office, where the captain, the chief and the lieutenant were still engaged in their ivory-tower conversation, and uttered two words to their shocked faces: "I'm done."

He placed his gun and shield on Captain Holland's desk and walked out, ignoring the cap's calls of protest, and as he made his way to the elevator, he felt a great weight lift off his shoulders.

Focus. Breathe. Aim. On what Agent Clopton had said.

She had informed them all in the meeting that Güero

Martinez, the man who raped, tortured, sold and murdered women from all over the world, had fled to Mexico. In the process, he had kidnapped his pregnant niece and the social worker that was trying to protect her. Since last being seen on surveillance cameras outside a gas station in Tijuana, Güero's whereabouts were unknown. Even worse? His ties with the Mexican Mafia would make finding him now nearly impossible.

"He's become a ghost," Clopton said, looking at Parker a full two seconds too long, as if to drive the point home.

Because they both knew she'd seen Parker's military file, and as such, she knew that in Afghanistan he'd been part of an elite unit tasked with hunting down some of the most heinous members of the Taliban and Al Qaeda.

The unit had no formal name. Instead, they were simply known as "the ghost hunters".

And Güero Martinez, fool that he was, had decided to become a ghost.

———

THE SUN WAS hot and centered between two wood slats in the rundown shack they were now being held in—or, more aptly, imprisoned in. Exhausted, Maggie Kincaid smiled with bitterness as she pressed her head against the splintery wood. Up to this point, she'd successfully managed to forestall her own rape while also protecting Luisa from harm. But there was no telling how long their luck would last.

It had been a week or so since they'd been taken from the warehouse in Hacienda Heights, the police sirens closing in mockingly on the site just as they pulled away. Why? Why hadn't she just waited for Detective Murillo to come that day? Why had she just charged in? Things might be totally different if she hadn't acted so rashly. Now look at things. Her life was in jeopardy for a girl she barely knew, and even in trying to help her she'd only managed to make things worse.

The drive from Hacienda Heights had been made mostly in silence before they'd arrived at another warehouse downtown, just off the 10 Freeway, where she and Luisa were unloaded and separated, Maggie tied to a water pipe that ran along the wall.

Güero had groped Maggie a few times in front of his henchmen before three old women arrived, each dressed in black coats, black shoes, black gloves and gray head scarfs tied at the side. The deference that not only his henchman but Güero himself showed the old women was stunning.

"Where's the girl?" the shortest old woman croaked in a nasty, disdainful voice.

Güero cleared his throat. "Down the hall, in another room."

"Why?"

Seeing Maggie, the tallest woman sneered then shook her head in amazement. "He was going to play first, weren't you, fool?"

Güero looked to the ground as all three women turned their attention to Maggie, their heads moving in unison, like a tiny flock of birds.

The short woman, who was actually bent over severely at the waist as if she suffered from osteoporosis, walked up to Maggie with an intense stare, her black irises almost blotting out the whites of her eyes.

"What do you see, Misha?" the tall woman asked.

Misha rubbed her bent back absent-mindedly. Her face filled with a sudden concern, before she mumbled. "I see the other side, Anastasia."

After studying Maggie further, Misha reached up one of her sleeves, pulled out a vile of liquid, removed the cork at the top of it and began casting the liquid in X-shaped patterns at Maggie's feet. It took a moment to register that the liquid was red, and another second for Maggie to realize it was blood. It struck the carpet of the office floor and instantly began to smoke.

Anastasia stepped forwards, shock in her voice as she looked at the smoke. "What's this?"

Misha leaned her chin back and tilted her head to the side before she replied. "She's not . . . normal."

Unable to take her gaze, Maggie looked away and towards the henchmen, who had all receded to the back of the room. Güero, too, had stepped back and was now by a nearby desk, his face a mask of worry.

"What do you mean, she's not normal? How so?" Anastasia asked, the "s" drawn out briefly, like a tiny hiss.

Misha looked to the final old woman. "Delva?"

The third old woman, who had a slight frame and so many wrinkles across her face that they almost looked drawn on, approached menacingly, removing her gloves as she did so. "She needs a touching," she said. Shooing Misha aside, Delva came forwards and reached up to Maggie's face with old, craggy hands that were covered in tattoos.

Maggie tried to pull away, but she was tied tightly. For a lady who appeared to be over a hundred, Delva moved fast, or at least her hands did. Before Maggie could dodge her again, the old woman's pruny fingers were splayed across her cheekbones, her pinky fingers digging hard into Maggie's jaw.

Then? Nothing. At least for Maggie. For Delva, however, the experience was evidently not pleasant. She shrieked and pulled back almost instantly. "Traveler!" she gasped.

Misha and Anastasia joined her in front of Maggie, the looks of ominous fascination on both their faces making her queasy. *Great. I've gone from a psychopathic rapist to three crazy old goats that are prob—*

That's when she noticed that each woman had inverted crosses tattooed at the base of their throats. She looked at Delva's hands, which were now folded over her chest defensively; large, black pentagrams were tattooed on the back of each of them.

Shit! They're witches!

It took crazy to another dimension. She and Luisa were quite likely in the hands of downright evil people, possibly even a cult.

Luisa began screaming from the room down the hall where she'd been taken by Felix. But her screams were more filled with rage than with fear. Things began getting slammed around in her room. There was the sound of a glass shattering.

Güero immediately motioned for two of his henchmen to investigate. Upon following his orders there was a chorus of arguing from Luisa's room, and when the henchmen returned one of them had Felix by the collar and the other had Luisa by the arms. Her top was torn and her bra pulled down at an angle over her ribs, leaving one breast awkwardly exposed. She fought one arm free to cover herself, her face filled with desperation as she looked to Maggie, her lower lip trembling violently.

There were scratch marks across Felix's face and forearms.

The old Güero was back instantly. As if the old women weren't there anymore, he marched across the room. Looking from Luisa to Felix he screamed, "What the *hell* is this?"

The old women, who had turned to stare at Luisa as if she were a prized goose, now focused their attention on Felix.

"Ahhhh," Delva moaned with a sick, perverted passion. "How delectable."

"What?" Güero snapped.

"Your boy here?" she replied with a chuckle. "I can see it in him. He's the one we've been looking for. *He's* the father of the baby."

Güero was Luisa's uncle, and he didn't even need to ask. Luisa began to sob the minute he looked at her, indirectly sealing Felix's fate.

Felix's eyes went wide with fear and he began to shout his denials. But Güero's eyes went wide, too; first with shock and dismay, then pure rage and, finally, madness. But it was a calm, scary sort of madness. Sighing, he slowly rolled up his shirt sleeves and began to methodically turn the rings on his fingers around, one by one, so that the stones were facing his palms.

Felix had evidently seen this little ritual before. "No, *jefe*," he mumbled in terror. "Please don't. Please!"

Maggie, seeing what was coming, looked to Luisa. "Close your eyes!" she said. "Close your eyes, Luisa!"

She did. Maggie did.

But horror comes in sounds, too.

And there was nothing like the sound of a man being beaten to death.

Chapter Two

FATHER SOLTERA MOVED WEARILY across the open meadow, which was still dark beneath the dead-light glow of the strange sky in this place, Ikuro and his violin still in his mind. In their haste to flee, they'd been forced to leave Ikuro unburied. A sacrilege back home, Father Soltera doubted that mattered much here. In this place, those who came were dead already in some ways, alive in others, and rites of passage meant little to those who were simply passing through. He had no idea how he knew this, but he did.

Michiko had remained quiet the entire walk. He glanced over at her a few times, one time finding her looking contemplative, the next, looking sad. Her slight features and pretty face no longer reconciled with the fierce warrior he'd seen in battle with the dire wolves. The power within her was great, and acted like a forcefield that reverberated outward before retracting back inside her. But it brought with it no fear, most likely due to the pure serenity of the creature it inhabited. She was an enigma with swords, but he was beyond relieved that she was with him. If she weren't, he would've been dead five times over by now.

When they reached the edge of the forest there was no hesitation. They plunged in at a spot that looked like a trail head, which proved to be overgrown in many spots. It barely mattered, as the trees were sparse. Before long, they emerged into another meadow, this one smothered in tall grass and patches of choking ivy. The trail continued and was hedged at the sides, as if someone—or something—maintained it.

Michiko stopped. "Wait."

He did as he was ordered but he didn't have to ask why. "I feel it too," he said, and sighed with relief.

She looked at him and nodded. The air here was filled with a peace you could actually breathe.

"Why?" he muttered softly.

"Why, what, *tomodachi*?"

"Why here? What makes here so different than back there?" He tossed a thumb over his shoulder. Then he added, "And please, no more mysterious *Twilight Zone* talk, okay?"

A quizzical look came over her face. "*Twilight Zone*?"

He shook his head. "Never mind. I just mean—"

"I know what you want, *tomodachi*. You want what all of your kind want: answers. Even though you should know full well by now that answers only lead to more questions."

"I guess that's true."

"My *sensei* taught it to me."

Father Soltera looked around before he replied, remembering countless hours in the confessional with people going round and round about their lives from one week, one month, one year to the next. "Your *sensei*?"

"Yes. You would like him. He helps others, much like you. He also says it is the great truth of the universe, this endless seeking. I've been dead for five hundred years, *tomodachi*. Still, I seek too."

"How? I thought heaven meant an end to all that."

She smiled. "Heaven?"

"Yeah. I mean, I believe. You do too, right?"

"Of course," Michiko replied. "And heaven is most certainly real. It awaits us all. But no one said that the second you leave the reality of your existence on earth that you go directly there. Some do, yes. But most have many more realities to pass through along the way."

"How is that possible?"

"Some—indeed, most—are not ready or equipped or prepared for the ultimate truth. They have too many memories that haunt them, too many weaknesses that would inhibit full transfiguration. So, the path that awaits them next is simply one that leads to less pain, and the one after that to lesser still. Like the path before you now." She waved her hand before them.

"You mean . . ."

"I will be here if you need me. But where you go next requires a solitary journey."

"Like facing another nightmare?" Father Soltera replied sarcastically.

The look of sadness came over her face again. "No, *tomodachi*. Like facing your only true love."

His throat clutched up and he swallowed hard. "What?"

"*Tomodachi*, did you not think for one moment that when your soul went wandering that it would not seek her, and in so doing, find the place where she was?"

"You mean—"

"Yes. She's been trapped here since her coma began. And you? You are the only one who can truly free her. And, I've surmised now, she is the only one who can truly free you."

Father Soltera looked down the path. "How?"

Michiko shook her head. "Later. For now? Just go."

He did.

As he stepped away from Michiko something between them tugged and snapped, as if all along there'd been a protective film over them and he was now separating from it. It took a moment or two for him to confirm this sensation; the air around him was suddenly much cooler and a mild pressure filled his ears.

He began walking hesitantly down the path, the soil growing

looser beneath his feet the further he went. Fear tugged at him. He glanced back to see Michiko still there. He wanted to turn back, but the fear tugging at his shoulder was not enough to overwhelm the curiosity pulling him forwards. Could it be true? Could Gabriella really be here?

He pushed on. As the forest closed in around him, his feeling of isolation grew. The path widened, then narrowed, then widened again before it cut through a thicket up ahead. He remembered being a boy and running through the woods behind his house in Missouri, when he would charge into the thickets with his friends, oblivious to what was beyond, until he wasn't. That was the blessing of youth: no apprehension of the unknown. But now? Now he was an old man. And the denser the woods, and the more the threat of the unknown, the greater the urge to turn back.

Vines were interwoven with the trees, crisscrossing in some sections in helix-type shapes that seemed unnatural. He steeled his nerves and pushed through. The path grew narrower and less cultivated, the trees on either side having overgrown it so much that it was almost like a tunnel now. There was a white light in the distance, creating a gradient down the tunnel. Where he was now, about halfway through, was the darkest point. Father Soltera kept his eyes on the foliage around him, and he was glad he did.

Slowly, arms began to slither out from it, fingers splayed and grasping, as if they belonged to people on the other side who had dropped a coin down here.

Except *he* was the coin.

Some of the arms were pale, others dark, some had streaks of blood, others looked as if they'd been torn or gnawed on. They reached out for him and he was about to turn and run full speed back to the protection of Michiko when instead a tremor moved through the air, the sensation you feel when someone is looking at you. It was a freeze-frame sensation set to the aperture of his heart.

It was the sensation he felt every single time he and Gabriella locked eyes, when the seeing *inside* of one another was still an awkward fumbling.

Except, this time, he *couldn't* see her. At all. Anywhere. Not yet. But she was there.

He sensed that he had to break through this thicket and out the other side before he could get to her. So, instead of fleeing, he carefully bobbed and weaved his way between the arms, realizing that some were broken at the elbows or wrists. It was obvious that people before him had come through here . . . and some of them hadn't made it. Somehow he knew they were now part of the woods and vines, reaching out for others. Again, a memory from his childhood came to him: playing catch-as-catch-can. The grips and holds.

Except here there was no letting go.

Just then, the fingertips from a hand he hadn't seen brushed against his neck. He jerked away a little too forcefully, and for a moment he was filled with terror as he felt he was about to lose his balance.

But it wasn't his balance that was threatening his demise. The path, too, was tilting from side to side, like some sick carnival ride.

He stutter-stepped until he righted himself, resenting the slowing reflexes of age, and suppressed the urge that came over him to run the rest of the way. Most of the broken arms were up there. Like sacrifices to the cause of this hellish little tunnel, they'd no doubt still be able to push or pull their victims to their doom. He moved on, this time with determination. The tilting of the path lessened, and the arms receded.

Before long, he was out the other side.

The path had turned to cobblestone. He wasted no time getting as far away from the tunnel as possible. Moving up the cobblestone he at first felt relief, but that was instantly ruined by the displacement of time and space around him. With each step he took, the world around him rotated: from day to night, from when the forest was young to when the forest was old, from times of fire to times of snow, from here to the other world, from life to decay, from Michigan to Missouri, from his boyhood to his manhood. A kaleidoscope of images turned with each of his footsteps.

He stopped walking and closed his eyes to give his mind time to recover. What was happening? How was this happening?

And that's when he heard her voice, soft as the rain on a quiet morning.

Leave the path, Bernie.

He looked around. The woods to his left were like a wall, but to his right was a wide-open field, and beyond the field was a lake. And in the center of the lake was a tiny island.

And on the island, Gabriella stood, dressed in jeans, a white t-shirt and a beige leather jacket.

Upon seeing him, she dropped to her knees. But Father Soltera did not do the same.

Instead, as if struck by lightning, he ran to her, kicking off his shoes as he reached the shore and plunging in the water. Crazy, foolish old man. There was no way he could swim that distance at his age. No way at all.

But he had to try.

———

CORCORAN STATE PRISON was a walled-off section of inmate housing, full of anger and bitterness, taking up three square miles of King County, California. Hector Villarosa thought he'd been to prison before, and technically he had, but after only five days as a resident here now, he was fully aware that this place was the real deal. This place was built to break you, even if you were already broken. It didn't care. His fellow inmates didn't care. As with any prison, the only one you could trust in here was yourself, plain and simple, but the added dimension for Corcoran was that even trusting yourself, your instincts, your perceptions, was a sketchy idea.

He was in his cell, blissfully alone. His cellmate, Roberto, had been sent to the Security Housing Unit, or SHU, for smuggling in heroine from his obese girlfriend, who had hidden it in a ziplock baggie that she'd tucked into the folds of her stomach fat. He hated Roberto. He talked too much about nonsensical bullshit and took no hints when you tried to keep to yourself. Still. Alone was no good either. Because alone only left you with your memories, and that was worse. Way worse. Like now, when his mind was turning back to the day of his sentencing.

Having pled guilty to all the charges levied against him, his sentencing hearing had come quickly: twenty-five years without the possibility of parole for the murder of David Fonseca and attempted murder of Hector's ex-girlfriend, Marisol Perez. In exchange for this, his public defender had managed to get the lesser charges of illegal possession of a firearm, evading arrest and reckless endangerment all dropped.

Not that Hector cared. He knew what he'd done, and The Gray Man had made it very clear the price that was going to be paid. At his sentencing hearing, as the judge droned on about the repercussions of his acts, Hector kept his head bowed. Only when Marisol's father stood to speak did Hector raise his eyes, and even then only briefly, for the hate-filled gaze that greeted him made him look away immediately. Just when he thought it couldn't get any worse, he got an update from Marisol's father he would've preferred never hearing: Marisol was paralyzed from waist down, would likely never walk again and was in speech therapy trying to learn how to form basic words and sentences with the throat that Hector had put a bullet through.

"Why did you do this to my little girl?" Marisol's father asked, his voice trembling with agony and rage. "Because you were *jealous?*" And it was the sound of utter disbelief in this last word that broke Hector down. He lowered his head again and fought hard against his own emotions.

David Fonseca's mother was next, and she had been no easier to deal with. She sounded stoned, probably on stress medication, as she shouted at him to raise his head and look at her. When he did not, because he could not, because his shame was like a fist on the back of his neck, she called him a coward in Spanish and then said what she had to say. "I want you to one day find yourself in hell, on fire, in eternal agony for what you've done to my son. I know it's a sin to say that, but I don't care. Not one bit. You . . . took away . . . my baby!" she screamed, before her family rushed around her to hold her up and her sobbing erupted into loud wails that beat at Hector's heart like a sledgehammer.

My God, what have I done? he thought. But God did not answer, nor did The Gray Man, who had abandoned him after his visit to Hector's cell, when he'd taught him prayers of prose. Evidently this moment, this time, was meant for him to face alone. Still, all the repercussions, all the consequences to what Hector had done was beginning to become very apparent.

When the judge announced that Hector would be serving his time at Corcoran, Hector barely flinched. He knew that was coming. Agents of evil, serving the very hell that Marisol's mother was damning him to, had already told him so. Because Curtis Ruvelcaba, the man who was Hector's gang mentor, was now also in Corcoran, after being transferred from San Quentin.

He was the man they wanted Hector to kill. The same man The Gray Man had tasked him to save.

The day Hector boarded the bus, he was in shackles both physical and mental. It was almost beyond comprehension. Because what The Gray Man was asking him to do was basically to go behind enemy lines, into a den of evil, and do something good. Plain and simple. And in a place like Corcoran, that was almost guaranteed to get him killed.

The three-hour drive up the 5 Freeway from Downtown Los Angeles had been made in pouring rain. Arriving in his orange jumpsuit, he was strip-searched and forced to change into the dark blue pants—stenciled with the letters "CD CR" and "PRISONER" running down the length of one leg—and light blue shirts of Corcoran's standard inmate attire.

That was five days ago, and so far he hadn't caught sight of Curtis anywhere. He was relieved for that. Hector had managed to lay low. He'd been kept alone a few days until they figured out how to process him, then left a day in his cell with no yard time until he'd been paired with Roberto. Yesterday had been Hector's first day mingling with the general population, divided as it was.

He laid back in his cot, laced his fingers behind his head and sighed. There were some books that were so accurate they were timeless in their truth, and Corcoran not only displayed but practically screamed the truths in *The Lord of the Flies*. This place was a cement island amid a sea of dirt. The men here were not children but acted like it. Power was taken by force, and life, in the final equation, was cheap. All that mattered, truly mattered, was what tribe you aligned yourself with to survive. Whites in the Aryan Nation or Nazi Lowriders, blacks in the Crips or Bloods, Southern California Hispanics called *Sureños* or Southerners, and Northern California Hispanics called *Norteños* or Northerners.

But in Hector's case, wouldn't you know it, even the north/south rules did not apply. Because Curtis was a Southerner just like him and it didn't matter.

A guy named Raul, another Southerner and evidently on Güero Martinez's payroll, had approached Hector that morning in the cafeteria, with two buddies and a smile on his face. "We know why you're here, *pendejo*. Do you remember why you're here . . . or do you need another beat down like our homies gave you back in County?"

Hector nodded, his wounds from that fight still not fully healed. "I know why."

"Good. We'll set it up in a lil time, get you a good shiv. You just be ready. Understand?"

Again, Hector nodded.

"Don't just bounce your head at me, bitch. Say it!" Raul snapped.

"Yeah. I understand," Hector said, looking at Raul with eyes full of weariness.

"Good. Next time you just bob your head around at me, you'll be doing it in my lap, *puto*. Got that?"

Hector wanted to punch him in the face, but he knew better. Instead, feeling like Piggy, he said, "Yeah. I got it."

Raul glared at him before he motioned his head to the rest of his crew, and they moved away.

Chapter Three

PARKER WAS IN THE ELEVATOR, riding down alone, when Napoleon appeared out of nowhere, right next to him. "You sure you want to do this?"

"Yeah," Parker replied with a stiff jaw.

"Vengeance is a double-edged sword, rookie."

Parker scoffed. "Don't I know it."

"You're thinking of the boy—"

"Yep," Parker cut him off, hoping that by doing so he could also cut off the memory of the Taliban boy back in the war, a child-sniper who killed one of Parker's best friends one day in the desert. The same boy Parker had hunted down and shot in the spine from five hundred yards away before leaving him to die slowly in the hot sand.

Napoleon shook his head. "I can't help you if it's vengeance you're seeking, Parker."

"I understand." But Parker's chest swelled with emotion. "But I have to do this."

"No. You are *choosing* to. There's a difference. But if you do it for the right reasons? In the right way? You won't have to go it alone."

"And what, exactly, qualifies as the 'right' way?"

"C'mon, Parker. Think first. Then shoot your mouth off."

The elevator continued its descent, the lighted numbers of the display overhead moving floor to floor. Parker turned to face his old partner, who was an angel of some kind now, or an agent of the afterlife. Napoleon's face and hair were the same, but today he wore a brown suit with a yellow shirt. "Someone's dressed up."

Nap nodded. "I had a funeral to attend."

Parker raised his eyebrows.

"Yep. The dead visit graves, Parker. To help some cross over, yes, but mostly to comfort those left behind."

"Someone you knew, then?"

"Yes. Gabriel Mejia. An old high school buddy. Died of a massive heart attack while eating breakfast at Denny's."

"Did he make it?"

"Make it?"

"To heaven?"

Napoleon looked serious. "That's above my pay grade."

Perplexed, Parker replied. "Well, were you at least there . . . in the end, I mean?"

"No. I wasn't. Someone else got him to the door."

"The door?"

"Yep. You die. You see the light, you follow the light. You get to the door. You go through the door. From there, it's all between you and what's next."

Far from being intrigued, Parker was suddenly sad, and the feeling confused him.

As the elevator reached the ground floor and the doors opened, Napoleon sighed and said, "Back to the point. Why? Why go after Güero?"

Parker took a deep breath, walked through the lobby, said goodbye to the desk officer for what was probably the last time, and exited the building out into the drizzling rain. The wetness kissed at his face and ears. When he looked at Napoleon, he noticed that the rain ran off him like glass. For the first time, Parker also noticed a very soft tan glow to his old partner.

I've gone crazy, Parker thought. *I'm seeing ghosts.* But he knew better now. *No. I'm not. On either count.*

"Still waiting," Napoleon said firmly.

Having mulled over his answer, Parker went with his gut. "Justice. That's why I'm going after him. For justice."

Napoleon nodded approvingly. "Right answer."

"You sound surprised."

"Yeah. I didn't think you were smart enough to get it right, to be honest."

Parker chuckled. "Well . . . screw you, too. Partner."

"Hey. Smarts ain't your department. They are, however, *hers.*"

"Hers?"

Napoleon bobbed his head over Parker's shoulder and blinked away just as Parker heard a woman shout from behind him. "Detective. Wait up!"

It was Agent Clopton.

The rain had gotten heavier, so he motioned her over to a nearby shuttle stop with a kiosk they could stand under. "What's up?"

Joining him, she ran her fingers through her cropped blond hair and nodded, looking nervous. Again, he noticed her sharp cheekbones. "Listen," she said, "you don't have to do this. I can still bring you on in a support capacity on our side or—"

"We both know that's not true."

"Yes, it is."

"Okay. Fine. You get me behind a desk in the Federal building, somehow, someway. No doubt over the vehement protests of that asshole lieutenant up there, who maybe gets you in hot water with your superiors."

She shrugged.

"For what?" he continued. "So I can push papers around a

desk, or do some internet research on Güero? Do you really think that's going to catch him?"

A look of defeat came over her face. "No."

They were alone in the kiosk when a shuttle pulled up. They both waved it off and it drove away.

After a moment, she spoke again. "But . . . your career."

"It's in a shamble anyway. It has been ever since I left South Central and caught my very first detective case in the cesspool that is East LA."

"The Hall Case, you mean?"

"Surprise, surprise. You've done your homework," Parker replied. But he thought again of Napoleon's words. She was smart.

"A lot didn't add up there."

He smiled. "Nor was it ever meant to."

"What's that supposed to mean?"

She was about his age, with a quizzical look that was intense. He looked her off. "You wouldn't understand."

"Try me."

His neck was tight with stress, so he rotated it between his shoulders before he answered her. "There were . . . uh . . . forces at work that . . . um . . . complicated things."

Both her eyebrows plummeted with confusion. "Forces?"

"Like I said, you wouldn't understand."

"I mean, from what I read, Caitlyn Hall was into devil worshiping. Some sort of ritual got her killed, right? Kyle Fasano was wrongly accused, blah, blah. Your partner disappeared in the woods in Monterey after a concussion or something. And so on and so forth."

He laughed. Hard. Then nodded. "Yeah. That's what happened, all right. And so on and so forth? Yeah, I guess that's one way of putting it."

"You saying there's more to it?"

"I'm saying you've heard what they wanted you to hear, as

best they could wrap a bow around a rather crumpled box of turds. That's what I'm saying."

"And?"

He shook his head. "Not a chance. Leave it alone. All of it."

Her eyes bore into him, as if she were either fighting the urge to interrogate him or pissed that he had dismissed her line of questioning. He realized it was probably a little of both. "Fine. I'll leave it alone. For now. But, shit, Parker. You caught a serial killer. You know how many of us at the Bureau would kill to have that one on our resumés?"

"No. I *helped* to catch a serial killer. In the process, a good man, a grandfather on the edge of retirement, died. And it was Tamara Fasano, not me, who finally brought Troy Forester's horror show to an end."

"C'mon. You're not giving yourself enough credit, you're the one—" She paused, then looked down and began to fiddle with her hands. He realized that this whole conversation had been a stalling tactic.

The sidewalk around them was becoming glazed with the rain. A group of uniformed cops passed on the way to the parking garage nearby. "What's really going on, Agent Clopton?"

She sighed. Her navy blue suit was fitted, with tight hem lines down her slacks to blue dress flats. Pure FBI, all the way. Finally, she replied, "I'm conflicted."

He bobbed his head. "Well, shit. That was honest."

"Yeah. I ain't big on sleight of hand, Detective."

"As of fifteen minutes ago, I'm not a detective anymore."

She shook her head. "You will be again. Someday. I'm sure of it."

"Yeah? Well, I'm glad one of us is."

"But in the meantime . . ." And now her eyes said she wished she were a better poker player. She looked around nervously.

The moment grew still between them. "In the meantime . . . what?" he gently prodded.

"If you're going to do what I think you're going to do . . ."

"You mean what you want me to do. What you *hinted* at in that conference room?"

"I absolutely deny—"

"Cut the shit, Agent Clopton. Ain't no one wearing a wire here, and besides that brown bird getting wet over there on top of that utility box? There ain't no witnesses."

Her face pinched up in anger. Not at him, he didn't think, but rather at something else. Finally, she spat it out. "I'm about the law. And so are you."

He nodded.

"But the other night? At the Long Beach port?"

The rain pattered around them as the air grew still. "Yeah?"

"They found another container. One not on the manifest or on our radar at all." Her voice sounded hollow. "So, we didn't get to it because we didn't know to get to it."

Parker said nothing. Instead, he waited.

"Fifty-eight women. Eighteen dead. Their container was buried in a stack. No one heard their screams. They were no doubt left there after the bust we made at San Pedro harbor spooked the whole organization. Though, I'm not sure I entirely believe that."

Parker leaned against the kiosk and crossed his arms. "Oh?"

"No. I think Güero did it on purpose. To punish us for inter-fering. To show us that he will always win. Because monsters like him never think they're going to lose."

"And?"

"And now it's even worse; he's kidnapped that poor pregnant girl. And the social worker? Do you know about her?"

Parker shook his head.

"Her name's Maggie Kincaid. Thirty-one. Recently moved here from New York after killing her ex-fiancé in self-defense after he'd stalked her for over five years."

Parker raised his eyebrows. "Damn."

"Yeah. Can you even imagine? Surviving that whole experience and then having the universe plop your ass right down in the situation she's in now? With Güero, of all people?"

"Yeah. It sucks. But you've already told me something about her that's very important to know, in light of her circumstances."

A chilly wind had kicked up across the grass and swept up and over the kiosk, rattling the plastic advertising billboards within it. "What's that?"

"She's killed before. Which means she can kill again if she has to."

"Good point," Clopton replied. "Which leads to my next—"

Parker cut her off. "I'm going after him. Yes. But one, you already knew that, and two, no one else needs to know that."

"You have ex-associates you're going to lean on, I take it?"

Parker thought of Melon, down in Cabo and living the easy life now. "Only one down that way. But he'll be enough." Then he smiled to himself, remembering Napoleon, and added, "Or maybe two."

"Or maybe three," she said.

They locked eyes.

"You realize that I can't draw outside the lines with you, right?" Clopton said softly.

Parker nodded.

She nodded back. "But that doesn't mean we can't color together."

He was surprised. "Yeah?"

"I'll be in touch."

When she walked away, Parker was speechless.

———

MAGGIE LOOKED across the shack at Luisa. Since Felix's murder, she had become the queen of one-word answers. At first this seemed normal. Just pure shock. But that had been nearly a week ago, before they'd been driven south of the border, and things hadn't improved much. Now, lying on her cot, Luisa was just staring off into the distance.

They had three guards. The same faces each day. All too big for Maggie to take on by herself. It didn't matter. She felt so weak that even her bones were tired, but her mind was still working, and that was a good thing. The guards rotated shifts, one of them always outside the shack door, another usually leaning against the black Escalade parked outside or sitting on a blue Igloo cooler that was dirty and cracked. The third guard was usually taking a turn getting some sleep in the Escalade.

On occasion, one of them would leave and come back with food and drinks for everyone. Always bagged chips or sandwiches, never anything in "to-go" boxes. There were no logos on any of the plastic wrap or the price stickers. That meant the closest thing nearby was probably a gas station with a mini-mart. These guys were professional, too. Not once did one of them come back with beer, tequila or anything else that would've impeded their senses and given her an advantage if she decided to make a move.

She had nicknamed the three of them Eenie, Meenie and Miney.

Eenie had broad shoulders and a handsome face that she was going to have no problem putting a bullet into someday, because he was all hands with her whenever he had the chance. Nobody in their right minds was stupid enough to touch Luisa after what happened to Felix. But it was also obvious that they were under some kind of orders not to touch Maggie, which kept her mostly safe. Still, whenever she needed her shackles loosened or asked to be escorted to the port-a-potty outside, Eenie was first to volunteer and snuck in every chance he got to "accidentally" touch her chest or ass.

It was better than being raped but still infuriating, and when she laid in bed at night and listened to the coyotes out in the desert yipping to one another, it was Eenie's end—and how she would affect that end—that lulled Maggie to sleep.

Meenie, meanwhile, was dumb as an ox and as thick as one, too. He had a block head and a crew cut, with beady eyes and a mouth too small for his fat cheeks. His voice was deep, but he rarely spoke.

The chatterbox of the group was the short and skinny Miney. He spoke mostly in Spanish, sometimes in English, and always had something to say. About soccer, or a job he had done somewhere for this person or that, or the weather, or how much he'd like to get word from Güero to be allowed to gang rape them both.

Maggie had tried repeatedly to find some redeeming quality in at least one of them that she could work on. A soft spot, a trigger for their conscience, anything. But she couldn't. They were flat-out evil human beings who liked to talk about killing people, making money and forcing women to do things they didn't want to do. After days now of listening to them intently, it was painfully obvious that they were simply barren people, living a barren existence.

She and Luisa were in a hopeless situation. At least right now. Which left Maggie mostly trying to fend off that hopelessness. It was obvious that Luisa had already surrendered to it. But Maggie couldn't. If she did, they'd have zero chance of survival. And she didn't want to die at the hands of monsters, plain and simple.

So she sat like a stone golem and watched them through the gaps in the wood slats and studied them carefully: the way they walked (Miney had a slight limp in his right leg), what their dominant hands were (only Meenie was a leftie), who was most likely to zone out with boredom (Eenie, for sure). They each had cell phones, which they played with while they sat around and charged in the car. That was good. It meant there was cell reception here.

When she got her chance, she'd go for Eenie's phone. He

was the youngest and therefore the most likely to bend whatever rules they were supposed to be following. If she could get his phone, she could make a call. But how? And then what? A call could be cut off, could take forever to connect, and she no doubt wouldn't have enough time to explain everything. And even if she had the time, she had absolutely no idea where they were anyway.

That's when a new idea came to her. She squinted, feeling the corner of her eyes tighten against the desert dryness that was gripping her face. Of course. Yes. It just might work.

Eenie was the one on duty now. Perfect. She knocked on the wall, making Luisa jump on the bed.

"What?" Eenie said, irritation in his voice.

"I gotta go to the bathroom."

For a second, she panicked, as Meenie began to stand up from the cooler. But she figured Eenie would want to be the one to take her, and sure enough, he waved Meenie off.

Eenie always kept his phone in the back left pocket of his dark jeans, and as he opened the shack door and escorted her out, she could see that it was right there. She steeled herself and let him walk her to the port-a-potty. When they got there, he, as expected, got his freebie in by pressing up against her from behind for a few seconds before he spun her around to take off her cuffs. Smiling at her, he motioned his hand to the bathroom door.

She nodded and said, "I'm gonna be a while, if you know what I mean," just to spoil his mood.

Once inside, she slammed the door as if she'd closed it all the way . . . then slowly reopened it, leaving herself a slit through which to see as he turned to the side, his back mostly to her, and pulled out his phone. Like he always did. Each and every time they'd done this little ritual before.

Routine. It was human nature. It was also what almost killed her with Michael, when he was after her that first year, but now it might actually be what helped her. Eenie's routine had thus far gotten her three of the digits of his phone's password code. Two, eight and nine. One more. She just needed one more. The port-a-potty was situated about twenty feet from the shack, in clear view of the shack. Meenie had not noticed that the door was ajar.

Eenie had out his phone but was looking out over the desert at something that had caught his eye.

Maggie rolled her eyes. *C'mon!*

After seconds that felt like minutes, he finally turned his attention back to his phone. His right thumb punching it out: Two . . . eight . . . nine . . .

One.

Maggie Kincaid closed her eyes and thanked God.

One part of her plan down. One to go.

Chapter Four

THE WATER WAS cool and blissful, and it splashed away the tears of joy spilling down his face with every stroke he took towards the island. It was okay to love. It was okay to care. It was okay to be here. It was. Wasn't it? The old voices of persecution and shame tugged at him like kelp trying to tangle his legs and drag him down. *Stupid fool, you aren't good enough, handsome enough, decent enough, young enough for this. And what of your oath? What of your faith? What of your God?*

He was tired of them, these voices. Even if they were "right" in some ways. What he felt, he felt. Sometimes that was enough. Sometimes "wrong" was relative, and the needle of your mind only pointed to where the gravity of your heart directed it.

Stroke after stroke he made his way to her, waiting for exhaustion to overtake him as his heart struggled in his chest and his legs kicked, heavier and heavier, against the water.

Breathe, he told himself. *Pace yourself. You have to make it. You haven't come all this way to die now.*

The thing was, the mere sight of her filled him with so much hope that he simply couldn't stop, wouldn't stop, swimming. He literally willed himself to the shore, and overcome with emotion, once he was there, he crawled to her. Still on her knees, she did the same, and they scrambled to one another like children before she wrapped her arms around him so tightly that she stifled his gasps from the effort of the swim. "Bernie," she said, her voice a tight squeak. "Bernie." It was her. The real her. Not a mirage. Not a twisted nightmare in disguise.

Then, knowing it was a sin but helpless to stop himself, he did something he'd always fantasized about, back home: he buried his face in her hair. That marvelous, sleek, shiny black hair caressed his face and dragged across his lips. It smelled of plums and lavender and he thought, surely, this would be the end of him, that his chest would tighten and the world would go numb and that would be just fine by Bernardino James Soltera. Death could take him. Like this. Right here. Right now. It would be a much better way to go than in the vessel of a body ravaged to pieces by the cancer spreading within him.

After a few moments she cried out in disbelief. "What are you doing here? How did you—"

He drew back and put the four fingers of his right hand gently over her lips, his thumb curved just below her delicate chin. Looking at her face, the soft cheeks, the thoughtful eyes and . . . there it was . . . that small, insecure little smile of hers. In seeing her, he felt so convicted that he had to pray. *God, God please forgive me, but I do love her so. Father, I'm so sorry, but I do.*

She pleaded with him. "Bernie? Please tell me how you got here."

"It's such a long story," he replied, his voice barely a whisper.

She reached up with both hands and wiped away his tears. "I want to hear it. All of it. I heard the song, Bernie! 'Ombra Mai Fu'? I heard our song."

Our song. So, it was true. She had felt it too, the bond between them, strung through the notes of music written almost three hundred years ago. Each of them a high note for the other's low. Playing beneath the canopy of an eternal orchestra.

"I played it each time I visited you, every month," he said. "Every time."

She nodded and smiled. "I heard. I don't know how, but I heard."

He choked back more tears. "I knew it. I just knew . . . if I played it, you'd hear it."

"I can't believe you did that: visited my grave every month."

Her words momentarily knocked him speechless. Gathering himself together, he took a few deep breaths, before he decided on a measured response. "Grave?"

An eddy of perplexity came across her face, mirroring those that were rippling here and there across the lake around them. "Y-yes." But that was all she said before she looked away, as if she wasn't sure she wanted to discuss it any further.

Father Soltera shook his head softly. "You aren't dead, Gabriella."

It was as if he'd slapped her. She recoiled from him and sat back on the tops of her feet. "What are you talking about?"

He looked around. He and this woman, they had been romantics back in the real world, yes, but they had also been sharp realists, occasionally teasing each other with the hard truths of things . . . as long as it wasn't the truth of the thing they felt between them. He owed her that honesty, that realism, that truth, now. "Surely, you didn't think this was heaven, Gabriella," he said, waving his hand at the world around them.

Her eyes widened in shock. "No, Bernie, I didn't," she said with a deep sigh. "I thought it was hell."

Again, he was knocked speechless, before he managed only one word: "Hell?"

She looked around sadly. "Every day I'm here. No food. No drink. No company save the fish that sometimes swim up at the edges of the island. There are birds, too, but they are too big to be real, I think, so I tell myself I'm imagining them. Besides that? It's just been me and the island. I've walked it. It's sixty feet by forty feet. The sand keeps me warm at night—during the day, it is as it is now. At night it glows. At first it was hard to sleep it was so bright, but I'm not sure you really sleep here, anyway. You just close your eyes and open them back up again sometime later. With nothing in between. No dreams. Not even any nightmares." She rubbed her eyes and grabbed one of his hands in both of hers. "I've been so, so lonely, Bernie. This place has to be hell, right? For the things I did in my life, for the . . . feelings I had for you, a priest. I mean, every time I heard your voice, reading things to me or playing our song, I thought surely I was being tortured."

He gripped her palms. "Gabriella, listen to me. This is not hell."

"It has to be! You're lying!"

"No. I'm not."

"Fine. Then if it's not hell, where am I?"

The million-dollar question. He glanced out across the water, to the area where he'd left Michiko behind. He could still feel her out there, somewhere, but she wasn't going to help with this moment, that was for sure. This one was all his. He thought about things for a few moments, feeling Gabriella's impatience, before he answered. "Your guess is as good as mine, but I think you're stuck, between your old life and the next."

"What? That makes no—"

"Gabriella. I'm sorry. I don't know how to tell you this . . . but your body? Back in the world? It's still there."

A look of stunned disbelief came over her.

"You're in a coma," he finished.

"You mean . . ." She faded away for a bit. When she came back, wonder was in her voice. "You mean I didn't die in that car crash?"

The sky glowed white with a purple tint, as if far off beyond the horizon a purple sun was floating. The air was slightly warmer, and he felt the sand sliding between his knees as he shifted his weight. "No. You didn't. You were seriously hurt, though."

Leaving one hand with his, she brought the other up to her mouth and asked the question he knew was coming. "How long?"

He tightened his lips with somberness before he replied, "Seven months."

The air came out of her in a long sigh that made her shrink in on herself. Her shoulders slouched, and her head dropped as the sobs came over her and racked her body like vicious blows. She fell forwards, into him, and he caught her up in his arms, and the questions she asked next were fired off so rapidly that they were almost unintelligible. "My mom? Is my mom okay? What do the doctors say? What are they doing to help me? Do they think I'm going to die? What about my sisters? Oh my God, what is this doing to my family?"

She stopped, then pulled away from him and gripped his arms in pure panic. "Bernie. My mom. This must be killing my mom, Bernie!"

He didn't want to answer but his face must've done so for him, somehow telegraphing the sad memories he had of her mother the few times he'd seen her, early on during his visits, and all the stories that the staff at the care facility relayed to him, of an old woman broken bit by bit with each passing day, until she was formally shattered by the visits to her daughter's bedside.

"Bernie," she moaned, "if I'm not dead, then I have to get out of here. Do you understand?"

"Yes," he said.

"How? How am I going to do that?"

"I don't know," he answered, looking from her face to the water all around them and back again. "But I have a feeling that's why I'm here. And we'll figure it out together, you and I."

She offered the tiniest smile of relief. "We will?"

He nodded firmly. "We will."

HECTOR AWOKE in the dead of night, uncovered, his fingers still laced behind his head, his shoulders numb. Realizing that he must've dozed off, he was marveling at the silence of the prison when he heard a creaking in the cot above him. This was nothing new—bunk beds in prison were notoriously loud—but Roberto was still in solitary. Which meant no one could be sleeping in the bunk above him, unless it was . . .

A pair of stubby legs swung down from above.

Sweet dreams? The Smiling Midget said, kicking his feet back and forth like a third grader on a swing set.

The weight of dread and terror that came crashing down over Hector was so pervasive that he could barely breathe. He tried to swallow but his throat locked up and his mouth went bone dry. *No, no, no, no, no, no . . .*

The Smiling Midget hopped down to the floor and turned to face Hector. *Yes, yes, yes, yes—me, boy-o! It's me, your old pal, to help with your rather jacked-up predicament here.*

It took a moment before Hector found his voice. "You can't be here. No way."

What? But I promised you, remember? Back at my friend Wally's house, when you killed him. Poor Wally. He paused as his smile went upside down. He added grimly, *But I promised you.*

Hector was so dazed that all he could do was shake his head in dismay.

I promised you that we'd finish things, you and I, on the inside, he said, his smile turning to a hateful sneer before his lips bounced gleefully back into place. *And, well . . . look! Here we are! Back home. On the inside!*

"No!"

Oh. Yes-sir-ee. The Smiling Midget chuckled. *Just the two of us. Once again I'm here to help your sorry ass survive.* He did a little carnival dance before he continued. *Because without me? In here? You, sir, are a dead man.*

Hector sat up. "Screw you, you little rat bastard."

The Screaming Midget reached out suddenly and touched

Hector's arm with the nubs of his right hand. Hector felt as if he were instantly on fire. He screamed and pulled himself backwards, across the cot, his back hitting the wall with a painful thump.

I've had it up to here with you, boy, The Smiling Midget said, holding his hand horizontal a few feet above his head. *Oops!* He laughed. *Sorry. I keep forgetting my real size.* He lowered his hand to just below his chin.

"Look. I don't need your help," Hector replied. And for the first time since arriving here, he called on the blue.

But no power came.

Shouldn't have let me touch youuuuu, The Smiling Midget teased. Then he sighed, deeply, before he added, *You're so green that you're simply* froggy, *my boy! C'mon, Hectorino! Be a good frog! Call on that stupid power of yours again. C'mon. Jump!* The Smiling Midget leapt effortlessly onto the toilet—*Jump!*—then on to the sink before taking one more leap to the tiny windowsill, the toes of his boots jamming hard into the cement as he braced his arms into the frame to hold himself in place, his neck craning sickeningly to one side.

Hector looked around, but The Smiling Midget was way ahead of him. *Ah. You're looking for your gray friend? That hurts my feelings, Hector. I was your friend first. And besides, he can't get in here anyway. Too much evil for his kind, ya know?*

Hector's legs felt weak, but he managed to get off his cot and stand. "What the hell are you talking about?"

Close! So close. Not what the *hell are you talking about, but what in hell are you talking about, Hector. There're two sides in this war. And this place here? It's behind enemy lines, boy.*

"Yeah?"

Yeah. And what they're talking about in hell, at least in my tiny corner of it, is the silly little gangster who was rotten to the core but now thinks he's a hero on a mission of some kind.

"Shut up."

The Smiling Midget's lips went tight, like a Kewpie doll's, as he jumped to the floor and widened his eyes, his head still stuck in a sideways position. *Hector. Hector. Hector.*

"Leave me alone."

Why? What would be the fun in that? The Smiling Midget shrugged and straightened his neck, the bones popping in place as he did so. *Your Gray friend? He doesn't realize that it's too late for you, Hector. You've been a good little soldier for our side for too long. That side? It's always so . . . naïve. So hopeful, and all that other nauseating crap.*

"I won't fail!" he screamed. Faintly, from far away, he felt the blue coming. Time. He just needed a little more time.

The Smiling Midget put his arms out straight and began to put one foot in front of the other, as if he were walking a tightrope towards Hector. Step by step, he made his way, until they were only a few feet apart. *Oh, yes, you will!* he said with a giggle. *I'm here to help you, before it's too late, because an old friend is coming for you, boy-o. She spared you last time because she was ordered to. But I got your back. And if we can kill Curtis before she gets here? It'll be all good.*

The blue was almost there. Hector prayed for it. Begged for it. *Please, please.* If it came in time, he could kill The Smiling Midget where he stood. If only—

The blue! The blue! The blue! The Smiling Midget shrieked in mock hysteria before he cast his arms wide like a vaudeville actor, threw his head back and screamed with mock glee, *Oh, the wonderful blue will save the day!*

As the blue finally arrived it sputtered in Hector's hands.

Like I said . . . you're so . . . damned . . . green. The Smiling Midget shook his head and blinked away. Hector sat and looked at the meager drops of blue that had pooled in his palms. He still had no training in how to use it. In how to do anything, really.

And if The Gray Man could not get to him to show him, he was doomed.

Chapter Five

AFTER TRUDY WAS FINALLY DISCHARGED from Huntington Hospital, being brought out to the curb against her protests in a wheelchair by a candy striper half her age, the mood had gotten quiet as she and Parker began the drive to Napa. Even though they had talked it over a dozen times, she was still not happy with being carted to her parents' house in Wine Country. So, after the obligatory hug and kiss hello, the debate began yet again.

"This is bullshit," she said, her voice heavy with post-hospital-stay weariness.

Parker sighed. "It's necessary."

She ran her fingers through her red hair, pushing it back. "I feel dirty and disgusting. I want to go home, my home, and take a long, hot shower. I don't see why—"

Knowing that this conversation was going to take an even harder turn in a few minutes, Parker decided to nip this particular phase of drama in the bud now. "Our home is shot to pieces, Trudy. There's still blood on the carpet and walls. Until three days ago, it was still a crime scene."

Silence. Cold and penetrating. The truth hurt, and the truth was that they would never live in that apartment again.

Together, yes. But there? No. The rain had gone back to a drizzle-dance, accompanied by a chilly sideways wind that had made Trudy grimace when Parker had loaded her in the car. It evidently still chilled her, as she reached up and redirected the heater vents as they drove down Walnut Street, the parked cars on the curbs whizzing by in alternating colors. Finally, she bit her lip and uttered one word. "Great."

It was one thing to survive what she had, quite another to come to grips with the aftermath. Parker knew this all too well. Trudy's struggles had begun the first time she saw the protective detail outside her hospital room. That's when it evidently hit her: life as she knew it had changed greatly, in ways she never considered, because of the love she had for Parker. Push comes to shove, all the romantic proclamations in the world begin to waiver a bit once it becomes clear that you can be killed for loving the person you love. Parker let her waiver all over the place the first few days, knowing full well that she would never give up on him, nor he on her.

Still. The details of the aftermath had to be worked out, and she had no idea that Napa was the least of the issues they had left to discuss. Luckily, or maybe not, they had a six-hour drive in which to discuss them.

Sadness crept into his voice. "I'm sorry, Trud."

He heard her breath catch in her throat as she swiftly wiped at one of her eyes. Her lower lip shaking, she took a deep breath and replied. "It's not your fault, Evan."

They merged onto the on-ramp to the 210 West, pulled around a white Nissan and accelerated into the flow of traffic.

"How are you feeling?"

"My head doesn't hurt anymore. Vision is fine. No more blurriness. But my face still hurts when I chew."

"The pain meds helping?"

"A little. Mostly with sleep. But they make me groggy as hell."

"You okay to talk? You want me to just turn on the radio for a bit?"

She didn't hesitate. "Yeah."

He nodded and put on her favorite R&B station, even though R&B to him was like a trip to the dentist's office. They drove down the 210 to the 5 Freeway, which he took north. After a bit, he looked over to see that she was resting her head against a sweater she'd placed between herself and the window and had dozed off. Good. She needed rest more than anything. She looked pale and weak and the sight of her like that threatened to resurrect his rage. *No. Not here. Not now. Not yet.*

It was when they were driving through Castaic, about forty-five minutes later, when the memories of him and Napoleon making this same drive, during the Fasano case, hit him. Up and down the 5 Freeway they'd gone, like dogs after a spooked rabbit, never realizing all along that they were tangling with forces way beyond anyone's comprehension. Then, after that, he'd used the 5 Freeway to go to Beaumont, too, a little town run by Sheriff Conch, to help catch The Bread Man, who had lived quietly in that town for years, killing dozens of women in the surrounding counties before being flushed out by happenstance, good police work and . . . here it was again . . . forces way beyond anyone's comprehension.

Nervously, Parker checked the rearview mirror, half expecting and also half hoping to see Napoleon there. And why not? Hadn't his dead partner come back to help teach him about those very same forces? Yes. He had. But he was nowhere to be seen now.

The rain was steady and made the traffic worse, but he was in no hurry. Trudy rested, and Parker drove, contemplating the path ahead of him and whether he was really going to take it.

He didn't have to wait long, however, for his decision to become crystal clear. It happened an hour later, when they stopped off at a Burger King so Trudy could use the restroom and they could grab a bite to eat. He watched her use her hand to cover the cuts and bruises on her face as she went inside. Shame and humiliation were in her eyes and Parker knew, right then, what he had to do. What he was going to do.

An hour later, back in the car with their bellies full, he decided to get the first part of what he had to say over with. She was sipping the straw aimlessly on a cup of Dr. Pepper when he told her he'd quit the force.

"You . . . what?!" she said, turning to him in utter shock.

"I had to."

"Why?"

"Because they were taking me off the case."

She was quiet for a moment. "What case? This case?"

"Yeah."

She put her drink in the cup holder of the center console and pushed her hands outward in small defensive motions to slow walk him through her thoughts. "Okay. So. Let me get this straight. You're on a case that almost gets us both killed. Why? Because you supposedly love your job. Then, when the shit hits the fan, you quit that same job?"

"No. That's not what I said."

"Oh?"

"No. I didn't quit because the shit hit the fan. I quit because they're not going to let me stay on the case and make things right."

"Make things right? How? By catching this lunatic?"

"Yeah!"

She licked her lips before making them a tight line. He knew this look; she was getting her Irish up. Not good. But also not a surprise. "Okay. So. For the record? Just so we're straight? I'm okay with this decision. I never saw myself as ever being with a cop and I get sick to my stomach every day you walk out the door to go to work, and quite honestly, I've never slept worse in my life. I am . . . *constantly* . . . worried about you. So. Cool. If you're leaving because you've suddenly decided to be a stock broker or to go back to school or some shit, fine. But that's not what I'm hearing."

Parker sighed. "Fine. What are you hearing?"

"I'm hearing that you had a childish meltdown with your boss and stomped off."

"That's not really—"

"Oh, but it is!" she said, her face incredulous as she blinked. "And why? Well, I don't know the rules of the police gig, but I'm guessing that having you stay on a case where your girlfriend has almost just been killed is a big no-no, right?"

He nodded.

"It is a no-no? Just to clarify, for sure now?"

He nodded again, resenting that he was being mocked but still aware that he was the one who had started this.

The thing about Trudy that amazed him, almost beyond belief, was that it never, ever took her very long to connect the dots that were in *his* head. He imagined them both old and gray someday, finishing each other's sentences. Except, well, she could already do that with him. She could read him like a book and earmark whatever pages that needed further focus, and as she sat there ruminating in the passenger seat, Parker thought she was doing just that.

"So . . . you actually quit because they won't let you go after him?"

He shrugged his affirmation.

Trudy put her head in her hands, her voice going flat and hard. "Please tell me you're kidding."

Parker cleared his throat and drove, the inside of the car suddenly feeling much too small.

———

MAGGIE EXITED the port-a-potty and squinted against the harsh sky above. She still had no idea where the hell they were.

But she could guess from the signs she'd seen thus far, which were all in Spanish, that they were probably in Mexico. She knew that Tijuana, Ensenada and Rosarito were popular touristy spots south of the border, but as Eenie grabbed her elbow and began pulling her back to the shelter, Maggie realized she couldn't even see a stray dog around their location, much less a tourist.

She forced herself back on point. The place was a dirt patch of pure boredom, which left no room for anything but routine, and if Eenie followed his, he would have his little perv moment when he got her back in the shack. She braced herself for it and told herself to just go with it for once. If it got her what she wanted, who cared. But there was a sickening ball of fear in the pit of her stomach that she might give too much ground and he'd get too excited and . . . She didn't want to think about that. But the pragmatist in her would have it no other way. She couldn't help but think about how she was not on the pill or any other contraceptive, so there was the very real possibility that if this whole ordeal didn't get her killed, she could still end up pregnant with some murdering thug's baby.

By breaking Güero's orders, the idiot had to know that he would get himself killed. But a man with a hard-on was the dumbest creature that ever lived. He might risk it. And if he did? Well, now that she thought about it, Güero's fantasy of having Maggie to himself would be spoiled and that would probably get a bullet put in *her* head, too.

Like it or not, though, her body was her greatest asset right now, not as an object, but as a tool. So she would use it.

Once in the shack, he guided Maggie to a spot in the corner out of sight of the cot where Luisa was lying, half asleep. Maggie's feet then tangled with his as he eagerly pushed her face-first against the wall. He pinned her wrists together and began dry humping her backside. Yep. Each time, he was getting more brazen. Going just a little further.

This was her chance.

She took it by pushing off the wall and swaying her hips to

encourage his grinding. He pulled back at first, no doubt shocked, then, excitedly, he let go of her hands, wrapped one arm around her waist while using his other hand to grope her chest. The plan was going perfectly, until the flashbacks came over her, like they always did. Like they had with all the men she'd ever tried to be intimate with in her life. Like they had with Michael.

The hands were different. The moves were different. In many ways, during her best moments in the past with the boys she thought she loved, they were even exciting for a few seconds.

The problem was her fear that . . . each man's intent . . . was the same. To hurt her. To use her. To violate her as a living, breathing human being. Like that monster of her childhood had. And that was the real crime of it: you could overcome the past but then, as the victim, you had to keep overcoming it, day by day and moment by moment. The therapist she had just begun seeing told her that the key was getting to the point where you could truly and completely redefine yourself from a victim to a survivor. And she had been doing well until . . . all this had happened. No real dates since New York but feeling healed and finally ready to meet a guy and share a kiss and see where things went.

But now . . . her stomach rolled with nausea.

She pulled herself back from the cliff in her mind with the realization that she was about to cry. No. That would blow the whole thing. So instead she quickly spun around, causing him to panic before she pulled him close and, suppressing the urge to vomit, buried her face in his neck. He tried to pull back, probably thinking about his boss, before his manhood overtook his better senses and he was all over her.

Perfect. She reached around and grabbed his ass, exciting him only more, as she slyly slid the dummy's cell phone from his back pocket. Once it was in her hand, she reached down and stuffed it into the side pouch of her workout pants and then began to scream with all her might. His panicked reaction was to cover her mouth, which caused her even more flashbacks.

"Shut up, you little bitch!" he whispered harshly. He pressed down hard on her mouth, jamming her lips painfully against her teeth, but it was too late. Luisa was up in a shot and began to scream, too.

Seconds later, Meenie and Miney came charging through the shack door, guns drawn. Seeing Maggie in his embrace, their faces went raw, and angry Spanish began flying in all directions. Eenie let Maggie go but glared at her as he did so. "I'll get you for this," he said in a frustrated voice.

"I hope you try," Maggie spat. As his cohorts pulled him away, she added, "Enjoy your blue balls."

He said some words to her in Spanish, no doubt insults, but even that was cowardly, as he no doubt knew she couldn't understand him. He was halfway to the door when Luisa came out of nowhere and punched him in the neck, which was as high as she could reach. She was strong for a little thing, and he arched his body in pain and tried to grab at her as Meenie grappled with him and pushed him outside with even greater urgency.

The shack door slammed shut and the cross bar fell into place. "Nice punch," Maggie said with a smile to Luisa. She smiled back, which was encouraging.

Maggie wasn't sure how much time she had for her idea, so she wasted none of it. Luisa's eyes went wide when Maggie pulled the phone from her pouch and punched in the code: 2-8-9-1.

Sometimes shit just went your way. Sometimes. And they were due a break, weren't they?

The display lit up. Luisa came over to shield Maggie and the phone from view of the shack door. "What are you doing?" she whispered urgently.

"Shh," Maggie whispered back as her fingers went to work. She had rehearsed this moment in her mind countless times and now she simply followed the steps. Forget about trying to make a call to someone. Screw that. She smiled. He had Facebook.

She logged him out and logged herself in. First break of the day? His Facebook was in English. She was right. Of the three, Eenie was the most Americanized. Probably was a citizen, or had at least grown up in the US. It was why the other two treated him differently. Regardless, had it been in Spanish she would've been ready for it. She had Luisa to translate. It just would've made things take a little longer.

She almost laughed when she saw the standard Facebook status question: "What's on your mind?"

Um. Not dying! That's what.

Luisa reached up with a tiny, stifled cry of excitement and grabbed Maggie's forearms as she typed a status update. But the words Maggie typed about their predicament darkened the mood for a moment. At least before Maggie clicked the "Check in" button and they both waited . . . for seconds that felt like weeks . . . for the dial on the phone to spin away. Only three bars of 4G but that was enough. It had to be.

The push pin came up at last: they were somewhere in Baja California near a place called El Centenario.

Maggie clicked "Share" immediately and almost began to cry as her status went live. That got the word out to all her friends, coworkers and family. One of them would see it and take action, surely.

Okay, okay. That's enough. You did it. Don't push your luck. He's gonna notice any minute now that his phone is gone.

But more than anything she wanted to DM Julie, so she did. "In El Centenario, Baja California being held by three men. With a girl from the shelter. Think they're heading south next but not sure. Been here three days. Call Detective Murillo or Klink. LAPD Hollenbeck Station. Get help." Her fingers were shaking as she held back a sob and she added one more thing. "I love you."

Outside she heard someone shout a bunch of stuff that

included one word she caught loud and clear: *"Teléfono!"* It was Eenie. He'd no doubt gone off to pout somewhere, reached for his phone and found it missing.

Luisa gasped. "He's asking them if they've seen his phone."

"I know, I know," Maggie replied. Heavy footfalls were crunching across the dirt to the shack. They were coming.

Hurriedly, desperately, Maggie signed out of her Facebook account and threw the phone side-handed towards the shack door, where it hit the ground and spun in a few circles before coming to a stop just as the shack door flew open. Eenie stood in the doorway, with Meenie and Miney right behind him, all of them blocking the light from outside.

Again, Luisa made Maggie proud.

"Que?" she screamed as she spun to face them all with her tiny baby-bump belly.

Eenie stepped in and looked around, the damned phone right at his feet.

Don't say anything, Luisa. Don't. It'll be too obvious. He has to find it for himself. When they walked in, all they saw were two women huddled off in the corner. They'll never know.

Maggie's heart dropped as Luisa began to open her mouth, but just then, Eenie looked down and saw his phone. With anger still on his face, he looked at Luisa. *"Cállate, puta!"* he screamed at her, before he spun and stomped back out.

Again, the shack door closed. Again, the cross bar fell into place.

Maggie and Luisa flew into each other's arms and hugged each other tightly. They'd done it. Word was out about where they were, and Maggie knew, just knew, that they'd come to help.

Or at least someone would.

Chapter Six

"TAKE MY HAND," Father Soltera said to Gabriella as he stepped off the island and into the water. The shoreline chilled his toes and the silty sand scrunched beneath his feet.

She complied hesitantly, her slender fingers gripping at his, the tips of her nails tickling his knuckles. Her face, that precious face, here at last, turned up to his with a sudden hope. His heart spun. Love. This was love. Plunging off to nowhere and everywhere. Together.

It was okay. It would all be okay. He could let go of all the things that kept him from letting go before, if what he felt was genuine. As long as what he felt was sincere. And it was, without a doubt, the sincerest thing he'd felt in his entire mixed-up life. This was the direction of every winding path he'd ever wandered down, the blind curve of every road, the turnoff to the ultimate view of the wilderness within him.

They made it waist-deep into the water before she stopped. "I can't move," she said with frustration. "I knew it!"

"Why? What's wrong?"

"I'm not allowed to leave the island. I've tried. Many times. I thought with you here it might be different. But, no," she said forlornly.

He couldn't believe what he was hearing. *This can't be.*

He pulled on her hand harder. She winced but put all her effort into trying to move forwards. Nothing. It was as if the soil beneath the water had suctioned her feet and wouldn't let go. Her face twisted with desperation as they struggled, tugging and pushing sideways, then upwards, until downwards finally worked, but only for the briefest of seconds.

Then, she was stuck again.

"No!" she cried out, her mouth drawn in sorrow, her eyes closed tight.

He stood over her for a second before slowly helping her to her feet. Her pants were soaked and her jacket wet, but he watched with fascination as the water coalesced and wicked off of her, as if she were dipped in wax. Clenching her fists, she leaned over and beat on her thighs. "This can't be happening! I knew it! I knew this was hell." She looked up at him furiously. "You're not real. You're not him. You were just sent to torture me, weren't you?"

"Gabriella! No. Listen to me. It's me. I'm here." And somehow, saying this aloud made it all more real for him, too. As if, up until now, a part of him was still holding on to the chance this was a dream. A mad, preposterous dream with fire-bellied cats, a female samurai, and dire wolves on the hunt.

She shook her head and looked away, as if to further deny him. "No. No, you're not."

He clutched at her arms and they both locked their hands on each other's elbows. "Yes. I . . ."

Seeing him hesitate, her eyes narrowed with suspicion. "You . . . what?"

Father Soltera sighed. "I was about to say that I came for you. But that would be a lie, wouldn't it?" he mainly asked himself before answering his own question. "Yes. Yes, it would be. I didn't come for you . . . and I wasn't *brought* to you, either."

"What does it matter!" She shook him loose, turned and walked back up to the dry sand.

He followed, but slowly, as he tried to figure things out. He mumbled the words again: "Didn't come. Not brought." How? He wanted to be here. Yes. But he had no way of willing himself to this place, of setting her as his destination on some sort of journey. No.

"How then? How did you get here, *Bernie*?" she said with sarcasm.

He'd had enough. "Look. We'll figure this out. But you know as well as I do that demons don't love, and demons don't confess. I've done both. So if this is hell, and I still don't think it is, but if it is? Then I'm certainly not an agent of it. I'm wearing a cross. I've prayed while I've been here. Even now, despite my feelings for you, I'm a man of God. Fallen, yes, but by no means forsaken!" And now his emotions were getting the better of him. His hands were shaking as he looked up at her with imploring eyes. "Do you understand?"

The hardness that had settled in her cheeks and chin quickly disappeared. She nodded gently and blinked away the last of the disbelief on her face. "Yes, Bernie. I'm sorry. It's just . . ." She buried her face in her hands and turned away.

He gave her some space, put his hands on his hips and mulled over her last question a bit more. How did he get here? *Didn't come. Not brought.* The words had him like a bear trap. Michiko had brought him. She had. *Wait. No. She brought you to the island, yes. But you awoke here, in this crazy world, first. She's been a guide, since the first moment you saw her. A guide.*

So, if he hadn't come here of his own free will and he hadn't been brought here by anyone, that could only mean one thing . . .

"I was sent," he said softly.

"What?"

He looked up to the sky, then out over the water. "I was sent. Yes."

"Who? Who sent you?"

Beyond that sky was the answer. Shaking his head in dismay,

he looked away and began walking up the island, seeking a distraction to his thoughts. He noticed a bunch of sand piles. "What're these?"

She shrugged. "I build sand castles when I'm bored, or pile sand to make a pillow when I'm really tired."

The breeze over the water cooled his face and combed through his hair as he walked around the island to the other side. There, heartbreakingly, she'd built a crude shelter with driftwood and rocks. In front of it was a burnt-out campfire. "You know how to start a fire?" he asked, surprised.

She scoffed. "Are you kidding me? No. It ignites every night by itself, then extinguishes each morning."

Curiosity overtook him. "By itself?"

"Yeah. It's a trip, I know. But it's done it since the first day I came here."

He looked out over the water again; it was flat as glass, save a few lazy eddies here or there. "Are there ever any waves?"

"Waves?" she said, perplexed. "No. Why?"

"Then where did the driftwood for your shelter come from?"

"It was here, too."

"The wood was already here?"

"Yeah. Not much of a shelter, but it helps on the cooler nights."

As a young man at seminary, he was known as a thorough, almost exhaustive researcher. It wasn't enough to know a biblical text frontwards and backwards, in Hebrew and Greek; he had to know its context and all the possible interpretations. At times, he would delve all the way down to the ideas in Aramaic. It wasn't that he was super-smart, though others viewed him that way. Quite the contrary. He studied so hard because he felt so dense at times, unable to understand anything. In time, he learned to allow himself to wait on understanding, because that was the true gift of the Bible: it read *you*, as you read *it*. As the living word of God, it knew when you were ready for certain truths and when you weren't. It was like a lifelong friendship with the best college professor you could ever have, ready with encouragement one day, advice the next, wisdom the day after that. And yes, sometimes, it gave you nothing, because nothing was all you could handle that day. And that was okay, too. He remembered his Bible with the blue cover, at home in his apartment, there on his nightstand, and all his scribbled notes inside it, written to himself like a journal to help him to understand things.

Like now. He wanted to piece things together, and sure enough, he was on to something and he knew it. "Do you mind if I look around a little?"

"No, of course not."

He motioned for her to follow as he walked further down the shore of the island. Besides more driftwood, it was barren, and as such, had no secrets to offer. But wait. Didn't it? He walked closer to the driftwood and instantly saw them snagged there: tiny pieces of colored thread, blazing oranges and yellows, dense blues and accenting reds. He knew these threads but not in this way. Not in this context. But he knew them. He did. How . . . how . . .

When it hit him, he gasped.

Gabriella came up next to him. "What?"

How was he going to tell her this? In what way could he soften the blow? There wasn't enough time to mull it over and he doubted it would've made much difference, so he shared his realization as gently as he could.

"These threads?"

"Yes."

"Have they always been here?"

"Yeah. I mean, I didn't walk to this side of the island for a few days, so I don't know if they were here before that. But it's weird, right?"

"Yes and no."

She looked at him quizzically. "What's that mean?"

He gently put his hand on her shoulder. "You're mother, Gabriella . . ."

"My mother?"

"She has visited you every day since your accident, so the staff tells me. I sneak in to see you once a month, to pray over you, to visit. And each month I see a new blanket laid over your bed, stitched and sewn in these same bright and beautiful colors."

As if she were trying to sew her way to you, wherever you were, he was going to add. But he stopped himself short as Gabriella's face melted instantly into a sea of tears. "What?" she choked.

"Yeah. To keep you warm. To keep you safe, the only way she still can: with a blanket. Like she no doubt did when you were an infant."

As they stood in silence for a few moments, Father Soltera felt the "rightness" of it. The research had been brief but correct. All that was left was to arrive at the correct conclusion, and that was not long in coming, either.

He cupped his hands over her cheeks and turned her face to his. "The fire? The shelter? All of it. To keep you safe. All of them byproducts of a mother's prayers. And that's the key, you see? She has prayed so earnestly over you, and I believe . . . I know . . . God our Father has heard. There is no doubt."

Gabriella wept. "How can you be so sure?"

Father Soltera chuckled softly. "Because I believe that's why I'm here, too. Your mother prayed for help." Father Soltera looked up to the sky, because there was always a sky, wasn't there? And always Someone on the other side of it.

He sighed, before adding, "And I was sent."

———

THE YARD SPLIT into four sections, four times a day, the inmates dividing like ants from separate colonies into their own groups. Hector had only lasted a few weeks in his sociology class in high school, but he didn't need it to know that when push came to shove, human beings almost always grouped together with those most similar to them – finding safety in what was familiar. The blacks, browns and whites all in their own corners; Asians and anyone else in the "other" category of the US Census in the last. It was like a chessboard of gang life: the outside world brought inside and boxed into a microcosm of violence.

Still not seeing Curtis anywhere, Hector made his way to a dirt patch in the worn grass next to a row of green wooden bench tables. The Fresno gangs had affiliations with some of the Los Angeles gangs, if he could find any. A group of six Latin men sat at one of the tables, tattoos running up their arms and necks, the demarcations of which he did not recognize. Four of them were playing dominos. The other two were watching with one eye on the game and the other on their surroundings. Prison life, man. It made you like one of those bug-eyed lizards, constantly looking in all directions. One of the men, bald with a long scar on one temple, sat at the table with his hands folded over the dominos in front of him. "What's up, lil homie?" he said, nodding at Hector.

"Not much," Hector said. "Jus' checking out the new digs."

The men laughed.

"Where you from?"

The age-old question asked by the very first gang member who ever walked the earth of the second gang member he ever encountered. Just a simple question that could just as simply get you killed. Hector balled up his fists in the pockets of his prison-issued jacket, just in case it was about to go off. "East Los, Fresno Street Vatos."

Silence for a few seconds. The bald man replied, "Twelfth Street. San Diego. My name's Philippe. This is Reverb, Sleepy-eye, Ocho and Juan. All SD or SD-affiliated."

Fellow Southerners. "We good?" Hector asked, still not sure after his run-in with Raul earlier.

"You still standing, ain't ya?" Ocho sniggered. He was painfully skinny, with wounded eyes that had large bags under them.

Hector did not unclench his fists. Better to be safe than sorry. But Ocho was right: with a six-to-one advantage, if there were any issues, there would be no need for them to be coy about it. They could jump him and whip his ass without even thinking about it. "Lots of eyes, huh?"

The other men nodded. "Everywhere," Juan added. But that was all he said. His voice was soft and his look unbalanced, like maybe he was trying very hard to hide the fact that he was more than a little crazy.

"Three towers, each side of the yard. Twelve guards around the circumference of the main lawn. But they're just for show," Phillipe spat, contempt in his voice.

Hector kicked at the dirt. "How so?"

"The tower guys got a boner to use their scopes. They gonna shoot you down long before their buddies have to roll up in here."

"We can turn on each other all we want in here," Ocho added, looking up at one of the towers. "They take bets on the outcomes, even set up some of the fights."

Reverb finally spoke, his voice deep and fitting for his large frame and wide shoulders. "But get near a guard, and well, this place has a rep for coming up with excuses for sending someone to the morgue."

A moment of quiet came over them.

"Your first time in?" Phillipe probed.

"No. Third. Other two times were county, though."

"Triple-A league," Phillipe said with a laugh. "Welcome to the big leagues, son."

The sun had finally tilted its way high enough into the sky to banish most of the shadows from the yard. What grass there was looked greener and the dirt patches looked browner. Other than that? Nothing changed. The chain link fencing all around them was still a dull and depressing shade of gray. The air was full of chatter between the other inmates, curse words and guffaws being tossed back and forth like hand grenades.

Some were shooting hoops on a paved court nearby with stark metal rims. No nets or chains to catch the ball here. The latter could be used as a weapon against someone and the former to hang yourself with when you'd had enough.

The occasional sound of metal clinked into the air as someone finished a set of reps on one of the workout benches across from the basketball courts. The black inmates had the gym area now, their shirts off and their muscles contracting with their efforts. A group of them had to be getting steroids from the outside, because even though everyone knew that the prison could get you in the best shape of your life, their muscles were beyond huge. One of the group, with a shaved head and small ears, was eying Hector intently. Not wanting to provoke him, Hector immediately looked away.

Phillipe evidently saw it and chuckled. "*Machismo?* Yes. *Estupido?* No."

"*Qué pasa, jefe?*" Ocho asked with smile.

And Hector suddenly remembered when he used to be called that. *Jefe.* Boss. By Bennie and Chico and the rest of his crew. No more. Just like that, he was back down the pecking order, all the way to the bottom.

Phillipe motioned at Hector. "Our new lil homie here. He's settling in, but he ain't dumb. Booker just looked him off. Cold."

All of them looked at Hector but only Sleepyeye, who still hadn't said a word, was smiling.

Hector knew the game: never show weakness, that was the rule. He shrugged in an exaggerated fashion. "Shit, man. I ain't no fool. Cuz got arms like a rhino . . . snap me in half any day. I mean"—and he looked at each of them, slowly from left to right, as he paused for effect—"any day he see me coming."

Sleepyeye's smile turned into a snigger. Reverb followed,

before they all joined in. "That's right, lil homie," Phillipe said. "*Cada perro tiene su día.*"

"Yessir!" Juan laughed too hard. "Every dog has his day, baby."

That was when Hector realized Juan was high. Probably meth, maybe acid. Whatever it was, it didn't matter. Hector had no doubt that Juan was bat-shit crazy, even when he was stone-cold sober.

"What you in for?" Juan asked.

So, it was time for credentials to be checked. Fine. Hector had rehearsed his answer. "Shot a fool in the face for hitting on my girl," he lied, because if he told them that he shot a guy that had stolen and banged his woman? Well . . . he was done for. No real man got cheated on. His woman wouldn't dare disgrace him like that.

"Hmm. Murder one," Phillipe said with a deep nod, like a proud uncle.

Hector looked at Juan and verbally pushed back. "You?"

Crazy Juan's face tightened and his lips went tight before he shrugged. "Raped my lil cousin. She was fourteen, but she was ready. She wanted it." His face loosened as his eyes went to look around at the memory. Then he was back. "Told the bitch not to tell. She did. So I raped her again, all weekend long actually, once I was out on bail."

The air grew still before, as per gangster etiquette, the rest offered up their crimes. Phillipe had murdered two rival gang members in cold blood outside a shawarma restaurant by Howe Park. Reverb was in for kidnapping and manslaughter after a carjacking gone wrong. He was then involved in gang activities at another prison and shipped here. Sleepyeye had followed a jeweler home from his shop in downtown Sacramento and murdered him in his driveway when the man had refused to surrender his briefcase full of gems and diamonds. Ocho had been busted driving a semi loaded with enough pure cocaine to get the state of Texas high. "Odds and all," Ocho said. "I made that run a dozen times at 10k each time, right in my pocket." He also was a transfer to Corcoran after he'd viciously assaulted another inmate in Folsom Prison for taking his cafeteria brownie off his lunch tray.

When they were done no one said anything for a while. Someone shouted loudly from the basketball court after hitting a half-court shot and someone else was whistling a Vicente Fernández song, "El Rey," by the water fountain.

Hector knew it was risky but he was getting impatient. So he mustered his courage and asked Juan, "You know a Curtis Ruvelcaba?"

All of them froze. With a squint, Juan replied, "Yeah. What if we do? What business you got with Curtis?"

Oh, boy. If only you knew, Hector thought.

Instead, he answered, "We go way back. In a good way. If you can get word to him that Hector Villarosa is here, I'd really appreciate it."

Again, Juan looked at him hard. But this time it was like a jealous uncle, not a proud one. "I bet you would," he said.

Chapter Seven

PARKER DROVE AS TRUDY YELLED. "Why on God's earth would you even *think* of doing this?"

He shook his head slowly and changed lanes before he answered. "You wouldn't understand."

"That's all you got? That's bullshit." Her hands were shaking and her voice quivered with raw emotion. This wasn't good for her in her current state. He wanted to stop the conversation, but it was too late.

"Trudy, look . . . I'm sorry. I'm not trying to be dismissive—"

"Oh! You're not? Really?"

"What do you want me to say?"

"That you're not actually thinking of going after this madman, wherever the hell he is. Just say that. Right now."

His silence was his reply.

"Honest to God, Evan," she said with a deep sigh as she put her hands over her eyes. It didn't work. Parker saw a tear race off her chin.

He realized that he had to at least try to explain it. "Trudy. Okay. Look. This guy? He won't stop. Can't you see that?"

"What?"

"He's crazy. He attacked the family of a cop—my girlfriend, yeah, but make no mistake about it: everyone in that squad room see you as my family. He knew that. The son of a bitch knew full well he was going to start a war by killing you. It's nearly as bad as killing a cop. In the criminal world it's nearly unheard of, as it causes way too much attention. The entire force comes after you, the Feds get involved . . . Like it or not, these scumbags are business people and what this idiot did is very bad for business."

"And?"

"And he has bosses that won't appreciate it. So maybe we'll get lucky and they'll off his ass. But probably not. He has a ton of connections and has been very good for them, too. They might give him a pass because you're 'just' my girlfriend. Who knows. But . . . and you need to listen to me now . . . I can't take that chance. Do you understand?" And now he realized that he was practically shouting too, as his own emotions came racing out of him.

"Evan—"

"No, Trudy. No! He crossed the line. He came after someone I love. You know me, Trudy. You do, damn it! How? How could you ever think that I'd let that stand?"

She wiped at her eyes and stayed quiet as she stared out the passenger window. Up ahead the traffic was thickening but at least they were finally reaching the outskirts of the storm. The sky was gray blotches and bloated clouds, but there was very little rain. The inside of the car felt like a two-person cocoon. Or at least it had. Now, the tension between them was so alive it felt like a third person had joined them.

"You can't just go after him blind and shit."

He laughed. "I have no intention to."

"I'm confused. Are you or aren't you—"

"Yes. I'm going after him. But not in some stupid-ass way."

She wrapped her sweater tight against her body. "You could be the one that ends up in jail, though. You realize that, right?"

Again, he stayed silent.

"You're crazy. This whole idea is crazy. Stop it. Now. I won't let you do this. I won't let—"

"He's kidnapped his pregnant sixteen-year-old niece, Trudy, and the social worker that was trying to protect her."

She looked at him stunned. "That—"

"Don't you pretend for one second that doesn't matter, Trudy. I'll call you a liar, right to your face."

"It's not your job to—"

"Word is, he's into demonic rituals. He may really just be after the baby."

That hit home. "Oh, God . . ." She sighed. And he was getting to know her well, too, because he knew fully that she was starting to give in. She just wasn't willing to admit it to herself yet.

An old, abandoned barn and a house that had mostly crumpled in on itself under the weight of its days flashed by as they drove. He briefly wondered why anyone would've ever wanted to move to such a desolate place as he gave the conversation a second to catch its breath. Then, he continued. "He's run south of the border—surprise, surprise. Probably hiding in his hometown or whatever. I dunno."

"So . . . what? You're going to chase all over Mexico looking for him?"

He bit his lower lip for a second before deciding to be as honest with her as he could. "I can't name names, for their sake, but it looks like I'm gonna get some help from someone with good intel and . . ."

She looked at him. "And?"

"I've got a friend down in Baja. We served together. He can help me on that side."

She stuffed her hands into the opposite sleeves of her sweater. "My God. You're really thinking of doing this." It was not a question. "Unbelievable."

"I have to."

"No. You don't."

"I have to protect you. Because he'll come again, Trudy. He'll try again. Then what?"

The road curved to the left up ahead. She seemed to be measuring her reply. "If you get hurt . . . for me . . . I can't—"

She was such a good person. Even now, still filled with the remnants of terror that Güero Martinez and inflicted upon her, she didn't want it to be about her. He should've known this would be her position. "Fine. Then what about the girl and the baby? I have to help the girl, don't you see? I have to help the social worker who, as far as I can tell, is one hell of a decent human being. If that's not enough, then don't I have to do it for the hundreds—did you hear me, Trudy?—hundreds if not thousands of women that he's taken from their homes, from their countries, and smuggled here as sex slaves?"

"They—" She was running out of argument, at last. He needed her to, because he needed her to be with him on this. He could not do this without knowing that he had her support.

"This guy is a rabid dog, running the streets. Someone has to put him down," he said softly.

"Why? Why do *you* have to?" Her voice crackled with emotion.

"Because I *can*. And if I can help, don't I then *have* to help, Trudy? Isn't it really as simple as that?"

She looked to the roof of the car. "It's not that black and white, Evan!"

"The hell it isn't."

She sighed heavily and crossed her arms. "Evan. Listen to me. You can't do this. You're not Jason-freaking-Bourne."

With that, he'd had enough. Pulling off the road, he slammed on the brakes and brought the car to a stop along an old wooden fence. Jamming the car into park, he spun and faced her. "You're damned straight I'm not! And do you wanna know why?"

"Why?" she screamed back at him.

"Because Jason Bourne is some damned character in a book, Trudy. And me? I'm *real*. And I'm about to prove to this son of a bitch just how real I am."

———

MAGGIE AND LUISA'S celebratory mood darkened just a few hours later, when another guy drove up in a white, dust-covered BMW. Hopping out, he began barking orders. Maggie decided to call him Moe. Suddenly, Eenie, Meenie and Miney began packing everything up in an excited fashion, happy faces all around as their time at the shack had evidently come to an end. Maggie's heart sank. She moved closer to the shack wall to peer outside between the cracks.

"What's going on?" Luisa said softly from behind her. She was coming out of it more and more, brought to life by the hope they now had in their social media post.

Maggie told her, then watched as a worried look came over Luisa's face, her eyes squinting into the sunlight that was pouring through the small holes in the roof, her face encompassed in countless dust motes stirred up from the floor as she shuffled her feet. "Shit! What now?"

"I dunno," Maggie replied. Not wanting to worry Luisa, she'd suppressed her real thoughts. *Well. It may be time for me to die. Dragging one person around Mexico is hard enough, no need to drag two— especially if those witches convinced Güero I'm nothing more than a distraction. And if that's the case, isn't this just the perfect mess? I may have to fight now, despite the very real risk of getting you or the baby injured in the process.*

The thought of fighting against such long odds provoked a shameful urge within her to just run if she got the chance. She'd already done enough for this girl she barely knew, hadn't she? It'd be wrong to abandon her, but when doing the right thing could cost you everything, it was okay to do the next best thing, wasn't it? Maybe if she got away, she could get help.

But who would protect Luisa in the meantime?

She's sixteen. She's just a baby, Maggie thought. *A baby with a baby. You just can't.*

Luisa startled her by grabbing her arm. "Maggie! No. This can't be happening. We just got that message out. Where do you think they'll take us next?"

"Hate to sound like a broken record, kiddo, but again, I dunno." Maggie put an arm around Luisa's shoulders.

It didn't take long for the four men to get everything together. In the process, it looked like Miney had ratted Eenie out to Moe, who looked irritated beyond measure. As he called Eenie over to him and clipped him, hard, with an open hand across his right temple, it was obvious beyond any doubt that he was the one in charge. With a guy like Güero Martinez to answer to, Maggie wasn't so sure that was such a good position to be in, and his actions now betrayed the pressure he was under. Eenie stepped back and looked as if he was thinking of retaliating before Moe unleashed a sea of Spanish that Maggie couldn't hope to understand. She looked at Luisa.

"You don't wanna know," Luisa said, her eyes going wide and her cheeks flushing red. "It's all bad words. He's super pissed."

The panic that was starting to rise in her was temporarily offset by hope as Maggie watched the argument outside escalate. This was good. If they fought among themselves then there'd be less of them for her to fight. After originally backing off, Eenie got in Moe's face and started shouting back. In the process, though, he didn't notice Meenie as he came up behind him. He lunged and pinned Eenie's arms behind his back. Miney pulled a gun and put it to Eenie's head.

The Spanish grew quieter, but no less intense. Then, without warning, Moe grabbed a full handful of Eenie's crotch and began squeezing. Eenie screamed and tried to squirm away, but with his arms trapped and a gun to his temple, he didn't have much hope. After a few seconds he reduced his screams to moans of agony before Moe finally let go. Then? More Spanish.

"He's saying, 'Do you understand?'" Luisa translated. "'This shit will get us killed. Forget about the little white . . .bitch.'" Luisa looked at Maggie sheepishly. "Sorry."

Maggie shrugged. "I've been called way worse."

"Yeah. Well, he said a lot of stuff before bitch, but I left that out."

A conversation between Moe and Miney began and the look that came over Luisa's face was alarming.

"What?" Maggie asked.

"They're . . . shit."

"Say it."

"Eenie's trying to tell him they should just kill you. Tell Güero that you tried to escape."

Maggie's panic came back with a vengeance. *I knew it.*

The only weapon she'd found was a quarter of a broom handle, not sheared but cut flat, that she'd found jammed into one of the floorboards near the corner of the shack. It would offer little or no distance from her opponent. Being this outnumbered, she needed distance to properly mount a good defense.

Luisa's eyes went wide. She suddenly began looking around for an escape. Then, apparently hearing something surprising, she spun back to look outside and her face began to relax.

"What?"

"Moe was asking which one of them wants to kill you and answer to Güero, because he wasn't going to be the one to do it and face the consequences of not delivering you safely to the boss."

"Any takers?"

"No." Luisa looked embarrassed again. "Um. Miney said 'no thanks'. That Güero is infatuated with you . . . wants to do . . . um . . . with you."

Maggie rolled her eyes. "Never mind."

Luisa put her hands over her mouth. "They've all taken a pass except . . . Thank God! Meenie's just said he's out, too."

Maggie exhaled and felt herself shaking. "Okay. Okay." She wiped her hand up over her forehead and across her hair. "Figures. Chickenshit can't do anything on his own but cop a feel."

"I'm so sorry, Maggie," Luisa said out of nowhere, a haunting sadness to her voice.

"For what?"

"This whole thing is my—"

Maggie hugged her. "No. We aren't going down that rabbit hole, okay? You had no idea your uncle was this evil, did you?"

Luisa buried her head against Maggie's shoulder and hugged her back tightly. "No. I swear. I knew he was in the gang . . . but this? No. The *brujas*—the witches—there are some in our neighborhood. Potion people. Silly stuff. But these ones? I think they're real."

"Real?"

"Yeah. I can almost feel their evil." And now she looked even more like a child. One who had watched one too many horror movies.

"Luisa, that stuff's not real," Maggie replied, hearing the lack of conviction in her own words, which was more than a bit unsettling. *Yeah. Exactly what "stuff" are you referring to, Maggie? What about the dreams of Father Soltera? And the boat? The dreams of the past, with the island, and your grandmother?*

"Yes, it is, Maggie. Evil spirits are everywhere. Even my mom would tell you that. On *Día de los Muertos*, we light so many candles in my house." Her breath rattled. "You can feel them, in our neighborhood sometimes. People die, or bad things happen, and the streets seem happy. Like every dead body found on a corner was led there by some sort of bad crossing guard."

"Luisa, don't get yourself—"

"I'm sorry I was lying on the cot so much. I'm scared, Maggie. And really, most of the time, I was trying to listen to what these idiots were saying. I should be stronger for us. I'm sorry."

"Don't be silly. We're gonna be okay, as long as we stick together. Help will come. I just know it. So all this time you've been listening to their Spanish? Tell me, what else were they saying out there?"

"Mostly stupid stuff about football soccer or poker games they'd won. But then, the more they talked? The more I didn't want to hear."

The air was getting stagnant in the shack as the heat outside rose. "Why?"

Luisa's face froze in a sort of desperate stare, off into the distance. Then, quickly, she looked into Maggie's eyes. "They want my baby, Maggie. The *brujas*, I mean."

Maggie felt her jaw drop. "What?"

"Yes. That's the only thing I have left now: hope that my uncle, of all people, will not let them do it."

"Do what?"

Luisa's eyes filled with tears. She shook her head, refusing to reply. Car doors were opening and closing outside. Maggie took another peek; they were almost done. They'd be coming soon.

Maggie turned back to Luisa and put their foreheads together. "Tell me," she whispered.

"They want to—" Luisa's voice caught in her throat and her lips trembled. "They want to cut it out of me."

A stone rolled over Maggie's heart as her body went ice cold. She was incredulous. "What!"

"He said no. Back at the warehouse. It was the only time he stood up to them. They said it was the quickest way for whatever sick ritual they're planning, but they didn't care how it happened, as long as it happened."

"As long as what happens?"

"I have to die, right when the baby is born. My death has to cancel out its life," she whimpered as she buried her head into

Maggie's shoulder. "But that won't happen, right? I have you and we'll find a way out of this, right?"

And you were going to run, weren't you? Maggie thought. As her shame returned, she took Luisa in her arms. "Yes," she replied with conviction. "You do. And we will."

Chapter Eight

FATHER SOLTERA WATCHED as Gabriella stepped forwards, fell to her knees and reached a hand out to run her fingers through the threads in the driftwood. As she did, a tiny gasp escaped her mouth and a sorrowful look came over her face.

His heart swelled again, both at her sadness and his own. How long had he been so distracted by his desire to escape, both his loneliness and his cancer?

Too long. In fact, the days had totaled a healthy sum long before he'd ever even met Gabriella. Now, however, the Holy Spirit had finally elbowed his way back into that space between his soul and his heart. It hurt. Badly. But it was also good. It was not fair now, nor had it ever been, to try using her as his escape. "Gabriella?" he said, too softly for her to hear, so he repeated himself. "Gabriella?"

She glanced up at him. "Y-yes?"

He knelt down and looked her in the eye. "Pray back to her."

"What?" she asked, timidly.

"Your mother. Pray back to her."

A quizzical look came over her face, but it was not cynical. "Really? Do you think that would work?"

Father Soltera smiled gently. "If God can answer her prayers to you, then I don't think it's much of a stretch to think that He could answer yours to her."

She nodded, and the torture in her eyes was swept away by a look of hope. She folded her hands in her lap and bowed her head. Father Soltera truly believed that somewhere back in the real world her mother might feel a twinge of peace, of comfort, for no reason at all it might seem.

But this was not the only reason why he wanted Gabriella to pray. Something told him that Gabriella had to begin reestablishing her connection with the real world, if she were to ever have any hope of getting back to it. Here, in this place, she'd abandoned her life. She'd been isolated, which was where the enemy always wanted you: isolated and lonely.

He also needed to have his own moment with God, didn't he? Yes. He did.

Unbeknownst to Gabriella, Father Soltera reached out his right hand and held it just above her head. Clutching the rosary around his neck with his left hand, he closed his eyes and opened a dialogue. It began with a tiny request of forgiveness, which, like a seed, unfurled into a prayer. *Help me save her, Lord. Help me be the bridge that gets her home. I hope that's why you sent me. I believe that's why you sent me. Please, Lord, let it be true, and please help me succeed.*

Around them, the waters of the island lapped against the shore, soft and gentle, back and forth.

It was while in seminary, as a young man, that he first discovered the depth and width of prayer. How it could be both clarifying and purifying at the exact same time, as if the cool waters of heaven were being dribbled down, through the creek of your soul, to form currents that would sweep away the twigs and rotting leaves within you. Each morning, noon and night, he and his brothers would pray in the small church chapel, and after a time Father Soltera believed that though he could only know his own prayers, he could feel theirs. In the air, like pollen on a soft breeze.

And now, he could feel Gabriella's, too. They were gentle, as he imagined they would be, the prayers of a child to their mother. The bond of the womb, sacred still. She began to weep softly. "I'm so scared, Mama," she whispered. And he was thankful to her for sharing, because he could then pray, in whispers of his own, right over her, one of his favorite prayers for addressing fear: one by Thomas Merton, from *Thoughts in Solitude*. "'I trust you always, though I may seem to be lost and in the shadow of death. I will not fear, for you are ever with me, and you will never leave me to face my perils alone.'"

He nodded softly, knowing that every word he uttered for her sake, he was also uttering for his, their shared existence in this place so far away from where they both belonged needing to come to an end, in more ways than one.

As if sensing his thoughts, she ended her prayers, sat on the back of her feet and looked up at him. "I never meant to fall in love with you, Father."

Startled, he looked away, then gathered himself. So now was the time for the words between them to finally be said. So be it. He nodded and looked back at her. "Nor I, you."

She looked at him intently, as if she always knew he felt the same but was finally relieved to hear it confirmed. "Why do you think it happened?"

"Hmm," he said with the tiniest of laughs. He took a few extra seconds to consider things before he answered. "Perhaps because you were at a place in your life where you needed an idealistic sort of love . . . and so did I."

A breezed picked up, blowing strands of her dark hair across her face, which she swept away with her hand. "You mean, it wasn't real?" And there was a tone of hurt in her voice.

Even now, in repentance, her beauty still called to him. Double-minded, he struggled for a moment, then replied, "No, it was real. But also . . . not."

"What do you mean? How could it be both?"

"It was a reality based in a fantasy. But it was mutual, you see. I don't know why but I think that makes it different somehow."

"A shared reality . . ."

"And a shared *fantasy*. That you could ever live down the stigma of seducing a priest from the faith or that I could ever live with seducing a congregant that trusted me with her deepest secrets."

"So . . . what, then? It was all evil?"

He shook his head as it all finally came into focus. "No. No. You see, God was in the love between us, Gabriella. Not in the sinful wanting but in the loving denying."

She tilted her head sideways, as if against the weight of her thoughts. "It's why I said I was going to leave the church and go somewhere else."

"And why I did not stop you. We both knew, you see, that it could never be. That sin was calling to us but we did not really want to answer it."

"How do you know that?"

He smiled at her. "Because if we did, we would've."

"Instead," she said, putting a hand out to touch his knee, "I saw in you a good man who could only be less because of me."

"And I saw in you a good woman who could only be more without me."

"So, you're saying . . ."

"That God works for the good in all things, Gabriella. I have seen it too many times in my life to deny it. That was the pain we both felt: God working within us to curb the path we were on, the one we both thought we wanted, until this happened." He waved his hand at the water around the island and the sky overhead. "Until the process was interrupted, in that car accident, by fate or chance, perhaps by the devil himself."

"So that I could come here and forever be trapped in wanting you."

"And I could remain behind, barred in the prison of a misguided passion for you, because that is how the enemy works." Father Soltera looked out into the woods and added. "By paralysis of the soul, through whatever means necessary."

Father Soltera knew now that he was the bridge home for Gabriella.

He had to get her home.

But as he looked out over the water and back to shore, he could feel the darkness there. Waiting. The enemy wasn't done with them yet.

Not by a long shot.

———

ON THE YARD, as Hector sat alone at one of the benches, The Smiling Midget paid him another visit. Sauntering up across the dirt-patched grass in black jeans, black boots and a white t-shirt, he smiled and asked, *Are you having fun yet?*

Hector looked around nervously. Knowing full well that no one else could see The Smiling Midget, he spoke under his breath. "We aren't doing this again."

What? You mean like before, when you were in that junior league prison, when I still had to protect your sorry-ass life from getting killed?

"Whatever," Hector mumbled.

How much more do you think you're going to need me here, Hector? I mean . . . this place is the big leagues. Sorry, but I don't see you making it to the end of the month here without ending up dead. Maybe in the showers, maybe in the cafeteria. Whichever. They gonna waste your ass, and you know it.

Rubbing his chin Hector gave The Smiling Midget a hard look. "Yeah? And why's that, smartass?"

C'mon, Hectorino. We both know why. You're too soft. Always have been. Curled up in bed whining about your mommy one moment, then pining over Marisol the next. All the while clinging to your books and stories, as if they could ever do anything to save you.

"Pfft! What do you know about any of it, man?"

I know that you snapped like a twig when you heard Marisol was getting it from another man. I know that much. And after all those days and nights we spent together in the last place? I know that you know full well your books can't do shit to stop a bullet or a knife. Ain't no bullets here, buddy boy . . . but there are plenty of knives. And they'll be coming for you. Trust. And when they do? You're gonna need me.

"No. Never again. Relying on you was the worst mistake of my life."

Oh, really? Think about that for a sec. How did things go the last time you turned your back on me, Hector?

"They went—"

They went to shit. Bennie, Chico, Burro . . . Marisol and David. All if it went to hell in a handbasket. You remember that. But it can get good again. As long as you remember why you're here. I mean . . . really, *here, Hector. Not the fairytale reason why the other side wants you here, because that ain't gonna happen.*

"Look, just 'cause you—"

Someone suddenly shouted at Hector. "Inmate 7558! Get your ass up!"

The Smiling Midget disappeared immediately.

Hector looked up to see a tall guard towering over him, the name "Clark" stitched on his uniform shirt. "I said to get your ass up."

"Where we headed?" Hector asked as he complied.

Clark seemed stiff, almost nervous. "You'll see."

This in turn made Hector nervous. As he was being escorted through the yard, he felt the eyes of the other prisoners' turning to watch him, trying to size him up or figure out what he'd done to get yanked from the yard. Once he and Clark reached the large metal door of the cell block, Hector hesitated. "Hey man . . ."

Clark pulled out his baton. "No, no, no. You don't dictate the stroll, my man, you hear?"

"Okay! Shit. Chill," Hector replied with a frustrated shrug.

Clark pointed his baton at the door and Hector opened it and walked through.

Clark followed, guiding Hector past an office and down a few hallways until they reached a set of double metal doors that led to an outside patio on the other side of the building. Clark motioned again with his baton. "You got a visit set up on the other side. Good luck."

As Hector pushed open the doors, he held his breath, not sure what to expect or how to react. Instead, when he saw who was waiting for him, he smiled. It was Curtis, who evidently seeing Hector's face morph into relief, laughed out loud. "*¿Qué onda, güey?* You shit your pants or what?"

Hector laughed, suppressing his emotions at finally seeing a friendly face. "*Nada, jefe! ¿Qué onda?*"

Seated at a small circular table with attached bench seats, the kind you usually saw at parks, Curtis looked good, but older. Hector saw it mostly in his eyes, which seemed wrinkled with weariness. His head was shaved and the dragon tattoo on his neck had been embellished on the inside. It was larger now, with red stripes. It was the only colored tattoo he had. The rest, nearly a dozen on his arms alone, were all black stencil on his brown skin, with one that matched one of Hector's, the letters "FSV" within a number four: Fresno Street Vatos forever.

Lanky but muscular, he stood confidently and walked over to Hector, where they engaged in the ritual of their gang's five-part handshake before they hugged. When they separated, Curtis nodded at Clark, who nodded back. "You got ten minutes."

"Got it," Curtis replied. Clark disappeared back through the double doors and they were left alone. "C'mon, homie. Come sit down real quick."

Hector did as he was asked, taking a seat opposite his gang's leader. The same leader that he'd been sent here to kill by the same forces of evil that infested this place, and the very same leader that The Gray Man had sent him here to save. It was a whole 'nother level of being screwed.

"How you adjusting?"

"I been better."

"Your cellie?" Curtis asked, referring to Hector's cellmate.

"Quiet kid. Southerner. Fifteenth Street. In the SHU now, so I'm having some quality me-time."

Curtis laughed. "But you're probably still sleeping with one eye open, huh?"

Hector nodded. "No joke. This place is a trip, man."

"Yah." Curtis looked at him hard. "It is."

Curtis took a deep breath. "Well, you'll be getting a new cellie soon, so hold tight."

"Who?"

"You remember Flacco?" Curtis asked.

A blast from the past. Hector raised his eyebrows. "Yah. Barely. He's old school, right?"

"He ranked pretty high when you were just a pup. Handled Echo Park."

Hector could recall a very tall, very thin man with long fingers, graying temples and dead eyes, like a shark, that used to frequent the neighborhood. He wasn't mean, but he wasn't friendly, either. "Yeah. I remember him. He's in here, too?"

"You remember them fools from Figueroa?"

"I do. That's right. He shot up a few of them."

"Killed them both for robbing his sister by accident."

Hector nodded.

"He went to Folsom for a bit. Got ordered to take out someone inside. Stabbed the dude to death with a steak bone his girlfriend smuggled in to him during a visit."

"A *steak* bone?"

"Yeah. We don't get no bones in here with our meat, ya know? Haven't for years. You can sharpen those bad boys up like a caveman. Makes a perfect knife."

Hector was a bit incredulous. "Daaaaaaamn."

"Anyway, after that, his life sentence got doubled and he got shipped here two years before I did. But at least you have an ally in your cell."

"Hmm. Sounds good but . . ." Hector hesitated and tried to push away the moves his mind was making behind his eyes.

It was no use. Curtis had trained him from day one and knew him too well. "My little homie," he said with a smile, "go ahead and say it. Let's see if you're game has gotten better or gotten stale. C'mon."

"Well. He was a shot-caller way back, when you were coming up. How he handle you being his shot-caller now?"

Curtis smiled, big and large. "There it is. Good 'ol, Hector. Trust no one and all that shit. You're like the Mexican Mulder, ya know? From that *X-Files* show, man!"

"The X-what?"

"It's an oldie TV show. I got all the episodes on DVD in my cell. Love it. We'll have to watch them. There's this little *chica* with red hair, his FBI partner? Oh, man. So hot. *En fuego, Holmes!*"

Hector laughed. "Dude, you crazy."

"Yep. Anyway, Flacco is old school. He knows the game. The big bosses say I take lead? Then I take lead."

"S'cool. Good to know, especially if he'll be bunking with me and knows my loyalty to you."

Curtis looked at Hector for a few seconds too long, like maybe he knew something. For a second, Hector panicked, but then he realized it could simply be that Curtis had gone a long time in here already and maybe had become just as paranoid as Hector.

"Yep. Anyway, we're running outta time. So, here's your quick rundown, just for perspective, okay?"

"Yeah. I'm listening."

"Okay. So. Eight out of every ten people in here will be right back here within five years of getting out. They process through the system like an Aflac rep. Someday you might want or get a transfer. It won't matter. 'Cause the same *vatos* trying to kill you in here? Even when they get transferred and you think maybe you're rid of them? They might transfer over right after you or have friends waiting for you there. You dig?"

Hector nodded. "Yeah."

"Get it in your head now: prison life, for you now, is the *only* life. Deals, trades, alliances? That's all that matters."

Hector shrugged. "How's that so different than how it is on the outside?"

Curtis nodded and looked out over the grassy area around them that formed a small courtyard. On one wall were lines of staggered potting boxes, each filled with herbs. On the other was a line of sticks with tall, vibrant tomato plants curving up their lengths and drooping with the weight of their harvest. By the back wall of the courtyard was a small garden of what looked like chili peppers of all kinds. After a few seconds, Curtis looked back to Hector.

"Simple, really. Two things make it different. In here, homie? In here there's no women and no retreat, you understand? And that's big. 'Cause that means there ain't no love and their ain't no rest, man. We like animals, just pacing back and forth, day and night, digging at the dirt for some hope, for . . . for . . . I dunno what word I'm looking for . . ."

Somehow, Hector did. "Humanity."

Slapping a knee with the knuckles of one hand, Curtis nodded vigorously. "Yeah, dog. That's it! Some humanity, man."

In the corner of the courtyard was a large avocado tree. A brown bird drifted down to it from above and landed on one of the branches.

When Curtis spoke next his voice was all business. "I want you to be careful. We're on different rotations but that's a good thing. It gives me some eyes on your shift, dig?"

"Yeah."

Then, somewhat ominously, Curtis added, "And one other thing: you fucked up out there, shooting up that kid over some dumb bitch. It's costing us all. We'll have to talk about that later, after you're settled in, you dig?"

Hector watched the brown bird hop between a few branches before it took back off into the sky. He lowered his head and nodded at the ground.

"I dig."

Chapter Nine

THEY'D MADE the rest of the drive to Trudy's parents' house almost entirely in silence, both needing their own space to figure out the answer to their disagreement by considering the Venn diagram that was their relationship. It was an awkward silence, but a silence they both seemed to know they needed.

The landscape around them had gone from patchy desert to lush farmland and the wide-open hills of Wine Country. Wooden fence posts stretched down either side of the highway, hemming in the occasional herd of cows or horses. They passed a few roadside stands and stores, closed now, and off the highway tractors could be seen here or there along with ranch-like homes that were painted fresh and bright. There was money in wine, for sure, and Parker guessed the cows and horses were just for show.

When they reached their off-ramp Trudy finally spoke, her voice sad and hesitant, her cheeks touched with color. "You can kill him to keep me safe and then what? Won't people want to avenge him? Which would mean I could end up in just as much danger, anyway."

Parker opened his mouth and then shut it, giving himself some time to process his answer so that it would come out calm and respectful. "You're right," he finally said. "Which is why I don't plan on killing this guy."

She inhaled deeply, then exhaled loudly. "You don't?"

"Of course not, Trudy. I'm not a killer." The last four words came out flat, because they weren't entirely true and they both knew it. He'd been to war. He'd killed plenty. His therapist had said that someday he'd have to confess the many truths of this fact to her. But now was not the time.

"Okay. But he's dangerous. So, you can't be sure that you won't have to kill him."

He nodded. "That's true."

"And you wouldn't be in that position if you weren't so damned . . . if you weren't so insistent on going after him in the first place."

"Debatable, and we both know it."

"How so?"

He gripped the steering wheel as he made a left turn into almost non-existent traffic. The road was wet in spots from a sprinkler system alongside it that was firing away in large, cascading streams. "He's come after me once, through you, already. If you think about it, had I gone after *him* sooner? Then what happened, wouldn't have happened."

She looked out the front window but said nothing, so he continued. "You can take it front to back, or back to front. Either way, something's got to be done. He's a monster, plain and simple. I go kill him, there could be repercussions. Maybe. But with the chaos this guy has caused? The cartel could just as easily be glad to be rid of him."

"That's a big gamble."

"Yes. But like I said earlier, killing cops or their loved ones is bad press, bad business, bad everything. At this point? In their jacked-up tribal existence? The cartel might actually think I have the right to do this."

"Do what exactly?" She put one foot up on the dashboard and uncrossed her arms.

"Go after him. Get him."

"*Get* him?" she pressed. She was obviously going to make him say it.

"Capture him. Bring him in. At that point, I've saved face and, more importantly to them, not cost them any face."

"And?"

"He has troops loyal to him. Just acing him on his own causes unnecessary drama. But once he's caught, everyone in that world knows that he's a liability. The cartel no doubt has plenty of people on the inside to take care of him, if that's what they want to do. At that point? The law will have done what the law does, and the bad guys will do what the bad guys do."

"What if you have to kill him?"

"Then I have to kill him. But I give you my word it will be as a last resort, no matter what."

She nodded, then reached out and put her hand on his. "Next to last," she said.

As they stopped at a red light, he glanced over at her, confused. "Next?"

"I get it now, why you're doing this. I'm scared, but I'm behind you. Especially now that I know you're not out to take another life as some sort of bullshit macho revenge. That being said? I don't want you to hesitate with this man, not for one second. You're right: he's a monster. And if you died because you were hesitating because of me . . . I could never forgive myself."

The light turned green and he followed the orders of the voice on his GPS, driving to the next corner and making a right onto a dirt road that led through a wide vineyard. He could see what he guessed was her parents' house about a quarter mile up ahead, its lights on bright in the middle of an open patch of land.

"Okay?" she pushed.

He nodded. "Okay."

Playfully, she raised her pinky finger to him as they came to a stop in the driveway in front of the house. "Pinky-promise me?"

He smiled weakly, his heart swelling, as he wrapped his pinky finger around hers. "Pinky-promise."

She leaned in close his face, wincing a bit in pain. "You do realize that pinky-promises are legally binding, don't you?"

His smile grew, and he barely got the word "yes" out before she kissed him full, long and hard on the lips.

When the kiss was over, he pulled back and said it, point blank. "I love you."

Now it was her turn to smile. Her lips turned up slightly, but her eyes were still full of worry. "I love you more."

He went to grab the door handle. "No," she said firmly. "This is not how you meet my parents."

"What?"

"As far as they're concerned, I had a friend drive me who couldn't stay to visit. You will not be going in there to answer to my father for what's happened—because trust me, he'll own your ass—or to make small talk with all the grim thoughts you have in your head right now. It would be wrong, and quite frankly, it would ruin the moment forever."

"But you're hurt and . . ."

She scoffed, opened her door and swung one leg out. "I can take care of myself, and I'll get my own bag. Just pop the trunk. You only have to do one thing, Evan . . ." Her voice broke and her eyes swelled with tears.

He grabbed her hand again. "What?"

"You come home to me. Do you understand?" She squeezed his hand so tightly that it hurt. "Come home to me."

Before he could reply, she got out of the car and shut the door.

He popped the trunk and heard her pull her bag out before she closed it.

Every instinct in his body begged him to get out, run to her and call the whole thing off. But he knew better. There was no running from this. No way to call a retreat from an enemy that was so insane or reckless. Güero was . . . a man of war.

As he drove back off the property, he mulled this over in his mind. Yes. It was true. Güero was nothing but the latest orchestrator of death in Parker's life. Al Qaeda. The Taliban. Murder and destruction, over and over. Misery caused by men determined to have their way, mostly in the name of money, couched in the name of war.

His therapist always told him that in order to be honest with others, he had to—absolutely had to—first be honest with himself.

This was the real reason why he'd opted to go after Güero this way, why Parker was choosing pseudo-military means over civilian means. Why he was calling on Melon for help, just like old times.

Because Parker's default setting was as a man of war, too. Because in Iraq and Afghanistan? There'd been hardly any justice served . . . and that's what was killing him. Slowly. From the inside out. And he had to exorcise that demon. Crime was a different kind of war and this was a different kind of enemy. But still, at some point, there had to be justice in this life.

And for that to happen, he had to be a soldier one more time.

In order to be a soldier for the last time.

———

MAGGIE TOLD herself to calm down when Meenie came through the door of the shack with Moe, both with guns drawn, and told her and Luisa to turn around and face the wall. Once they complied, their hands were zip-tied behind their backs and they were marched out to the Escalade and loaded up.

In her mind she began begging with God not to let it be too long of a long drive from where she had push-pinned their location on Facebook. Something told her to relax. If she really thought about it, they had Eenie's phone ID now, which meant the police could probably track it. If, that was, he didn't get sent off somewhere else. That would be bad.

The sky was a loud blue, with hardly any clouds. After about a fifteen-minute drive through nothing but barren hills on a wide dirt road, they came to a stop and the doors of the Escalade flew open. Maggie was pulled from one side, Luisa from the other. Before them was an old house, mostly made of brick and adobe, painted a sun-bleached tan. The windows were shuttered and the lawn, if you could call it that, was all dead grass surrounded by a few hedges that were not long to follow. There was a path that cut through the lawn and to the front door, and as they were ushered along Maggie saw that over the door, painted in red, was a pentagram. The red was too stark, almost maroon, and smeared in places. Blood. She told herself it was probably from an animal of some kind, but she wasn't so sure. Luisa, walking just ahead, saw it too and tried to put on the brakes, but it was no use. Moe grabbed her roughly by one arm and Miney by the other. She screamed and Miney used his free hand to cover her mouth. Maggie didn't even try. Around them was nothing but open desert and what had once been farmland of some kind, with no other house or person in sight.

The weight of their predicament was obvious. They were in a foreign country, far away from help, stripped of any US rights they'd become accustomed to. These guys were serious, Mexican Mafia types, which meant they probably owned any nearby town and its inhabitants anyway. They could run, they could escape, but to where and to whom for help? *Nowhere,* she thought, and her despair multiplied. *Nowhere and to no one. You're completely screwed, Maggie. You've gotten yourself into one you can't get out of this time.*

The door to the house flew open, shocking Maggie out of her thoughts, and what was there took a while to compute. It was a woman, yes, but she was beyond pale. Her face was painted with some sort of chalk. Her eye sockets were small but worst of all, by far, were the piercings in her cheeks and lips, almost too many to count, so that when she looked upon Luisa and smiled, the sun caught the piercings in a wave of tiny glimmers. She reached out with one hand, her long fingers slender and tipped with long nails. As Luisa struggled violently to pull away, Maggie struggled just as hard to get to her but Meenie had her in a tight grip.

They were forced into the home, where the three witches from the warehouse were waiting: Misha on a chair to the left, Delva and Anastasia on a frayed and worn blue couch to the right. The room was lit by diffracted light through the shuttered windows, which were partially covered with sheer black drapes. A large lamp in the near corner was turned on, spreading a cone of yellow across the floor, which was carpeted and filthy with the outside dirt. Between the witches was a folding table with bones and stones on it.

"Ah. Here she is again. Finally. Lovely, lovely girl," Delva said, gazing upon Luisa, her voice clogged. She cleared her throat of phlegm and continued. "Bring her to me."

Luisa was having none of it. Her adrenaline kicked in and she doubled her efforts at escape. Moe held tight but Miney lost his grip on one of her wrists. Luisa spun towards him, raking her nails across his face in the process. He screamed and grabbed at her hand, over and over, trying to catch it like a wild bird, as she swung it at him, missing a few times before connecting again, this time with his lower lip, which went plump almost instantly. He cursed and nearly tripped.

At the sight of it all, incredibly, the witches began to laugh, hollow and wicked, in a round, like a children's tune. This only frustrated Miney more but it didn't matter. The woman with the piercings closed the door, crossed the room unceremoniously and slapped Luisa hard across the face. Shocked, Luisa fell back into Moe.

"Easy, Sonia! Easy!" one of the witches screamed from the couch.

In the far corner was some sort of display altar, covered in dead flowers and surrounded by dozens of candles in staggered rows, shorter ones to the front, taller and fatter ones towards the back, each with dried dribbles of wax. There was a photo at the center of the altar, but Maggie couldn't make it out. She did, however, see an upside-down crucifix on the opposite wall, and the sight of it made her think of one thing: Father Soltera. She hadn't reached out to him in a long time. Not because she hadn't wanted to but because she hadn't . . . been moved to. That was probably the only way to say it, if not the best way.

She did now, and his presence was nearly immediate. Distant, but still there. She had a childhood notion come to mind, that of tying a long piece of string between two tin cans to make a crude telephone. Sometimes it worked, but sometimes the connection was too weak, the string . . . not taut enough. Another realization come to her from out of nowhere: she and Father Soltera, their connection, was based on need. Or, more accurately, the level of their need. Contact could only be established when a certain benchmark for that need was met.

The witches stood and gathered around a pitifully resigned Luisa, who was now whimpering unintelligibly. Maggie stopped struggling as Sonia turned to look at her, sneered and said, "What do we do with this one?"

"She's special," Delva croaked. "I think her blood will prove to be a very special gift The Master has given us for the ritual."

Maggie knew it would do no good to panic. Still, her mind began to dissolve with fear. Eenie held her in place as she did everything she could to wrench herself loose.

All while Delva laughed and laughed.

Chapter Ten

THE SKY around them folded over on itself, first in one layer, then five, before it spread back out again, as if it were a massive sheet being whipped flat. The air crackled with energy, like sparklers on Fourth of July, but invisible and all around them. Father Soltera turned to look back at the mainland and saw Michiko there, sitting cross-legged, her wrists on her knees, her palms face up, watching.

"Who is she?" Gabriella asked curiously.

Father Soltera shook his head. "I don't know, entirely."

They walked to a small dune edged with grass and sat together. "How did the two of you meet?"

"I first saw her in the hospital, after . . . ." He paused.

"After what?"

He looked at her. "Gabriella, I should tell you something. I was attacked. Stabbed, I think."

"What?" A look of concern flooded her face.

"Yes. There's a young girl, Luisa, from my congregation. She became pregnant with a . . . less than honorable man, is the best way I can put it. He wanted her to abort the baby and when she hesitated, he threatened her. I tried to help, so he came after me."

"What happened?"

Father Soltera grasped at the memory of that night. "I-I don't know, really. I mean, I remember him coming towards me and I was grabbed from behind. I felt the knife go into me a few times, and then things went black."

"That's horrible," she said as she hugged him.

"I woke up a little later with people all around me . . . on the street. I think I bled a lot. Then I passed out again until I was at the hospital, and"—he motioned to Michiko—"there she was. Telling me stuff."

"What stuff?"

The energy around them had dissipated. The water, which had been restless, now went flat as glass.

He sighed. "That I wasn't going to die. That it wasn't my time."

"And then?"

"Then I was here, in this place. Off in the woods that led to here."

She looked around them. "I've wondered, so many times, what's out there."

He shook his head. "You don't want to know."

Rubbing the back of her neck with one hand, she asked, "Well, now that you're here, what next?"

He sighed heavily. "I think I have to leave."

"What? No! No, Father. Don't leave me here all alone again. I can't take it." And the way she said it, with such desperation, made him waiver. Instead, he looked back to Michiko and the shore.

"It's why she's waiting, Gabriella."

She shook her head, back and forth, like a terrified child. "No."

Father Soltera felt as though Michiko was right there in his mind, counseling his thoughts, showing him the truth. "I think it's the way—the only way—to get you back home."

"How? How are you ever going to get me back home?"

"We had a connection there, you and I. It was broken. I came here to reestablish it, and now, I guess like some kind of electrical current, it needs to be grounded again."

"Father, I can't—"

"You have to, Gabriella. You have to be strong and trust in the Lord. And I have to get back home and . . ." He struggled through the different ideas in his head. It was no use. He looked to Michiko and called to her in his mind. *What? What exactly do I have to do?*

She told him.

Nodding softly, he said, "I have to go back and bring the energy of this place back with me to bridge the divide."

"What are you talking about?"

He was still staring intently at Michiko. "Yes. Yes, I get it. If I bridge the divide between here and there . . . yes."

Gabriella seemed torn. "If what you're saying is true . . ."

He looked into her eyes. "If I can get back, your soul will be able to cross over that bridge, back to your body. From this place and back to your life."

Michiko stood and took a stone out of a small satchel on her waist and began using it to sharpen her long sword. The time for talk, verbally, telepathically or otherwise, was evidently over. And he was okay with that. Because now, at last, he could finally see a clear direction.

He walked in a semicircle. "Yes! That's it. This is how it must be, Gabriella. This is how what's between you and me finally—" But he stopped himself from finishing, fearing that she was not ready to hear the rest of what he was beginning to suspect.

"Finally what?" she prodded.

He thought again of Felix coming towards him with the knife. He'd been scared, but hadn't a part of him, way deep down, almost welcomed it?

The sky rumbled but there were no storm clouds to justify it.

The cancer. The loneliness. The chemo. The pills. The five

stages of grief, over and over . . . by himself and for himself . . . until he lost count. Then? The cruel ray of sunshine in the form of this woman, standing right before him, the hope of a love, an escape, that could never be. That only ended up compounding his pain. So that by the time Felix arrived, by the time death came to visit . . .

He pointed to the trees. "That forest is full of people who gave up on life, in one way, shape or form. I've counseled many over the years that had such thoughts, of taking their own lives. But sometimes the surrender isn't always . . . proactive . . . is it?"

She looked away.

"Tell me," he said, giving voice to a fear he'd had all along, "the accident— on the freeway, with the semi-truck—how did it happen?"

"What do you mean? It blew a tire, it swerved into me . . ."

"And?"

She squinted at the memory, looked away, then looked back. At it. At him. "There was nothing I could do."

He said nothing. Because he didn't have to. Because they both knew what this place—this stifling, haunting place—was for, and there was no use hiding it any further. Father Soltera, he'd been sent here, for her. But Gabriella? She'd arrived here because she shared something with all the other lost souls he'd encountered so far on this strange journey.

Her eyes filled with tears as she set her jaw defiantly, seeing the accusation in his face. "I did everything I could to avoid that accident."

Again, he said nothing.

She stepped towards him and began beating him on the chest. "I did! Don't you look at me that way! Don't you dare judge me! I did all that I could . . ."

"I know, I know," he said softly, tears filling his eyes now too. "I'm not judging you."

He'd been a priest a long time. He'd been a part of countless confessions, and each one was different in many ways: in what they said, in how they said it and how much they meant it. Except the moment when they were ready to confess something to themselves. Then it was always the same. Something special happened, almost every time; a clarity came to their eyes that was so bright it was almost like a light, as if the Holy Spirit were a beam flickering in their pupils. He watched it happen in Gabriella's eyes now.

"The road was wet. It was raining. I was . . ." Her cheeks tightened against the sadness overcoming her. "I was listening to our song. 'Ombra Mai Fu.' Loudly. Really loudly. I didn't hear the tire blow on the semi as clearly as I should have but it didn't matter. Because, because . . ." She fell into his arms and buried her face in his chest.

"Say it," he whispered into her ear, like a lover. A true lover. Not one who gives passion, but one who offers freedom. Absolution. Grace. Hope. "Say it."

"I didn't *want* to avoid it—the crash, I mean. I didn't even t-try," she cried. "I hit the brake, but only for a second. Then I figured, why the hell not? What was there to live for anymore? Thirty-two years old. A useless job. No man had ever found me good enough, and I hated myself for caring about that, but I was tired of being alone. And now, I was a sinful piece of shit who'd tried to start something with her priest! Seriously? My priest? Who does that? Who? But then to . . . how could I have . . ."

"You weren't—"

Her sobs subsided as she cut him off. "How could I have done that, Father? Just give up like that? What I did to the people I love. My poor mom. She'll never know how much . . ."

He pushed her away. "Yes, she will, Gabriella. She *will* know how much you loved her and I'm going to see to it. I'm going to get you out of here, if it's the last thing I do."

"But how in the world are you going to do that?"

They were so engrossed that neither of them noticed Michiko had somehow crossed the waters and was now standing next to them. "He will do so by crossing through The Whiting Woods and finding The Stairway," she said solemnly. "But your time together must end, now, if it is to work. We must go. We are running out of time."

Father Soltera hesitated, then looked at Gabriella and mounted up within himself all the courage his soul had left in it. "I've got to go," he said.

She let go of him reluctantly and wiped at her eyes. "Okay." As if to pep him up a little, she smiled encouragingly. "See you soon!"

"Yeah." He nodded with equal encouragement and a little smile of his own. "You bet."

As he turned and walked to the water with Michiko, he realized that he hadn't really lied. He'd simply substituted one truth for another.

He'd see her again. Someday. But not here.

————

HECTOR HAD FORGOTTEN how night in prison comes on like a creeping fog: through the bars in the windows, caressing the walls of the hallways, lingering at the edges of every cell until it finally rolls in, making a dark place even darker, until it permeates your soul. Hector hated nighttime in prison and though he was liking his solitude, he was also feeling like he was ready for the cellmate Curtis had promised. Flacco, anyone, would be welcome company right about now.

He sat at the tiny desk in the corner of his cell, a copy of *The Brothers Karamazov* open before him under a small reading lamp, unable to concentrate enough to read and distracted by the discomfort of the metal chair he was sitting on. Rubbing his hand over his face, he closed his eyes and tried to deny it, the night. But it was no use. It was the loneliest, saddest part of the day, when you were left with only your thoughts. Of what you'd done to other people. Of what you'd done to your entire life.

You could barely fathom the sun coming up the next morning, much less contemplate the years and decades stretching out ahead of you now like a long road to hell.

But it's not a road to hell, Hector. It's a road to redemption.

He opened his eyes and looked over his shoulder. The Gray Man was standing with his arms folded and his back against the cell door. But his image was snowy, like the static signal on a bad black-and-white TV set.

"It's about time you showed up."

The Gray Man dipped his head to one side. *I know. But as you can see, this place . . . it is hard to infiltrate.*

"I thought you could do anything."

He grunted. *And who ever told you such a thing?*

"I dunno." Hector shrugged. Turning sideways in his chair, he could not hide the relief he felt, to his core, at seeing him. "I'm just glad you're back."

Good. But I can't stay long. There are a lot of lines in play this time.

"Lines?"

Human lives are like intersections, Hector. They cross and re-cross in some cases. You're all so busy getting to where you're going that you rarely ever see this.

"Yeah?"

His image faded, squelched, then blurred before he was back again. *Yes. And the activity in my . . .*

Hector squinted at him with curiosity. "What were you going to say?"

The Gray Man suddenly looked sad. *It's nothing, my boy. I'm just getting far along in this journey, is all.*

"What? You mean, like, you're getting old?" Hector said teasingly.

It worked. The Gray Man smiled. *That's what I used to call it, yes. Now I know better.* He looked up, then back to Hector. *Now I know that the entire journey is not about aging; it's about evolving.*

Hector stood and stretched his back, which was killing him

from the chair. "Yeah? That don't make much sense because, man, I don't feel so young no more."

Well. Aging happens. Yes. The body withers. But to what, is the question. To this state I'm in now or—

"To the state of that little bastard that's back after me?" Hector said, referring to The Smiling Midget.

The Gray Man nodded. *Exactly. And from there? The process continues.*

"What do you mean?"

Never mind. We don't have time for idle chatter. You've been in contact with Curtis.

"No. C'mon. Look where I'm at. I know you're in a hurry but I'm not. Because the minute you leave?" Hector said with a huge sigh. "I'm gonna go back to slowly going crazy again."

Hector, we should be working on your training with the blue. You will need it.

"Please," Hector said, looking at The Gray Man seriously, emotion cracking his voice. "I need something to understand besides just survival, man. I don't care about no blue if there's no purpose for all of this . . . of life . . . anyways."

The Gray Man looked down at his shoes and nodded. Then, uncrossing his arms, he put his hands in his pockets. *Okay. It's not all that complicated, really. Your little friend is doing as much evil as he can to advance in his kingdom.*

The idea reminded Hector of his Xbox for some reason. "You mean like leveling up or something?"

Well. I've never heard it put quite that way, but yes, I suppose you could describe it like that.

"And you?"

It's different.

"How?"

Your friend does everything out of selfish desire and ambition. With hate and pride he seeks promotion, to do greater harm, to become a greater evil. His kind and the place he serves is all about perpetuating greater pain and sorrow.

"You mean . . . like in the world?"

No. More like in the world within *each one of you, Hector. By doing that, the world outside will naturally follow.*

Hector leaned against the edge of his cot, facing The Gray Man, waiting for him to continue.

The crackle of more static came as The Gray Man looked around them, as if seeing through the walls and checking that the coast was clear, before he continued. *The path I am on is about peace and redemption, about serving others and a greater good. It does not seek to grow and overcome anything, but rather to be a seed and become something. One must* become *before one can* overcome, *do you understand? The evolution of the soul is continuous.*

Hector squinted with confusion. "I'm not sure I follow."

Don't play the street thug with me, Hector. You understand full well. I'm on a path to my . . . next level, as you put it. So are you. Neither of us should forget that one can go the other way, too, at any given time. Free will does not end on earth. If that were true, then how could Lucifer have made the decision that he did?

"Shit, man. That's heavy. Lucifer?"

The Gray Man shook his head. *I'm saying too much. You shouldn't be hearing this.*

"Then why are you telling it to me?"

The Gray Man removed his fedora with one hand and used his other to dust the top of it off before he replaced it. He looked sad again. *Because I'm running out of time.*

Alarmed, Hector tensed. "Time?"

Yes, Hector. I've watched over my little section of the universe, your city, for long enough. It's time for me to move. It happens. I just didn't expect it to happen this soon. We don't have nearly enough time to train you . . . and with the challenge coming your way, it will be crucial.

"So then why is it happening?"

His image cut out and staggered in static flashes across the room before it became fixed again. But his façade was much snowier now, and only getting worse. A pensive look crossed

The Gray Man's face. *We must have faith, Hector, always, in one very important thing.*

"And what's that?"

That the Lord works for the good in all things. All things. Always. For me, most recently, it happened with Kyle Fasano. The love he had for his wife, the choice he made in the end. It affected me, you see? It reminded me of something I'd left behind. And now I'm seeing it again with you, in even more ways.

"Seeing what, man? Quit talking in riddles."

Your humanity, Hector. Kyle's humanity. It's a beautiful thing, but it beckons to a part of me that is long gone. My role, the role of those like me, is to lead and guide you all, when you need to be, when you ask to be. To help you to evolve. We cannot waiver in that task. When we do? It's okay. We, too, can repent and be forgiven. God loves us all, in the roles we each serve. And I suppose I'm telling you all this because you've seen enough to know that it's all real: good, evil, heaven and hell. It's not a bad thing that I'm leaving. It's best for me now, at this time, to do other things. And you're my last.

"Your last what?"

My last millionth.

Chapter Eleven

JUST AS PARKER began the drive back home, and while mulling over when he'd call Melon in Cabo, his cell phone rang.

It was a restricted number. He tensed. Was it possible that Güero would dare to call him again? He braced himself as he punched the answer button on the steering wheel. When he heard Clopton's voice, he sighed with relief.

"It's me. You got a sec?" she said.

"Yeah," he replied.

"You figured out any details, yet?"

"I was just starting to. I'm thinking about—"

"I don't want or need to hear any of it," she said bluntly.

He nodded to himself. Of course she didn't. "Oookay."

"Here's the scoop. We have a task force down that way working in conjunction with the Mexican government and the DEA. Mostly on the cartels. But they'll have intel. Maps. And a burner phone in case you get into any trouble. Your contact will be a guy named Jim."

Parker laughed. "Jim?"

"It's a nice name."

"And as generic as they get."

"And you were expecting something different?"

"Good point. The burner phone is a nice touch, too."

"How so?"

Parker shook his head as he stretched his neck against the stress that was just beginning to grip at it. "Um. Can you say 'plausible deniability'?"

Clopton sounded irritated. "Again, he acts like this is his first rodeo."

He pulled around a Prius that was laboring in the fast lane and hit the gas. "Yeah, yeah. You get any further with the case?"

She mumbled something, then replied, "We busted a few of his local cronies, who won't talk they're so damned afraid of this guy. So, we still don't know what happened to the girls that were smuggled into Long Beach. But from what records we found in one of Güero's warehouses? It looks like this guy was pulling a container a *week* into the Southern California area." She took a breath as her voice grew angrier. "But even worse than that? You wanna hear it?"

"Shoot. Might as well tell the disposable guy what you can, while you can," he half-joked.

"Oh, please. Trust me, I wish I could be the one to go after his ass and not you. I really do. It makes me sick that I can't. But I can't. The chickenshit ran. And, well, I got these other containers to track down, you understand?"

"I do."

"So, do me a favor and don't play the sacrificial hero on me. We both have a common interest. We're both going to help each other to serve those interests. Period."

He sighed. "You're right. No more joking around. So. What were you gonna tell me that's worse?"

"Alejandra. Remember that name. She's sixteen. We found her during the warehouse bust I just mentioned, in one of twenty client rooms at the back, built out of two-by-fours and plywood. They had no lights, these rooms, and it took me, a translator, two agents and an FBI psychiatrist to calm her down long enough to get her statement. She was hysterical. All she kept saying was '*Manos! Manos! Manos!*'"

Parker squinted at the road, not wanting to hear anymore, but knowing he was about to.

"That . . . and freakin' numbers. In Spanish. *Ocho, ses, quatro.* Over and over. We finally find out that it was because she was always kept in the dark, back there, in that shitty plywood room. And the only way she knew how many men were raping her at one time? Was by counting the number of hands on her body, holding her down."

He grunted in pain at what he as hearing. "Oh, man. Clopton, I—"

She either didn't hear him or didn't want to hear him. Cutting him off, Clopton let it all out. "I want this guy. I want his damned head on a pike. If I've got the legal means to do it, and a few semi-legal ways to make the legal part happen? You best believe it's gonna happen."

"Fair enough. We're both on the same page, then. Now what?"

"LAX to Cabo San Lucas, because we both know who you're going to see."

He smiled. *Shit. She does her homework.* Still, he did not confirm anything but simply said, "Go ahead."

"When you get to Cabo, go to a restaurant called Señor Nachos. It's across from El Squid Roe. Ask for the lobster tacos. They don't serve lobster tacos but never mind, just make the order and wait for Jim to arrive with your intel, got it?"

"Got it. But one thing before you go, Clopton?" Parker said, suddenly remembering his talk with Trudy.

"What?"

"That whole head-on-a-pike thing? I get it. I really do. But I'm not going down there to kill him, okay? This is hopefully gonna be a simple snatch and run, got it?"

She laughed. "I understand. A simple snatch and run? With a guy like Güero? I hope you pull it off, I really do. Because that head-on-a-pike thing? I really, really want it to be *me* that gets that honor. In a courtroom. In front of a judge. Before he goes into a hole as dark as the ones he likes to put women in."

"And your superiors? How they gonna be down with this? Or, for that matter, the judge in that courtroom?"

"With this guy's track record of horrors? I won't need much. Hey. We put the word out down there; one of the guys that's gonna meet with you is a DEA informant. Official record will show that he reported Güero's location and a private citizen made the arrest."

Parker grinned. "A private citizen?"

"Yeah. Your buddy, if he jumps on board with you. Regardless, said citizen, for his own safety against the murderous bad-guy cartel that Güero works for, will have to be a John Doe, with only a short written statement. Our DEA station chief signs off on it down there, I sign off on it up here. Done."

"Shit. You really are coloring with this one, Clopton. And pretty much with only the red crayon."

She laughed. "Yes and no. Sometimes the rules can be blurred. And don't forget The Mayan and your partner, Campos."

His eyebrows shot up. "Yeah?"

"Yeah. You may think that Güero had no direct connection to that shooting, and you're probably right, but in a lot of people's minds on this end? Güero was in a club where a cop was shot and nearly killed. Period. And you know what that means, right?"

"What?"

"It means screw the red crayon. I get to use the whole box."

With that, she hung up.

The drive from Napa went quickly enough. Along the way, Parker made a stop in Los Banos to get some gas. Seeing a Chipotle nearby, he hit the head, then grabbed a carnitas burrito and a root beer, which he ate while sitting alone at a plastic table scratched up with graffiti.

Once back on the road, he found traffic on the 5 Freeway was wide open at this hour, and with the landscape buried in the dark of night, Parker played his music and bathed in the reflections of the dashboard lights off the interior windows, one of which now told him it was just past midnight.

Wearily, in the corner of his eye, he noticed that the lights appeared to be bending into an outline of someone in the passenger seat. The outline thickened and filled. Napoleon had returned.

"How long you been sitting there?" Parker asked.

"The whole ride," Napoleon said.

"What?"

Napoleon laughed. "Man, you're gullible, Parker. You actually think I have time to sit here for a long cruise down the highway with your ass?"

Parker smiled. Then chuckled. The car grew quiet for a second as Napoleon's tan glow became more obvious in the darkness. Parker noticed him looking out the passenger window. "What is it, Parker," he finally said, "with you, me and this freeway?"

Parker nodded. "I was just thinking about that earlier . . . Our drive up and down this road chasing Fasano."

"Good times," Napoleon said with a smile.

"The best," Parker replied with a scoff.

Again, Nap grew quiet. Looking contemplative, he spoke again. "It's all so different now."

Parker glanced over at him. "What is?"

"The world . . . everything . . . when you see it from this side."

"How so?"

"I dunno. It's kinda like watching a play that you've only seen parts of before. You can see some things coming in the story, in between parts that are a total surprise."

"Sounds awkward. And hard."

"Yeah. But the hardest part is the context."

"Context?"

"Yeah. I think it's part of my training, to be honest. Does that make you feel a little better? Hearing that you're not the only rookie, now?"

Parker eased his Camaro into the slow lane and set the cruise control at seventy. The road ahead was wide open, with only one set off taillights far up ahead in the distance. He looked over at Napoleon. "Ha! Training? Who's the lucky one that got the job of training your ass?"

"You remember the gray guy in that driveway?"

"At the Brasco house? No way."

"Way."

Raising his eyebrows, Parker sniggered. "Better you than me, man. That dude . . ."

"What?"

It was Parker's turn to take a long pause. "Look. I'm not the easiest person to get to know, I get that. But the whole God and religion thing? When you've seen what I've seen? It's hard to accept, you know what I'm saying?" Napoleon nodded gently but said nothing as Parker continued. "I mean, over there. The bodies. The body parts. The medics trying to tell guys with seconds to live that they'd be fine? How can that shit happen in a world with a God who exists at all, much less one who is supposed to *care*? And that's sorta how I felt about things and figured I would always feel about things. Then? That gray guy appears in that driveway and turns it all upside down."

Nap smiled. "How so?"

Parker sighed. "Because he's proof, man. Like, I dunno, evidence. And now? You? You're more proof. And, dammit, I preferred not . . . not . . ."

"Not knowing."

"Yeah! Exactly. Because, sometimes, having the answer isn't enough. You know that. Just like at a crime scene. Once you get the how . . . now you need to know the why."

"You might want to be careful with that one, rookie,"

Napoleon replied. He looked back out the passenger window. "You might not be ready for the answer."

———

MAGGIE FORCED AWAY her panic and told herself to focus. *Be tactical. Assess the situation.*

Delva was the leader of this little "we've watched too many horror movies" crowd, that much was obvious. So, she'd be the first one Maggie would have to kill. Misha was so feeble she could be eliminated with only a shove, but Anastasia somehow seemed stronger than she looked. The length of her arms would make it harder to get in close and her frame seemed solid. She'd have to be taken out with a foot sweep, to get her low enough to incapacitate. Mr. Saw, her Taekwondo instructor, had always said that a level opponent was an equal opponent. If done quickly, the foot sweep would probably mean a broken hip or shoulder.

Her pulse was racing right along with her thoughts. Maggie took a deep breath. Then another. Was she really thinking about attacking three old ladies? About actually killing one of them? Yes. She was. When trapped in a "do or die" situation, most people will do whatever it takes not to die. If that meant biting Miney's nose right off his damned face or putting a pencil in one of Anastasia's eyes? So be it. She was going to get the hell out of here, with Luisa, no matter what.

Delva had both hands over Luisa's stomach, which barely had a bump. You'd never know she was pregnant just by looking at her.

"I can feel its heartbeat all the way from over here," Sonia said.

Maggie didn't even look her way. Because Sonia was a different kind of problem. There was something about her that conveyed pure, unfiltered danger. She should be the one that Maggie took out first. Not Delva. But in this case, the strongest would have to wait to last. Because she would be the hardest fight, it would have to be one-on-one, without the three old ladies getting in the way.

You are absolutely kidding yourself! You? By yourself? The four women, maybe. But aren't you forgetting something: the four thugs with guns all around you?

Her panic began to rise again. Back at the shack, four-to-one was bad enough math. She'd come to accept that in the hopes things would somehow get better, in a bullshit Disney sort of way, but now it was eight-to-one. She exhaled in defeat.

Sonia walked across the room as Delva rolled Luisa's shirt up and over her breasts, then touched Luisa's stomach. "I can feel it there. Waiting. Pondering. We must call to it."

"To what?" Anastasia asked.

"The child that will inherit the baby's body."

Maggie perked up her ears.

"Which child is that?"

"The Master will know who to call, and from which land to call it."

"In hell, you mean?" Anastasia asked. Perhaps in her early-sixties, she was the youngest of the three.

"There are many lands, in many places, Anastasia," Delva replied in a professorial tone. "The Master works all things together, as best he can, to the evilest outcome he can."

"Yes, he does, doesn't he?" Misha murmured from across the room.

"It's really quite blissful when you see it happen," Delva said dreamily. "Somewhere, right this very second, she awaits. A spawn not yet called. Maybe she will come directly from hell, though I doubt that, as the spirit's power would be too much for a fetus to contain. So. Maybe she'll come from The Broken Valley, or The Dark Castle or perhaps even The Hanging Forest. But she will come."

"I can't wait," Anastasia said. She spread her arms wide. "Well? Should we get started?"

With a nod from Delva, Anastasia began to chant and Misha went to the altar, where she began opening various small jars and pouring some of the contents of each into a black bowl that looked as if it were made of stone. Using a small pestle to grind the contents down, she then cured it over the flames of one of the candles, moving from one ingredient to the next. The altar seemed aglow in orange and yellow flickers as the room grew darker, the light revealing countless wrinkles and scars on Misha's face.

"Make sure you get it right," Delva said.

Misha grunted and barked back at her, "I will. I will."

"Bring her to the chair," Delva ordered Moe, who complied. After easing Luisa down, he stood aside, sweat beading on his forehead. Up to this point, he, Eenie, Meenie and Miney had all stayed silent. But, despite his apparent nervousness, Moe's curiosity seemed to get the best of him.

"What happens now?" he said to Delva.

There was something in the way that Delva looked at Moe that was just plain bad. A menacing look came over her face, as if he'd overstepped his bounds, and then, on a dime, her voice turned friendly and cheerful. "Oh! You want to know what's next, do you?"

But Moe wasn't fooled. He took a small step back and shook his head vigorously, looking very much like a man who wished he could travel back in time and take his words back. "I'm sorry, no, no, no . . ."

"No, no, no . . ." Delva said mockingly, before cranking her head to the side. "It's good to know. Sometimes. I mean, you've had the courage to ask, so you deserve an answer, don't you think?"

"No!" Moe shouted. "I'm sorry. I made a mistake."

"Yes," Delva said in a deep voice, as she dropped her chin and glared at him. "You certainly did."

She nodded quickly, and in a flash Sonia stepped forwards. Proving what Maggie suspected, that she was the most dangerous of them all, Sonia pulled a long dagger from the folds of her garment and ran it straight through Moe's back and out his chest. He gasped in shock and agony as Sonia stepped in close behind him and supported his skewered body.

"*Madre mia!*" Meenie cried out.

Maggie looked at him. Then Eenie and Miney. Surely, they wouldn't stand for this. Maggie waited for them to do something. To pull their guns and start shooting. But they didn't. Instead, they stood frozen in place. Meenie's hands were shaking.

Delva stepped forwards and put a long finger under Moe's chin. He spat a little blood as his terror-filled eyes stared into hers. "So . . . it's Ernesto, *si?*" she asked, revealing Moe's real name. "You wanted to know, so here it is: we are mixing a little drink for the girl. The drink will help the baby grow faster. We will cut the baby out at the right time, when the spawn arrives to inhabit it, and we will raise that spawn to kill, aaaall the days of its life." She cackled, looked to the ceiling and then back at Moe. "She will be trained to kill as many as she can, as beautifully and cruelly as possible."

Ernesto's eyes began to roll back in his head but Delva was having none of it. "No! You don't get to die yet!" she commanded. And, placing a hand on his temple, she brought his gaze back to her somehow. "You haven't heard the rest of what I have to say, and the rest is the most important part, Ernesto. It will impart in you a truth you will need in order to make it home, to The Master's domain, for the pain and loathing that awaits you there that will aid you in becoming what you are meant to be next. Are you ready, Ernesto?"

Ernesto shook his head vigorously as tears filled his eyes. Sonia bore down on the dagger, causing a fresh wave of agony to shoot through his body. He grunted and tried to cry out but Delva covered his mouth as she finished. "Ernesto, here is the truth of your life: your mother was a whore. She slept with half the men in town and your father let her, because he was a weak man, a pathetic man. So pathetic, in fact, that he was never really sure he was your true father."

Miney looked away, as if ashamed on behalf of his companion, and so did Eenie. Ernesto's eyes, meanwhile, widened in shock again. Except this time, it did not look like the shock of bodily pain, but rather of mental agony. Hurt. Sorrow. Betrayal. Denial. Belief. They all flickered there, like the flames from the candles around the altar, right before he grunted, vomited blood over Delva's hand, and died.

Delva cackled with glee as she licked the blood from her fingers, one at a time, as though it were dribbles of ice cream.

The room went nearly silent for a moment, with only the sound of Misha continuing to mix and grind away at her concoction. Delva spoke to Sonia. "Take him to the back room, spread the blood from his body around the sacrificial altar in two circles. Then cut his head off and place it at the foot of the altar, are we clear?"

Sonia nodded, not with the look of a subordinate but as a resentful equal. She half-carried, half-dragged Ernesto through a black curtain at the back of the room.

Through it all, as if totally oblivious to her surroundings, Anastasia kept murmuring her chants in what sounded like foreign languages. The air in the room grew heavier, as did the darkness. Eenie began to look like what he really was: a young little pervert in way over his head, worried now that he might never see old age. Miney stood completely still, his hands folded behind his back, as if determined to await orders while avoiding being the next one killed.

When she was done, much to Maggie's dismay, Misha gathered ashes from all around the alter and sprinkled them into the cup. Giving it one final mix, she turned to Delva. "It's ready. Make her drink it quickly."

They're crazy. It is *some damned cult. Those ashes . . . whatever else is in that thing . . . it's going to force Luisa's body to abort the baby. Or worse, it might kill them both.*

"No!" Maggie screamed, trying to break away from Meenie again. It was no use; he was almost twice her size and picked her up like a rag doll. Evidently not wishing to attract any negative attention his way after what had happened to Ernesto, he slammed Maggie violently sideways against the nearby wall before bringing her square against his chest again.

Seeing stars, Maggie felt instantly woozy. *Okay. For that, you son of a bitch, you are the one who gets to die first.*

Then the blackness of unconsciousness overtook her.

Chapter Twelve

ONCE FREE FROM THE ISLAND, Father Soltera found the
swim back to the shore of the mainland to be much more diffi-
cult. The water seemed thicker, as if it didn't want to relinquish
its hold on him or allow him to leave. He was also missing the
extra shot of adrenaline he'd had earlier upon seeing Gabriella
again. The elation. The hope. Sadly, they were gone now, too.
Still, he pumped his legs and swung his arms against his fatigue,
weighed down by his sorrow as much by his clothes.

Jesus was a man of sorrows, he reminded himself. *This is my
path. It's what I must do. And with God's grace, I will do it.*

Michiko had teleported across the water and was waiting for
him near the tree line, crouched in front of her sword, which
she had stabbed into the soil in front of her. He couldn't tell if
she was praying, but her head was bowed. It occurred to him
that she could've helped him cross the water if she'd wanted to,
but she hadn't. As if he had to do this for himself, for some
reason.

Her voice spoke softly in his head. *Yes and no, tomodachi. I can
help. But never more than you help yourself. The majority of the effort must
always be yours.*

"I'm exhausted," he said with deep frustration, sputtering water as he struggled on.

Try, tomodachi. Because I sense that I must conserve my energy.

Father Soltera grunted, feeling the lower half of his body sinking more and more. No one was supposed to swim weighed down like this, much less a frail, sickly old man. But despite this fact, he was embarrassed. The swim, at most, was a hundred and fifty feet. Still, he was gasping for air, his heart pounding against his lungs, for what seemed like forever, before his right hand finally scraped against the pebbles of the shoreline and he clawed the rest of the way to land. Drenched, he fell face-first into a patch of grass and struggled to hold it together.

Breathe, tomodachi.

"My heart. The swim."

Your heart suffers from more than just the swim.

He began to cry, against his will, the pain in his soul too much to bear now, knowing that Gabriella was still right behind him, standing on that shore, watching him, perhaps wanting him to come back, like he wanted to go back. Perhaps they could both just deny it all. Just stay and be two people on an island in a Neverland that would lead to nevermore. How many people in life had made the exact same choice? Anything but loneliness. Anything but despair. He didn't dare lift his head and look back, because if . . .

Shhhhhh, Michiko whispered as she knelt next to him. Reaching out one hand, she touched him gently on the back of his neck. Instantly, warmth began to spread throughout Father Soltera's body, from a deep place at the center of his body in a blossoming flame of energy that made its way to every pore on the surface of his skin. *It is the "if"s that kill, tomodachi. The "if what"s and the "if then"s are all demons of a most vicious kind.*

After a few moments, he felt the warmth move beyond his skin. It was as if his clothes were being turned into an electric blanket. Steam rose off him as the water from the lake began evaporating. Even his socks, which had been drenched only moments earlier, were now completely dry.

He wiped at his eyes. "Is that what you were saving your energy for?"

She laughed and spoke aloud this time. "That? That was nothing, *tomodachi*."

He got to his knees and slowly stood. His shoes were behind him, where he'd kicked them off earlier, but so was the tunnel . . .

"Walk into the forest. I will get them for you," Michiko said mercifully.

Father Soltera did as he was told. Making his way into the forest, he felt cool soil and soft pine needles crunch beneath his feet. Deeper in, the branches overhead began to thicken, blocking out the light of the dull sky and casting him in shade as he made his way to a large boulder and sat down. Like a child, he'd gone far enough into the forest to have complied with Michiko's request, but not so far a cry for help wouldn't be heard.

He heard a twig break at the edge of the forest and looked up with relief, hoping to see her. Except . . . Michiko should've been coming from the direction he was facing. The sound had come from . . . behind him.

He turned his head and instantly caught sight of her. Stunningly, horribly, it was La Patrona. Back again. The last time he'd seen her, she'd been standing at the foot of his bed back in his apartment. Torturing him with his own thoughts.

She smiled wickedly. "Hello, Popi." The smile turned into a sneer. "Word around town is that you killed my sister."

Instantly, Father Soltera was reminded of The Gossamer Lady, lying there next to Ikuro, her severed head still trying to speak, her lips moving in silent words.

"They weren't silent, Popi. She was sending me a message, telling me who you were and what you and your little sword-wielding whore had done to her."

"No," he replied, his voice a coarse whisper as he half slid, half fell off the boulder. For a moment he thought La Patrona was alone, absent her brood, but then he saw them behind her, all the little girls with bruises and cuts that had surrounded his bedside, back in his church apartment, in what now seemed like ages ago.

They were each peeking eerily out from behind separate trees, their giggles echoing back and forth through the air. Quickly, almost impossibly so, they moved from tree to tree, in blurs of movement, back and forth, here to there, their feet scurrying through the fallen leaves.

"Yessss," La Patrona hissed, her black hair falling along her jawline and down across her shoulders. "They're coming for you, Father. And pretty soon? They're going to be playing catch with your beating heart, once they're done carving it out of your duplicitous, lustful chest."

"No! Stay away from me!" he commanded as he rose to his feet.

"Tabitha?" La Patrona shouted.

All the girls stopped moving save one. She came forwards. She was wearing dirty pink sweats with a white top that said "Super Star" in faded glitter letters across the front. Her brown hair was ratty and tangled, her face a pasty white that only made the horrid deadness of her black eyes all the starker. "Yes, Mother?"

La Patrona glared at him with so much hate that it was almost a living thing, snaking its way through the air. "Kill him!"

Tabitha laughed gleefully. "Yes, Mother."

Then, incredibly, she crawled up the tree next to her with blazing speed, like a four-legged spider, her fingernails digging into the bark with rapid, scratching sounds as she gripped with the sides of her feet. She launched herself onto the thick branch of a nearby tree and began moving from tree to tree, growing closer to Father Soltera each time. He backpedaled away. "Michiko!"

La Patrona laughed and leaned back. She was wearing a white tank top this time, with worn blue jeans and black motorcycle boots. Digging her thumbs into the pockets of her jeans, she shook her head at him. "Really? You're going to call on that whore to save you, after she brought you here to visit the *other* whore on that island? Ah, men. So. Damned. Pitiful. You're as boring and predictable as the rest of your kind. We're either supposed to be your mommy or your lover, your rescuer or your pacifier. All the needs in your weak little minds."

"Shut up!" Father Soltera screamed. "I don't care what you say about me, but don't you call either of them that!"

"There ya go!" La Patrona spat. "A little manly-manliness, right before the end. I like it. But here's what you fellas never seem to understand: we don't want to have to deal with all your damn needs and wants aaaall the damned time, massaging your egos and satiating your horniness. It's exhausting. And, well, I can't speak for all my kind, but all *I* ever really wanted?" She paused and looked around at her little brood before she locked eyes with him. "Was children."

With that, all the other girls leaped into the trees began to follow Tabitha, the entire pack of them on the attack now.

He looked around for an escape but saw none.

Meanwhile, Tabitha dropped to the ground briefly and picked up a large stick. Opening her mouth sickeningly wide, her lower jaw cracked and dropped on each side as her lips curled back, revealing rows of small razor-sharp teeth, which she then shaved across the stick, back and forth, until she'd fashioned a crude stake. Then she jumped back up into the trees and continued her advance.

But Father Soltera noticed that the closer the children got, the more they slowed down. Something was inhibiting their speed.

It became evident what it was when blue lines began to cut across the trunks of random trees. Moving from right to left across the woods, Michiko's sword was slicing through the trunks as if they were cheesecloth. In time, a few of the trees that some of the brood had leaped on were toppled, crashing sideways and sending the girls screaming off to one side or the other.

Eventually, Michiko came to a stop directly in front of Father Soltera, her left leg straight out, her right leg bent at the knee, both feet firmly planted, with her *katana* lifted at a downward angle behind her head, ready to strike.

La Patrona seemed thoroughly unimpressed. "Ah. I have waited a long time to meet you, Woman of the East," she said with a smirk.

"Demon," Michiko answered with a tight voice. "There are some meetings you should never wish for."

———

HECTOR CHEWED on his lower lip and stared at The Gray Man. "What do you mean, I'm your last millionth?"

Exactly that. My time training others is coming to an end. And that is why we must get this right, you see. Because you are in great danger. Listen. For now, I want you to practice pooling the blue.

"How?"

Call on it from inside yourself. Concentrate. You'll feel it. When called, it calls back. Work on channeling it to your hands but also your mind.

"But. I mean . . . how?"

The Gray Man's image went scattershot again. The snowy façade now pixilated violently, causing his voice to cut in and out.

I'm running . . . time . . . You must try . . . practice .. .first . . . then shoot . . . angles . . . there are . . .

Hector shook his head and put out his hands. "I don't understand."

His cell vibrated violently, as if it were stuck between two magnets. Slowly, The Gray Man's image hardened. But his face twisted with the effort. *The evil creatures of this place have noticed me more than ever. They know I'm around now and are trying to fix my position.*

"What were you saying?" Hector replied, sensing the urgency.

Practice calling, then pooling the blue. Then let it go. In time, try to shoot it from your hands. But keep the angles short and don't let the power from either hand cross to the other.

"Okay. But how long does it take to learn to use it?"

Everyone is different. Most take some time. Kyle Fasano learned quickly.

"Who? Man, I don't know nothin' bout no Kyle Fasano," Hector said with frustration.

No. You don't. And you wouldn't. Two different people, in two entirely different parts of the city once.

"Once? Is he dead?"

The Gray Man chuckled. *No. He moved away. I hear he's getting along though. He made his choice and now he's working his way through it, one step at a time, and becoming a better person for it.*

"Choice?"

Never mind. It's not yet time. What's important is that I need you to learn it quickly, like he did. Because you're not the only one I'm training right now. There's another, who will take my place, who is about to go up against an evil as great as the one you are facing.

Hector was stunned. "What?"

Yes. The enemy is putting all his effort into this. An incredible amount, really.

"Why?"

The Gray Man seemed contemplative. *Because of me. Because he wants to stop me from moving on . . . from going to where I've always wanted to go.*

Hector shook his head in dismay. "Where?"

The Gray Man smiled. *Ah. Hector. So tough. So young. But you're smart. You've managed to ask the what and the why and the where. So there's only one question left, isn't there?*

Hector thought for a moment, then looked at him with surprise. "Who?"

The Gray Man smiled. *Exactly. She was the only "who" that ever mattered to me, and I've waited so long to get back to her. To love her again.* He paused, looking desperate from just a split second, before he added, *For the victories I've helped secure against the enemy? He would like nothing more than to stop me from getting to her. Just like he would like nothing more than to see you fail in your efforts to save Curtis, or in my friend's efforts to take my place. We cannot let that happen, son. To any of us. Do you understand?*

"Yeah. I got you. I get it now," Hector said, clenching his fists.

Good. Now. There's a detective you met a little time ago.

"A detective?"

Yes. In the driveway of your shop on Winston Street. He was investigating Hymie's murder.

Hector thought about it. "Yeah. I remember. There were two of them. A Mexican and some white boy."

The Gray Man tightened his lips. *His name is Detective Parker. He's involved in something separate from you but could use your help.*

"My help?"

Yes. I can reach out to him but it's better if you do.

"Why's that?"

Because you will need him, in the long run.

"Oooookay," Hector said, shaking his head in dismay. "What am I supposed to reach out to him about?"

You know of Güero Martinez?

Hector raised his eyebrows. "Who doesn't? We all do. On the street he's kinda a sick legend. Crazy mother—" He stopped himself. "Sorry."

At least you're trying now, The Gray Man replied. *Yes. Güero is sick, indeed. And aligned with a level of evil that has grown disproportionally to what anyone can handle. Anyway. Detective Parker is going after him.*

"Ha! Good luck with that. Dude's a whole 'nother level of

crazy. This detective don't need my help. He needs to back off and go get a drink somewhere."

Neither of which are options. And in case you haven't noticed, I don't traffic in luck, Hector. Just for the record.

"Yeah. Got it," Hector said wearily. This whole thing was getting crazier and crazier.

He used to work out of the LAPD Central Station.

"Used to?"

Suddenly, the heavy static returned, forcing most of The Gray Man's lower torso to disappear. *It's a long story,* The Gray Man said, sounding irritated as he looked up and around. *But I've officially run out of time now. So . . . use one of your calls and leave a message for him with Detective Murillo. Tell him it has to do with Shilo. He'll get the message to Parker and you'll get a call back.*

"Shilo? What does that—"

Just make the call and leave the message.

"And what am I supposed to tell him when he calls back?"

You'll know it when the time comes.

Hector was dumbfounded. "You can't be serious right now!"

In reply, The Gray Man vanished.

Chapter Thirteen

PARKER SPENT the rest of the drive into Pasadena catching Napoleon up on things with Efren. There wasn't a lot that Nap didn't already know, and it became quickly obvious that whatever free time he had outside of his time training with The Gray Man was spent checking in on his little nephew. He even knew a few things that Parker didn't. Namely that Efren has kissed his first girl—Maria—after walking her home one day after school. "You should've seen them, Parker," Nap said, a dreamy look coming over his face, "nervously holding hands the whole two blocks from the school to her house. They lit up, man."

"Lit up?" Parker asked with a chuckle.

"Yeah. It's beautiful, ya know? Love in its purest form. They were both a light pink glow the whole walk, then bright pink with a shock of red with the kiss. And, I mean, that kiss? It was barely a peck. But I thought for sure Efren was going to faint when he turned to walk back home."

Their laughter filled the inside of the car. It was a good sound and Parker embraced it. Taking a good, long look at his old partner, Parker realized that he was finally ready to fully embrace Napoleon's reality. "Hey, man."

"What?"

"It's good to have you back."

Napoleon gave a little shrug. "Yeah, yeah."

"No. I mean it."

"What? You gonna try to kiss me now, too?"

"Yeah, right."

A teasing look came over Napoleon's face. "Hey. All I'm saying is you're lightening up all pink and stuff, man."

Parker shook his head. "Screeew you."

"You better slow your roll, Parker. Jus' saying."

"This guy," Parker said to no one, "he thinks he's got jokes."

The 210 Freeway was partially closed to construction, but they made it to his apartment in short order. As Parker pulled into the underground garage, he felt a tightness come over his entire body.

"Take a deep breath, Parker. In fact, take about ten of them."

Parker nodded. Coming back here, after what had happened, was not entirely different than letting his mind wander back to the desert in Afghanistan.

The complex had quickly been cleaned up and repaired, except for the "Arroyo Villas" sign out front, which still had bullet holes in it. But his apartment, being a crime scene, took a little longer to clear. The front door and living room window had been replaced, but the bedroom door was still off its hinges. He'd torn down all the yellow tape and thrown away his shattered furniture but he hadn't yet replaced it, which created empty spots in the house that only served as reminders of what had happened almost as much as the broken wood and glass would've.

The landlord had also waited for as long as possible for the insurance people to get all their photos, so the bullet holes inside his apartment had been filled but not yet painted over. Parker wondered if his apartment manager, Susan, was going to be politely asking him to move soon, as a number of the other tenants had completely freaked out over what had happened.

"Do what ya gotta do. I'll be back soon," Napoleon said. Then he was gone.

Parker finished his breathing exercises, then quietly went up to his apartment and packed a duffel bag with a few days' clothes and his phone charger. It was nearly 2:00 a.m. He hadn't slept but he could probably do that on the flight, which he immediately booked on his laptop. LAX direct to Cabo, just as Clopton had instructed. Leaving at 8:45 a.m., it would be a two-and-a-half-hour flight. It was too early to call Melon, so Parker took a hot shower. The long drive had only added to the tension that had balled up in his neck and shoulders like knots strung across the rope of his muscles. Letting the hot water do its work, he felt his mind going numb as his body began to completely uncoil.

He wanted to work and plan and do all the logistics, but his mind was having none of it. By the time he got out of the shower and toweled off, his fatigue hit him square, and he reconsidered his idea to wait for the flight to sleep. Still, he dressed in running sweats and a plain blue t-shirt, so he'd be ready to go when he awoke. Then, like a zombie, he packed his laptop in his duffel bag and carried both it and his tennis shoes over to a stuffed chair in the living room and collapsed onto it. It wasn't the most comfortable chair in the world, but he'd slept on boulders, crates and on the inside of rumbling C-30s, so it would do.

The last thing he managed to do was set his cell phone alarm to 6:00 a.m. This would give him enough time to make it to the airport for his flight.

Then? His mind went as black as the night.

When his cell phone began to sing its song to wake him up four hours later, his eyes popped open with stunned fatigue. He'd need more sleep for what was coming, and he reminded himself the flight would provide it. Now, though, it was time to hit to the road.

On the freeway to the airport, he called Melon, who answered on the third ring.

"Dude! Heading to my favorite panga now. The tuna are biting. What's up?" Melon said bluntly, his answer revealing why he sounded so awake at this hour.

"I need help," Parker said, equally bluntly.

A few ticks of silence followed. Sounding concerned but also very much like a man having his life interrupted, Melon replied. "What kind of help?"

Parker smiled. Old buddies were one thing. Old war buddies quite another thing entirely. The military lingo never went away, and you always spoke in code. "What kind of help?" was a totally innocuous and expected question at this point in any normal conversation, but they both knew that Parker would be asking for the fishing report right about now if this were going to be a normal chat. Something was up by the way Parker had gone straight in, and Melon knew it.

"I'm having a tough time. Love on the rocks . . . and all that."

And there was the actual code.

Melon picked up the dance. "Like the drink or like the song?"

"No, man. I'm talking the song, all the way."

"Hmm." Melon cleared his throat and added somberly, "Good. I'm not into pussy drinks, anyway."

"You cool if I come in for a visit today?"

"Today, huh?" And now he sounded a bit alarmed. "Yeah. Sure, man. Sounds bad."

Then, just in case the call was somehow being recorded by someone or anyone, because that's how ops worked—always assume exactly that—Parker added some garbage. "Yeah. I quit the job and lost the girlfriend."

"Shit. Talk about running the table, huh?"

"Yeah."

"What time you getting in?"

"Flight leaves at 8:45 a.m. Number 1102. United. I can—"

"I'll pick you up at the airport. You can fill me in then, buddy."

"Fair enough."

"Just one thing, though."

"What's that?"

And now Melon, whose voice was stiffer than usual, was obviously throwing in some garbage, too. "This is gonna make me miss my panga. The tuna are biting, asshole. So, you owe me dinner."

"You got it. See you soon."

"Affirmative."

The line went dead. Parker sighed.

The bowels of the 110 Freeway were constipated with the usual weekday morning commuters, and he had to suffer through most of it to get to the 105 West to LAX. He despised this drive. The cloudy skies remained but there was no rain.

Thinking he saw a flash of beige light, he turned his head to the passenger seat. "You there?"

Nope. Once again, things were not as they seemed. And for anyone monitoring this trip, things were not as they seemed either. On the surface? He was flying to see a friend in Cabo to cry on his shoulder about losing his girl and to get career advice.

In reality? It was likely that no sooner had Melon hung up the phone, he'd called his panga captain, who was guaranteed to be a local, and not only pushed the reservation out three hours but also booked an extra spot for Parker. Not because they were actually going to go fishing, but because it had to *look* like they had gone fishing. And Melon would know this. Full well. Because together, he and Parker had done this before, many times, to nab or take out one terrorist leader or another. And they always began with a song.

"Porcupine Pie." "I Am . . . I Said." "September Morn."

Every mission had code words that had something to do with Mr. Neil Diamond.

———

SLEEP, Maggie's familiar friend, had been forced upon her this time.

She could tell because when it came naturally it was black, deep and refreshing as a spring well. Anything could happen and her depth of perception was a Wi-Fi signal with full bars. But the few times she'd passed out or been knocked out in her life, including this time at the hands of Meenie, the blackness was always tinged orange around the edges, shallow and dry as fall leaves.

She could still see things here, but the images were often vague or inconsistent: a seesaw tilting back and forth in a sound-less wind, a child chasing a bicycle, headlights in night traffic. The images spun across the diorama in her head until one image looked familiar: Father Soltera. He was still lying in his hospital bed, his eyes closed, but he was no more in that room than she was, Maggie could feel it. Absent his body, his mind had gone wandering. But where? Back to that place she'd seen before, with the big wolves and warped sky?

No. Somewhere else. A place where something he wanted had been, but she couldn't figure out what. She willed herself to focus but was hit with another round of stunning images. Her breast, cupped in Mario Ewing's hand after the junior high dance. Wanting to feel excited but instead feeling violently ill. Blaming it on the Hi-C punch, the finger sandwiches or the strobe lights inside the dance hall they'd left behind. Back before she discovered the dark secret inside herself. Then a hard right turn across the hills of Virginia, just outside of Charlottesville, when she'd gone backpacking all alone and run into a family of racoons next to a muddy green river.

None of these images were important now. She knew that.

Now, all that mattered was Luisa. And the only one that could help her was the one she'd just lost her grip on. So, again, she reached out to Father Soltera, like a child sticking their hand through a hole in a tree, feeling around for a bird's egg. All fingertips. Gently. Gingerly. So as to do no harm. Because she knew, when you were this deep inside your own head, you could do untold amounts of damage if you weren't careful.

Finally, she found him. He was in danger. Again. The poor man's life had been nothing but a sequence of dangers since he'd met Luisa. She felt Father Soltera's fear and remorse come crashing down over a part of him that was in aching pain. The selfish, human part of him was resenting what life had brought him to, but in many ways, from the moment she'd met him that first time at Eden Hill Women's Shelter, Maggie had known he was special. Different. Kind, in a voluminous way, as if the love of God was not something he wore, but something he was. It was his eyes that gave it away. The way they asked something with only a glance, or saw not some things but all things, with an empathy that was profound.

But that meant little now, because he was under attack. All alone and . . .

No.

Someone was with him. A woman . . . of sorts. Yes. An Asian woman.

When Maggie's mind took her in, it immediately recoiled. As if it were not prepared to even conceive of such a thing, much less see it.

And then the woman noticed her, too. Her head whipped towards where Maggie's consciousness floated up above them, and Maggie's soul trembled, to the core.

The woman was beautiful, with long black hair tied back in a ponytail with a strip of leather, a few wisps of it crisscrossing over the creamy white skin of her face and framing her dark, almond-shaped eyes. She was a warrior, not only of this world but . . . She was wielding a long sword of some kind, that was glowing white. And her eyes glowed. And the wings on her back, folded in tight, glowed white, and she knew what Maggie was going to say (*Please tell him Luisa's in danger and she needs his help*) and she answered immediately in a way that Maggie did not want to hear (*His path is to save another now. Your path is to save the girl*).

And then the dark sky with all its sharp edges collapsed in on itself in quadratic angles, corner over corner, and Maggie was both glad and sad, because she'd seen a light that she had always believed in but had never fully embraced, and it had looked upon her not with disappointment but with reassuring love. And like with one of those paper fortune tellers you played with when you were a kid, being folded in and out with various answers to the only question that mattered—were you liked by that special someone—Maggie had found the answer she'd always hoped for. And it was all good.

Until she woke up to Luisa screaming at the top of her lungs, her eyes wide, a gray fluid spilling down her chin and neck. The witches were holding her down and trying to force her to drink their concoction but having little success, until one of them evidently had enough and grabbed Luisa around the throat and squeezed so tightly that her mouth opened to gasp for air.

An adrenaline that was almost otherworldly coursed through Maggie's veins. Her left temple hurt from being smashed against the wall, but it didn't matter. She rammed her skull backwards suddenly, a move totally unexpected by Meenie. Probably still thinking she was unconscious, he had relaxed his grip on her just enough for her to arch her back into it. She felt her head smash into his nose and heard a crack of bone just before he howled and instinctively let go of her. Wasting no time at all, she spun and caught him flush in the forehead with her right elbow. He went down in a heap, but the room was full of guns and both Eenie and Miney trained them on her immediately. Eenie looked like he was begging for her to make a move, his finger dancing on the trigger.

None of that mattered. What did matter was that all three witches had been distracted just enough for Luisa to squirm loose. Getting one arm free, she swung her hand at the bowl and sent it flying across the room, splattering its contents all over the floor. Delva shrieked with rage as her sisters struggled to get Luisa back under control. Maggie stood, frozen, waiting for anyone to get close enough to attack, but no one did.

Meenie was still on the ground, thrashing around in pain. "You . . . stupid little . . . bitch!"

"Get up, fool!" Misha screamed at him.

As he tried, Maggie turned sideways to fend him off, half expecting to get shot and surprised when she didn't. Eenie took aim but Delva shouted at him. "No! Wait. We might need her."

"What?" Anastasia yelled.

Delva slowly, patiently, walked over to a table and picked up a pair of long sewing scissors. With a smile, she walked over to Luisa. "Hold her hand still," she said to Anastasia, who complied.

"No!" Luisa yelled. She began whimpering as Delva opened the scissors and placed them over the pinky finger of her hand.

Looking at Maggie, Delva went from smile to full grin. "This little piggy went to market?" she asked, raising her eyebrows.

The situation was obvious. Surrender or they'd start cutting off Luisa's fingers, right in front of her.

Maggie glared at them all and stepped back against the wall. She placed her hands in front of her in full compliance as Miney twist-tied them together.

"There," Delva said. "Now wasn't that easy?"

"But——" Anastasia began to protest.

"But what? Remake another batch. We can wait. And then? She'll drink it for sure."

"How? Why?" Misha asked, contempt dripping in her voice.

Delva walked over and lifted Maggie's left hand. Putting

Maggie's index finger between the shears, she looked at Luisa. "Hey, little girl? See this? Tell me. Is *this* little piggy going to have to go to market?"

Luisa's face melted with despair as her eyes filled with tears. Calmly, with a look of utter defeat, she shook her head and said, "No."

Chapter Fourteen

LA PATRONA GLARED at Father Soltera over Michiko's left shoulder. "You think this one is worth saving, Woman of the East?"

"What do you care what I think? When have you ever cared about what anyone thinks? All you care about is causing hurt and pain."

Taking two wide steps to her left, La Patrona's hands disappeared into her clothing. When they reappeared, she was holding two long knives with black handles and silver blades. Michiko matched her steps and smiled. "You seek to fight a sword with knives?"

"Yes and no," La Patrona answered. "These blades are for my two little warriors who have practiced with Mommy the most. Tabitha? Come here. And you too, Addie."

From the woods the girls came, still looking a bit stunned by the havoc Michiko had caused. Tabitha was the first to arrive. Dropping the wooden stake in her mouth, she reached up and took one of the knives from La Patrona's hand as the girl named Addie came bear-crawling in from the left with feral grunts. Her hair was blond, with smeared patches of blood from head wounds that had long ago clotted. Her eyes were also black, but one of them was completely missing an eyelid, giving her a half-faced permanent stare.

La Patrona caught him staring and took a dig. "Head wounds are a bitch, Mr. God Man. Your little whore out there on that island can tell you that."

Father Soltera held his tongue. There was too much tension in the air and he didn't want to be the one to spark anything or rush Michiko into battle until she was ready.

Tabitha glared up at La Patrona with awe and envy, but it was an evil sort of look that held zero love and all the promise of betrayal the first chance she got. Perhaps after she grew up, if such a thing were possible in hell, or perhaps when La Patrona turned her back on her one day for a second too long. Next to her, grunting again, perhaps incapable of talking for some reason, Addie took her blade from La Patrona and stared at it with glee. Then, disgustingly, she stuck out her tiny tongue and licked it.

"Okay, then," La Patrona said with a sigh. "You girls go on and play now. I want the man cut up in pieces, please. Arms first, then legs. Save his head for me when I'm done with the little samurai here, okay?"

"Yes, Mother," Tabitha replied dutifully. Addie nodded her head vigorously. The girls split wide, one to the left flank, the other to the right, leaving Michiko with too many fronts to defend. Glancing from one girl to the next, she backed up a step, evidently trying to cut off their paths towards Father Soltera.

Now empty-handed, La Patrona reached back into a void that opened up behind her and produced a black leather vest full of throwing knives and stars, which she calmly put on, locking eyes with Michiko the whole time. "You know, when your man got to hell? I had him. Many times. He was good, you know. We all wanted a piece of him, but I was one of the few who had earned enough chits with The Master to get a taste . . . just a taste . . . of all the love he had for you."

Michiko's blade lit a bright, hot white.

"And by taste, I literally mean it," La Patrona added, widening her eyes with exaggerated joy. "I mean, his heart was like a filet mignon. Rare. I only got a nibble, but boy did it run with the juices of all *your* love, too."

"Liar!" Michiko screamed, just before she charged.

La Patrona smiled victoriously, as if she'd properly baited her opponent, but the smile was short-lived. Michiko halted her advance on a dime, sidestepped to the left and swung her sword perfectly to strike the charging Addie, who thought she had an opening. The girl erupted in a ball of red flames and disappeared.

"How? How did you do that? You can't send—"

"I can do many things, demon spawn. Having wandered your lands, I know its coordinates just fine. She's been teleported there, and she won't be back anytime soon."

Her face going from shock to rage, La Patrona reached into her vest and flashed two small throwing knives in each hand, which she cast at Michiko with stunning accuracy. Three were deflected by Michiko's sword, but the fourth found flesh, striking her in the left side. She winced and turned to strike at Tabitha, but it was too late. She had breached the right flank and was charging directly at Father Soltera.

Michiko grabbed the short sword in her belt, crouched and threw it sideways towards Tabitha. It struck a glancing blow off of her calf but that was all. Still, it was enough to at least slow her. But the move had cost Michiko two more strikes from La Patrona's throwing knives, one to her left thigh and the other to her left shoulder. Four more blades came, but these Michiko deflected off into the trees with her sword.

"Run, *tomodachi*!" Michiko shouted. "Look for the stairs, just beyond a narrow river, underneath Japanese elm trees. Go!"

Father Soltera hesitated, not wanting to abandon her, but the look in her eyes was commanding, so he turned on his heels and began sprinting as fast as he could.

That was when Maggie Kincaid came to his mind, like a vast weight. Then? A vision of a room and three witches and evil men was projected, like a movie, against the dark green forest canopy around him. What it showed made his heart stop. Maggie was tied to a post. And Luisa . . . Luisa was on an altar, about to be . . . harmed. The witches were gathered around. They wanted her baby.

"No," Father Soltera said under his breath.

They were drawing an incision line on her stomach.

"Noooooo!" Father Soltera screamed, falling to his knees immediately. He sucked air, then clutched in agony at his temples. But now, on his knees, he was eye-level with Tabitha, who had stopped not ten yards away to watch the vision, too.

The witches in that far-off place looked up suddenly. As if they saw her just as she was seeing them. Then one of the witches, the one that Father Soltera sensed had the most power, made a beckoning motion to Tabitha. "Come, child," she said. "We've been waiting for you. Come." And her words came in a raspy echo that seemed to vibrate in the air.

Tabitha looked at him and their eyes locked, for the briefest of seconds, before she looked to the woods beyond him. "Run to The Stairway and come to us," the old witch said encouragingly. "Then you can drink all the blood you ever wanted."

Gleefully, Tabitha abandoned all pursuit of Father Soltera, indeed she charged right past him and towards the woods beyond.

"Michiko!" Father Soltera screamed as he tried to scramble to his feet.

Father Soltera saw Michiko swiftly pull the blades in her body out with one hand, spin and hurl them at La Patrona, who stumbled backwards in the effort to fend them off.

Then, incredibly, Michiko spun again, this time casting a ball of iridescent light at Tabitha. It struck her square in the back but did not knock her over or vaporize her. Instead, it seemed to be another time warp of some kind. Tabitha, looking stunned and extremely frustrated, was reduced to moving in super-slow motion, her darting eyes the only thing that remained in real time. Her right foot was slowly rising from the ground, her left foot slowly digging in, her arms now looking as if they were pumping their way through wet cement.

Father Soltera scrambled backwards on his back, unable to banish the vision, still seeing Luisa screaming and crying for help.

"Oh, Father. My God. No. Please. No. Help them."

Tabitha was struggling mightily to speed up her advance. To make her way to the same place he was trying to get to: The Stairway. The gateway out of here and back to the real world. If she got their first . . .

La Patrona hurled a throwing star at Michiko's head, which barely missed, before producing four more knives. Again, two in each hand, balanced there between her thumbs and the bridge of her index fingers. Balancing, waiting.

Michiko glanced over at Tabitha and Father Soltera with grave concern in her face before being forced to turn her attention back to La Patrona. Michiko took her sword and spun it in swift circles, twice to her left side and twice to her right. As if trying to provoke the fight to a conclusion.

"I'm going to kill you, little angel," La Patrona said with sneer.

Michiko lowered her chin and spat on the ground with contempt. "Promises, promises."

———

HECTOR SAT at a table in the corner of the cafeteria, not by himself but keeping to himself, as he contemplated a line in the book opened up before him. Sometimes it helped him to say the words out loud. They stuck in his head better that way for some reason. But in here, he wanted to keep the process more private, so he whispered them instead: "Your pain is the breaking of the shell that encloses your understanding."

He'd made the call to the LAPD's Central Station as The Gray Man had told him to, and now he was sick to his stomach. The breakfast tray before him was stark and depressing, consisting of hash browns, two hard-boiled eggs, a slice of toast, a banana and a small boxed orange juice. He'd filled a Styrofoam cup with coffee, but it was so bad he'd only managed a few sips. It was too bitter, even with five packets of sugar, and was now trying to claw its way back out up his throat. Using his spork, he pushed around one of the hard-boiled eggs on his plate, mindlessly guiding it over the hash browns and down the curving length of the banana.

Detective Murillo had been in (Hector was hoping he would not be) and he listened carefully to the message (Hector was hoping he would call him crazy and just hang up). For a cop, he sounded pretty chill, until the call was nearly over. Then he'd pressed a bit. "What's going on?" he said, his voicing sounding hesitant. But then, like a man who knew he didn't want to know what he didn't want to know, he'd just as quickly said, "Never mind." Then he hung up.

What was getting to Hector now, more than the demons in the hallways or the creatures he was now beginning to see working the perimeter of the yard outside, was the feeling he had inside himself. It was a weight—no, a burden. Like an inner demon. The heavy burden of knowing that he'd taken another man's life and—maybe even worse—the feeling that the burden was permanent. It was never going to fade away. It would be with him every morning when he woke up, the knowledge that, because of him, another human being in the world was never going to wake up again. The burden was a special kind of pain: pervasive and haunting. He was beginning to feel that it was going to be too much to bear. Period. But he had to try.

So, again, he repeated the words from Kahlil Gibran. This

time, three or four times, not noticing that Curtis had come up behind him. "What's that you sayin', lil homie?"

Hector cleared his throat and answered sheepishly. "Just some stuff I read in this book."

"Ah. My man, Hector. Always with the books, huh?" Curtis said with a smile and a shake of his head. Sitting down across from Hector with his breakfast tray, he somberly added, "Tell me something, lil homie: did any of those fancy-ass books of yours keep you from ending up in here?"

Hector shook his head. "No. I guess not."

"Nope. They didn't. Books are for rich folks who have gardeners and worry about getting oil spots from their car on the driveway. They ain't us, Holmes. And we ain't them."

The bars over a nearby window were casting shadow lines from the muted sun outside across Curtis' face. Hector took a good long look at him. His mentor. His leader. His left ear was missing a chunk from the lobe which a little gangster over on Eleventh Street had bitten off while on the losing end of a fist fight. Under his left eye were three teardrops, back when such markings were fashionable and bragging about your kills was a badge of honor. Back before the Feds brought the same RICO laws into play that they'd used against the Italian Mafia in New York to start breaking up the LA gangs. Now, gang markings naming your affiliation or claiming your exact deeds were photographed, cataloged and documented. Like inked on rap sheets. And, as such, they were more frowned upon.

Curtis' head was freshly shaved and his dark brown eyes, as always, were lying flat below his eyelids, which were darker than the rest of his face. His smile, which he had just flashed at another inmate walking by, revealed crooked teeth, one top front tooth covered with a gold cap. As he dug into his breakfast, Hector also noticed his hands. Over the knuckles of his right hand were tattooed the letters H-A-R-D in black. On the knuckles over his left hand, the letters L-U-C-K. Beneath each knuckle on both hands were the repeating card suits in color: a spade, a club, a diamond and a heart. He looked the same, in many ways, but still seemed different somehow.

"So," Curtis said as he took a bite of one of his hard-boiled eggs. "What'd your defense attorney get you?"

Hector laughed. "Not much. The DA tabled nixing the death penalty for a full confession on his own. Yeah. My guy chirped about me being under the influence of alcohol and all that, which helped muddy the waters. But I'm thinking, ya know, a good attorney maybe coulda kept me from a life sentence."

"Maybe. Probably not likely, though. You killed that dude and crippled Marisol, bro."

Hector winced. "Don't say that, man."

"What?"

"Don't talk about Marisol," Hector said, anger flooding his voice. He still couldn't process that part of it. Not at all.

Normally, back out on the streets, Curtis didn't take well to being told what to do by a subordinate. But, again, Hector noticed he had changed. After looking like he was going to press the topic, he instead leaned back and fell silent. After a few moments he calmly said, "I told you we were going to have to square up on that."

"Dude." Hector put both hands flat on the table and took a deep breath. "I can't talk about her. I can't, bro. Not yet."

Curtis looked him up and down. Hard.

"Please, bro," Hector added respectfully.

Finally, the old Curtis flashed back. The older brother, sometimes even the father figure, something Hector never had, looked at him with both care and not a little bit of contempt. It was a look that said "I got you, but you've disappointed me" at best, "You're pathetic and weak" at worst.

Unable to bear his gaze, Hector looked away and forced himself to choke down his breakfast. Because he did feel pathetic. And weak. But he didn't care anymore.

"So," Curtis said with a deep sigh, "I'm bringing you into the fold. You know that, right?"

"I was hoping so," Hector answered quietly, "but I wasn't totally sure."

"Yeah. Me neither."

Hector looked up, wounded.

Curtis smiled. "Just playin', lil homie. Don't get your panties up your ass crack, bitch."

But it was a reminder of how cruel Curtis could be if he was mad at you. Joking about leaving a guy uncovered in prison was not cool, and Curtis had the sway to tell everyone to stay away from Hector if he wanted. That would leave Hector with no affiliation and the same death sentence he'd managed to avoid with the DA.

"Fill me in on the outside," Curtis mumbled as he began peeling his nearly spoiled banana.

"I gave Burro the lead."

Curtis laughed. "*Pinche* Burro?!"

"Yeah. I know. But he was hustling the hardest, every day out there. Like always."

"Burro's a grunt. Of course he hustles. He's too stupid to be anything but a grunt, though. He challenge you?"

It was a trick question. That was old news that Curtis would know by now.

"Yeah. I beat his ass back into line. Then . . . this."

"And what's that mean to those that are loyal to—"

"I made Burro swear to leave Bennie and Chico untouched when I was going down for the shooting."

"You don't really believe he'll do that, do you?"

"I figured maybe, as long as they backed off and let him be. When I was in court, I had a chance to speak with them both. Told them to stand down and lay low."

Curtis smiled. "Because you knew, didn't you?"

Hector looked down. "Knew what?"

"Shooooooooot," Curtis said with a chuckle. "All them books

you read, homie? You know what they don't change about you, Hector? Not one bit?"

Swallowing hard, Hector looked back up at him. "What?"

"You are one ruthless bastard, my man. I mean . . . shit. Hymie proved that. You're own cousin. Set his ass up to get straight-up aced. I mean, I was both impressed by that and . . . I dunno, man. That's some chilling shit right there. I figured, ah, Hector's learned some of his lessons from me a little *too* well!" Curtis laughed so hard that he rocked back and forth in his place at the table. "But then this: on the same night that you shoot your girl, you go and promote someone to take over the gang that you know I'm never going to accept—which means Burro's headed for a ditch somewhere."

He'd brought up Marisol again, but Hector knew better than to challenge him this time. An awkwardness had joined them at the table, and Curtis' eyes were a bit wild now as he went on. "Man, homie. You know what? Now that I think about it? Maybe I'm wrong. Maybe them books are teaching you up real good. 'Cause, I mean, that's some stone-cold chilling shit right there, Hector. You a killer . . . planning even *more* killings . . . as you were *getting ready to kill* someone. Sh-eeeee-it!" He squinted at Hector. "Maybe I'm underestimating you, homie. Maybe I been underestimating you all along."

Hector wasted no time. He knew better. Gritting his teeth, he looked firmly and seriously at Curtis. "I'm loyal. Always have been. I have never, ever betrayed you. Marisol was my only screw-up and I'll make it right. I will. But even Hymie went down because *we* agreed it had to happen. That was my blood, man. But so are you."

"Hector—"

"Nah, man," Hector said, throwing his hands up in the air and half standing, his heart filling with a tidal wave of emotion. "Just do me, right now. If anyone is going to kill me, Holmes? Let it be you. Let the only person that probably ever cared about me in the world be the one to check me out of the world."

A few inmates at a nearby table looked over but everyone else was lost in their own conversations. Curtis looked them off. When his gaze returned to Hector, it had softened. *"Calmaté, Holmes* . . . I get it. Stop with the drama. I believe you. Now sit down."

Hector did as he was told.

Then, with the last bite of his banana, Curtis nonchalantly said, "Anyway, we'll deal with the Burro situation later. Right now, we gotta talk about Flacco."

"Flacco? What? Did his transfer to my cell get hung up or something?"

Curtis gave an alarming grimace as he looked around quickly, then leaned in close. "We got orders from up on high."

A slow nod came from Hector. He knew that grimace and he knew it meant nothing good.

Curtis sighed. "Flacco's gotta get aced."

And there it was.

"Shit! What?"

"Yeah. I know. He did something to upset the big guy. I dunno what, and the whole thing sounds kinda shaky, but you know how it works."

"When?"

"Tonight. After dinner. In the cafeteria."

Hector held his breath. What was he going to do if Curtis asked him to do the deed? He needn't have worried. When Curtis spoke next, his face was grim. "And it's me that's gotta do it."

"You?" Hector said, feeling stupid for being surprised. Of course, it was Curtis. This was it. This was the moment that Hector had been sent here to stop: Flacco's murder.

"Unusual, I know. But some parley of some kind is in play, up top. I do this, I get more time, but another step up the ladder, too," Curtis answered with a sigh. Then he said something odd that resonated with Hector instantly. No. Not *with* him, but *in* him. Hector felt the blue in his veins pulse ever so slightly.

"It ain't pretty," Curtis said, "but ever since that Güero guy showed up years ago it's been getting uglier and uglier."

At first, Hector was thrown off by his body's response. He felt slightly nauseated, but he concentrated. The blue was pulsing now. This was important. Someway. Somehow. "Yeah. I know. Dude's like some sorta mystery or some shit. What's his story, anyway?"

Curtis cleared his throat and looked around. "Man. You don't wanna know, lil homie. Trust. The shit this guy does . . . I seen it once, at a party over by a warehouse in Hollenbeck. End of the year party or some shit, celebrating our splits and stuff. Everyone was high on coke and booze, so it mighta just been that but . . . this is when he was first getting started, dig?"

Hector leaned into the story and nodded. "Yeah."

"He's showing off. Has some honey half naked on his lap, tossing bills around like he's in a rap video. Then? He sees this damn cat. No joke—a black cat. It come up to him like they're best friends and without even hesitating, do you know what he does?"

"What?"

"Picks it up and snaps its neck!"

"Nah!"

"I know, right? People flipped the hell out. Some thought it was funny, others were just straight trippin'. But this fool? He ain't done. You know what he does next?"

"What?"

"He gets up. Puts the cat on a picnic table—now, remember, I'm watchin' all this shit go down right in front of my face—and he starts blabbing some mumbo jumbo. Then? He waves his hand over the dead cat and up it pops, good as new."

Hector twisted his face if disbelief. "Shut the hell up, man!"

"No. And I'm telling you . . . everyone heard that cat's neck snap loud as a shotgun blast, man. I almost hurled. And it went limp instantly. But then, check this out, I ain't done. The honey that was on his lap? She goes down the path of pure stupid and says she thinks it was a parlor trick of some kind. 'How'd you do that trick, baby?' she asks. Then when people tell her it had to be real, she makes it worse. 'Nah. That was fake you fools,' she says." A glassy-eyed look came over Curtis' face. "And Güero, he looks at her and starts turning his rings in."

"His what?"

"He wears rings like crazy. Three or four on each hand. They got weird symbols on them. Anyway, I didn't know it then, but that's his thing."

"His thing?"

"Yeah. When he's about to go off? Like, ya know, go psycho? He turns them rings in, towards his palms. I guess so as not to damage the stones or diamonds. And right in front of us? He beat that girl to shit. Jacked up her whole face. Blood on his hands up to his forearms before he stopped because—and this is when I knew this dude was for real, homie—no one, not a single damned person at that party tried to step in and stop him or even cool him off. They just let him pulverize the hell outta that bitch. People say he still has her, holed up back in his hometown in Mexico. Had her ruined face filled with studs and piercings to always remind her to never question him again."

Chapter Fifteen

PARKER WAS AT THE AIRPORT, finally clearing the TSA line, when he saw them: a group of three men, still in their military fatigues, working their way from the Vroman's Bookstore pop-up shop nearby to the Panda Express in the food court just up ahead.

Of mostly equal height, one of them was Caucasian with blond hair and the other two looked to be Hispanic, with their hair cut the shortest. They moved in unison, probably subconsciously, as they were now in a civilian setting that was safe and that did not require such a united front. They were Army, for sure, but too far away to determine what unit or rank. It didn't matter, really. Parker's eyes had seen the image of them and a switch had flipped, somewhere in the back of his mind, to a reveal a similar one from his memories.

Parker, Baer and Molchan were at Outpost Keating, the night before the attack. They were walking together, much in the same way, as they crossed the hot sand of the base, making their way from the mess tent to their temporary barracks for the night.

Somewhere between talking about football season and which drinks they were going to guzzle over poker that night,

Parker took a moment to really look at his fellow soldiers. His friends. His brothers. It was just a quick appreciation of things, nothing more. But, since all moments are forever framed by those that follow them, it was a moment now of innocence and reflection. Less than twenty-four hours later, all three of them would find themselves in the firefight of their lives, and all of them would survive it at the price of never being the same again. They'd seen plenty of battle and plenty of casualties in the times of their tours, but none on the scale or with the ferocity of what was coming their way.

Big sun. Massive desert. Small lives.

Feeling dizzy, Parker quickly made his way to his gate, making sure, making damn sure, not to look at the soldiers again. He took a few deep breaths, like an asthmatic trying to fight off the inevitable betrayal of his lungs, and downed a swig of water from the bottle he was holding before he found a seat and collapsed into it. The pressure in his chest continued to mount, but this wasn't asthma, it was the threat of an approaching panic attack, and the first time he'd felt this way since Beaumont when he'd ducked into that bar for a few beers before The Bread Man case had erupted.

Life was funny, and life was cruel. That night, the poker tent had been filled with the laughter of men who would be using the same throats the next day to be screaming orders or screaming in agony. What was it that Molchan called it? "The fickle finger of fate"? Yeah. But at least for that night, things had been good. They'd talked of sexual escapades between shots of tequila, while raising and calling each other's cards, which made or broke their fortunes. He could still remember, all this time later, the clinking of beer bottles over toasts for this or that, and Lynyrd Skynyrd's "Need All My Friends" blasting on the MP3 speakers in the corner.

Rope yourself back. Hand over hand. Pull yourself back, he told himself. *Remember what the doc says. Leave the past where it's at between therapy sessions, for now. You'll be strong enough later. But not now.*

He was early to the gate. A group of about eight people were crouched over their laptops or phones at a charging station and maybe a dozen more were near the check-in desk. He was seated alone, near the concourse. A few men in suits walked by, one of them casting a glance at Parker then looking away quickly when their eyes met. A woman in a black sweat suit and white sneakers wheeled her bag past him and to a row of chairs beyond, paying him no notice as she chortled into her cell phone to someone about where she'd hidden the house key for the dog walker. A cold sweat hit Parker. It started across his chest before rolling over his shoulders and down his back.

"Shit. Keep it together," he whispered to himself. "Hold it together."

But then a plane taxied by, gunning its engines ever so briefly, sounding nothing at all like an F-15 but not having to, thanks to what his therapist called "flashback by association". Logically the sounds were dissimilar, but even more logically? The mind heard a plane. Plain and simple. And just like dominos of a different color can still fall together, so too did the sky outside the window over LAX and the sky beyond the boulder he was hiding behind at Outpost Keating, just two blue skies of a different time and different place.

And with that sky came bullets, exploding all around during that ambush, for what seemed like an eternity, before those F-15s finally arrived with the fury of the gods, ripping through the clouds with vengeful intent. There to save them. But mostly, only to save what was left of them.

Parker closed his eyes against an onslaught of images that came next: a bottle of German liquor that one of the younger soldiers, Stanton was his name, had brought to the game. Strong stuff that burned the whole way down. Stanton had drawn a royal flush one hand and chewed a toothpick while he played, like some character in a western movie. The next day he'd been strafed across his body and was dead before he hit the ground. The bastards had then used him as target practice from their positions in the high ground. Knowing it would mess with the heads of their enemy. Knowing someone would crack and try to get to him. That someone had been Carlisle, from Nebraska, who had no luck at cards and no luck at being a hero, either. He hadn't even made it halfway to Stanton before he caught a round in the back and tripped face-first to the ground. They were just beginning to use *him* as target practice too, one bullet shattering his left elbow, another his right thigh, when the F-15s arrived and blew the enemy to pieces along with the hillside they were hiding on. So. There was that. But last Parker had heard, Carlisle had a prosthetic arm and was a raging alcoholic. So. There was that. Too.

A family of four, on full vacation vibe, came walking up. Mom. Dad. Two teenage boys. Then they realized they were at the wrong gate and changed course, heading back down the concourse. He was probably never going to have that life. That perfect, domestic life.

"Pull your head outta your ass," Nap said from his seat right next to him.

Parker nearly jumped out of his skin. "Shit!"

"Sorry, but you needed a good shock. You'll have that life. Someday. You'll get well. Like anything else in life? You'll have to do the work. But you'll do it."

Parker leaned over, his elbows on his knees. "Yeah. Whatever. I'm not so sure, partner."

"Yes, you are. You just gotta quit holding off doing the work. You're dragging it all out, rookie."

"It's too much to do it any other way."

"You mean like when you go to the bar? Or buy a six-pack? Or sneak a shot of brandy before you go to bed?" Napoleon said, shaking his head. "I tried that route, Parker. Trust me. One drink becomes a thousand and all that happens is you start refilling all that pain with new pains. Stop. Now. While you still have a chance."

Shaking his head, Parker sat up in his chair and cleared his throat. "It's cool. I'm fine. I'll be fine."

"No, Parker, you won't."

"Look man, I said—"

When Napoleon looked back to him there was something different in his eyes, something penetrating and overbearing, yet somehow still tinged with love. His old partner was the same, but not. There was a power now that resonated from him. "I'm not your therapist, Parker. I don't need to ask you to tell me what's inside you. I can *see* it, okay? And it's like a cancer that's eating you alive."

Parker looked at the ground before nodding firmly. "Okay. I hear you. I do." Moving to change the conversation, he said, "So, you on lunch break from training with your gray friend?"

"Hmm," Napoleon said grimly. "Yes and no."

"What's that mean?"

"He's working with a guy—kinda like the situation with Fasano—you wouldn't understand. Regardless, his efforts are proving too daunting, to say the least."

"Why? Guy doesn't want to listen or something?"

Napoleon chuckled. "No. That'd be my situation with your sorry ass."

"What? So you're saying that I'm—"

"No. Your situation's different. I'm learning—or supposed to be learning—how to counsel someone. Ya know, in the everyday sense."

Parker smiled skeptically. "Everyday sense?"

"Yeah. We're all around you, all of you, every day, ya know? Waiting to help. All any of you have to do is ask. We can't wave any magic wands and only some of us can pull off an actual miracle, but still. Who knows? Maybe all we can do is get you through the day, but that's something, right?"

"Yeah. I guess it is," Parker replied. "But this guy's situation is different?"

It was Napoleon's turn to look out the concourse window. As

his eyes traced a plane taking off into the sky, he nodded. "Yeah. You could say that."

"How so?"

Napoleon thought about it for a second before he replied. "Well, Parker. He's pretty much a kid in a twenty-something's body. A lost cause on pause. He's surrounded by evil, with a mission to carry out, in a prison where practically every other cell?"

"Yeah?"

Nap looked back to Parker with a grim look, and what he said next made Parker's stomach drop.

"It's like every other cell has a Bread Man in it, Parker."

———

THE CRAZY-ASSED WITCHES had seen something, up in the ceiling or something, and Delva called to it. "Come," she'd said, before more spooky talk about a stairway and blood being spilled and so on. Maggie had followed their gazes but saw only wood-beam rafters and a section of puffed straw that was evidently this home's version of insulation.

All Maggie knew for sure was that it was scaring Luisa worse. The poor girl was looking up and around with bewildered dismay before Maggie screamed to her, "Just close your eyes, Luisa! Ignore them!"

Evidently having had enough of Maggie's interference, Delva ordered her to be ushered into the room behind the black curtain, where she was tied to a thick wooden support beam in one corner. This room was decorated even worse than the other, with walls that were painted in a mix of chaotic colors and images, like a *Día de los Muertos* exhibit on acid. More inverted crosses of all sizes were hung on them. In the center of the room was a large wooden chandelier with round sconces that held several candles, none of them lit yet, so that the only light was cast in from the next room through a crack in the curtain.

She remembered that this was where Ernesto had been dragged, and sure enough, there he was, his body piled like yesterday's garbage along the wall to her left . . . his head missing. It was too dark to see where it was now, and she was thankful for that.

In the other room she could hear them remaking their ash-based concoction, the sound of the pestle grinding away again accompanied by Luisa's occasional whimpers. Maggie had never felt so helpless in her entire life which—for *her* life—was saying a lot.

It was obvious that Eenie, Meenie and Miney were scared shitless of all the women around them; Sonia had killed the fourth member of their quartet. She had a big dagger and knew how to use it. But, still . . . against their guns, what was a dagger? And why be afraid of three little old ladies from Halloween Town with their witch-themed clothes and behavior? All silly hocus-pocus. Carnival shit for the weak-minded.

Still, seeing as they were Latin and most likely raised in Latin culture, gangster thugs or not, the three men had no doubt gone through the same Catholic Church rites and rituals that Maggie had. There was a certain . . . reverence . . . for the mystical. But this crap was off the charts. The only way to explain why these men hadn't killed Delva, Sonia and the rest with ease by now was because they truly believed that they could call on evil spirits and powers. It was the occult that gripped them now, so much so that when Meenie had dragged her in here and tied her to this damn post, his hands were shaking the whole time. More than once he looked at Maggie with a hope-lessness in his eyes that she imagined must've mirrored her own, his face changing from a mask of fear to a mask of worry, one second to the next, as he mumbled something about "the job".

Maggie smirked bitterly at the memory. *Yeah, Meenie. I'm guessing that you regret taking this one, huh? No matter how much Güero is paying you.*

But she didn't have this same irrational fear that they did. Okay. If she were honest? The inverted crosses really bothered her. But beyond that, survival had to take precedence over fear. If she could just get a hold of one of their guns . . .

The curtain shifted, casting a beam of light across a large cement block nearby that was probably the altar they kept talking about, and then she saw it: Ernesto's decapitated head, three flies combing back and forth across it until one was brave enough to cross his eyebrow, dance over his eyelid and settle down directly on one of his eyeballs. Her stomach rolled. She diverted her gaze. Around the rest of the altar was a moat of some kind, now smeared with blood, which led to a channel that ran across the floor on the other side of the room and to the outside. She could make out some carvings at the base of one of the corners of the block. They were ornate and looked like owl heads of some kind, but the rest of the block was too hard to make out in the dim light.

Before long, the song and the chants began again. Luisa screamed. Maggie got up on her knees and pulled with all her strength against the post to loosen the ropes. All to no avail.

There was a gurgling sound, then Luisa was choking. A lot. Then she was crying and begging for them to stop. She yelled in pain, probably as they forced her mouth open again, and then there was utter silence for a minute, which felt like a decade, before Luisa's crying came back and turned into a full-fledged wail.

Maggie Kincaid put her head against the post, closed her eyes and found her way back to all those days of Sunday school, growing up Irish Catholic in an Irish Catholic church. *Lord God, Our Father. Please. Save her. Help her. I'm begging you. I can't do this alone. We need help. Please.*

Round and round the prayer went in her head, crossing her lips in whispers, reminding her of catechism and holy water. Her and her little sister Julie. Simpler times that were actually very complicated times, as it turned out. But none of it important now, save for the belief that God was always just one prayer away. Contradictory or not, Maggie wasn't so sure she was down with the idea of demons and devils roaming the world, but she believed in God's light at her core.

Finally, someone spoke. It was Sonia.

"What now, strange ladies?"

"We wait," Delva croaked.

Then, as if to drive just one more dagger into Maggie's already fading hopes, she added, "For the girl from The Hanging Forest to find that Stairway and join us. Once here, the fetus will have a host. And we will have succeeded."

Chapter Sixteen

FATHER SOLTERA WATCHED in terror as the fight before him broke out, knowing that his job was to run and find The Stairway, but now he had the added pressure of getting there before Tabitha did. Because if that vision was correct? If she got through? She'd head straight for Luisa.

La Patrona spun around and unleashed a swath of throwing knives in a tight arc. Michiko swung her sword, matching the arc in reverse and managing to deflect all the knives save one, which struck her in the forearm. She grunted and swiped it out of her with one hand as she advanced a few yards into another volley of knives, this time six in all. Four missed, one glanced off her left shoulder and the other sliced a deep line across her right temple. Father Soltera noticed immediately that the blood from Michiko's cut was pure white, not red. She grimaced and advanced another ten feet, closing the distance between her and La Patrona by half now.

"He killed my sister!" La Patrona shrieked, before reaching to the belt across her chest and producing a handful of throwing stars. Sneering, she cast them with a wicked flick of her arm. They came out of her hand in a wider arc than the knives, but it was as if Michiko had not only expected this move but was counting on it. With blinding speed her sword darted down to the nearest star, up to the next closest and then finally down to the middle star. The sound of metal on metal was not dull and thick, as it had been when she deflected the knives, but lighter and tighter. *Dink, dink, dink!* Like tiny ricochets. And that's exactly what they were.

Incredibly, each throwing star was struck and redirected by Michiko's sword right back at La Patrona, one striking her in the right hand, which she used to protect her face, one into her right thigh and the last one into her chest. She stumbled backwards. Her face melted into rage. Looking to the trees towards the rest of her little darlings, she shouted, "Kill her!"

But Michiko was having none of it. Reaching to her side, she produced her *tanto* blade. Spinning to the left, she struck it against her *katana*, producing a sound wave so forceful that it sent the girls flying and more trees toppling. Then. Silence.

"Your brood is knocked unconscious," Michiko said softly. "And you are wounded. What now, hell spawn?"

La Patrona's eyes glowed red. "You dare to mock me?" she said.

The ground began to rumble and shake. Father Soltera watched in dismay as, one by one, each shard of broken wood, each splinter of every branch, each piece of chipped bark levitated off the ground, moving around and behind La Patrona in a wall of hundreds of natural daggers.

Michiko's eyes combed over them with defiance, but her confidence was erased when she glanced over her shoulder to see Father Soltera still standing there. "I told you to run!" she yelled. And this forced him to move. Because she had never yelled at him before, with anger in her voice, nor was there any mistaking that her anger was tinted with a tone of deep concern.

He spun on his heels and launched himself into the forest, past a still-hindered Tabitha, running as fast as his legs could carry him, as the wooden shards collapsed in a shower of death over Michiko. *No!* The selfishness of his next thought filled him with shame. *How do I make it out of here without her?*

He found a clear path beyond the deep grass of the meadow that led off to the right. Following it, he couldn't help himself again; he looked behind him. He was awestruck by what he saw. Michiko had formed a dome of white energy over herself that had protected her from the daggers. With the full force of the attack deflected, advanced again on La Patrona. He watched through the tree trunks as their bodies collided, La Patrona using her wide, bronze wrist bracelets to form an "X" over her head and catch Michiko's sword and trap it. They struggled from side to side before La Patrona lunged like a vampire at Michiko's neck. Michiko pulled back just in time, counter-intuitively collapsed the distance between them by relaxing her arms, then put her hip into La Patrona's stomach and flipped her, up and over, to the ground.

Father Soltera glanced quickly ahead. The path widened for a bit but still ran closely alongside the meadow. Still running, he looked over occasionally, careful not to trip. La Patrona barely rolled out of the way of what would've been a death stroke by Michiko's long sword, then she tried to stand, stumbled backwards and righted herself in time to get off three more stars. They burried themselves into Michiko's stomach and chest. Crying out in pain, Michiko relentlessly counter-attacked, gashing at La Patrona's right thigh with her *tanto* blade before striking her across the forehead with the handle of her long sword. In return, La Patrona punched Michiko in the face.

Father Soltera pushed on. He heard a loud *pop*, as if someone had just burst a soap bubble, and he looked back again.

The efforts of the battle, of the dome she'd generated against the wooden shards and the wounds she'd suffered, had evidently taken effect on Michiko's power; the forcefield that was holding Tabitha in place had burst and she was now swiftly, ruthlessly in pursuit of him again, running on all fours like an animal, the blade her mother had given her now clenched between her teeth.

Run. Run as fast as you've ever run in your life! He told himself. And he did. For the length of what had to be a football field, he abandoned himself to nothing but the idea of getting away, his feet pumping against his age, his heart struggling to keep up. He ran and ran. Up ahead, there was a large opening into a canopy of woods, but his spirits dropped when he saw a hill leading up to it. He wasn't sure he could make it up that hill.

Tabitha was suddenly on his back like a feral monkey, her legs wrapped around his waist, her arms around his neck, her head next to his. She began viciously thrusting her cheek against his face, incredibly using the knife in her mouth to stab at his neck, grunting and screeching with a horrifying glee that was only matched by the intensity of her efforts.

He reached back to grab at her, to pull her off. After all, he might be an old man, but she was still just a child. No more than ten years old. Surely, he could wrest her off him. He realized he was done for when she let go of his neck with one arm and grabbed the knife out of her mouth. She raised it high, ready to plunge it deep.

And that's when La Patrona came hurling through the forest, end over end, exploding through the trees like a cannon-ball. Fire and lava erupted from her in bits and pieces, and Father Soltera realized that this was the manifestation of her blood. Blood from hell, that pulsed with hatred and burned with sin.

She came tumbling into the opening ahead, finally coming to rest at the base of the hill.

"Mama!" Tabitha screamed.

La Patrona, barely conscious, looked over at them. Her legs were broken and sideways, one arm limp at her side. She reached out towards Tabitha without any sort of care or concern but with one final order. "Kill him!" she groaned.

He felt Tabitha raise the knife. But at the same time, Father

TONY FAGGIOLI

Soltera saw something that filled him with complete awe.
Michiko was swooping in, on wings as bright as her glowing
blood. She grabbed Tabitha's wrist and wrenched her off him.
The force of the move was so violent it sent Father Soltera
tumbling to the ground.

"No!" La Patrona screamed, as Michiko flew with Tabitha
towards her. Incredibly she was still struggling, trying to get to a
throwing knife, when Michiko grabbed her too. A large gap in
the air opened up next to them, a portal of some kind, that was
white around the edges and led to total blackness beyond. The
void within was howling violently with celestial winds. Michiko
hurled Tabitha at the portal, but Tabitha caught a thick tree
root on the ground in her small, clawed hands, held fast, spun
and took off back into the woods.

"Tabitha!" La Patrona screamed. Michiko tried to throw the
broken body of La Patrona through the portal, too, but with a
guttural growl, the demon woman clawed at the ground, desperately trying to hold on. Seconds later, bursting white globs of
light, the rest of La Patrona's brood, all unconscious, came
cutting through the forest and through the portal, striking La
Patrona and loosening her grip on the ground. All of them were
sucked into the portal, which closed instantly with a sucking
sound.

A few seconds passed before Michiko folded in her wings
and fell to her knees. He scrambled towards her and slid,
catching her in his arms.

Her eyes fluttered open. "You are okay?" she said weakly.

"Yes. And you?"

"I will be okay. I just need time to heal. Leave me here. Get
to the gate."

He cradled her in his arms and put his forehead to hers.
"No. I'm sorry. I can't. I will never leave you . . ."

Michiko smiled sweetly. "Nor forsake you."

They were alone together, a simple priest utterly amazed at
all that he had just seen with an angel asleep in his arms.

164

AFTER BREAKFAST, Curtis and Hector went to the yard to get in a workout. Shoulders and traps. It had been a while since Hector had lifted and it felt good. They alternated sets while a number of the other inmates stopped by to talk business with Curtis. Some things relating to the inside (the latest shipment of heroine had been placed in Ziploc bags and put in butter containers, the butter being melted and poured back in so it set around the bags before being delivered to the prison's cafeteria) and some things relating to the outside (two members of a rival gang in Chino Hills was secretly doing drug runs into a few Downtown LA clubs as a side hustle, and therefore had to be dealt with).

Hector quietly marveled at his boss, who had morphed again into the same ol' Curtis: funny but lethal, engaging but rude when he was done speaking with you. The contemplative, slightly remorseful Curtis from earlier was nowhere to be seen. He wanted one thing done one way, another the other, and as long as you did what you were told you were good.

His minions rotated on by with handshakes, disguising the work chats with bullshit chatter, just in case anyone was listening in, then they slowly drifted away. Hector noticed more than a few of them eying him up and down, probably wondering who the new dude was and why he had such instant access to the top. No one gave him the stink eye though, at least not yet, which was good.

After their workout was complete, Curtis dabbed a towel on his head and bobbed his chin at Hector. "Here he comes."

A man walked up from behind Hector who was about six-foot-four and weighed, maybe, one hundred and seventy-five pounds. It was a look that earned him his nickname. With his long arms and lanky legs, you'd have never guessed him for a killer. His eyes were small and dark. His face was pockmarked and wrinkled. At age forty-five or so, the wrinkles were a bit too heavy, but that was the gang life for you. "I gotta have a private chat with him, to set things up right for tomorrow, so go take a walk."

Hector did as he was told. He took a stroll across the yard to the water fountain for a long drink and splashed water over his face and across his scalp. Feeling a presence behind him, he turned around quickly.

The Smiling Midget was standing there and flexing his biceps. *Hey, Hector? Do you think I got my swoll on?* he asked with a laugh.

Hector shook his head and tried to walk past him, but The Smiling Midget cut him off. *So, what's with all the lovey-dovey friendship talk with the guy you're supposed to kill?*

"Get out of my way," Hector replied.

I mean, this ain't adding up for my side, Hector-Me-Boy! They're starting to get concerned and all, know what I'm saying?

Hector stepped around him, stuffed his hands in his pants pockets, and began walking the perimeter of the fence line. "Your side needs to back off."

The Smiling Midget double-timed it to stay in step beside him. *No, no, no, Hector. Don't go doing that. They'll send* her, *then we're all screwed.*

"Pfft! Send who?" Hector shrugged with irritation.

Never mind. Just trust me. Don't go there. She's bad news.

"What's it matter to you, anyway? Ya little freak!"

For the first time, The Smiling Midget seemed genuine in his reply. *Look. Hector. We go back a long way and all. I did good getting you through prison the last time, didn't I?*

"I guess."

You guess?! Without me, you'd be dead! That guy woulda killed you.

Hector thought about it, then shook his head. "So you say."

No, man. It's true. And what about dealing with the dude that got your girl to betray you? We took care of him, too. I got props for that one.

"Yeah. Great. And what about Marisol?"

The Smiling Midget's reply was absent any happiness but

also noticeably absent any regret or sadness. *That one's on you, ya know. I had nothing to do with that.*

"No?"

No, man. I'm serious. He reached up to run his tiny fingers over the chain link fence as they continued walking. *Think about it. If I had? More points to me. I'd have actually looked better, dude. But no, you went rogue on that one, buddy.*

"I'm not your buddy."

Yeah. C'mon now. Don't blow this. Just kill him. It'll be quick and easy, and from there? I promise you, your time here will be spent with no pain and no suffering. I'll get you chicks on conjugal visits, all you want, a solo cell for your whole term—complete protection and peace of mind for your entire sentence. No one will even try to hurt you.

Hector took a deep breath and surprised himself with his hesitation. It sounded good, he had to admit. "What's in it for you?"

The reply came with a shrug. *I get to stay, for one. And I don't have to answer to her. If she comes? That means I've failed. That's bad for me. Then I have to go back.*

"Back where?"

You know where. And I don't like it there. It's hot and all about punishment. I like it out here better. Where I can play.

"Look, you don't seem to get that I'm not on your side in this."

But you could be. You should be. Fine. I'll sweeten the pot. No guilt. None. About anything that you did. I can take it all away. You'll sleep like a baby.

Hector's walk down the fence line slowed immediately.

The Smiling Midget nodded encouragingly. *Yeeaah. That's it. You're getting it now. A life sentence is a long time. No need to suffer. It's easy really. Here's the plan. There's a shiv waiting for you in the library. Ya know, your favorite place! It'll be inside a copy of* Moby Dick. *Get it? Sidle up next to Curtis—I'll tell you when, so you're not on camera and the coast is clear—then just stab him the kidney. Nice and deep. Then break it off in him. He'll be done for.*

"I dunno," Hector said, looking out over the yard to where Curtis was sitting and talking.

Yeah, you do. And here's the thing . . . you have to do it tonight. After dinner. Or else, she's coming, man. Then? It'll be too late. For both of us.

Hector looked at The Smiling Midget. "Tonight, huh?"

Yeah, The Smiling Midget replied with a shrug.

"Why tonight, exactly?" Hector asked, just to take a dig.

Just like that, The Smiling Midget was smiling no more. *You know why,* he said forebodingly. *Got it?* he pressed.

"I got nothin'," Hector answered. He turned to walk away.

The Smiling Midget shouted after him. *You don't do it, Hector, then you got no idea what's comin'! No idea at all!*

The threat caused a knotted ball of foreboding to settle in Hector's stomach. And what The Smiling Midget was promising him . . . he couldn't deny it was tempting. Could he actually do it? Abandon this whole "millionth" thing? After all, what had The Gray Man promised him except suffering and training and growth and all that shit.

And what about Curtis? Could he really take him out?

Hector suddenly remembered the way Curtis had talked down to him, over breakfast, and how he'd rubbed Hector's nose in what had happened to Marisol.

What was it Curtis had said? That Hector was "going to have to answer for that". Yeah. That was it.

Well, Hector thought, *what if I'm tired of answering to shit, Curtis? What if I'm tired of answering . . . to you?*

Chapter Seventeen

PARKER WAS STILL SITTING UNCOMFORTABLY in the airport, though much more composed now, when his cell phone rang. It was Murillo.

"How you holding up?" he asked, sounding genuinely concerned.

"I'm doing okay, man," Parker replied. "Heading out of town for a bit to get my shit together."

"Oh? Where to?"

"Cabo."

"Nice. Well, for the record? Have fun and all that . . . but none of us here agree with you leaving, including the cap."

"Oh, yeah?"

"Yep. He's sitting on your paperwork. On the down low, he told us to tell your union rep to slow everything down, too, as much as possible. He thinks in a few weeks your head will clear and you'll come around."

"Hmm. That's what he gets for thinking."

Parker could hear Klink say something unintelligible in the background. "What'd he say?"

"He said you're being an asshole."

Parker laughed. "Tell him I love him, too."

"He's right, Parker. You're a good detective. Napoleon knew that. You were his last trainee. Don't forget that."

It was a gut punch that hearkened back to respect for the dead, and it would've been more effective if that very same dead person wasn't visiting him these days. Still. It hurt a bit. "I know. But taking me off the case was—"

"Was one hundred percent by the book. Everyone here knows that and so do you. The DA would've been in a horrible position—the entire case on this guy completely jeopardized—if you were allowed to go after him. Bias and—"

Parker was getting irritated. "Yeah, yeah. I know. How goes it, by the way? The case, I mean?"

There was an awkward silence for a few seconds before Murillo answered with obvious reluctance in his voice. "Nothing new."

"Uh-huh."

"Don't 'uh-huh' me, Parker. We're busting our asses over here. After what he did to Trudy? We'll get him."

Not before I do, Parker thought.

Then, because life was funny that way, and a person could sometimes put two and two together without realizing it, Murillo came dangerously close to the truth with a laugh and a joke. "If you happen to see him in Cabo, let us know."

Parker smiled. *You're a good detective, Murillo. That's gonna hit you. Tomorrow. Or maybe later this week, when you're two bites into your fried chicken sandwich at Lucky Bird in Grand Central Market, or at one in the morning when you wake up suddenly and say 'How did I miss that he chose, of all places, to go to Mexico to take a break?' and it'll make you so mad that your subconscious knew it well before you did.*

Still, just to be safe, Parker covered his ass. "Unless he happens to be on another panga ten miles off shore and fishing for bluefin tuna? I doubt that's gonna happen."

"Oooh. Fish tacos."

"And the best sushi. Right there on the deck of the boat, still a tad salty from the ocean."

"Damn. Well. Whatever. Just promise me that you'll think about it, Parker. Fair enough?"

"Fair enough. Is that the only reason you called?"

"Nope. The main reason is Inmate 7558 at Corcoran State Prison, otherwise known to you as Hector Villarosa. He called me, desperate to speak to you."

Feeling his face twist with surprise, Parker sat up in his chair. "What?"

"Yep. Says he needs to talk to you about what went down at The Mayan."

Parker went from stunned to flummoxed, barely managing to repeat himself. "What?"

"I'll text you the number of the prison."

"Yeah. Okay. But I'm not in the mood for convict tears right now, man. I'll call him when I get back."

"You sure? He sounded pretty insistent that he needed to talk to you right away. Told me to tell you that he was calling about . . . Shilo or something? Who the hell is that?"

Parker felt the blood in his veins go ice cold. "Come again?"

"Yeah. 'Shilo.' Name like that, I thought you'd know right away. Doesn't sound like it though. A witness at the club that night, maybe? Or, Klink said he read in the report that you and Campos filed when you visited Hector's warehouse over on Fresno Street that the dude liked quoting poetry?"

Wrong, wrong, wrong. Parker looked around, expecting to see Napoleon, but he was gone again. This was getting insane on more levels than he could count. How? How could Hector Villarosa have known to toss out a Neil Diamond song? The people around him, the check-in counter staffed by two pretty blonds, the luggage stacked nearby, it started going sideways. Just like it had that day on the freeway, when he'd seen that glowing creature taking the car crash victim off and away. Except this time the . . . eeriness . . . wasn't from seeing something, but rather hearing something. *Shilo? Incredible.* He barely managed the words he needed to end the call. "Okay. Text me the number. I gotta hit it."

"You got it. But Parker, if this guy gives you anything pertinent to the case somehow—"

"I know, I know. I'll get it to you right away." Parker hung up.

A woman in a black business suit, white blouse and navy blue pumps that had been trying to flirt with him earlier and was seated across from him was now looking at him with concern.

He felt weak and sweaty, like he might pass out. He pulled himself together and wiped his hand across his forehead. A little kid, maybe five, was chasing his older brother around a bench of chairs, laughing and yelling as he did so. Their mother and father, both seated nearby, were thumbing through magazines, the mother occasionally tossing an eye in their direction, looking wary of possible injuries.

When his phone buzzed with Murillo's text, he looked down at it and deciding to go all in or not in at all, he punched the number and let it dial out. The prison guard manning the main line forwarded Parker to the Visitors Information Desk, where a man with a very deep voice, identifying himself as Sheriff Thomas, answered the phone. After taking down Parker's information, he told him that inmate Villarosa was out on the yard. Calls were supposed to be scheduled in advance, but Parker pressed, telling Thomas that Hector might have information crucial to an ongoing case. *Never mind the fact that I just identified myself as Detective Parker, which I'm not anymore. Screw it. I didn't mean to. Force of habit.* Thomas softened his stance and said they'd fetch Hector, bring him in and have him call Parker back in fifteen minutes or so.

Parker still had time until his flight began boarding so he sat . . . and waited.

It took twenty minutes before his phone rang. Again, he played the role. "Detective Parker."

And again, he was floored. The man on the other end of the line said, "I thought you weren't a detective anymore, man."

He vaguely recognized the voice. "Hector?"

"Yeah. It's been a while, huh?"

How did he know that I'm not a detective anymore?

Parker grunted. "Yeah. It has. But how'd you know that? Did Murillo tell you—"

"No. Our friend in the gray suit did."

Again, another shot to the head. This was too much. Parker leaned back in his chair, wanting to puke but afraid to move. *This isn't happening. It's just . . . not . . . possible.*

"You still there?" Hector said solemnly.

But Parker wasn't. He was too busy running thoughts around in his head, like the little boys around the bench of chairs nearby. *The Gray Dude is involved. How? How does . . . dammit, just say it . . . how does an angel align himself with a cold-blooded killer? What. Is. Going. On. Maybe I'm off base. Maybe he's just referring to—*

"And by 'our friend in the gray suit' your referring to . . ." Parker blurted out.

Hector sniffed and yawned loudly into the phone. "Ah. Man. I dunno. This shit sounds so crazy you ain't never gonna believe me when I say who this guy is and what he—"

"He's an angel," Parker said suddenly, as much to himself as to Hector. It was time to quit pretending and denying. Again. Maybe this time it would stick.

Silence. Long and hard. "So you *do* know about him? Bro, this is nuts. I keep telling myself that I'm just seeing things, or at least I did tell myself that, but it goes both ways 'cause I can see the other side, too, man."

Parker didn't want to know. Still. He asked. "The other side?"

When Hector spoke next, he was practically whispering into the phone, his voice full of fear. "Man. They everywhere. Demons and shit. This place is full of 'em." His voice dropped, and he sounded depressed. "I'm starting to think it'd just be easier to join 'em instead of fight 'em, man."

"Nah. You don't know me, man. But trust me when I say: you don't want to do that."

"No, huh?"

If anyone were to hear this conversation, they would surely have called the men in white coats by now. *Got one looney in Corcoran, the other one at LAX. Round 'em up!*

But Parker realized that the real loons were the ones that missed all this stuff, happening every day, all around them. You could turn a blind eye all you wanted to. But, eventually, you'd see.

"You still there, Detective?"

"Yeah. I'm here."

"Just say it. You think I'm crazy, don't you?"

Parker sighed. "No, Hector. I don't. Not one bit."

———

MAYBE AN HOUR PASSED, maybe two. Maggie couldn't be sure. Her head hurt, and she had to be careful when she leaned it against the post she was tied to; in the right spot she could rest, but if she hit the wrong spot then pain would lace itself across her eyes and face. All those Taekwondo classes and thus far she'd spent most of her time getting her ass kicked, first at that warehouse in Granada Hills, that damned place she never should've gone to, then all the way across the border to this little shantytown in the middle of nowhere. History was repeating itself. Men groping her. Men abusing her. Except this time, women were involved, too. Three crazy old ladies and a psycho bitch with a face full of piercings.

Her frustration was growing by the minute. She'd already tugged and pulled at the ropes binding her hands to the post so much that her wrists were red raw and throbbing. She thought of giving it another go but she'd found a position, lodged against the pole with one shoulder resting against the wall, that was semi-comfortable. She was exhausted, but afraid to go to sleep. Luisa needed her and the last thing either of them could afford was Maggie wandering back to wherever Father Soltera was and maybe getting stuck there this time.

She tried to keep herself awake by staring at Ernesto's decapitated head. It was a morbid solution, but it worked for a while, until, like all horrors, the effect began to fade. Death was already turning his face plastic-looking, almost unreal, and as the very early stages of rigor-mortis set in, his cheeks began to tighten. Only the flies, still feeding on him and laying their eggs, ruined her ability to chalk him up as a wax figure now.

She looked to the ground for further insect-based denial to her fantasy that she wasn't really in a room with a dead person; a long trail of ants, about an inch wide, was snaking in from a crack in the floor of the house, over to Ernesto's body and up one of his sleeves. Maggie was marveling at their organization when her eyelids began growing heavier and heavier.

Then sleep claimed her as its own again, as if it were a mother she never knew, and she a daughter that could never escape.

This time she did not go anywhere. This time she slept like a "normal" person who was struck with utter exhaustion: deep and heavy into a blanket of blackness.

Someone was speaking. "Is she ready?"

Her eyes shot open. It was Güero, in the next room.

"Yes, yes she is. No thanks to you and the comedy of errors it's taken to get to this point."

"Where's Ernesto?" Güero asked, sounding angry.

"He overstepped his bounds," Delva said calmly.

"What?"

"So I had to have your lover kill him."

Güero sounded enraged. "What!"

"I was only following orders," Sonia said in a fearful voice.

"Orders?!" Güero yelled.

"If it was my choice," Sonia said, "I would've killed the *puta* in the other room, too. How dare you bring some little whore you want to sleep with into *my* house."

Maggie heard a loud slap and Sonia cry out. Then two thuds as Güero began using his fists on her.

"Enough!" Delva yelled.

Sonia was whimpering. "I'm tired of you always hurting me."

"Remember your place, *puta*. You're only alive because I allow it."

"Alive?" Sonia screamed. "Look at my face! Look what you did to my face!"

Another round of slaps and thuds. "Do you think I care about your face? Do you think I care about you, at all? Do you even realize what you've done by killing Ernesto? Besides being my right-hand man down here, he's the cartel leader's nephew, you stupid bitch!"

Sonia screamed in fear, probably because Güero was advancing on her again. Delva shouted, "I said, enough!" Except this time a massive rush moved through the house, the air rapidly displaced, as if a suppressed explosion had been released. It caused the walls and roof to vibrate and the curtains to the next room to fly open. Through all the dust and dirt that plumed up from the floor, Maggie could see Misha dabbing a washcloth on Luisa's head as Delva glared at Güero, his face twisted in rage and glaring back at her.

Well. In the movies this would all work out splendidly. They'd just kill each other off and I could ride out of Dodge with Luisa on the back of a horse. But that's not going to happen, is it? Maggie thought.

As if the world was reading her thoughts, Delva went soft, showing that, elderly or not, she still knew how to turn a man's ego against him. "Güerito. When? When are you going to realize that you're beyond these worldly concerns of the cartel?"

Güero huffed and puffed a few times before replying, "It's

complicated. You never should've ordered it without my approval."

"Yes. Yes, I know," Delva replied, waving her hand across the room and then to Güero. "But all of this is for you. When this is done, and you have the child? All we must do is get you somewhere safe with more money than you could ever need. The cartel will never find you, we'll see to it with our spells and our friends. Then, you can raise her and have her as many times as you want, and trust me, when this child grows up? She will be all you'll ever want. No other woman will ever please you again. You will serve The Master and she will serve The Master . . . and the evil you will do together? Oh. My old bones shudder with ecstasy at the thought."

Maggie closed her eyes in disgust and dismay. How? How were there really people like this in the world? It didn't seem possible until you read all the articles about kidnappings, saw all the news reports of the serial killers, or jumped for the umpteenth time when your phone exploded with an Amber Alert. No. It was true. Evil was real. And though she still wasn't ready to go down the rabbit hole of demons and hobgoblins, she didn't need to. Evil was right here, in this house, not twenty feet away. It didn't matter if it answered to the moon or to Satan himself.

Because it was answering to somebody.

Her energy somewhat refreshed from her nap, she scrambled to her knees and began pulling the rope up and down against the post again. Nothing. Except her efforts had caught someone's attention.

The curtain, which had fallen partially closed again once the disturbance in the air passed, was pulled wide open and there, in a blue suit with a starched white shirt and red tie, was Güero looking down at her. "Hi there, baby," he said with a big, fat smile.

"I hate you!" Sonia screamed from behind him, her voice dripping with jealousy.

"Leave her be!" Delva shouted.

Maggie gritted her teeth and jerked towards him, wanting to hit him more than anything in the world.

His smile grew so wide that it seemed almost inhuman. "Yes! Still feisty. After all you've been through? Incredible. I can't wait anymore. I want a taste. Just a little taste," he purred, his eyes so full of lust that he was completely blinded to Ernesto's body and head nearby.

"You can't," Delva said, this time, incredibly, almost pleadingly. Up until now Maggie had Delva pegged as highest on the totem pole around here, especially the way Güero had deferred to her back at the warehouse before they'd killed and cut Felix into pieces. But now? Now she sounded genuinely concerned.

Güero turned sideways and looked at her. "Why not?"

Delva looked at Maggie. "Because she's been . . . touched. By the other side."

"What are you talking about? She hasn't been out of our sight since—"

This time, as Delva spoke, Maggie met her gaze. "No. She was touched by the other side a long time ago, to protect her from an evil that was being done to her."

"Whatever. Who cares. So what?"

"So . . . you will risk involving forces we do not want or need here, you stupid boy!"

The room froze. Eenie, Meenie and Miney all looked to Güero, their faces showing that they were relieved by his return. Anastasia and Misha walked slowly to Delva's side. Sonia rose from the ground and wiped tears from her eyes.

Go ahead, Maggie begged. *Pull that dagger, Sonia! Cut out his cheating heart!*

"I listen to you only because The Master has told me to, hag. Know that."

"Yes," Delva sneered, "and The Master is all that matters. You've worked too hard to get this far. I'm trying to help you."

The house went quiet again as Güero looked to the ground, then at Maggie, then back to Delva. "So, what, then?"

Delva's face was painted with somberness. "If you were smart, instead of trying to have relations with her, you'd kill her. Not now, but right at the end of the ritual. We could use her blood, touched as it is, to heighten the effects on the child. And by then? It would be too late for the other side to help her."

When Güero looked back at Maggie, the lust in his eyes now gone, and when he spoke it was a crushing blow to Maggie's distant hopes for a Hollywood ending where the bad guys killed each other off in stupidity.

"So be it," he said firmly.

He closed the curtain and Maggie was back in darkness.

Chapter Eighteen

FATHER SOLTERA KNEW time was the enemy now. He had to get to The Stairway, to home and to two frail bodies: his own and Gabriella's. Worse still, somehow, someway, Luisa was now wrapped up in all of this. As he cradled Michiko in his arms, he looked desperately to the woods. Tabitha had gotten a good head start on him.

"You cannot let her get through," Michiko whispered.

Father Soltera looked down. "What?"

"You must go, *tomodachi*. She must not breach The Stairway before you do. If she does, she would have access to the girl and her baby."

"How do you——"

"I can see it all in your mind." She coughed weakly. "And your concerns are merited. In addition, if she gets through, she could seal the door behind her, trapping you here forever."

Shock numbed his mind, momentarily distracting him from the fight within himself between the urge to chase Tabitha and the duty to stay and protect his friend. "Michiko, I can't just leave you here!"

"I will be fine," she said, as her body lit up in a soft goldishwhite light that pulsed over the outline of her body. "I just need some time to heal."

As if to confirm this statement, Father Soltera watched in awe as bits of the aura left the outline, combed over Michiko's wounds, and then came back. Tiny dots that, with each pass, were healing her cuts and gouges a bit at a time. He looked into her eyes and saw strength. She nodded firmly. "Go."

Jumping to his feet, he turned and ran into the forest opening where he'd last seen Tabitha. As he did, something in the woods moved. Something big. It was no natural stirring on the forest floor. He looked around but saw nothing. A branch cracked. But it was from above, from somewhere up in the forest canopy. He looked up and squinted, trying to see what it was. Again, nothing. Sighing, he asked himself how many terrors could this place throw at them? Then he immediately regretted even thinking the question.

As he ran down the path, he saw no sign of Tabitha. At her age, even without that head start, she'd have a clear advantage of getting to The Stairway ahead of him. Fear, anxiety and a building sense of desperation began to overtake him, yet he was thankful for it. Because he knew what to do with these things, had trained himself over the years to counter them with only one reaction: prayer.

And as he ran and prayed, Michiko's voice came into his mind immediately. *Be strong, tomodachi. Take heart.*

The sky above began to crackle with energy. A lightning bolt splattered across the sky in staggered, swiftly disappearing sections, and thunder rumbled through the woods as a storm began to form. It occurred to him that everything here was sudden. Life. Death. Safety. Danger. Clear skies one minute, full-fledged storms the next. As if this place were suffering from a series of mood swings, as if he and Michiko were stuck in a massive subconscious that was made up of all the dead who were stranded here, lost, marooned and alone. Teetering between the depression of their decision and the madness of its consequences.

He felt a sadness creeping over him before he countered it with one thought: no one was beyond saving. Especially if those they left behind loved and hoped and prayed enough to reach them. Wasn't Gabriella proof enough of that? And what of Ikuro? How many lonely songs had he played on that violin, refusing to go back to his tree and hang? Knowing—believing—that someone, someday, would come.

His knee caps groaned in their sockets as the uneven terrain of the path began to take its toll. He pushed on, wiping at his face, as scattered raindrops pattered down on the upper leaves of the trees and fall below. Something told him to look up again. Something was up there. Looking. Watching. He could feel it.

As the rain began to make its way in dribbles down the tree trunks, Father Soltera realized the rain was colored. Yellow, blue and red hit the ground and mixed to form glowing puddles of green and orange. But he noticed that the rain did not fall straight down like the rain back home, but instead came in at angles and changed direction along the way, sometimes more than once, so that it was a zig-zagging sort of rain, like wet fireflies.

After a while, as he ran, he looked down and saw shoe tracks staggered in sections of the path that had gone muddy. Feeling this to be proof that he was running in the right direction, he mustered his strength and picked up his pace.

As he went deeper into the woods, the air became cooler and more still. Sounds carried further, and again, in the distance, up the trees, he could hear branches breaking. He looked up with dread, half expecting demon-possessed monkeys to be swinging from tree to tree. But. Nothing.

He pushed on. Crossing a shallow creek, he found more shoeprints that wove off to the left and up a steep hill. Seeing that he could get where they led without forcing his old legs to take the hill, he went straight and picked up the trail on the other side, desperation growing in him as his lungs fought to keep pace with his heart.

There's was no way, simply no way, that a little girl with all that youthful energy wasn't going to beat him there, much less one that was supernaturally gifted. The path wound down into a gully with heavy underbrush to the left and thick tree trunks to the right. Vines hung from the trees all around, giving the area a jungle-like feel. In the distance he could hear running water and felt encouraged. He was parched and his fatigue was growing by the second.

As was his desperation. Resignation clawed at what was most likely his demise. Stuck here forever, tortured by his failure to save Gabriella, a wandering man forever lost.

And that was when he saw her.

Tabitha had stopped about fifty feet up ahead and was craning her head slowly, from side to side, up and around. With her back to him he couldn't see her face, but the image of her there, in her pink sweats and her hair down the back of her white shirt, made her seem almost innocent.

Until more branches snapped again, up in the canopy—she'd heard whatever it was, too—and he saw the inhumanely rapid way in which she twitched her head . . .

First to the left . . .

Then to the right . . .

Then to the left again . . .

He froze.

A feral growl escaped her. The sound grew and grew.

Fear unfolded within him. But not of what was up in the trees. No. But in the way the little girl before him dropped her head and raise her shoulders.

And then turned slowly around to face him.

———

HECTOR LOOKED CAUTIOUSLY AROUND. Two guards were

with him. A woman with short hair stood outside the door; an Asian man with white hair sat at a nearby desk across the room, cautiously thumbing his way through an issue of *Sports Illustrated*.

Upon hearing Detective Parker's words, that he did indeed believe all the crazy shit Hector was confessing to him, he felt very much like a man on a violently bucking bull. He was sick to his stomach again. Was he really doing this? Was he really talking to a cop? About gang business? Like a rat?

An overpowering urge to hang up the phone came over him, and he was just about to succumb when the thought of The Gray Man helped him rein in his panic. This was important. Somehow. To stall, he asked a dumb question, "Okay. To be clear. We're both talking about—"

"Yes," Detective Parker replied, sounding as uneasy as Hector. "We are. Though I think we're both still having a hard time getting our heads around it."

"Ya think? No shit, homie."

"Yeah. Well. It's real, okay? I'm dealing with stuff on my end, too."

Hector squinted at the wall. "Stuff?"

"Never mind."

"On, no. I don't think so. No secrets, Holmes. I told you mine, now you tell me yours. That's gotta be the deal."

"I don't think so," Detective Parker replied flatly.

"Then screw it, man. Screw it all."

"Hector—"

"No!" Hector shouted, sitting up in his chair and earning a hard glance from the Asian guard over his magazine. Hector lowered his voice. "You don't get to just say we're in something together without saying what that is."

A long, uncomfortable silence followed. Hector sighed. "Man. I can wait as long as you need to. I only have, oh, thirty or forty years with nothing better to do."

One word followed, and from it anyone could've been able to tell that Detective Parker was pissed. "Fine."

"And?"

"You remember my partner?"

"Yeah. I met him. The Latin Loverboy that came with you that day you visited my shop, right?"

"Nah. That was Campos. You got his ass shot up, by the way, at The Mayan that night."

"Wrong place, wrong time, I guess," Hector said, falling on the old habit of silly bravado laced with uncaring. But he didn't mean it and his words made him sicker, so he immediately followed up on his trash talk with a qualifier. "I mean. Ain't no way I shot him."

"No. You were too busy trying to ace your ex and her new boyfriend."

Hector caught a string of expletives inside his mouth and swallowed them back down. "Nice," he finally spat out, with no small measure of contempt.

Another uncomfortable silence followed. When Detective Parker spoke again, he completely surprised Hector. "Forget it. I didn't need to go there."

"Yeah. And I ain't hearing no apology either."

"Nor will you. Now or ever."

Hector chuckled. "Maaan . . ." But in truth, the detective had just earned huge points for not kissing ass. He was right, Hector did what he did. And it was wrong. Period.

"Anyway. I was talking about my *other* partner."

Hector was confused. Screwing up his face he said, "Your other partner?" Then it hit him like a ton of bricks. "Oh. You mean from the *park*?" he asked incredulously.

"Yeah. Evergreen Park. That one."

The bull kept bucking and Hector just kept trying to hold on for dear life. "You're not trying to say—"

When Detective Parker replied it was like a man just trying to spit it all out at once. "He's visited me. More than a few times. A lot, actually."

The overhead fluorescent light flickered a few times as the

detective continued. "So there ya go. We're Even Steven."

Hector was speechless for a few moments, then, looking to the ceiling and shaking his head, he managed a reply. "Man. This is insane. Totally . . . insane. Is this really happening?"

"Yep."

"How?"

"I wish I knew. But I don't. It's . . . uh . . . above my pay grade."

"Anyone hears us talking, they gonna think we straight-up crazy. You know that, right?"

"I know. But who cares. Let's get to it. Why'd you reach out to me? Your message says something about The Mayan." He hesitated, before adding, "And . . . Shilo?"

"Yeah. I just said that for cover. Figured it'd get you to call back. But, really, I called because he told me to—the gray guy, I mean. Told me to use that name. Said you're going after . . . someone."

This time the silence that followed was long and deafening before Detective Parker replied. "You on a visitor's phone?"

Hector caught his tone immediately. It was obvious Detective Parker was worried about the call being recorded. Being on a phone at a guard's desk, the odds were not likely. But, still, he lowered his voice to reply. "No. I'm in one of the guard offices. But, I mean, with what we've already discussed? Does it really matter?"

"Good point. Yes. I'm going on a little trip. Do you know who I'm going to see?"

"Yes."

"Then what can you tell me about him?"

"What do you mean?"

"Any inside info? Hometown, bases of operation, safe houses, etc.?"

"Well. He's from Michocán, but I doubt he'd be there. Operates in and between all the gringo spots down there . . . Tijuana, Ensenada, Mazatlán . . . good business." Hector looked nervously at the guard, then whispered the rest, "Don't know of any safe houses, though. Sorry."

This information obviously disappointed Detective Parker. "Well. Shit. What *do* you know, Hector?"

Hector thought hard. "I've only seen him, from a distance, a few times. But each time he was traveling with a group of four bodyguards. I've heard that they're super tight. Anyway, he lets them do the dirty work."

"Okay. That's something."

"I also hear he likes to move at night and . . ."

"All rumors, man. I mean, when it comes to rumors, ya gotta consider the source. It's mostly all bullshit, Hector. If you don't have location intel, then I need target intel. His quirks. His tendencies. His habits."

Hector shifted in his seat and rubbed his free hand back and forth over his head. "Hey. I'm trying, man." Then, it hit him. *His habits!* Of course. "Hmm."

"What?"

"Well. Maybe it's just a coincidence but . . . I was just talking to a guy today who is def in the know. But, I mean, he just told me a story."

"About?"

Hector told Detective Parker the same story that Curtis had told him, down to the last detail about how he beat the girl and what led up to it, not sure why but feeling that it was pertinent information. When he was done, Detective Parker was quiet yet again.

"You still there?" Hector asked.

"Yeah. Just thinking. That it?"

"That's all I got for now. But if you end up facing off with him . . ."

"Yeah. I'll know what's coming. Good. Okay. If you think of anything else, call the station and leave me another message," Detective Parker said. Then, oddly, he asked something Hector never expected. "How you holding up?"

Hector was so stunned he could barely reply. "What?"

Detective Parker repeated the question. "How you holding up?"

Hector looked around, feeling almost as detached from reality in discussing his feelings with a damned cop than he did speaking to The Smiling Midget. "Uh. Okay." He looked to the ground. "I guess."

"Well. I gotta go . . . but hang in there."

As Hector suspected, the detective's caring was fake. "Yeah, yeah. Whatevs."

"No. I mean it, Hector. If that gray guy is visiting you?"

"Yeah."

"You must be doing something right. Don't stop."

Nodding to no one, Hector cleared his throat. "S'cool."

"And one last thing, Hector?"

"What's that?"

"You said your story, that maybe it was just a coincidence?"

"Yeah?"

"My partner is sitting right here with me. He wants me to tell you that there's no such thing."

The line clicked off as Detective Parker hung up.

Chapter Nineteen

PARKER AWOKE MIDWAY through the flight to Cabo with a dull headache. He'd managed a sort of twilight sleep after forcing his entire conversation with Hector Villarosa to the back of his mind, but it hadn't been easy. Like it or not, there was a connection now between him and a murderous felon and at first it was hard to stomach.

Until he realized that in some circles he'd be viewed as a murderer, too. Though he could argue the rules of war for much of his body count, there was still that day recently when he'd come very close to killing Tic Toc, the Korean gangster who'd fled him and Campos early on in their investigation. And some of Güero's thugs had been body bagged at Parker's apartment complex after he'd rescued Trudy.

Self-defense. Those were self-defense kills and you know it. They have nothing in common with what Hector did at The Mayan.

And it was true. But truth be told, Parker was scared now. Napoleon was one thing, but the reappearance of The Gray Man was quite another. He represented a bigger sort of truth. One that had eyes less likely to parse sins so easily. Killing was killing, and that truth up there, in the stars? It knew what few others did; it knew what Parker had done to that sniper-kid he'd hunted down across the Afghan desert. That was most definitely a murder.

Which means you and Hector aren't all that different after all, doesn't it?

"Shit," he whispered under his breath, causing the passenger next to him, who had her face in her Kindle, to glance at him. He motioned for the stewardess. When she came over, he fought off the urge to ask for a beer and instead asked her for a cup of coffee and any snack they had.

He had the window seat, so as she walked away, he pulled open the shade—annoying Ms. Kindle Reader even more—and looked out over the clouds below. It was bright and sunny but none of it was enough to erase the story that Hector had told him of what Güero had done to that girl at that party. There was a . . . viciousness to it that was a bit too much. Perhaps it was that he'd done it to her in public, no doubt multiplying her horror since no one tried to stop him, which Parker found detestable.

And then, there was the disturbing way in which Güero had turned all his rings in to his palms. That was a perp move right there. The move of a man who didn't want to risk leaving signature marks from his rings in the flesh of his victim that could later be used as forensic evidence against him.

Which meant two chilling things: one, he'd probably done it many times before, and two, by fear alone he had amazing control over that crowd. Men like Güero always had some sort of sick charisma, some grip over their subjects. There were so many similarities—ruthless, sociopathic, violent, murderous—between Güero and many of the terrorist leaders that Parker had dealt with that it was spooky. It was as if the war had followed him home in the form of a sick doppelganger who Parker was meant to run into on the streets of East LA sooner or later. Run into and . . . end.

Run into and kill.

No! That's not an option. You promised.

He smiled weakly, he'd made a pinky-promise, and what was it Trudy said about them again? That they were "legally binding"? Yeah. That was it.

Except, he was no longer a man of the law, was he?

He suddenly wanted that beer now even more.

He sure could use Napoleon's company, but he'd disappeared again right after the end of Parker's call with Hector.

When the stewardess returned, she had his coffee and a bag of salted peanuts. He frowned. But it was better than nothing. He spent the rest of the flight looking out the window, sipping his coffee and wondering what Melon would look like now. It had been a few years. Had he stayed in shape or gained weight? Would he be up to the task ahead, or hell, even be down with doing it at all?

An hour and a half later, once his flight touched down and he debarked the plane, Parker had his answers. He was halfway down the arrival tunnel when he saw him. Wearing a dark blue t-shirt and tan khaki shorts with flip flops, Melon was still a short, stout and a compact collection of muscles. His eyes were narrow and dark, but his biggest feature was a massive grin, which was always trending towards mischievous. "My man, Park!" he said with a deep chuckle. "Adonis has arrived."

Parker cursed at him and before they shook hands and gave each other a quick hug. "Damn. You haven't changed a bit. You look the same."

Melon shrugged. "You were expecting . . .what, exactly?"

"I thought you'd be a fatass by now."

"And I thought the same for you. But you know how it is . . ."

And Melon let it hang there as Parker nodded. Neither one of them needed to say it. They just knew. Most people worked out to get fit. But a man who went to war and came back in one piece usually worked out for one main reason: to make himself tired enough to get some sleep.

They left the Cabo International Airport and made their

way towards a winter-green jeep with a tan canvas top. A collection of stickers from various fishing villages, ports and charter vessels covered the back window. "Damn," Parker said, "I had no idea you were such a fishing junkie. I mean, I don't recall you talking about it much in country."

Melon grabbed Parker's bag and tossed it in back, then motioned for him to hop in as he did the same. "Yeah. I wasn't until I moved here. I was gonna open a bar, maybe, or a jet ski shop."

"That part I remember. And?"

"One day I decided just to try it. Tuna fishing, I mean. I'd heard so many times that they're a fish that puts up more of a fight than any other in the sea, even marlin, so I gave it a go. Invested in a local captain and his charter boat."

"Ya got hooked—pardon the pun."

"You could say that," Melon replied as they pulled out to the main highway. Parker noticed the signs said they were driving towards downtown Cabo. Melon added, "I mean. The fishing is killer. But . . . I also kinda had a moment, I guess."

Parker raised his eyebrows. "A moment?"

"Yeah. Dude. It was crazy. But one day I was out at sea. We were, like, twenty-five miles offshore, fishing a huge patty of kelp. I'd had a beer and was feeling chill when it hit me."

"What?"

They hit a pot hole and bounced around for a bit.

"It was a perfect day and the sun was up full, clear and bright. That same sun that used to beat us down so mercilessly over there, ya know . . ."

Parker nodded and swallowed away the lump in his throat. *Big sun. Massive desert. Small lives.*

"And . . . dude! I was totally at peace, man. Out there, on that water, the boat rocking back and forth, the chain from the anchor sliding through the guide rail. I had my pole. I had a beer. Life was good, ya know? And I loved that feeling so I go out as much as I can now."

"You found your safe place," Parker said, remembering the urgings of his therapist for Parker to do the same. To find a spot in the world where his past couldn't find him, and visit it as often as he could, until the past no longer bothered to visit.

Melon looked at him funny. "My what?"

Parker squirmed. "It's nothing. Just something I read in a book."

"One of them Oprah books it sounds like to me, dude," Melon said with a mocking laugh.

"Yeah, yeah. Probably."

"Were you reading that during your mani-pedi?"

Parker laughed loudly. "Okay, eaaaaasy now, Corporal."

"Oh! Not even here a half hour and he's already pulling rank?" Melon shot back. In his best Forrest Gump voice, he added, "Yes, sir! SAR-geANT!"

This caused a fit of laughter that filled the car as they shook their heads at what Parker guessed was the mutual realization that they'd picked up right where they'd left off, as if the years that had passed by were nothing. And they weren't. That was a good feeling.

"You set up good here?" Parker asked.

"Yeah. Bought a small house with some of my VA money. Ain't getting rich, but making decent money. Enough to keep the belly full and the cable on. You?"

"Work, as I mentioned, is a bit of problem right now. But there's this girl . . ."

"Ohhh, shit. The opening four words of every man's downfall."

Parker told him briefly about Trudy. Mostly just the basics.

"How'd you meet her?"

Parker replied, "During . . . uh . . . an investigation."

"Really? No shit."

"Yeah. Long story, but basically she was a friend of one my suspects' wives." Parker hesitated, realizing too late that didn't sound too good.

Melon jumped on it. "Wow, the plot thickens. So, you're a *bad* cop?"

"No. No, I'm not . . ."

"Uh-huh."

"I'm serious. The suspect ended up being completely cleared. The relationship started after the investigation was closed."

Traffic around them was light. A group of seagulls flew overhead as a kid on a rickety bicycle rode by on the opposite side of the road.

"Ah. Okay."

"But not before she shot and killed one of the real perps."

Melon jumped. "What? Dude. This chick took someone out? No. Way!"

"Yeah. She was protecting some kids he was after."

"Damn. Well. Sorry, man. I've never even met her but I'm already gonna have to steal her away from you."

"Ha! Your ugly ass wouldn't stand a chance," Parker shot back.

Melon chuckled as he made a turn off the highway. They made some more small talk as the road stretched out ahead of them and then they drove in silence for a few minutes.

Parker was looking out over a row of houses, feeling the cool sea air through his open window, the smell of salt foreign and exhilarating. Melon was pretty much the same as he remembered.

But, with his new life, would he still be down with the real reason Parker was here?

As if on cue, Melon broke the silence and nonchalantly said, "So? Who we going after and why?"

———

WHEN GÜERO HAD LEFT the room, the curtains hadn't closed completely, leaving Maggie with a thin gap through which she could see into the next room. Luisa was still in her chair. Delva and the others moved in and out of sight at random.

The roar of large trucks was coming from a distance. The adobe house they were in muted most of the sound at first, but as the trucks pulled up, the house vibrated so violently the thicker grains of dirt on the floor bounced up and down.

"They're here," Misha said, looking out the window.

"Two trucks, correct?" Güero asked.

"Yes," Delva said, "one for the wild and the other for the tamed."

What the hell does that mean? Maggie thought. Maddeningly, no one in the other room said anything to clarify the comment.

"What now, sister?" Anastasia said.

Delva scoffed. "You know the answer to that as well as I do. We prep the room while the girl sleeps."

A flurry of shuffling feet broke out and then the curtains were pulled completely open, the brightness temporarily blinding Maggie this time, as she hadn't been expecting it.

Güero was barking orders. "You guard the door," he said to Eenie. "You other two, go outside and secure the trucks. Tell the drivers to wait until we've checked the cargo."

Both Meenie and Miney replied in unison. "Yes, *jefe!*"

Delva came into the room with Güero, who again looked at Maggie as if he could only see her one way: naked and as an object of his perversions. She looked away.

"You!" Güero barked at Sonia.

"Yes?"

"You did this," Güero said, motioning down at Ernesto, spooking some flies off his face in the process.

Sonia was beside herself. Pointing at Delva, she answered, "Under her orders, yes."

"Ah. Always with the excuses. Stupid *puta!*" Güero said. "This better go quick, then. We don't need word getting back to the cartel any sooner than it has to that he's dead."

Sonia didn't look like she appreciated being called whatever he had just called her. Again, Maggie began to wonder if Sonia was the weak link in this posse. Her contempt for Güero was growing alongside her obvious jealousy of Maggie.

But Sonia's contempt was clearly rooted in longing. The kind a jilted lover has until the object that they supposedly hate shows them a little hope of the love they used to have. If Güero did that, Maggie had little doubt Sonia would throw herself at him again. Even after what he'd supposedly done to her face. It would be shocking if Maggie hadn't already seen it countless times at the women's shelter back home, women who had come in beaten to a pulp, leaving only days later to run back to the very men who had threatened their lives.

Maggie tried to stay as close to the post as possible and made no sudden movements. She simply watched carefully as Misha filled a large bowl with water and carried it over to Anastasia, who dipped a rag in it and began wiping Luisa down. First her face, then her neck and shoulders, before finally getting her hands and arms. Misha followed along with each step, using a dry towel to dab up the wetness.

Misha looked up. "One of you get the henna for me."

With a nod, Anastasia complied.

Maggie winced in confusion. *Henna?*

Güero noticed her. "What are you looking at, you little whore?"

Maggie looked down and said nothing.

"That's a good girl. You're lucky to be alive, you know that?"

Maggie stayed frozen.

"Answer me!"

Against the urging of every cell in her body, Maggie forced herself to nod, suppressing a sneer as the bastard laughed at her.

"Yeah. Not so tough now, are you?"

How tough do you expect me to be when I'm tied up to a post, you chickenshit? Maggie wanted to say. Instead, she closed her eyes. She had to stay calm.

Play the long game, Maggie. You lose it and get shot in the head then you'll be absolutely no help to Luisa.

It was true. She needed to focus on the positive and—believe it or not—there was plenty so far. One, the perv that had been touching her all the time had been ordered to stay away from her. And the murderous rapist who was fixated with her had been convinced to leave her alone, too. By now, countless abuses, including gang rape, could've happened to her and all she had was a bump on the head and some scratches and bruises.

And Luisa was still alive. There was that, too.

Chapter Twenty

THE COLORED RAIN fell all around them, bouncing off leaves and arcing to the ground, as the lightning did another dance across the otherwise barren sky. Tabitha looked at him and seethed, her little chest going up and down, her knuckles popping as she extended and protracted her fingers, over and over.

Father Soltera was holding his breath so firmly in his lungs he could barely exhale. *What do I do now?* he thought.

Tabitha began a slow, laborious walk towards him, her head tilted to one side, her eyes as vacant as a wild animal staring down its prey.

"What?" she croaked. "Letting Joaquin Murietta go, so he could do what he did to me, wasn't enough for you, Father? Now you want to remain stuck here, too?"

"Listen," he replied in a weak voice, her use of Joaquin's name rocking him to his core. "No one wants to leave you here, young lady. No one wants you to . . ."

She kept advancing as she talked. "Live in hell? Because that's where I've called home for a long time. After Joaquin was done."

Father Soltera blinked. Something did not compute. It took

a split second to register but when it did, he felt stupid for not catching it sooner. He'd suspected it but was never quite sure. But now, he had his proof. "You never suffered at the hands of that monster, and you are no child."

She dropped her chin with a look of offense. "Uh . . . excuuuse me?"

"The way you speak, the words, the intent, they are beyond the years of the mirage you inhabit. You're like all your kind: a liar. A liar serving the king of liars."

"Yeah? You think so? Well, if that were true then tell me this, tell me—"

He suddenly remembered his teachings at seminary. When it came to demons, you were never to speak to them. To engage, debate or try to convince them. Ever. Because doing so also meant doing the one thing that could be a fatal mistake: listening to them.

They had centuries of practice and you . . . did not.

"Stop!" he screamed. Then, stepping backwards, he began to recite a prayer by Thomas Merton.

The prayer seemed to hurt her, but still she was coming. When she was only thirty feet away, he began looking around for something, anything to defend himself with. He needn't have bothered.

He'd just taken a step over a small log when a series of vines began to snake their way across the forest floor. No. Not vines. Roots.

His right ankle was wrapped immediately by two thick ones that began to squeeze down, hard, on his flesh and bones. Crying out, he dropped to one knee, realizing too late what a bad idea this was as a clump of finer roots clutched his fingers and claimed his wrists with stunning speed.

"No!" Tabitha screamed.

He looked up to see that she was being entwined as well. A series of roots had spiraled up around her feet and around her calves. She teetered and fell sideways, a mask of shock on her face.

More roots came at them, like a herd of slithering snakes, from all directions. He struggled to get up, fell, and tried again with a shout of frustration. It was no use.

Tabitha, meanwhile, still had one hand free. It was her dagger hand, and she began using it to stab at the roots.

That's when, clear as day, Father Soltera heard the forest scream. Not a tree, not a branch—the entire forest cried out in a shriek that split his eardrums. Then another sound ricocheted between the tree trunks in a lingering thud not unlike the antlers of a rutting moose. *Knock, knock, knock!* the sound came. *Knock, knock, knock!*

Something groaned. The woods above them shifted.

Father Soltera looked up, and what he saw there made him question his sanity entirely.

————

WHEN HECTOR WAS DONE SPEAKING with Detective Parker, he was sent to the library for cleaning duty. He was not the least bit surprised. Like most new inmates, cleaning duty was a rite of passage. But this was the first time he was assigned to the library and he knew that The Smiling Midget, or perhaps whoever worked for the prison that was under the influence of Güero Martinez, had made this happen so that he could get to that copy of *Moby Dick*.

And the shiv.

After pushing his cleaning cart through the entryway of the library, he straightened the vacuum, which had fallen sideways a bit, and grabbed his cleaning rags. He had been here a few times already, but as a reader. Now, he used the rag and a bottle of Windex to wipe down a long row of desks with banks of computer monitors on them, taking care to focus on the keyboards, which were filthy with dirt and grime. The computers were nearest the entrance and usually under close supervision: no social media sites worked, nor any porn sites. You signed on and off via the librarian, who sat behind a nearby counter with a speckled Formica top, and when you were done, a print out of all the sites you had visited online was reviewed before you could leave. Only inmates up for appeal who had been granted the rights to defend themselves were given any extra privacy, and even then it was minimal.

The librarian today was a young hipster with over-sized, wire-rimmed glasses that were fashionable these days. Hector had sold many a bag of H to guys who looked just like him, outside concerts at Hollywood Forever Cemetery or in the alleys behind trendy restaurants in Los Feliz. This one wasn't too much of a douche, though, and the week before he'd even helped Hector find a copy of *West with the Night* by Beryl Markham, which Hector had read about in a newspaper article and was so far finding a great read.

Today, however, the librarian was in a mood. "They usually clean the computer desks last," he said in a huff, as if it mattered one bit what got cleaned in what order.

Hector bobbed his head, sighed and went back to his cart, which he pushed past the periodicals section and towards fiction, which was divided by genre for some dumbass reason, one of which was "CLASSICS," which, um, wasn't a genre. This annoyed Hector more than it should have, as did the fact that the classics were now divided not by author name, but by book title. New to the prison, he wasn't about to make waves, but he was determined to see this all made right someday.

Scratching his head, he removed the vacuum cleaner from the cart, plugged it into a nearby socket and began vacuuming his way down the aisle until he reached the "M–N" section and found the copy of *Moby Dick*. He was willing to bet, oh, a month's prison wages that nobody in here ever read *Moby Dick*. The shiv was right where he was told it would be. A purple toothbrush, its handle had been sharpened into a wicked point.

Electrical tape was balled up thick on the brush side to form a crude handle that allowed for a solid grip. He swiped it and put it in a pouch on the cart, then covered it with a few packs of paper towels.

He was turning to vacuum his way back out of the aisle when he just couldn't help himself. He quickly grabbed the copy of *Moby Dick* and flipped it open. He was wrong, but not entirely. It had been checked out. Three times. Twice by a guy named Elias, back in the mid-80s and most recently in 2004 by someone named Samuel. Three times in over thirty years. It was almost tragic.

Two hours later and he was done with the entire library, cleaning the main counter last, under the watchful eye of the hipster, who evidently felt bad for snapping at him earlier. "Hey, you want this?" he asked.

Hector looked down at the hipster's hand, which was holding out a can of Pepsi.

"Really?"

"Yeah. It's an extra one from the fridge in the break room. Still cold."

Hector slotted the broom he had in his hand back in one of the holes in the cart, bobbed his chin and took the Pepsi. "Thanks. What's your name, man?"

"Wayne."

"Wayne, huh? That's a white-boy name for sure. I'm Hector."

It was Wayne's turn to bob his chin as he shuffled some papers around on the counter. "Nice to meet you, Hector," he said.

Then, he froze. Literally. In place. One hand an inch off the counter, the other hand reaching for a slip of paper, his head partially down and his eyes staring downward, his head tilted like a mannequin.

A chill ran over Hector. Setting the Pepsi down, he took a step back.

Are you really still deliberating? The Gray Man said.

Hector turned around. "About what?"

The Gray Man looked at the cart. *About what you've hidden in there. About what the other side wants you to do with it.*

"Listen," Hector murmured as he shifted his gaze away from the penetrating stare of The Gray Man, "I'm not sure I can do this, is all."

Do what?

"Be . . . a millionth or whatever. Ya know. Save someone, be good."

We've talked about this already. We've—

"I know, I know. I remember. But, man, my whole life?" Hector said, looking back to The Gray Man. "My whole life I've done wrong. I've screwed up. And now Marisol . . . what I've done to her. I mean, I appreciate you believing in me and all, but I'm not sure I'm worth all your efforts, Gray."

The Gray Man nodded a few times before tilting his head. *Call on the blue.*

"What?"

You heard me. Call on the blue. I'll help you this time.

Hector paused, then did as he was told. Like calling on your lungs to freeze in place or for your mind to fix on one thought, the blue was an internal part of him now, both physical and ethereal. He could actually . . . feel it cooling him from the inside.

Good, The Gray Man said in an encouraging voice. *Now, bring it out. Just tell it where to go, like you tell your foot where to step or you head which way to turn.*

"Oookay. Okay," Hector said. The moment was a little fearful, like the first time you set off on your bike without the training wheels. But, before long, a cool liquid with the consistency of motor oil began to pool in his hands. He turned his palms up and gasped. All the lines in them were carved in dark blue, and his fingerprints were alight on the tips of his fingers.

Do you see that, Hector Villarosa?

"Yeah," Hector said with wide eyes. "Yeah."

That is a force from heaven. There. In you. A part of you.

Hector nodded. Turning his palms towards one another, he watched in wonder as the blue reached out to itself, in slender strands, from one hand to the next. Pulsing. Vibrating.

Do you think such a power could dwell in an evil person, Hector?

Hector shook his head.

Men do good things, Hector. Men do bad things. God sees it all. And if He has ordained you for this mission then I, for one, am not about to question Him, The Gray Man said in a somber voice. *Are you?*

Hector shook his head, slowly at first, and then firmly.

Good, The Gray Man replied with a small smile. *Now. I've asked others to help me shield this room, for a short time, so I can provide you with some training. Are you ready, son, to finally grab a hold of your destiny?*

Hector looked at The Gray Man and for the first time in as long as he could remember, there was no hesitation in what he wanted to do with his life. "Yes," he said. "I am."

Chapter Twenty-One

MELON HEARD the plan and didn't even hesitate. He was down. As they drove into downtown Cabo San Lucas, Parker was relieved but also a tad concerned. It had been a bit too easy to get him on board, to be honest, as if Melon were spoiling for a fight. And this made Parker wonder just how well, despite the talk of sweet senoritas and fishing charters, his buddy was adjusting to civilian life after all.

In the distance, sitting in the ocean like an old statue, was what Melon had called El Arco, a huge, arch-shaped rock formation that sat where the Pacific Ocean became the Gulf of California. The ocean was a dazzling dark blue and picturesque beneath the clear, light blue sky. Parker had nearly forgotten what the sky looked like with all the rain and dreariness of LA the past two weeks. The seagulls that were flying ahead of them down the road now sped off to join a huge flock that had gathered at a dock in the distance, where a charter boat had pulled in and fish grizzle was being tossed over the side. It was a feeding frenzy of seabirds, with their white and gray feathers, gliding, diving, crisscrossing and even colliding at times, all to get a bite.

They arrived downtown and parked. Melon opened the

back of his jeep and unzipped a black duffel bag. "I packed light for now. For what you've got planned we'll have to swing by my house. I've got a few gun lockers in the basement that'll have more than enough of what we need."

"Got it," Parker said, as Melon handed him a 9 mm Czechoslovakian-made CZ-75 that made Parker grin widely. "No way."

"Your favorite, right?"

"Yeah. Broke my heart when I found out it wasn't on the approved firearm list for the LAPD. Still got mine at home, though."

"That gun saved your ass a few times, right?"

"No doubt."

"Figured you might appreciate having one down here," Melon added, slapping Parker on the back before he tucked a Colt .45 into the belt of his shorts and pulled his t-shirt over it. It wasn't disguised as well as Parker's, which was covered by his Puma sweat jacket, but Parker wearing a jacket in paradise made him equally conspicuous. But neither one of them was going to be left vulnerable. After locking up the jeep, they walked a half block down Morelos Street to Lázaro Cárdenas, where they entered Señor Nachos, the restaurant Clopton had told Parker to go to.

Across the street was El Squid Roe, which Melon said was a hard-core party bar for the college crowd. It was pretty much empty save for a few folks sipping Bloody Marys to conquer their hangovers.

"Now what?" Melon asked.

"We go in and order lobster tacos, which they don't have on the menu. That's the cue, I guess."

Melon smiled. "The name is Bond. Melon Bond."

Parker laughed. "More like, Douche. Melon Douche."

When they entered the restaurant more than a few people took notice. They weren't young, but they were both big and fit. A waitress, leaning against the counter next to the food station, gave Parker a smile. He looked her off and caught the eye of a passing waiter with slick black hair and dark skin. "You can sit anywhere," he said, as he hurried off with two armfuls of plates towards a table full of raucous people.

Training was instinct, instinct was training. They both automatically went to a table that gave Parker a clear view of the entrance and Melon a clear view of the emergency exit. Parker wasn't the least bit worried about Clopton being dirty, but that didn't mean her contact down here hadn't been flipped, or worse, been discovered, killed and replaced with someone who was going to show up with a crew of men with murderous intent. After all, they were, once again, in enemy territory. Except this one was owned by drug cartels dealing mostly in cocaine instead of terrorist cells dealing mostly in poppies for heroine.

The waitress who had tried to flirt with Parker came over. Evidently determined to make a second run at him, she stood so close that her hip touched his shoulder as she asked if they wanted any drinks. Before Parker could say anything, Melon ordered them two Modelos. She scurried off before Parker could make the order and he raised his eyebrows at Melon.

"What?" Melon said. "One beer helps the aim, man. And . . ." He looked around carefully. "I need a few more minutes to size this place up before you say the magic words."

Parker nodded and looked out the window, which was open to the outside, a roll-up door recessed into the ceiling. Outside, a few couples rode by on bikes, touristy types, laughing and joking. A group of three Mexican girls, maybe thirteen or fourteen, had gathered on the opposite corner, their hair too made up for this time of day.

"Hookers," Melon said, evidently having followed Parker's gaze.

"You're kidding me, right?"

"Nope," Melon answered, a chagrined look on his face.

"Please tell me you haven't—"

"Nah, man. C'mon. They're children. I have a hard enough time—" Melon began, but then he stopped himself cold.

Parker was gonna press, but he knew better. Whiskey Dick was bad enough, but War Dick was even worse. It wasn't manly to live with it, much less to discuss it. But like it or not, they were still only human. Be it the depression or constant lack of sleep, things didn't always work the way they used to. It had taken Parker almost a year to get back to normal after he'd returned home, and even now he sometimes worried that he'd let Trudy down if he or she picked the wrong night to make amorous advances.

"It happens, dude. To us all," Parker said, without looking at him.

Having finished his scan of the room and evidently finding no danger, Melon leaned back in his chair. Digging a finger into a crack in the table, he gave a defeated sort of nod. "That damn place," he said with barely a whisper.

"Yeah," Parker said.

"How'd you do it, man?"

"Do what?"

"Come back from that chaos and become a damn cop, of all things?"

Parker pursed his lips and thought about it for a second. "I dunno. It wasn't easy at first, I'll tell ya that."

"No?"

"Shit, no. The hardest part was that first year on street patrol, not seeing a threat around every corner."

"Yeah. Makes sense. You weren't in country anymore but . . ."

"But that didn't matter. My body wasn't in country anymore, man. But my mind? My mind was one thought, one memory, one blink of an eye away from that place."

"And now?"

"Not as much, but still . . . not as seldom as I'd like."

Melon nodded and looked out over the bay, a scar along his

jawline oddly delineating his face in the sunshine. "Mm-hm. Same here, if that helps. I can be out there, miles off the coast, with the tuna finally biting after days of nothing, totally at peace —like I was telling you—and it'll hit me. It might be the rotors from one of the tourist helicopters in the sky, sounding nothing like a Blackhawk but then again just enough like one from that far away to take me back. More often, though? It's the blood on deck from a fresh catch or the way a tuna fights when you finally gaffe them and get them on deck. Just gasping for air. Gulps of it. Like . . . you know." He paused and took a deep breath. "How 'bout you?"

"Before, it was coming up on a group of bangers—I started in South Central LA—and it didn't matter that they were black, wearing red or blue hoodies and looking nothing like any grunt in Al Qaeda or the Taliban. I perceived them as deadly threats from the minute I pulled up in my patrol car. They might just be sitting around and bouncing a basketball back and forth, but to me? One or all of them *had* to have a gun and they *had* to be wanting to use it on me *at that second*, you know what I mean? The assumption that they were up to no good was maybe reasonable, but the assumption that they all had murder on their minds? It was irrational."

"Irrational?" Melon said with a chuckle. "What's that?"

"Exactly."

The waitress came back with their beers and gave Parker a third smile, proving that she was the thirstiest one of them all.

The smile disappeared when he ordered the lobster tacos. Her face went hard as stone and her hand froze over her notepad, the pen poised in mid-air, before she wrote nothing and said, "Yes, gentleman. We'll get those ordered right up." She fled to the waiter they'd seen earlier, who was at the counter filling salsa bottles, and whispered to him. He looked up surprised, then came over to them.

"Gentleman, I just wanted to let you know that it's going to take about twenty minutes for your order. Is that okay?"

Melon took a swig of his beer and gave him a wink. "No problem."

When he walked away Parker looked at Melon and said, "Never, ever, did James Bond wink so obviously at a contact like that."

"I know," Melon said with a shrug. "The damn Brits always were far more sophisticated than us."

"So, why'd you do it?" Parker asked.

"Because I wanted to make a personal kinda connection with him. Just so he'd know."

"Know what?"

"That he'd be the first one I shoot in the face if he sends the wrong people here."

———

THE LIGHT WAS poor in the direction Luisa was facing, so Eenie was ordered to rotate the chair she was in. This allowed Maggie to get a glimpse of her face. She was still sound asleep, despite all the chatter and commotion. Something in what they'd forced her to drink had probably knocked her out. They hadn't eaten since they'd been moved from the shack, which meant that whatever was in that concoction had mostly hit an empty stomach, no doubt heightening the effects. *Well. It's not actually an empty stomach, is it?* And this thought only made it worse. Maggie worried about the baby. Luisa was still in her first trimester, the time when she was most vulnerable to miscarriage.

With the heavy drapes drawn in the outer room, it was hard to get a fix on the time, whether it was day or night. The flames on the candles of the display altar flickered against wicks of unequal length, some tall, some barely stubs of fire, the newer wax dribbles of the candles running over or alongside the old.

"Why?" Maggie muttered, getting to her knees. "Why are you all doing this?"

"Shut up!" Güero shouted.

But Delva looked at her with a cruel fascination. "Do you think that your God is the only one that gives blessings, child?" Her eyes narrowed. "Because he's not. Mine does, too."

"We don't have time for this," Güero said, his voice full of impatience.

"No. We don't. But the trucks are here. And the potion is doing its work on the fetus. We're almost there. Get things prepared," Delva said, waving her hand at the stone block in the room without taking her eyes off Maggie, "while I enlighten this pretty little creature."

"Ah! What for?" Güero scoffed.

"Because she's going to die today, and it's always best when something knows ahead of time that it's going to die. Be it a girl or chicken. The eyes . . . they go wider in the end. It heightens the fear and thickens the blood, too, like syrup." Her gaze was just as perverse as Güero's, but in a different way entirely. "And that kind of blood, *mijo*? It tastes much better. Goes down like a fine wine, actually."

"You're all sick," Maggie said. "Sick and crazy."

Delva's smile ominously thinned before she broke into a churlish giggle. "And what, exactly, is wrong with being sick and crazy?" she purred. "Anyway. As I was saying. We are blessed too, by our Master."

Güero was pulling ropes across the stone block. "Seriously? Blessed, my ass. This whole thing has been total chaos since I left LA"

"Yes. And that is where The Master does his best work: in chaos, *mijo*. Because chaos is subterfuge. It provides cover for the darker dealings until . . . Why, look at her Güero," Delva said, walking over to Maggie and lifting up her chin. "All you could see was her sex. But no. She is a touched one. Touched, I say. Oh. You have no idea the power we can gain from her in the end."

"The end?" Maggie said, scared now, but nudging her to continue.

"Yes. The others we have brought here have been for this task or that. To protect our interests or the interests of our friends."

Maggie's shock was immediate. *The others?*

Just then, Güero opened a trap door over the stone block. The natural light that spilled in momentarily blinded her before it lit the stone block up in full detail, finally revealing a sacrificial altar made of carved stone. Smooth on the top, it stood about four feet off the ground and was more like a curved table than an altar. At each corner, wooden posts had been inserted into the stone. To each post was tied a length of thick rope. Along its side, in sections, were Aztec-like markings, some painted in bright red and green, others carved into the stone.

How many people have died looking up at that trapdoor? Maggie wondered before Delva interrupted her thoughts.

"You see, blood is life. It gives it and it takes it. Sometimes, like tomorrow morning, it has to be taken in order to be given."

"Tomorrow morning?" Güero said. "I thought we were doing this tonight! Why do we have to wait?"

Delva waved both hands at him with frustration. "Because, you idiot! The timing was ruined when the dumb little bitch destroyed the first batch of potion. Now that it's in her, we will resume with the rest of the process. First? We paint the girl. Then? We paint the altar. Once the girl's body is finally ready? Then we bring in the animals—"

Maggie's heart sunk. *Animals? Oh, God.*

"—then the wrathful things. They come next."

Wrathful things?

"After that, it'll be like a wicked play!" Another giggle, but this one laced with glee. "You'll see. The breach will happen, and everyone will play their part. And then?" Delva's face was covered in moles and deep scars, some of them so wide that they looked like nail scratches. She bunched them all up now in a sickeningly layered grin. "Then we take the baby, and right at that moment, at that *second*"—she lifted Maggie's chin painfully high, exposing her neck—"we cut this one's throat and fill that bowl over there with her blood."

Maggie's eyes followed Delva's. In a carved recess of the altar there was a large wooden bowl.

"Why? I mean, you said it would heighten the effects on the child. But why?" Güero asked curiously, stepping back and looking at the bowl as well.

"Why?" Delva said, as if it were the stupidest question anyone had asked her in her life. "Because it'll be for the baptism, of course."

"Baptism?"

"Yes, *mijo*. This is how we've been blessed. Before? It would've been a baptism of just normal blood. But to do the ritual with the blood of a touched one? Ah. You'll see. The baby from this womb will be an agent of hell of the highest order." Delva cackled.

As Maggie looked into her eyes, she realized that Delva, contrary to appearances, was not raving mad. She was cunning. She was the smallest and weakest looking of the bunch, but she was by far and away the most dangerous. Because in her— through her—something evil emanated. Something that was just using her as a shell. It was a notion that Maggie was completely uncomfortable with. Hell. The devil. You couldn't just believe they existed without believing they were also at work, each day, in the world. Could you?

Because, deny it all she wanted, Maggie knew evil. She knew it . . . intimately. She had made its acquaintance both as a child and as a grown woman. Maybe that's why she'd been so eager to reject things earlier, when she'd dismissed all their voodoo like silly Halloween beliefs.

But she knew those eyes that were looking at her. They were familiar . . . Somehow, they were . . . "No!" she whispered in terror, her eyes going wide with recognition.

"He still watches you, you know?" Delva said. The smile

drained from her face and was replaced with a look of complete, overwhelming and utter contempt.

"No. Shut up!" Maggie said, closing her eyes against his. Because Delva's eyes were *his* eyes now, she could feel it. *That's impossible. Insane!* But they were.

Delva chuckled. Then, leaning over to Maggie's ear, she whispered, "What was his name again, sweetie?"

NO!

"Michael. Yes. That's it. Michael. Part of his agony is in being forced to watch you, all the way from hell. Isn't that . . . sweet?"

Maggie's lower lip trembled, and despite her best efforts, a single tear escaped her left eye.

She cringed as Delva leaned in and licked it off her cheek with a leathery tongue.

Chapter Twenty-Two

FATHER SOLTERA TOOK two large steps backwards. *My God, what—*

But the question was barely out of his mouth before it was answered. Off to their right, first one, then two, then five trees toppled sideways, gashing through tree branches nearby with sharp cracks and brittle explosions.

Coming through the forest was a creature seemingly beyond the grasp of even his worst nightmares. About twenty feet tall, it was a blended mix of cracked wood and flesh. Seemingly without knee joints, it stepped stiffly and quickly across the forest floor. Everything obstructing its path was simply pushed aside, as if a force field of some kind was moving out ahead of it. It had a barrel chest that led up to a pair of featherless wings, reduced to bone and tendon. Spread wide, they had sharp tips. Its thick neck was curved bone, covered in thorns at least four feet long. Its head was all skull, its mouth agape and its eyes hollowed-out holes. From the top of its head, on the left side, protruded a horn that bent downward towards the ground. The horn on the right side appeared to have been snapped off and what was left of it was merely a jagged stub.

Father Soltera was beyond shocked and falling headfirst into dismay. *This is what's been watching us from up there, beyond the tree line, this whole time!*

Even more startling was the fact that Tabitha seemed as terrified as he did. She looked up, then around, seemingly for an escape route. But why, if both she and this thing were evil?

Something told him that this demon was too stupid to discriminate between him and Tabitha. It had evidently claimed this place and would kill anyone who tried to come through.

The creature shrieked and spread its wings out wide, forty feet across, almost upon them now. That seemed to be all Tabitha could take. Glancing at Father Soltera, she sneered, tugged free of the roots, then spun and headed back into the woods. The Wood Demon thrust a wing at a dead log on the ground, pierced it with a spine of bone and launched it at Tabitha. It barely missed her as she ducked back into the tree line.

Father Soltera

moved to chase after Tabitha, but the creature cut him off. Thrusting forwards, it let loose a raw growl.

There was no way he could win this fight. He thought of retreating, of running back to get Michiko, but that would mean completely surrendering his pursuit of Tabitha.

And Father Soltera was tired of running.

It seemed like he'd been running from the moment he'd arrived here. Felt nothing but terror.

He looked around. This place was all about fear. Yes. Manifestations of his own deepest fears.

First, The Hanging Forest and his fear of death. Even before the cancer, funerals always left him with a feeling of futility. Then came The Gossamer Lady with her dire wolves and his fear of lust. Then came the island and Gabriella and his fear of falling in love. And now, here again, was just one more fear. The fear of being small, weak and powerless. A fear that stalks you through the dark woods of your subconscious, telling you that you're not capable, that you're not strong enough to face the monumental challenges of life. Instead, you'll spend your miserable little days on this earth trembling beneath the weight of it all. Fear. This giant creature was made of it.

Father Soltera was sick and tired of it.

Hadn't he told his flock, so many times, that fear was the opposite of faith? His heart swelled. Yes, he had. And at some point, you must walk that walk, not just talk that talk. Because it really was that easy, if you were willing to let it be that easy.

Father Soltera smiled wearily and muttered, "Because the choice is always ours."

He was here, in this spot, alone, for a reason. As for Tabitha? He had to have faith that could still get to her and stop her somehow.

But first, he had to deal with this horrid beast before him.

The woods stilled as The Wood Demon moved sideways across a thicket, the branches and thin trunks of the trees there groaning beneath its weight before releasing a sound wave of cracking wood. If he got too close it would simply crush him. It was . . . a giant.

And this reminded Father Soltera of one moment in scripture. Just one.

Had not little David, all by himself, uttered a prayer as he stepped out to face Goliath? Amid all those who didn't think he had a chance . . . what did David do?

"He ran *towards* Goliath," he said under his breath.

And so, too, did Father Soltera with his Goliath. With this demon intent on stopping him from getting out of here. Old man or not, he already had what he needed: his faith.

And so it was that he ran at The Wood Demon with a prayer (*God, please be our rock and our shield*) and a bit of Ephesians, the Word of the God, the same God that he had served his entire life and, he was sure of it now, would serve until his dying breath.

Advancing, Father Soltera screamed, "Finally, be strong in

the Lord and in His mighty power. Put on the full armor of God, so that you can take your stand against the devil's schemes. For our struggle is not against flesh and blood, but against the rulers, against the authorities, against the powers of this dark world and against the spiritual forces of evil in the heavenly realms."

The effect was instant; the words he uttered had caused The Wood Demon pain. It howled with a rage so loud that it shook the trees violently. Its dead wings flapping uselessly, The Wood Demon suddenly let loose a staccato of click-calls that pierced Father Soltera's ears. And then it charged him, flinging its skeletal wings forwards, trying to clamp down on him with them, the thud of bone hitting the earth filling the air as they just missed him.

It lunged backwards as it prepared to swing itself forwards at him again.

Father Soltera smiled.

His sling was his voice and his stones were The Word.

"Therefore, put on the full armor of God," Father Soltera continued, "so that when the day of evil comes, you may be able to stand your ground, and after you have done everything, to stand firm."

Again, The Wood Demon recoiled. Spreading its wings wide, it launched the barbed tips towards him. Most of them missed, but one struck him in the shoulder, gouging into his flesh.

It hurt. He still pushed on. This time, with a grimace.

Michiko had left. He could feel it.

Which meant she believed in him. That he could do it.

The creature was fully upon him. Father Soltera didn't flinch. Instead, he gritted his teeth, did not look away, and began to recite more and more scripture. Words, alive, powerful, lethal, began to strike the creature as if they were flaming arrows.

"The Lord is my rock, my fortress and my deliverer!"

Bits of The Wood Demon caught on fire. Tiny embers at first. Screeching, it slammed its wings to the ground. The force reverberated across the forest floor, casting leaves up in a cloud storm and knocking Father Soltera onto his back.

He rolled over, got up, and continued.

"He will never leave you, nor forsake you. Do not be afraid; do not be discouraged."

The embers on the creature caught and blossomed, provoking more cries of agony. Opening its mouth, it roared, and the soundwave cut into the tree trunks all around. The trees began to fall, helter-skelter, on all sides. Two to Father Soltera's left, one to his right, their boom so forceful that he was lifted off his feet.

But he was not struck, nor did he fall again.

Instead, he stood firm. "Don't fear, for I have redeemed you; I have called you by name; you are mine!"

The flames spread, up and over The Wood Demon. The creature wobbled, then advanced. But only barely so, its face twisted in total confusion.

How many poor souls, Father Soltera wondered, *have come through here, trying to get to The Stairway, only to be killed by this creature?*

As if in answer to this question, as more of The Wood Demon's bark began to burn away, bits of charred white began to show through.

Bone. That's bone!

And as more of it burned, more and more bone became visible.

It teetered. Then, letting out a final groan, it toppled, now completely ablaze. As it struck the dry wood and leaves on the ground it erupted into an inferno.

Father Soltera watched the flames and sighed with relief.

Just like the boy with that giant.

Not much of a fight.

It made sense, really. Almost all the fight with fear was within yourself.

Realizing that there was no time to relish in his victory, Father Soltera yanked at the roots until he was free and ran to the area of the woods he'd seen Tabitha disappear into.

———

THE GRAY MAN had left the library quickly, saying it was too dangerous for him to stay and he would try to meet Hector in his cell again later. So once Hector had finished cleaning the library he returned to his cell, where sure enough The Gray Man was waiting, staring at the floor as if contemplating something.

"You okay?" Hector asked.

Yes. Just thinking of how best to proceed.

"Let's just get to it."

The Gray Man walked over and took hold of Hector's wrists. Hector felt the power in his hands.

Let the blue gather in your palms. This will allow you to concentrate the beams when you release them.

"Okay," Hector replied. He didn't admit it, but he was tired. He tried half a dozen times to get the blue warmth that came from his core to flow to his wrists. Each time, it made it partway up his forearms before it faded.

Focus, The Gray Man said.

"I'm trying to. I can't get it!"

Keep at it.

His image was starting to crackle and break up again, which only distracted Hector more.

The forces here are even more aware of my presence now. Your little friend is helping to orchestrate it.

"Why doesn't he just come and attack you?"

The Gray Man smiled grimly. *You mean, after I nearly killed him the last time he saw me?*

"But doesn't he have a lot more help here?"

Yes. And if it came to that he could launch an all-out offensive. But he's outranked in power. He would need a higher demon to help him. Until then, it's all a matter of blocking my signal and keeping me away from you as much as he can. Now. Again. Focus.

Hector did. This time, the blue made it to his wrists before fading. "Better, right?"

Yes. But not good enough for proper combat.

"Did the other dude have this much trouble . . . what was his name?"

The Gray Man shook his head. *Kyle Fasano. No. He had a rough start, but he was a natural. It came to him . . . stunningly fast, actually.*

"Why?"

I do not know.

Hector's arms were aching and going numb from all the surging and receding power. "Give me a sec, man," he said. Taking a step back, he shook the pins and needles out of them.

The Gray Man sighed in frustration. *We don't have much time.*

"I know, bro. But it hurts. I'm sorry I'm not as good as the Fasano guy."

It is not about being better or worse than anyone else. Each of you has your own path.

"Each of us?"

Each millionth.

"What does that mean?"

The Gray Man went snowy, then blipped in and out of the cell a few times before his image became fixed again. *It means one becomes a millionth, evolves as a millionth, and then either advances on the path or not.*

Hector stretched and leaned a hand out against the cot. "So? Were you a millionth?"

Yes.

"For what?"

Never mind.

"Okay. But . . . you chose to advance, I take it? Whatever that means?"

Yes. When my mission was done, I decided that I had no reason not to. So, I chose as you say. I advanced.

"Was that a long time ago?"

Yes.

"How long?"

It doesn't matter.

"At least tell me why I'm your last."

The Gray Man walked over to Hector, his gray suit seeming to glow softly, as he motioned for him to sit. Hector complied as The Gray Man leaned against the wall directly opposite him and folded his arms. Looking at the ground, he murmured. *Hector, Hector, Hector.*

"What?"

Nothing. I should've known. You were always a curious child. You and all your books. Wanting to escape, yes, but also wanting to learn. Such vast . . . wasted . . . potential. But not anymore.

"Why?"

Because you have been, are being, redeemed. And as for why you're my last? I've simply reached a point where I want to move on.

Hector thought hard for a second. "You mean . . .?"

Yes. I'm through being an agent between here and there. I wanted to help other tortured souls like myself. Some I have been able to help, some I haven't. Eventually, I was called to train other millionths, and that I've done as well, as best I could. But just like each life on earth has a span, so too does the life of a millionth.

His image went translucent. He looked around, then back to Hector. *It's really quite simple, my boy. Some of us who get to go to heaven go straight there; others take a detour. I wanted to stay behind, to help others, you see, who maybe might not get there without that help.*

Hector shook his head. "Why would anyone wait to go to heaven? I mean, I never even thought about the place because, well, the life I was leading, man? I figured I never had a chance of getting there anyway."

The Gray Man smiled. *Exactly. But now you have that chance, don't you?*

Bringing his hands in front of him again, Hector called the blue forwards. Calmly, he guided it towards his palms, almost making it the whole way this time. "Yeah," he said, "I guess I do."

Chapter Twenty-Three

JIM, the man who Clopton said would show up once the lobster tacos were ordered, joined them a half hour later. Wearing brown Bermuda shorts and a light green Tommy Bahama shirt, he looked like any other tourist, his aviator glasses hiding his eyes as he pulled up a chair and gave Parker and Melon each a fist bump. No handshakes. Nothing formal. Nothing to suggest that business of any kind was taking place, just three old chums in town to relive their college days and maybe do a little fishing. Jim was built like a swimmer, lean but in good shape, with a tan face and taut biceps.

From there, their conversation was straight and to the point. "You guys have pulled a full house on this hand, I'll tell ya," Jim said with a small shake of his head as he removed his sunglasses.

"How's that?" Parker replied.

"We got a vector on the Kincaid woman and the girl yesterday."

"How?"

"Family and friends blew up local law enforcement from a Facebook status that Kincaid managed to post somehow."

Parker was incredulous. "No way."

"Way."

"Damn," Melon said.

"Yep. Even push-pinned it on the damned map for us."

Melon let out a small whistle as Parker looked at Jim inquisitively. "And?"

"Well. We obviously couldn't wait for you at that point. Clopton contacted me, I scrambled a team. Little dirt town called El Centenario, just outside of La Paz. Took three hours to get there and by the time we did, they were gone."

Parker exhaled. "Shit."

"Not to worry though. We had the phone's SIM key by then. They're traveling through some pretty rural areas of Mexico, meaning reception is brutally spotty. We lost them for a bit, but when we finally got them back online, they'd moved about fifty miles south-east, to an area outside a town called San Juan de los Planes. We were going to head there today before Clopton confirmed that you'd arrived."

"Why didn't you just go after them straight from the last hot spot?" Parker asked, taking a sip of his beer. The waitress was looking at them, but not in any ominous way, and she certainly wasn't flirting anymore. Jim motioned for a beer and she disappeared into the back.

"They took a route through known cartel territory. They woulda had scouts the whole way in—we woulda been seen, for sure."

Melon was picking at the label on his beer. "So, how's that any different now for us, if we go in?"

"They've come to a stop at a small mostly abandoned ranch. We got a satellite pass. The property has one large home, mostly caved in, at the front of the property. But they're in an adobe house with a side barn, built further inside the perimeter."

"Go on," Parker said.

"We don't have a head count yet, but the satellite images initially showed four men, one who we think has the cell phone Kincaid used."

Melon looked at Parker first, then back to Jim. "She used one of *their* phones to post?"

Jim nodded. "Yeah. Balls, huh?" he said as the waitress brought him his beer and set it on a coaster before heading off to a different table.

"Balls for sure," Melon replied.

"Anyway. We also caught three women coming in and out of the house. Impossible to tell their age. But you didn't draw the ace of spades until today.

Parker smiled. "Güero?"

"Yep. Between you and me, Clopton was crazy torn on this one. Obviously, she was going to place highest priority on the Kincaid woman and the pregnant minor. But Güero wasn't with them then."

"No?"

"No. And we couldn't figure out where he was. Our intel initially had him at a safe house outside Tijuana. But they shuffled the deck there with a six-car pickup, each car splitting off in different parts of the city. We couldn't track them all, just two, and we guessed wrong on those two."

"Pretty sophisticated move, though," Melon said suspiciously.

"Exactly," Jim said with a hard nod. "The guy's file says he's as paranoid as hell. So maybe it's just that."

"Maybe?" Parker pressed.

"Well. It wouldn't surprise anyone if he had sources inside law enforcement all over the country. And he works for the cartel, which would have plenty of government help, too."

"Great," Melon mumbled. Then he shrugged. "But yeah, no surprise."

Parker leaned forwards, grabbed a tortilla chip and dipped it in the salsa before taking a bite. "So . . . we're dark down here?"

"Me and my people aren't. But you and he are, for sure. That's how—"

"Clopton wanted it. I know."

"Which means we have to go in alone," Melon said.

"I'm afraid so."

"Gee. That's wonderful," Melon said, sarcasm dripping in his voice.

"But there's a lot of good news here and I mean that."

Another group of tourists walked by, a few families with beach chairs and towels. Behind them was a pack of college kids, the girls in tiny bikinis and the boys, with tight bellies, in swim trunks. Parker smirked. It was good to be young. He looked back to Jim, who was no doubt ex-military like they were and who probably knew not to bullshit things. "Like?"

"First, there's a limited presence there. Güero came in a white Range Rover with three additional men, each of whom has set up a perimeter around the house. Then there's the four dudes and three other women inside the house. That's it, as far as we can tell. There's one other car, which arrived there first, a black Escalade. Second, the dude with the cell phone we've been tracking? He snuck a call out to some girl in Cancun. Discussed the women he was 'bodyguarding' in the present tense, which means Kincaid and the girl are most likely still alive. Lastly, the cartel chatter is telling us that they're losing patience with Güero."

"Really?"

"Yeah. He's earned them some very big money, but he's gone off the deep end it seems."

"How's that?"

Jim took a long pull on his beer. "Dude's into devil worship or something. Rituals. Rumor is, he's using his own product—"

Melon wrinkled his brow. "Product?"

"Yeah. Maybe too much of the drugs, getting high and whacked out—wouldn't be the first time one of these types became his own best customer—but also the girls."

"What do you—"

Parker cut Melon off. "Oh, man. I'm telling you right now,

you don't want to know any more than what I've already told you."

Melon shrugged. "You can never have enough info, man. You know that, Park."

Jim grew quiet. "Yeah. Well . . . rumor has it he's been sacrificing some of them."

"Bulllll-shit," Melon replied.

Parker sighed and leaned his head back. "Told you. Man. Even I haven't heard that one, yet."

"Yeah. May just be a bunch of urban legend bullshit, but supposedly a girl in Cerritos, California and one last month in Tijuana. Evidently, he's trying to create some sort of demon-succubus creature or some shit."

"What the hell is that?" Melon exclaimed.

"Isn't a succubus a female vampire?" Parker asked, confused.

"With a wing-nut like this, is it any wonder he's confusing his monsters?"

Something struck Parker. An idea. He voiced it before he could trap it in his mouth. "Or trying to crossbreed them."

They all grew quiet for a minute before Jim cleared his throat. "Well. There's a nice thought. Anyway. Effort in futility. We all know vampires aren't real."

And Parker almost smiled, because Jim had been specific, hadn't he? Vampires? That was silly stuff. But no comment whatsoever on the demon part of that equation. This was another vote for Jim being ex-military. Because once a man has seen the death and destruction cut loose with the wild abandon of men at war, there's no longer any doubt that evil, in one way, shape or form, existed. And Parker was chastising himself, internally, for not coming to this realization sooner within himself. He didn't need angels to appear or his partner to come back from the dead to show him there was way more going on in this world than many realized. He already knew. But, like any inconvenient truth, it was easier just easier to deny it.

"So . . ." Jim continued, exhaling through his nose, "the cartel is thinking of taking him out."

"Ha!" Melon said. "Even the bad guys have a limit on how much bad they can deal with, huh?"

"Evidently."

Parker said one word. "Leverage."

Melon nodded. Jim nodded and replied, "Yep. You nab him, get him to us and we play him some of these taped phone calls that show him his own people are planning to make him worm food—"

"He's more likely to give up the ghost on all their operations."

"Yep."

Parker rubbed his chin. Clopton was smart, for sure. "So, what's the plan? Because the Kincaid woman or the girl could be next, and I don't want to get there too late."

"Short ferry across the Gulf to the mainland. One of our guys is waiting on the other side. We can get you there by dusk today. I can get a cache—"

"We already have all the weapons and gear we'll need," Melon said, matter-of-factly.

"Okay. Good. Anyway, you go in. We'll be off-site a few miles—"

"Just far enough away to drive off if things go south for us, like nothing ever happened, or close enough to swoop in and claim the credit, if things go well?"

Jim looked at Melon with mild shock in his face.

"What, man? You think this is our first rodeo? We know the game. Go on."

"That's not how it is, but whatever. We'll be off-site. As soon as you radio out that you got him, we'll come in and get you all out. Car evac to a pickup point, then helicopter transport across the border."

"Good luck keeping that quiet from the Mexican government."

"By then, it'll be too late for them to do anything about it. We'll toss a cover story on it and remind them of the US federal dollars they're getting. They'll be butt hurt, pout for a few weeks, and get over it."

Parker finished his beer and looked out over the street and the sea beyond. "It could get messy."

"I know. We're ready for that, too. Clean-up team will be waiting with us."

"Okay. Give us an hour to get to my house to get the gear together, then send someone to pick us up. Because I don't want my car or anything else about me tied to this. I'm assuming you know where I live by now?" Melon said.

"Yes. And while we're on that subject?"

Melon looked at him with a smirk. "Yeah?"

"I get why *he's* doing this," Jim said, motioning his head towards Parker. "But why you?"

Parker watched as Melon and Jim eyed each other for a moment before Melon replied, "I go where my brother goes."

Jim did not smile. Instead, he gave a small nod and said, "And where my brother before him goes."

The table grew quiet. There was no point in asking Jim anything about himself. He was no doubt with The Agency, a Langley operative, so any answer he gave you could be a lie anyway. But this last comment pretty much cemented his pedigree, if nothing else; he was ex-special ops, for sure. So, when Jim spoke next, Parker gave him the benefit of the doubt that he suspected Melon would now give him, too. "If this thing goes sideways, I'll give you all the help I can possibly give, I promise you that. Definitely more than Clopton or any of the other Fed geeks would rubber stamp. That being said? Don't fuck this up."

The waitress came over with a large plate of carne asada tacos that no one had ordered. Probably standard operating procedure for when Jim met operatives here. They ate quickly, because food was important before any mission, and then said their goodbyes until later.

As he and Melon walked back to the jeep, Parker's thoughts turned to how quickly things were moving. Way quicker than he expected. He'd barely landed in the country and they were already making a move. Insane. And it was all because of that Kincaid woman. A Facebook post using one of her abductor's phones? It was incredible. He didn't even know who she was, but already he knew one thing about her.

She was a smart, smart girl.

Chapter Twenty-Four

ABOUT A QUARTER MILE over uneven terrain later, breathing so hard that he felt his lungs might explode, Father Soltera finally saw The Stairway.

There, about a hundred and fifty feet on the other side of a narrow river, it was framed by a huge patch of overgrown Japanese elms. Just like Michiko had said. There was no missing it because, most striking of all, it was bathed in moonlight. Vivid, bright moonlight, as if night were the only thing that could ever puncture this place from the outside. It cast an eerie glow down the steps, stopping hard right at the base of the steps, as if no longer permitted by some invisible law of the forest to advance.

His heart sunk. What if Tabitha had made it here and passed through already?

He needn't have worried. He heard her before he saw her, grunting with frustration as she moved into view with a clay jar in her hands. Shattering it against the steps, she then began shifting through the shards.

He noticed that there were actually bits and pieces of shattered clay everywhere, tan and brown shards creating jagged points of reference amid all the deep, dark shadows. There was no way she'd broken that many jars already, so what was going on?

He resisted the urge to charge across the river, tortured by the knowledge that he was so close to home but knowing that he wasn't about to leave Michiko behind.

"Michiko!" he whispered, hoping that she could hear.

There was no reply.

Between him and the other side, staggered across the river, were a series of stepping stones, all made of marble of various colors and patterns. The stones looked slippery and dangerous. "I don't know if I can cross that," he said to himself.

Tabitha looked up, saw him and snarled with obvious rage and frustration.

There was something about the clay jars that was holding it up, but he didn't know what.

"You won't succeed, God Man," Tabitha screamed. "You can't. I'll kill you as soon as you cross over so just turn and go back to your little island."

He shook his head at her.

"No?" she yelled across the river. "Then come on then!"

Not allowing himself to hesitate, Father stepped out onto the first stone.

Shame filled his body instantly. There was no mistaking it; the emotion was moving up through his foot, from the first stone, and through his body. Shame. So much shame. For the past. For the present. In him all along, like bruises that never healed. That time could never reach.

"I can't go on . . ." His feet were slipping on the rock, and his momentum was carrying him forwards, so he had no choice. The second stone brought another emotion: sorrow. It, too, carved into his heel and up his leg, first into his stomach and then to his chest, where it clutched his heart in a strangle hold. He felt his lips turn south and sadness crease his brow but still he pushed on, over another stone that made him feel brutally lonely, and two more that produced melancholy and regret, before he found himself halfway across the river.

I can do this! he said to himself, like when he was a teenager in summer camp, afraid to take a rope bridge across a dipping valley outside Lansing in Michigan. Except that wasn't the best moment to recall, was it? Because he'd turned back, hadn't he? His knuckles white on the ropes and his mind blasted with terror, he'd turned back. Causing a backlog. All the kids behind him mocking him as one of the camp instructors helped him back to the entrance.

He felt woozy and began to tip backwards, as if to force himself to fall back towards the shoreline, before he felt her small hand center itself between his shoulder blades.

"Keep moving, *tomodachi*!"

Bliss filled him. It was Michiko.

He glanced over his shoulder. "Thank God you're back."

She gave him a tiny nod. "Yes. But I am too weak to help you much, Father. I barely made it here."

He looked at her face, which was slack. She looked feverish.

Turning back to the river, he stepped across another two stones, one of pain and the other of loss, and he was now only three stones away from the other side. He could do this. He could.

The next stone, however, was one made of utter and complete desperation that climbed up and over him like a wild animal. He struggled and was falling sideways when he felt Michiko reach out with her *tanto* blade and place the flat side of it against his shoulder, steadying him with incredible strength. He couldn't be sure, but he also thought he felt her give him another little nudge, and the next stone wasn't much better. It was one of guilt. Joaquin Murietta came to dance in his head, as did the images of all the little girls Joaquin had murdered and all the faces of their family members, some who came to Father Soltera for comfort, never suspecting that it was he, by way of the sanctity of the confessional, who had let their child's murderer get away.

He was a bad person. A bad man. Unworthy of God or anyone. A destitute creature who was meant for this place—to hang from a noose, or to be perpetually hunted by all the dire wolves that roamed here, or to have his eyes clawed out daily by the Fire-Belly Cats.

No escape. No justice.

"You are not damned, Bernie," Michiko said. "Just lost. Now keep going."

Consuming anguish overcame him. "Why? What's the point?"

"Because," she said softly and calmly, despite their circumstances, "you are almost found."

He took a step to the final rock and was not the least bit surprised that it was made of nothing but terror. Here he was, all the way across the river, almost safely to the other side, and inexplicably he spun and tried to run back the other way.

Michiko gripped him by his arms and steadied him yet again, but he was full of nothing but a want of survival as he tried to push past her. In her weakened state, she seemed barely able to stop him. Then, incredibly, she did something he never expected: she embraced him. Then, she lovingly shushed him, like a child. "Shhhhhhhhhh," she said softly. "Shhhhhhhh." The sound was comforting, and it caused him to look into her eyes.

And what he saw there was the light of heaven. Still. Patient. Encouraging.

He turned around and leapt with that encouragement, over the stone of terror and to the shore beyond it, as Michiko came up right beside him.

Tabitha charged him immediately, baring those small razor-sharp teeth that protruded so unnaturally from such a tiny mouth.

Michiko stepped between the two of them and grappled with Tabitha as she lunged. They fell to the ground and began to wrestle with each other, Michiko barely able to hold her at bay, and that's when Father Soltera realized how weak she really was.

"Get to The Stairway. Hurry. Please!" Michiko said with great effort as Tabitha tried biting at her face and throat.

Father Soltera made his way to The Stairway. At the top of the steps was a massive oak door with a huge iron rung in the center and a keyhole just below it. He stumbled up the steps with desperate relief to the door, grabbed the iron rung and pulled.

Nothing.

He tried, again and again, with a strength juiced with adrenaline. Nothing. Panic swarmed over him as he glanced all around with shocked confusion. "No!" he screamed with frustration. He looked to Michiko, whose face was twisted in dismay.

Behind them, the river splashed in waves as Tabitha separated herself from Michiko, stumbled backwards and began to giggle uncontrollably. "No way out, God Man!" she cried. "There's no way out!"

———

AN HOUR LATER, and they'd made some progress. Hector was able to pool the blue in his hands, just like The Gray Man had wanted. From there, he could form small orbs, about the size of tennis balls.

But throwing them was much harder. He'd charred the wall across from his cell door with only three successful tosses. It was just like learning how to throw a ball, expect these balls were coursing with energy and stuck to your hands, which forced you to adapt your timing before you released them. It was awkward. So far, much to his frustration, if he tried throwing as he would a baseball the orb would veer sharply left just before it was about to hit what he was aiming at.

The Gray Man, whose image had been going out more and

more sporadically, also seemed a bit frustrated. *I must go,* he said suddenly.

"What? Why?"

I can no longer hold the forces here at bay. I had to get at least one good training session in with you, but it's taken a lot of focus. And the other one I am training is going to need me, soon. I must get to him.

"Wait! You can't just leave me here. Dinner is going to be soon and—"

The Gray Man looked pressed upon. *I know, Hector.* Casting a somber glance at the shiv, he looked into Hector's eyes. *But you know what to do now, right?*

Hector nodded. "Yeah, man. I know."

I'll be back as soon as I can.

"What? I mean, what about my mission—"

Hector, all this . . . The Gray Man said with a sigh as he motioned to the charred black spots on the wall from Hector's training. *It's the least important part of the process, do you understand? The real key to any mission is getting a millionth to conquer whatever it is within them that's keeping their heart from speaking to their soul.*

"But—"

You're already there, son.

"But what if you're not here when—"

If I'm not back in time, just remember that your mission is not that complicated. You just have to know your right from your left.

Then The Gray Man was gone.

Stunned, Hector paced around in his cell a few times, then practiced forming the orbs in his hands a little more, marveling still at the brightness of the blue and how the cores went pure white if you held onto them long enough. By closing his hands, he could cancel them out completely.

Feeling tired, he lay down on his cot and tried to sleep. It was no use. He was too stressed about dinner and what Curtis was about to do. When he'd tried to ask The Gray Man earlier what he should do to stop him, his only reply had been, *You must wait for the moment to reveal itself before the answer will reveal itself.* It was cryptic as shit and it only stressed Hector out more.

He made his way to his desk and was stubbornly trying to ignore the clock while he worked his way through another chapter of *West with the Night* when The Smiling Midget stepped through the bars of his cell with a grim look on his face. *Tsk, tsk, tsk,* he said. *I'm so disappointed in you, Hector.*

"Get out of here," Hector said, without even looking up from his book.

Without warning, the book was ripped by an invisible force from his hands and pinned to the far wall. The Smiling Midget began opening and closing his fingers, and as he did, pages of the book were ripped out by the handful and tossed to the ground.

Hector glared at him.

Don't give me that pissy look, you stupid boy, The Smiling Midget said in a tone Hector had never heard before. *I tried to ask you nicely, but . . . nope.*

"What are you talking about?"

I can still smell him here, The Smiling Midget spat. *That stupid gray ghost of yours. I don't know what you two were doing or talking about, but forget it, whatever it was.*

"What's it to you?"

What's it to me? No. What's it to you, *dumbass? You see the clock?*

Hector glanced at the alarm clock on his desk. It was five minutes to dinner time. "What about it?"

You got to do the right thing, boy.

"Not the way you mean it, shorty," Hector said.

Don't argue with me. I'm done asking. You get that shiv ready. Then, when the dinner bell rings, you get down there and kill Curtis. Plain and simple.

Hector looked at the ground and all the torn pages of his book. With a sigh, he stood. "No," he said.

The Smiling Midget's smile was gone. In its place, warping

like a blur, was his true face, sinister and menacing. *Oh? Is that right, you little shit?*

"That's right." Hector thought for a second. The Smiling Midget had said something very interesting, hadn't he? Yes. He had. "What are you going to do about, *chaparrito?*"

The Smiling Midget's face blurred again and his eyes began to burn red. From his mouth snaked a long, sharp tongue, which he stuck out mockingly in Hector's direction. *I tried, boy. I tried hard, at the last prison, at this one, to show you your one true path. But no. You wouldn't listen. So? I'm done with you, boy. Time to check you out and call it a bad mistake.*

Slowly, his fingers began to elongate into claws. As he began to advance across the cell, Hector let him. The closer the better.

When he was about six feet away, his little black-shoed feet began to quicken. It was only when he'd launched himself at him that Hector called on the blue. It came to him instantly, he guessed more from the urgency of the attack than from the training. Whichever, the blue shot into his hands just as he grabbed The Smiling Midget's arms. Originally intending merely to hold his claws at bay, there was instead a much bigger effect: he blew The Smiling Midget's arms off completely.

Flesh and bone went flying in all directions as the little man shrieked and fell backwards with horror.

That's fitting, Hector thought. *I wonder how much horror he's caused others?*

As he advanced on him, The Smiling Midget looked at Hector's hands with disbelief. His arms gone, he kicked backwards across the floor with his feet and used the stumps where his elbows used to be to guide a bloody retreat. Hector loomed over him.

"You talk too much, *chaparrito.* You made a big mistake telling me that you didn't know what I was doing in here with my friend. That told me he'd shielded us successfully, and you'd have no idea what was coming."

C'mon, Hector. Let's not get crazy!

"Not get crazy? Fool, we way past that."

Hey! Hey! No! The Smiling Midget cried out, desperation now in his face. *You owe me, man. I saved you . . .*

Hector called the blue into two orbs, one in each hand. "I don't owe you nothing. Everything you did, you did for yourself."

The Smiling Midget had backed his head into the bars. *You're not going to win, Hector. There's no way.*

"Yeah? We'll see, I guess. No. Take that back. Only one of us is going to see, actually. 'Cause you ain't gonna be around much longer."

His face filling with the rage of defeat, The Smiling Midget turned his gaze upwards. At first, Hector couldn't understand what he was doing. Until he saw the cell door lock glow red and the metal begin to melt.

"No!" Hector screamed.

The Smiling Midget grinned. *He who laughs last, Hectorino, laughs—*

He didn't get a chance to finish before the orbs Hector threw at him completely incinerated him.

Slowly, as his blood, bone and flesh began to disappear, Hector realized that his tormentor, for so many months now, was gone at last. Gone forever.

But not before he'd screwed up Hector's life just one more time.

With his cell door lock completely fused shut, the dinner bell rang.

Chapter Twenty-Five

THE OLD PICKUP truck that they were in was painted a faded two-tone of red over white and was the very definition of nondescript. A layer of dust covered the hood and side mirrors. Their driver was a Hispanic man in his late forties with gray hair over his temples who'd identified himself as "Juan"—with a smile that said that wasn't his real name—and his clothes were just as dusty as the car.

He let them load the gear they'd picked up from Melon's house into the bed of the truck before he began driving north with a lead foot through town and then out the other side, to a lonely, winding dirt road that climbed a short hill before leveling off into what appeared to be a semi-desert wasteland. Perhaps it was the shrubs and tumbleweeds or maybe it was the fact that he and Melon were both in their desert camos and their tan shirts with long sleeves, both of which matched their surroundings. Either way, Parker began to feel a little queasy.

Central Baja California was a different kind of barren than the Afghan desert, for sure, but there were enough similarities to make small memories in his mind fall like dominos: rock formations that cast long shadows; ditches that carved in all directions;

clay colored dirt littered with rocks; and a pale blue sky punctuated only here or there by a few solitary clouds.

"Roadhouse Blues" by The Doors was playing on a cassette tape in the 80s-era radio and Juan was bobbing his head happily to the music, as if he were driving them out to harvest avocados instead of to a place of possible violence. It dawned on Parker that this was the attitude of someone who really had no dog in this fight. The gringos. The cartel. They were always gonna do their thing and he was gonna do his.

They were sitting three across in the front cab, Melon in the middle, and it was only while making small talk that Juan made things more complicated than that when he revealed that the cartel had killed his brother and nephew fifteen years earlier, over a missing stash of weed. Parker curved his lips to convey his apologies, but inside it was just another domino falling; like Waheeb or the countless others who agreed to help the enemy, everyone had an agenda, a grievance or an old score to settle.

Jim Morrison took a tape-hissing break for a few seconds before "When the Music's Over" came on next. With his window down, Parker let the hot desert air blow over his face and ears. "How much further?"

"About an hour," Juan said.

Parker nodded. Melon nodded. A hawk circled in the air, looking for something down below to snack on. The road ahead curved left, then right, as the wheels of the truck hummed beneath them.

Juan cleared his throat and spoke with a slight Spanish accent. "We'll go over the logistics as we get closer, but the idea is to park about two miles out and walk the rest of the way in."

"You're going in with us?" Melon asked, sounding surprised.

"Shit no!" Juan said with a chuckle. Talking to the roof of the truck, he added, *"Pinche loco Güero!"*

"What'd he say?" Parker asked curiously.

Melon smiled. "That he thinks I'm a gentleman and a scholar."

Juan laughed. Melon laughed. Knowing he'd been lied to, and feeling a bit clueless, Parker managed a chuckle anyway.

"I will sit comfortably at a distance, thank you very much," Juan continued. "With a satellite phone. And then I will tell them if you succeeded or failed."

"Nice," Parker said.

"That's all?" Melon teased Juan.

"I will do that and eat my Subway sandwich, which I packed in the cooler right there," Juan said with a smile, pointing at a blue Igloo that was between Parker's legs on the floor. "With a Pepsi."

Melon nodded and said. "Okay. *Pinche puta.*"

The smile disappeared from Juan's face. "Hey, *cabrón*, I just—"

"He's just busting your balls," Parker said, holding up his hand. "Truth be told, we don't want or need your help. We'll be fine."

"I hope so," Juan said flatly.

"Hope so?" Parker shot back.

"Yeah. These guys where you're going? They is bad news."

Melon gave a tiny smile. "Well . . . we ain't exactly the funny papers, *muchacho.*"

"Hmm," Juan managed. Then the truck fell into silence as they drove their way through another half dozen Doors songs before the cassette tape ended. Juan flipped it, and on came a collection of 70s hits. Some good. Some bad. Parker wasn't much for classic rock unless a pool party and BBQ were involved. What they were about to do required at least some classic metal. Maybe a little Metallica or Pantera.

As he watched the landscape go by, offering up a few abandoned homes and dozens of cactus trees, Parker went over their inventory in his mind. With three gun-safes in his basement, Melon had spared no expense in his little collection, not even with the Busse survival knives they each had strapped to their right thighs. In addition, in the back of the truck were two military-issue fully equipped M-4s, with grenade launchers and Nikon M-223 scopes, good for up to six hundred yards. They'd brought plenty of extra rounds for their ammo belts but only a few of the grenades, to be used in the most extreme of situations, because, well, there were hostages involved and grenades had a hard time discriminating between who they were supposed to blow up. They also had flash-bang grenades. How Melon had come across such ordinance Parker didn't know, and he didn't want to know. Night vision goggles were in their backpacks, along with bottled water and protein bars, just in case things dragged out past sundown, which they both were both hoping to avoid if at all possible.

"Unchained" by Van Halen, arrived just in the nick of time before Parker dozed off, and ended just as they pulled off the road into a patch of dying cypress trees that offered sparse shade beneath their anorexic leaves.

No one had to ask if they were there. It was obvious that they were, and each man started going about their business. Juan pulled a duffel bag out from behind his seat, rifled through it and produced an old .357 Magnum, a pair of high-powered binoculars and the satellite phone by which he would either call in their success or their demise.

Despite the fact that he'd given them Jim's name and description when he'd picked them up, there were no instant friends in country, so they both watched Juan carefully as he put on a shoulder holster. Once the .357 was safely strapped in and nullified as something that could be turned against them, at least for now, Parker and Melon got back to suiting up, double-tying their military boots. When Juan saw their helmets, he gave a surprised look, but they said nothing; with the high likelihood of bullets flying around, keeping your brain together inside your skull was more important than making a fashion statement. Also, there was no mistaking the psychological impact it would have on a civilian target. Yeah, they were going after mobsters, but even mobsters weren't prepared for fully geared Army

Rangers to come dancing into their front yard. They would need that surprise as an edge before they began taking out targets.

He suddenly heard Napoleon's voice from somewhere off in the ether: *No killing.*

Trying not to let Melon see that he was startled, Parker turned and murmured under his breath, "Do you know how impossible that's going to be?"

Self-defense is one thing, Parker. And I mean Imminent Self-Defense. But that's it.

Parker shook his head and sighed. "Great."

"What's that?" Melon asked.

"Nothing. You ready?"

"Ready," Melon said with a nod.

Juan looked them both up and down, sternly, and shook his head. "*Pinche gringos,*" he said, this time with a smirk.

Then the three of them began making their way into a small valley where, in the far distance, they could see the adobe house that Jim had described earlier.

———

IT WAS RIGHT about the time Maggie foolishly began to think things couldn't possibly get worse that they brought in the goat. Brown with white stripes over either side of its mouth and cheekbones, it had sky-blue eyes that reminded her of—

No. Don't go there.

Zossima.

Her beloved cat, murdered by her psycho ex-fiancé, was the one area in her head her therapist had suggested they avoid, for now. It was too painful. Zoss used to be her best buddy, and the way he used to look at her after a long day at work, or cuddle in her lap while she read in her reading chair, always seemed to make life a little better.

The goat bleated suddenly, making her jump, as Eenie forced it into the house and guided it towards the altar. They had tied a crude rope around the goat's neck, not unlike the rope that they'd tied Maggie to the post with, and in a weird way this made her identify with the goat. Both of them were captive. And, according to what Delva has said earlier, both of them were destined for sacrifice.

Her heart sank as Delva nodded at Anastasia, who pulled a long knife with a white handle out of a case next to the altar. Spitting on it, she walked around the altar slowly, scraping the knife over each corner.

Maggie loved animals of all kinds. They were innocent, vulnerable creatures that never hurt anyone with any sort of malice in their hearts. For survival, yes. But never malice. And though she thought it was probably wrong to think this way, she couldn't help herself. This was going to be at least as hard, if not harder, than listening to what they'd done to Felix back in the warehouse. Yes. Murder was murder. But God only knew how many people he'd killed himself by that time. And after what he'd done to Father Soltera it was hard not to think—sinfully, she knew—that he finally got what he had coming to him.

But this goat had done nothing, to no one. And as it bleated a second time it seemed to look around the room with a dense, animalistic confusion, before those blue eyes fell on Maggie and she looked away.

No. Not dense. She felt a sob catch in her chest. *Innocent.*

"Are you ready?" Güero asked.

"Yes. You step back. We've done this many times before," Delva said. "Misha?"

Misha stepped forwards and took the rope from Eenie, who seemed more than happy to hand it over and retreat back into the main room.

The goat bleated again. The room grew quiet.

Delva held a wooden bowl in both hands as Misha yanked the goat's head up and grabbed its chin, fully exposing its neck.

Maggie stared at a crack in the floor and told herself that

this wasn't happening. A little denial was okay. Everybody had some, sometime. She wasn't here in this house and neither was the goat. This was all just stuff happening in her head. Lame to call it a dream. Even lamer to call it a nightmare. Especially when she trafficked in dreams and nightmares all the time and knew one full well when she saw it. No. This was just a little trip down a winding road—

The goat screamed.

Hell.

Sounds of a struggle followed.

Just like Felix, who had begun to swing his fists wildly when he knew he was done for, after Güero had turned the rings on his fingers in and attacked him. Before Güero's goons had held him in place.

Kicks. A primal sort of cry.

Again, like Felix, begging for his life as Güero beat him to death with his bare hands. Like a sick, savage brute.

Gurgling sounds followed.

Then death.

Maggie closed her eyes tight as she heard liquid filling the bowl.

"Yes, yes . . ." Misha said. "Perfect."

"Anastasia, put the knife away. Grab the brush, right there. Now, cover the entire altar with the blood. Side-to-side strokes only. Misha? You handle the prayer."

"Really, sister?" Misha said, sounding pleasantly surprised.

"Yes," Delva said. "You did the cut. You earned it. Drink a cup of the blood first, to bless your tongue."

Evidently, she did as she was told.

"Eh!" Güero said with a voice of disgust.

"Oh, *mijo*," Delva chastised him. "So sensitive."

Misha suppressed a laugh.

Delva spoke again. "You there!" she shouted.

"Yes?" It was Eenie again.

"Go get three chickens now. I will need their warm, still-beating hearts next. Hurry!"

Maggie heard Eenie scramble outside.

Chickens? Chickens were next. And what about after that?

The room was quiet for a bit before Maggie heard the sound of a brush, going over and over, across the stone surface of the altar. That's when she made the mistake of finally opening her eyes.

As she did, instantly, she saw that Luisa had awoken and was staring right at her, with the same, accusing look that Zossima had that fateful day, when she'd come home to find him lying in her apartment.

How, that look said, *have you let this happen to me?*

Chapter Twenty-Six

FATHER SOLTERA FORCED himself not to panic. To focus.

"You're doomed! You'll never escape this place!" Tabitha yelled.

He looked at Michiko. "I can't—"

I know, tomodachi. Leave her to me. I will buy you time. You try and figure this out.

Michiko attempted to draw her sword, but Tabitha was upon her again, obviously intent on not allowing that to happen. They spun and fell back into the water as Father Soltera did the hardest thing he ever had to do.

He walked up the stairs and turned his back on them, to better study the door.

The door. Which was locked.

And a door that was locked needed . . .

"A key," he said softly.

He looked around at all the jars, many of which Tabitha had shattered and some of which looked as if they'd been shattered a long time ago. As if . . .

He ran over to one of the jars. The top was sealed with a clear wax plug. But inside he could see a key, clear as day. Excitedly, he lifted the jar above his head, intent on shattering it to the ground, before something told him to stop.

No. It couldn't be that easy, could it? If it were . . .

He looked to the door. It hadn't been opened in a long, long time. Moss and vines covered almost its entire surface save for the wood at the front. The handle, too, was old and very rusted. Looking to the creases and seams it was obvious that they were filled with foliage and dirt.

He looked down at the jar in his hand again, the key glinting at him from beyond the wax.

"Do it!" Tabitha screamed. "Get the key!"

Father Soltera didn't need Tabitha's encouragements to cause his suspicion. He'd come upon it all his own as he squinted at the jar. How was that possible? How could a key glint from beyond a wax plug? It couldn't.

Unless it wasn't a real key.

He sensed immediately that what was in his hand was evil. That if he shattered the jar? It would be the end of him.

The fight behind him broke out again. He didn't want to distract Michiko, but he couldn't help himself. "Michiko?" he said, asking for guidance.

I cannot help you, tomodachi. I don't know this place any more than you do. All you can do—her voice in his head broke off as he heard her grunt loudly behind him—*is follow your instincts.*

He nodded. His instincts told him to put the jar down. He didn't know how it could hurt him if he shattered it, but it could.

Running from jar to jar, he saw some that were empty, but some still contained gold, silver or bronze keys. Some of the keys were round, others square, and a few were skeleton keys, which caught his eye the most.

One in particular almost felt like it was the one when he looked up for some reason, back to the door, and noticed for the first time that the lock in the door . . .

"It's way too big for *any* of these keys!" he shouted with surprise.

His hands trembling and his mind caught in a seesaw of trying to stay calm enough to think and trying not to completely panic over how the fight behind him was going, he ran back to the door, half tripping and catching his balance along the way.

Once at the door, he looked more closely at it. Horrifyingly, he could see deep gouge marks that looked scratches, as if some people who'd gotten here had tried to claw their way out. Then, stuck in the brick wall to the right of the door, nearly covered with ivy, he noticed two old and rotting wooden spikes, like the ones from the tips of The Wood Demon's wings. How many people had made it this far, past that creature somehow, only to be killed by it in the end?

"*Tomodachi!* Hurry!" Michiko shouted.

Not in his head. Aloud, this time. And panicked.

He looked over his shoulder to see that Tabitha had pinned Michiko into a neck of the river. The wounds she'd received from her battle with La Patrona had all reopened, and white blood was spilling from them.

Tabitha was bouncing, up and down, on her chest, determined to force a wooden branch across Michiko's throat.

He took two steps towards them, but his instincts kicked in again. Still, his resolve almost waivered until he saw Michiko clearly shake her head at him.

He turned around, back towards the door . . . the *covered* door.

That was it! He ran up to the door and began using his fingers to pull all the moss, dirt and ivy clear of it. Bits of it came off at a time as soil became stuck beneath his nails. Still, he scraped and scraped at it all, until, at last, a series of bamboo wheels, eight in all, came into view.

He froze, completely stunned for a second.

On the wheels were numerals. Greek numerals.

His mind spun in every direction before it came to him. Of

course: a combination. You needed a combination to unlock the door.

Banging his hands over the wheels, momentarily excited by his realization, he closed his eyes and tried to think. What combination? Why a combination?

The fight behind him continued. Tabitha screamed out in pain as Michiko grunted with exhaustion. Water splashed.

Focus. Focus. Focus.

Why . . . why were the numbers in Greek?

How fair was that?

Not that this place, or any place, had to be fair. But, still, whatever dead zone this place was, it was obvious that many people came here, from all places, races and . . . times. If poor Ikuro had made it this far, being Japanese, how likely would it have been that he would know Greek? Not likely at all. And unless the whole idea of The Stairway was a complete lie, unless there really was no escaping this place, ever, then this meant something.

This meant that the wheels were personal. They had to be.

Because who else would be likely to know Greek . . .

Than someone who had been forced to study it in seminary for years.

Like a priest.

Eight digits. He blinked. Michiko screamed with rage from behind him as the sound of fists on flesh, punches being exchanged, followed. He blinked again. *Think, Bernie! THINK!*

Eight digits. Personal.

Too short for a social security number. That was nine digits.

His birth date! Day. Month. Year.

That had to be it.

He ran his hands over the wheels, most of which rolled beneath his fingers with little effort. The last two stuck before he managed to loosen them and get them into place.

Then, with a smile, he stepped up and looked at the door.

Nothing happened.

Again, he remembered seminary. How they'd been trained that what was least obvious was most obvious. Scripture. Context. History. You started with the obvious and worked your way backwards, because that was often the right path. So . . . what was obvious . . . the *most* obvious thing . . . about this place?

He took a deep breath. *Think, think, think.* He said the words over and over again, almost like a prayer.

The answer came to him like a gunshot: you came here after you died. Or sort of died. Or half died. The point was . . . your first day here . . . was your last day there.

He opened his eyes. *God, please let it be true. Don't let my friend die, Lord. Help it to be true.*

What was the date of his last day back in the reality he once knew? The day that Felix had stabbed him? It was the same day that he'd visited Gabriella's bedside. And that was always on the last day of the month.

And what month had it been?

February.

He punched in 0228 and the full year.

Again, nothing happened.

"No!" he screamed. "This can't be! It can't—"

His mind was caught in a cobweb of panic when he told himself to stop.

Wait. Wait. Wait. Hold on a second!

He'd left Gabriella and stopped off on the way home, hadn't he? Yes. Late at night. Then caught the bus. By the time he'd gotten near home . . . it had been well after midnight, hadn't it?

"Yes. It had been nearly two in the morning," he whispered to himself. "Two in the morning the next day."

His hands ran over the wheel frantically to change the numbers.

When the door disengaged with a loud boom and an over-whelming bright light began to spill out from around its frame, he was so shocked that he tripped and fell backwards down the stairs.

Rolling over on to his stomach, he looked up to see that Tabitha had her hands around Michiko's throat. She looked up with a feral scream at Father Soltera, her face laced with hatred, but then immediately became spellbound by the light. She looked down at Michiko, as if trying to resist the urge to finish her off, before she looked back at the now opening door.

"C'mon!" Father Soltera shouted. Getting to his feet, he waved his arms at her. "C'mon. You wanna go. You know that! C'mon, you little monster! C'mon!"

Unable to resist, she leaped off Michiko and began to run full speed to the doorway, which was open all the way now, casting light in all directions across the forest, which seemed to be shriveling in response to it.

As she came, fast and hard, Father Soltera ran to the side of the doorway and yanked at one of The Wood Demon's spikes. Stuck in the ivy it took a few tugs, but with his adrenaline surging, he was finally able to wrench it loose.

He turned, and seeing her coming . . . he hesitated. What if she really was the spirit of some poor, demented child? Did it matter if she wasn't? Was murder ever allowed? Could he really do this? Could he kill?

He didn't have a choice. His vision of Maggie and Luisa had made it clear; if he didn't stop Tabitha then Luisa was doomed. Gritting his teeth, he steeled himself for what was coming, determined to do whatever it took to stop Tabitha from getting through the doorway.

He needn't have bothered.

As she ran towards him, her eyes full of determination to get past him and through the doorway, Michiko's *katana* shot through Tabitha's chest from behind. She vaporized with a stunned look of pain on her face.

The *katana* fell to the ground.

Father Soltera looked past it to his friend, who had thrown

her sword from on her knees. Her shoulders were slouched, her head was down, and she was looking at him through her hair, which had fallen over her face. With one arm she was clutching the other. "I just . . . needed time . . . to draw my sword," Michiko gasped. "It is good now. Leave now," she said, as she wobbled in place and then fell sideways into the gravely dirt next to the river.

He shook his head, walked down the stairs, picked up her *katana* and went to her.

The door behind him began to slowly close.

"*Tomodachi*, you are risking everything . . ."

"For a friend," he said, as he scooped her up in his arms.

He was old and weak and frail, but he had to do this, no matter what.

He turned and half ran, half stumbled with exhaustion up the stairs. With just enough of a gap remaining, he tilted her at an angle and squeezed them both through the doorway before it closed completely.

They were through and free, at last.

———

HECTOR STOOD and looked at his cell door, melted now to the frame, his frustration only mounting as he heard all the other doors of the cells around him open up in a cascading melody of metal on metal, from right to left, top floor to bottom floor.

His door tried to open, but it was hopeless. The electrical current sent to it to disengage the locking mechanism sputtered and the gears inside the door groaned with protest. He was trapped.

He ran to the bars and began screaming for help but all the other prisoners on his level funneled by, some with shrugs, others with smiles on their faces.

"Sucks to be you," one of them said with a chuckle, causing a bunch of them to laugh out loud. "I'll eat your dinner for you, homie. Thanks for the seconds!" someone else shouted out with a chortle. But then, Hector noticed a few of them look over with hateful grins, their eyes nothing but black orbs. One guy, with thick eyebrows and a narrow chin, slowly drew his finger across his throat and turned away.

"You got lucky, anyway, man," the other one said. Heavy-set, he held out his pudgy hands. "Power's out in the other block so they're mixing up the chow line with guys from that side."

Hector was staring at him intently, noticing the black orbs in his eyes as well. The man stepped to the bars and added with a smile full of gold teeth, "You know. Guys like Flacco. You know Flacco, right?"

Then he laughed, causing his belly to bounce as he disappeared down the stairs to the first floor.

What do I do now? Hector thought, leaning his head against the bars. This was it. This was the moment that had been manufactured by Güero's people to give Curtis the chance to take out Flacco. "Power outage, my ass," Hector seethed.

He looked around, trying to buy time, then told himself to think. He couldn't feel The Gray Man anywhere nearby, but he had to try. "You there?" he asked.

Silence.

Down below, the chatter of all the inmates coming together at the cafeteria door grew. His cell was on the second floor, so he could only see the far corner of the bottom level. The door at the far end opened and in came a stream of prisoners from the other block. Looking intently, Hector could see none of them was Flacco, and he was just beginning to hope against hope that something had gotten screwed up, when in Flacco came, fifth from last in line, his hands in his pockets as he exchanged a few informal "hello"s with some of the other inmates.

Stepping back from the bars, Hector took a deep breath. He knew that the blue was his only way out now. He called a few orbs to his hands and grabbed the bars, intent on summoning enough power to blow the door off its hinges, but after half a minute it was obvious that he needed way more power than he'd learned how to master yet to pull his idea off. Instead, he noticed that, beneath his grip, the blue melted straight through the metal, leaving two hand-sized holes in the bars.

The guards below were shouting at everyone to get in order. Three lines, instead of the usual two. Curtis was down there somewhere, he was sure of it, slowly working his way towards Flacco. He'd have his own shiv, ready to strike.

And then? Then it'd be too late.

Hector looked at the bars and blinked. Of course.

Dropping to his knees, he called two more orbs and repeated the process, four feet further down on the same two bars he'd already melted. This caused two four-foot sections of bar to fall with clangs to the floor on the catwalk outside his cell. The hole was still too narrow, so he repeated the process on the two bars on either side of the existing hole. Four more orbs later, and he had a hole that was big enough to crawl through.

Once out on the catwalk, he ran at full speed down to the stairs, taking them in twos and fours.

But his path was blocked. Two guards were on the way up to his level, no doubt alerted by the jail's security system that his cell door had malfunctioned. When they saw him coming, they looked surprised.

"Hey!" one of them, stout, with a blond crew cut, yelled.

A few inmates looked over, but Hector couldn't have cared less. He saw Flacco, just past them, still near the end of his line of prisoners. Scanning the rest of the crowd below, Hector saw Curtis just as he jumped out of the front of his line, a row over, and began weaving his way up Flacco's line. Smooth and swift, like a shark, he was coming. Some of the other prisoners, no doubt recruited by Curtis in advance to facilitate the attack, began to move out of the way or nudge other prisoners off to the side.

Hector began running down the stairs again, straight towards the guards, which did not make them happy. They each pulled out their batons. "Stop!" the other guard, short and muscular, yelled.

A few more prisoners saw Hector coming but Curtis didn't. When Hector saw him again, he had the look of a man with fixed, almost blinding attention on the task at hand. It made sense. Flacco was a very dangerous target and Curtis would know that he'd only get one chance before he'd have the fight of his life on his hands.

The guards flew up the stairs towards Hector, one of them actually getting close enough to swing at him, barely missing, before Hector leaped up and over the railing. The drop to the ground wasn't that far and he took it easily, landing smoothly into a roll, like a kid on the playground, before he got to his feet again and charged towards Curtis, who had now closed the gap between him and Flacco with incredible efficiency.

Hector was close to the lines but not close enough. He wasn't going to make it in time. In desperation, he was about to yell out to Flacco to run or get away, but then Hector realized that would only help Curtis by distracting his target even more.

So instead, with complete disbelief that he was doing it, Hector called out to Curtis.

"Curtis! Don't do it!" he screamed at the top of his lungs.

And this time, everyone heard. The guards behind Hector were closing in. All the other prisoners stopped talking and turned to look at him as he came running across the lobby towards the cafeteria. Seeing the commotion, the guards near the entrance fanned out as one of them blew their whistle to sound the alarm.

But Hector only saw one person. One face.

Curtis was looking at Hector with burning betrayal in his eyes.

Chapter Twenty-Seven

IT WAS A TWENTY-MINUTE WALK IN, measured and slow, to the "one mile out" mark. Because there was little or no cover, it was mostly done at a crouch. When they reached it, Juan settled down onto the ground with his backpack and combed the area with his binoculars. He needn't have done it on their behalf. Parker and Melon had both gone down on one knee and were doing the same with their own binoculars.

Things were mostly how Jim had described them earlier. A dirt road led to a wooden fence made of decrepit wooden posts. There was a gate to the property that was open, and beyond the gate was an old, abandoned house. Beyond the house, further inside the property, there was an adobe house with a wooden roof, and beyond the house there was a small barn, the doors slightly open but unguarded. A white Range Rover was pulled in to the left of the house and a black Escalade was backed in next to the barn.

What was different was concerning, though. There were two large delivery trucks to the right of the property, one behind the other. Jim had mentioned eight men, including Güero Martinez. Three of them were supposed to be sentries, but there was actually five of them now: one isolated at the entrance to the property, two at the front door of the house and two standing next to the backs of the delivery trucks.

"What do you make of those trucks?" Juan asked.

"I was about to ask you the same thing," Parker said.

"Odd."

"Yeah. You could say that. But between them, the barn and the Escalade, if we come in from the east, we'd have a ton of cover."

"Getting there is going to be the problem," Melon said.

"Spider crawl," Parker said flatly. "Probably for a half mile or so east, then north before coming in from that side on a westward path."

"Bellies the last half of the way," Melon replied.

Parker did the math in his head as he imagined Melon doing the same in his. They looked at each at the same time and said, "Two hours."

"What?" Juan said incredulously. "Two hours?"

"Minimum," Melon answered. "That guy at the front of the property is both a good and a bad thing. Good, because he'll be the easiest to take out."

"Yep. He's separate from all his buddies," Parker said.

"But he's also the most bored and least distracted, and therefore the most likely to notice movement as we're coming in."

"We a go?" Melon asked.

"We're a go," Parker replied.

So that no errant ray of sun could glint off the barrels if they were strapped to their backs, they instead strapped their M-4s to the front of their torsos.

As they got into tight crouch positions, Juan gave them a mock salute and said, "Don't let the rattlesnakes bite you in the balls."

"Thanks, *chavala*," Melon grunted, earning a scowl from Juan as they walked off.

"Shit," Parker said with a sigh, "is there anyone you don't find a way to offend, dude?"

Melon smiled. "Not if I can help it."

They moved in good time, over shrubs and rocks, alongside boulders to rest their backs and then on again, slowly and laboriously over open dirt patches. Parker kept his eye constantly trained on the sentry at the front of the property. When the sentry turned away or looked down, Parker, in the lead, would pick up the pace. When the sentry looked out in the direction of where they were, Parker would freeze, and Melon would too. Again, Parker had memories come his way, and again he pushed them away. But there was no hiding the fact that he'd missed this . . . feeling. It was the feeling of the hunt. And the game was getting closer and closer.

Eventually, after carefully crawling through a collapsed section of the fence at the far east end of the property, they came in as planned, just behind the delivery trucks, a little more than two hours later. Nostalgia aside, it had been a long time since Parker had done this and as he looked at Melon, he realized the same was true for him; they were both drenched in sweat, their faces and arms covered in dirt. The sun had been a relentless companion the entire journey, both threatening to reveal them and cooking them alive in the process. Parker's back and quads were killing him, so he laid down for a second and took a break.

"What now?" Melon said, before exhaling deeply.

Looking under the delivery truck nearest them, it was easier now to see what they were up against. Once again, Parker realized Güero was old school. Just like the goons at his apartment building when they'd gone after Trudy, these guys all had Uzi submachine guns. It was a glamour weapon of the 80s, not very accurate and almost a collectible now. But Güero must've seen a movie where all the tough guys had them, and the image must've been part of his idea of how your goons looked when you were finally branded The Boss Man.

All four of the sentries were wearing them loosely, barely paying attention to things, and even more interesting, the sentry at the front door looked like he wanted to be anywhere on earth but there. Best of all, his view of the back of the delivery trucks was next to zero. From his vantage point the only guy he could most likely see was the sentry at the front of the property.

"So," Parker whispered, "you got eyes on the guy at the front of the property and the guy at the front door. I got these two." Parker motioned at the two goons guarding the delivery trucks.

Melon nodded.

It was all about stealth . . . and watching your prey. The goon at the back of the truck was looking the wrong way when Parker came up behind him, and that was good. But Parker had to wait, patiently, for the one at the other delivery truck to turn away and spit some chew before he made his move. Moving in quickly, Parker cracked the goon nearest him over the back of the head with the butt of his knife. He dropped like a stone into Parker's arms and Parker laid him down in the dirt. Without pause, he swiftly advanced to the second goon, but he was a little sloppy, scuffing a rock with his left boot at the last instant. The goon turned in shock, but it was still too late; Parker got him in a choke hold and bent his neck forwards, just enough to cut the oxygen supply to his brain. Shortly thereafter, he slumped in Parker's arms, also unconscious. Wasting no time, Parker dragged him next to the other goon, removed their Uzis, checked for other weapons, then zip-tied their hands and feet and gagged them, even though it was doubtful that either of them would be waking up anytime real soon.

He was just turning to check on Melon when Parker heard the familiar *phut* sound of a silencer. He looked over just in time to see the sentry at the front of the property collapse, his head partly blown off.

Parker's mind raced. *Shit!* He hadn't told Melon about non-lethal measures. "That's not on me," he murmured to Napoleon.

There was a moment of silence, then Nap's voice, sounding disappointed. *Not entirely.*

Evidently having seen what happened, the sentry on the porch was just opening his mouth to yell something when a puff of blood plumed from the back of his head and painted the door of the house. He crumpled to his knees, his eyes in a death stare before he hit the ground.

The second sentry at the door got off a few shots, ducked and ran for cover.

Dammit! Parker thought.

Some things never changed. Just like before, it was always Melon who started shit. Always. And it was Parker's job to come in and mop up the ensuing chaos.

But as he stood with his M-4 and began to advance on the adobe house, he realized he was actually fine with it. Partly because it was too late to do anything about it now anyways, but also because he'd missed this feeling, too. The point in every battle when there's absolutely, positively no turning back.

It was time to dance.

———

MAGGIE'S HEAD WAS BOWED. She was trying to block out the sound of the chickens the witches were now slaughtering. Luisa, drugged and mumbling, was flat on her back on the altar, one hand stretched off to the side, her fingers clutching spasmodically at the air. She turned her head suddenly and vomited onto the floor. "M-M-Maggie," she moaned.

"Why did she puke?" Güero asked.

"The drink was only to prepare her stomach. We don't want to harm the baby, obviously."

"Is she giving birth now?"

Delva scoffed. "No. Not yet. The baby is much too premature. We will induce labor after all the rituals are complete—they will speed up the development of the fetus."

Luisa tried to turn onto her side, but Delva pushed her down.

Güero looked around. "So . . . what next?"

"She will be bathed in blood, practically immersed in it, by the time we're done," Anastasia said from behind him, a wicked glint in her eye.

"Yes," Misha said with a deep sigh. "Once immersed, we will call on the moon to bring us the power we need to call on The Master, who will send us the spawn that is to inherit the baby's body."

"Yes. Inherit," Delva said, "and infest."

"With the ability to curse all that is good," Anastasia added.

"At that point, at that perfect moment, we will make her drink the blood . . . and this will provoke the birth."

Luisa screamed out. "It's dark in here. Someone help me. Where am I? Hello?"

"It's begun," Delva said.

"Is that all it will take?" Güero asked.

"No. The wrathful things are needed now."

"Okay. The whores are outside in one of the trucks," Güero said softly.

Delva nodded. "Good. Send one of your men to get a few. Have they been used yet?"

"No," Güero said. "Just shipped in."

"Ahhh," Delva said with a sickening smile. "All the better, right ladies?" She laughed, looking at Misha and Anastasia, who chuckled in return. "Afraid. Desperate. And mostly unspoiled."

As quietly as she could, Maggie pulled and tugged, twisted and contorted the ropes. They were old, and the wooden post was dusty and splintered. She had to be able to get loose somehow. She had to, or they were done for.

Güero began to ask something. "Will she be . . ."

Delva looked at him out of the corner of her eye. "The baby will grow to be the most beautiful woman you have ever seen, Güero. She will give you the sex of the gods, warm and deep, like the soil of the earth, and together you will produce spawn that will lay waste to tens of thousands of souls. Her love will be so dark that you will never love another again."

"Yes," Güero said calmly. "I can't wait."

"But you will have to. For years. The child will grow at twice the normal rate, but you will still have to wait. Do we have an understanding, Güero? You'll have to wait."

"Yeah, yeah. I know. We've already talked about it. I'll wait. There's plenty of women to keep me entertained until the moment arrives. Until the child is grown."

Sonia suddenly spoke up. "What are you all talking about?"

"Why, it's about his new lover, about to be born and bred for the moment, silly woman," Anastasia said.

"Sister!" Delva admonished her.

"What did you say?" Sonia asked, a look of deep hurt coming over her face.

"Oh. It doesn't matter, child. Men will be men, after all. You should never expect them to be any better than their worst selves," Misha interrupted.

"No! No, that can't be right. What are they saying, Güero?"

"Nothing," Güero said dismissively.

"You can't be telling me that I let you do this to me . . . to my face . . . all the crap I've put up with, moving down here and helping to manage all these girls before they're shipped to you . . . so that you could . . ."

"Shut up!" Güero said.

"No! I'm done shutting up. You promised to marry me. You said we'd have children!"

Maggie was stunned. Sonia's anger grew and she continued shouting.

"I let you do this," she yelled, waving her hand over the piercings, "because you said it was the only way another man would never want me, that it wouldn't matter because you . . . would never leave me!"

Apparently unable to help herself, Anastasia sniggered.

Güero looked away and back at Luisa, and that's when Maggie saw the unholy lust in his eyes. His own niece, pregnant at that, and he was looking at her that way, too. Maggie's revulsion was instant. She continued to work on the ropes.

"Look at me!" Sonia screamed.

"Girl," Güero said, turning to sneer at her as he did so. "Don't you dare give me orders. You were nothing when I found you and you'll always be nothing. A dumb, babbling little hood rat. That's your problem—you never shut up! Anything I ever told you was to just get you . . . to . . . shut . . . the hell . . . up!"

Something in Sonia's face, in her eyes mainly, reflected the level of utter betrayal that she felt. Maggie could see it coming. She was cracking.

"You son of a bitch! I should've known you never cared about me. Ever. Fine. If that's how it is? Then I'm done caring about you!"

With that, she pulled out her dagger and began to charge Güero with a look of utter disdain, and for one brief moment, Maggie had hope again that something unexpected like this was going to save them. One of this bastard's own was going to betray him and stick him like a shrimp on a kebab. And as Sonia came on, full of fury, she came close. So. Very. Close.

Until Misha and Anastasia both drew long, curved daggers of their own from their cloaks and turned on her. Sonia, evidently too blinded by her passions, hadn't expected this, or maybe she never expected two frail looking old women to be able to move so incredibly fast, but when they began stabbing her mercilessly, she let loose a blood-curdling scream.

Eventually, as her own weapon was knocked free and Sonia was left completely defenseless, the daggers began to do their work. Over and over again, the thump of metal into flesh sounded out as Sonia's screams morphed into pure terror. Then, when she began begging for her life, the unimaginable happened; they all began to laugh. Güero. The witches. They all thought it was funny.

Maggie wanted to just shut down. Close her eyes. Close it all out. But there was no time for that.

While they were all distracted by the action, she began tugging violently at the ropes. It was true; they were loosening. They weren't coming undone yet, but she could crouch now, and with a little more effort she could stand, for sure. She pulled and pulled. If she could get them loose enough, she could maybe shimmy up the pole and work them off another way.

When the stabbing was finally over, Sonia's body was a bloody lump on the floor. "Foolish, foolish girl," Anastasia said. Looking at Güero, she added, "She really felt hate for you."

"Yes," Misha said, "and it's that hate that will now carry her to hell."

"Yeah, yeah. Whatever," Güero said. "Let's get on with it!"

Instead, Delva froze and cocked her head to one side.

"What is it?" Güero asked. "Hurry up already!"

"Shhhh!" Delva said.

"Sister," Anastasia said. "Do you feel it, too?"

"Yes," Delva said.

"What? What's going on?"

"The spawn. Something has gone wrong."

"What?" Güero replied, anger in his voice.

"No. It . . . can't be," Delva murmured.

The room filled with a strange sound. Barely there, but growing, it took a moment to register with Maggie before she realized it was the distinct sound of wood scraping on the walls. From all around them.

"No!" Misha hissed.

Maggie's jaw dropped as all around the room, in methodical succession, every single crucifix began to right itself. Slowly, deliberately, carefully. As if each one was being touched by some unseen hand.

"You will leave the girl alone," a voice said from the shadows in the far corner of the room.

"I will . . . not!" Delva screamed, her face twisting with rage as she spun and glared into the corner.

Maggie watched in awe as a man stepped out of the shadows wearing tan pants and a blue short-sleeve shirt. He appeared to be Latin, with dark skin and salt-and-pepper black hair, which was disheveled. He had sad eyes, like those of a St. Bernard, with large bags under them.

Who's this guy? Maggie thought.

"You dare to come here alone, creature of the light?" Delva mocked.

"Alone?" the man replied. "No. Actually, I haven't."

And that's when something outside the house exploded and all hell broke loose.

Never in a billion years would Maggie have thought that such a sound could bring with it so much hope, but it did. Her head shot up and she saw everyone in the house panicking. Eenie and Miney pulled their guns and faced the door as the witches screamed.

Someone was coming to help.

At last.

Chapter Twenty-Eight

FATHER SOLTERA AWOKE BACK in the real world much as he had awoken in The Hanging Forest. Eyes open, suddenly. One place one instant, and another place the next. But no hesitation was in him at all. Not even a little bit. He sat up instantly.

I'm running out of time. I've got to get to her!

He struggled out of bed, pulling the IV needles from his arm. He had to get to Gabriella. Had to touch her and bridge the gap. Just one touch and he could free her to come back to the world and finish her life. She still had so much of a life to live. Not like him. His days were done now. He looked around for Michiko, but she was nowhere to be seen. As wounded as she was, he imagined that she had gone off to wherever angels go to heal.

A stout Filipino nurse rushed into his room in a panic. "Sir! What are you doing? Stop!"

"I've got to get out of here!" he insisted with a gravelly voice.

"Stop it! Lie back down," she said, trying to guide him back to his bed. "You're in no condition to be sitting up and walking. You'll open all your wounds!"

He pushed her away, desperately and a little too hard,

almost knocking her over. "I'm sorry. You don't understand. There's something I must do. Someone I have to get to."

"Catalina! In here!" she cried out. Footsteps were coming from down the hall, causing him to panic as he made his way to the closet, feeling weak and off balance.

A janitor and another nurse, this one Latina, rushed into the room.

The first nurse stepped forwards. "Sir. My name is Ana. Please, get back in bed."

"Ana? Good. That's a pretty name. Now, Ana. Please tell me. Can you force me to stay here?"

Ana ignored him and instead looked worriedly at the other nurse. "Catalina, help me get him back in bed."

The janitor was a tall black man in a gray shirt. His name badge said "Rudy." Even though he was close to Father Soltera's age, Rudy looked easily strong enough to wrestle him back to bed. For a moment, a brief and painful moment, Father Soltera felt helpless.

Then, like three lights from a distant shore, he saw them: Ana wore a gold crucifix around her neck; Catalina's was silver and on a beaded chain; Rudy wore an empty cross, made of marble, on a leather cord knotted at the side.

Even here, even now, his savior was with him. All around him, in fact.

It was time, truly time, for his walk to Calvary.

"You are all believers," Father Soltera said, as he calmly walked to the closet.

"Father," Ana said, almost pleading with him now.

"No. Listen. I have to do something, to save a soul and maybe even help save my own. Do you hear me? Do you understand!"

The three of them stood there, stunned, speechless, before him.

"There's someone I absolutely must see. Now. As quickly as I can get to her. Someone I was trying to help before all this all happened," he added, waving his hand over his sick and sore body.

"Yes, but—" Catalina tried to protest.

He looked at her with earnest sincerity. "Child. This is God's work. Do *not* get in the way."

Once at the closet, he opened it, expecting a hospital bag of his clothes, like the few other times he'd been in this place. After his surgery. During a particularly brutal reaction midway through his chemo treatments. Instead, there was only a small bag, on a hook and . . . he saw a navy blue suit, hanging over a pair of polished black shoes. Then it dawned on him. Of course they wouldn't have the clothes or shoes he was wearing the night Felix had attacked him. Those were no doubt a bloody mess.

"How did this get here?" he asked.

"The woman from your church, Carol, your secretary. She brought everything."

"But . . . why did . . ." he began to question, because he was obviously a long way from being discharged by their looks, before it dawned him. "These were for my funeral, weren't they?"

There was an awkward silence before Ana spoke up. "Father, you've been in critical condition for a while. Completely unconscious. What's happening right now with you? It's practically a miracle."

Then it was Rudy's turn. "Sir. Please. You're in no condition to be trying to help anyone. If you give us her name, maybe we can have someone bring her here and—"

"No!" Father Soltera said firmly. Grabbing his suit, he made his way to the bathroom, where he dressed in pain, sure that the stitches in his ribs would split wide open when he tried to put on his pants. As he buttoned his shirt, he looked at his body; it was cut and torn, stitched and bandaged in so many places that he looked like Frankenstein. Blood trickled from a few wounds, but it didn't matter. He put his white dress shirt on, then his jacket. Tossing the tie to the ground, he opted to slip his shoes on without his socks. Bending over that far would be too painful.

As he made his way back out of the room, they were all still waiting for him. His shoes were untied, the laces threatening to catch, but he didn't care. Instead, he made his way back to the closet, where he found the small bag he had seen earlier. In it was his wallet, keys and cell phone. He grabbed them and turned to the door.

"Wait!" Catalina said.

He turned towards her, about to lose it, to tell her to just leave him alone, when incredibly Catalina bent down on one knee in front of him and tied his shoes.

"There's discharge paperwork he needs to—" Ana managed weakly. But her face was a sea of concern.

"Never mind all that," Rudy said, a sort of calm resignation now in his voice. "You go on and get, Father. Go do what you have to do."

Nearly overcome with relief, he managed to nod at each of them. As he reached the doorway he stopped, turned to them, and in a choked voice he said, "May God bless you all."

Then he limped down the hall, got onto the elevator and pushed "L" for Lobby, his body feeling a bit chilly and his vision momentarily blurry.

Once in the lobby, he pulled out his phone. It looked dead and he prayed that was not the case, that maybe someone had just turned it off for him. When the phone came on with a few bars of charge left, he sighed with relief. There was only one app he needed. Pushing the Uber button, he smiled, thinking of how Luisa had teased him for not knowing how to use the app, ages and ages ago, back when this whole thing had started.

The Uber driver was five minutes away, which wasn't normally a long wait, unless you were as big a mess as he was. Father Soltera leaned attentively against a pole just inside the doorway of the main entrance, not wanting to stand outside in the night air, but not wanting to miss his Uber, either.

He was on the lookout for a driver named "Moshe" who was driving a black Lexus. When it finally pulled up, Father Soltera went out quickly, inhaling the blissfully fresh rain air through his nostrils as scattered raindrops tickled at his scalp. It was good to finally be on his way, but he already felt overwhelmingly exhausted. He was telling himself to push on, that it'd be fine, when he fell to one knee, his hand outstretched to the cold, wet cement, trying to prevent himself from totally teetering over. Two strong hands helped him to stand, and when he looked up, he saw that it was Moshe, a comforting smile on his face that looked similar to the photo on his Uber profile. "Let me help you up," he said calmly.

Father Soltera was in no position to argue, so he grabbed onto Moshe's forearm as, together, they got him back to a standing position. "I'm fine, I'm fine," Father Soltera said, energized by embarrassment. "Thank you. I feel better now." Then he made his way to the Lexus and got in the back seat.

Getting into the driver's seat, Moshe said, "Okay, sir. Where to?"

"Haven Home," Father Soltera answered. Then he gave Moshe the address and watched as the GPS on his cell phone, which was mounted to the dash, came alive. The display said that the drive would only take eleven minutes. Father Soltera sighed. It could've been worse, much worse, on a rainy night in Los Angeles. Still, eleven minutes felt like eleven years.

They drove through traffic in silence until they arrived and briefly exchanged goodbyes, Moshe offering to help again and Father Soltera politely refusing.

But as the Lexus pulled away, he instantly regretted turning Moshe down. Father Soltera realized that between his confusion and his fever, he'd asked to be dropped off too far away from the building. His legs were giving way and his side was bleeding, the blood like syrup, gathering on his hip and spreading to the small of his back.

He had to make it. Silly, silly, stupid, dumb old man. He had to make it. He would.

He took three steps and felt the world tilting on him before he regained his balance. He made it another ten paces up the sidewalk, then fell sideways, catching the top of a newspaper stand to steady himself, oh so briefly, before he careened over to a lamppost and held on for dear life. By sheer will alone he made it up the sidewalk, through the entrance and to the elevator. Leaning his head and body against the call button, he took long, deep breaths, his lungs wheezing in his chest and his heart pounding away.

When the elevator doors opened, he half fell into it, thankful that there was no one else around. The world swam in his head as the elevator ascended to her floor. When the doors opened with a ding, he took two steps out. Feeling his dizziness overwhelming him completely, he managed to make his way to a large cafeteria cart just up ahead before he began to cry. He wasn't going to make it. Not even close. How? How could this happen? No.

"No!" he murmured, looking up to the ceiling. "Do not do this to me, Lord. Please!" Stifling his cries in his sleeve, he added, "Please don't do this to me, I beg of you."

He felt a deep chill cover his entire body, from the core of his chest to the pores of his skin, forcing him to shiver violently.

He was dying. In utter desperation to reach Gabriella, he let go of the cart and thrust himself onward, barely managing a single step before he fell sideways and slammed against the nearby wall, his fever-burned forehead smearing softly on the cool, high-gloss paint.

Body going cold. Head on fire.

Heartbroken.

IT WAS Flacco's turn to look betrayed as he traced the look

from Hector to Curtis, saw the shiv in Curtis' hand, and easily put two and two together. Still looking determined, Curtis began to advance on him. The other inmates, sensing a fight was coming, broke ranks to let Curtis through, but Flacco retreated as he took off his sweatshirt and wrapped it around one of his hands, evidently to use as a shield against the shiv. In the process, he backed up towards Hector, who now had enough time to get between the two of them.

Again, Hector shouted, "Curtis!"

"What, man!" Curtis said, his voice full of frustration. "What the hell is wrong with you!"

"Just . . . stop!"

"Why? Who you with, lil homie? Who turned you against me?" he asked, his eyes moving back and forth between Hector and Flacco. "You two set me up?"

"I dunno what the hell you talkin' about, Holmes," Flacco said, his voice as deep as a baritone.

The two guards that had chased Hector down the stairs almost got a hold of him, but he spun away, leaving them both in the middle of the loose triangle he, Flacco and Curtis had formed.

"Now let's take it easy, fellas," the guard with the crew cut said.

"Yeah. Just chill," the other one added, as his blue eyes looked past them and towards the cafeteria doors for backup. A third guard was there, his nod a non-verbal cue that help was on the way, but he held his position.

A voice came blaring over the intercom systems. "Ground! Ground! Ground! Inmates to the ground. Now."

Just then, one of the side doors flew open and in charged a dozen guards in riot gear, beating their batons against their tactical shields. Two of them had tear-gas guns and the threat of it seemed to do the trick. Many of the other inmates began dropping to their knees and then facedown on the floor.

"You punk-ass traitor!" Curtis yelled. He tried to charge

Hector. The two guards in the middle of them all intercepted him, one of them striking Curtis' forearm with a baton and knocking the shiv out of his hand. The shiv skittered across the floor, but Curtis wasn't through. With a scream of rage, he tried to bull through the guards, his hands reaching out in a death clutch, as if he were trying to get to Hector and choke him.

When he was fully subdued, Hector, sensing he was next as two other guards came his way, did the unthinkable; he ran to Curtis and tried to embrace him, over the arms of the guards holding him in place.

A wave of commands and shouts to separate erupted from guards all around.

"What are you doing?" Curtis spat.

"Listen to me—"

"No, homie. I ain't listening to nothin'! You gonna get me killed now for blowing this!"

"I'm sorry," Hector said. "I had to, man."

A sea of hands grabbed and clutched at them. Hector fought them off.

His neck the only thing that he could move now, Curtis bared his teeth with contempt. "You had to? What do you mean you *had* to?"

Hector saw his opening and took it. It was short and it was brief, but he lunged between a few of the guards and hugged Curtis over his shoulders. The tussle forced him close enough to say the answer in Curtis' ear. "To save your soul, man. I had to save your soul."

As he was finally ripped off and struck by countless batons, Hector saw the look of shock and confusion on Curtis' face as he was pulled away.

A baton struck Hector in the jaw, almost knocking him senseless, but he struggled no more.

He'd done it. He could feel it. He'd somehow accomplished the mission The Gray Man had told him was his . . . and it felt good. His friend might never forgive him, but now Curtis would have a chance to . . .

A buzzing came through the air in a low pitch that quickly climbed higher, filling his ears so sharply that he feared it would pierce his brain. He recoiled as he clutched at his ears, trying to plug them with the balls of his fists. The buzzing grew louder and louder, like the reverb from a broken amp, until Hector felt like even his eyeballs were vibrating beneath the onslaught.

At first, he thought that it was the baton strikes. Too many, all at once, about his head and face . . . until he realized that the blows had stopped completely. He'd closed his eyes against the reverb but his ears were telling him that all around, something was going terribly wrong.

The screaming came in a growing chorus from the rest of the cell block, at first a few stunned yips, then cascading shouts of pain sprinkled with curse words that eventually became full-throated screams of agony. The chorus built and before long it was joined by an orchestra of other sounds: tear-gas guns going off, plastic trays clattering to the ground, light bulbs exploding, doors slamming, shouts for backup and another alarm was tripped.

"Order! Order!" the voice on the intercom commanded, until, terrifyingly, that person began to scream in agony over the microphone, too.

The cell doors were next, opening and slamming closed, over and over again, like percussion instruments keeping time to a song of utter madness.

Somehow managing to stand, Hector summoned the blue without even realizing it. Cool liquid rushed to his eyes and filled his eardrums. Finally, able to see and hear, what Hector took in all around him was almost beyond imagining. Some inmates and guards were rolling on the ground, writhing in pain as they clutched at their heads. Others had managed to stand, somehow, and were running in circles, like wild animals, incapable of reason. Pockets of violence had broken out, with the heartier guards and prisoners locked in battle, throwing punches and pulling hair. One guard screeched as a prisoner he was wrestling bit his ear off and spat it, like a shriveled prune, across the floor.

Out the corner of his eye, Hector saw the flickering image of snow and static, and his heart leaped at the hope that it was The Gray Man, come to help.

Instead, it was just the three TVs in the rec room down the hall, their volumes on full blast with nothing but noise.

Some of the men at the farthest end of the cell block, where the tear gas was spreading, had evidently reached their limit. Unable to cope with the pain of the buzzing and the agony of the tear gas, they each took turns, four of them, running straight into the wall at full speed, knocking themselves unconscious in the process.

The blue filled Hector's entire body now, leaving him immune to the buzzing. But it was obvious that it was only growing worse; the barred windows near the top of the cell block shattered, as did the tiny windows in each cell, the *pop, pop, pop* not unlike massive pieces of bubble wrap being squeezed by invisible fingers.

Which weren't invisible for very long.

When he saw her, he told himself he should've known this was coming. The Smiling Midget had told him that "she" would come if Hector didn't do his bidding, but the little rat bastard was always so full of lies that you never knew when he was telling the truth.

It was The Black-Veiled Nurse, levitating twelve feet off the ground, near the guards' station to the right, her arms spread wide, her fingers tensed tightly. She looked down at him and smiled. "Why, hello there, Hector! Isn't this quite the soirée ? I mean, isn't all this pain the sweetest thing?"

She floated down towards him as the blue in him surged so much it was almost painful. She was a threat. A huge threat that he wasn't prepared enough to fight.

She touched down to the floor and, while looking over at a guard that was babbling incoherently, she continued, "But do you want to know what's even better? Madness. Madness is the most delectable agony of all. I mean, look at them." She giggled gleefully as she stared out at the battlefield of her own making. "They're going to tear each other limb from limb, you know. Limb. From. Limb! That is, if *you* don't do your job, Hector."

She steered his eyes with a glance over to a nearby lunch bench that had been tilted upright. Pinned to it, seemingly unaffected by the buzzing, was Curtis, his eyes full of shock and disbelief.

Someone down the hall was calling for his mother. Just like in the hood. As soon as someone got shot, or right when they realized they were going to bleed out and die, they always called for their moms. Why?

"Because one of the greatest lies ever is that mommas make the pain go away," The Black-Veiled Nurse replied, evidently reading his thoughts. "Did you know that Hymie called out for his precious mama, too, Hector? Cried out for his mama like he needed his diaper changed."

"And he did!" a random inmate lying nearby said, as if under her control. "Because he shat himself, homie. Right there on that sidewalk, as he was dying."

"Where *you* sent him to die!" another inmate-turned-puppet said with a chortle.

"And what of your mother, Hector? Did she ever make the pain go away?" The Black-Veiled Nurse asked, before pursing her lips with mock sadness. "My poor, poor little baby!"

Feeling completely outmatched, Hector called for The Gray Man. But . . . nothing.

"Well," The Black-Veiled Nurse said, "that didn't take long. I thought you'd at least put up a bit of a fight before you called on your stupid little angel."

"Hector?" Curtis screamed with fear as he struggled against

the invisible force that was holding him firm against the table. "What's goin' on? What's happening?"

Feeling the blue in him building, Hector's mind was scrambling for what to do next. He hadn't really used it that often, and as such, he had no idea how it could be utilized in the current situation.

The Black-Veiled Nurse looked over at Curtis. "Oh, honey. This? This is the moment right before Hector here does what he was supposed to do."

She whipped up her hand and tossed Hector, like a rag doll, into one of the nearby vending machines with a loud crash.

Then, taking two, small steps forwards, she added with a smile, "This is when he kills you, Curtis."

Chapter Twenty-Nine

PARKER WAS HALFWAY to the house when he realized that Jim's intel wasn't very good. Actually, it was shit. Having heard the scream of the sentry at the front door, men seemingly came out of everywhere. The one from inside the house he expected —there were supposedly three in there—but the one that came piling out of the passenger seat of the Escalade, a huge man, not so much. Even worse were the other four who came from—

The damned barn. I shoulda know when it was unguarded. And the doors were partially open. Probably the other shift, trying to get some sleep.

The gunfire started immediately, tufts of grass and dirt exploding all around them. Parker was just about to take cover behind one of the delivery trucks when he heard a sound that shocked him. People. No. Women. It was a chorus of female voices. Screaming. Screaming from inside one of the trucks.

"You hear that?" he shouted to Melon.

Busy returning fire, Melon shouted. "Yeah!"

"Cover me!" Parker yelled. His best bet was the Range Rover, which he barely reached in time. The back window exploded from a round and a sea of *chink, chink, chink* lit into the air as the car was strafed on the other side. Lying on the ground, he assessed their situation. Big Boy was between the Escalade and the house, firing from behind a bunch of wooden crates. The four guys from the barn had fanned out. All were armed. Two had taken up positions behind the Escalade and the other two had split off, hard charging to the east to outflank Melon. Parker looked for his next move, but there wasn't one. He was pinned down, tight, and that's when he noticed Melon loading the grenade launcher.

Their eyes met but Parker didn't even hesitate. He nodded firmly.

Melon blew the Escalade into pieces, sending Big Boy flying across the front porch and out the other side. The two goons next to the Escalade had seen it coming and escaped most of the explosion just in time. Just then, another goon came rolling out from inside the house, a Glock pistol in hand. He shouted to Big Boy and the goons who'd escaped the Escalade explosion and they all began advancing on Parker's position with confidence.

Too much confidence.

Parker whipped his head to the right to see that Melon was pinned down by the two goons who'd been trying to outflank him. Bullets were exploding everywhere around him. Parker turned to give Melon cover, knowing this would jeopardize his own safety and not caring one bit. Melon needed no coaxing. Seeing his opening, he jumped to his feet and ran full tilt to the Escalade to join Parker.

"I'm not sure that was your best move, buddy," Parker said with a grimace.

"Only move I was going to make," Melon replied.

"That truck is full of women, I think."

"I know. And it sounds like a lot of them."

"They locked in?"

"Yeah. Those doors are latched tight."

"Dammit!"

"You said this guy traffics them, right?"

"Yeah. But why here? What's there to traffic here?"

"I dunno, man, but we gotta do something to save our own asses before we can save theirs."

Parker nodded and made his decision. It was a reckless one, but the only one left. *I've gotta make a run for it. And soon!* But this time he wasn't speaking to Melon. Instead, he was speaking to Napoleon, who he sensed was nearby somewhere.

He moved effortlessly, his mind off, his body on autopilot. The way he'd been trained. The way he'd spent hours practicing.

The men before him were the enemy. He came at them with his M-4, laying down a line of suppression fire at their feet. Then, when he was close enough and his clip was emptied, he came at them with his hands. Under normal circumstances, this would've been suicide. But these were not normal circumstances.

Big Boy was to his left, and as the biggest and strongest of the bunch, he had to be neutralized first. The man was just advancing on the front of the Range Rover when Parker jumped up, knocked his gun sideways as he fired, and struck him with a vicious throat punch, his larynx collapsing under Parker's knuckles. He fell to the ground gasping in panic.

The goons nearest him now had him dead to rights. They took aim and fired . . . but their guns did not go off. They just clicked and clicked. Not like they were jammed, but like they were empty, and the look on their faces was so far beyond shocked, so far beyond this being even within the faintest realm of possibility, that it was almost comical.

With Parker advancing, and now having no other choice, they charged him, screaming with rage. Parker spun sideways and slid through a spot directly between them. As he did so, he brought his left elbow up, around and down on the back of the neck of one goon, sending him to the ground unconscious. The other goon tried to turn around, but Melon shot him twice in the side. He went down in a heap.

"This is taking too much time," Parker shouted to Melon.

"Affirmative."

They both knew that in any hostage situation, it was crucial to get to the rescue stage of the operation as quickly as possible. But this was not happening, and with a guy like Güero, each second that passed was another second closer to him putting a bullet in the head of the girl, or Kincaid, or both.

Just then, a barrage of bullets came Melon's way, pinning him down against the rear wheel of the Escalade.

Another delay.

———

MAGGIE WATCHED in wonder as the sad-eyed man stepped forwards and, using his hands like a conductor, began to move things telekinetically about the room. First, two chairs were sent crashing into Meenie, the first to his chest and the second right to the back of his head as he tried to flee the house. He went smashing into the wall and then down to the floor, unconscious.

Meanwhile, all around her, the crucifixes began to glow white, yellow and gold, as if each one was tearing a seam not only in the house, but in the universe.

Was she dreaming again? Had she fainted? Was this all just another vision in her mind?

No. No. And no.

"My God," she said under her breath.

The ground began to shake as Eenie ducked a wave of candles from the small altar in the living room, their flames aglow, their hot wax exploding upon hitting a crossbeam and the far wall. Maggie looked at his face for proof. Proof that he was seeing this, too. That she hadn't lost her mind. His face was a mask of awe and panic as he dove behind the altar.

Luisa was still bound to the altar by her wrists and ankles. Anastasia was coming at her with one of the daggers, perhaps to kill now what could not be brought forth. It didn't matter. A dome of pure, white energy covered her instantly. Anastasia, undeterred, was trying to stab through the dome when the sad-eyed man clenched his right hand, clutching her with the same invisible power, and threw her up and through the ceiling.

Miney had just run into the house and saw her body exploding through the wood. "*Dios mio!*" he screamed, falling sideways. On his hands and knees, he crawled back outside.

In the middle of it all, Delva seemed thoroughly unimpressed. She simply stared at the sad-eyed man as he moved in on Güero, who stood, with full machismo, his chest out, in the center of the living room.

As the sad-eyed man lifted his hands, a red and orange grid formed in front of Güero, who was now grinning widely. "Your God's got nothing on my girls," he taunted.

"Is that so?" the sad-eyed man replied. He glanced at Misha.

"Delva?" Misha cried out, the concern in her voice betraying the fact she did not have nearly the same amount of confidence as Güero.

"Hey!" Delva yelled, distracting the sad-eyed man. "Psst! Looky here!"

The ground was undulating and a whir from some other place was echoing across the air. Maggie looked to the cracks in the walls, but they were too bright to see through.

The sad-eyed man glanced her way and that was probably his first mistake since arriving. Because Delva's face flashed with a revelation. "Ah!" she said, with a grim smile. "Crows, is it?"

Immediately, a small black portal opened up over the man and . . .

No. This isn't happening. I am dreaming. It's a nightmare. Yeah. All I have to do is find the Latin here, to prove it. Someone. Please. Speak to me in Latin.

But no one did.

Instead, a flock of twenty or thirty crows came pouring through the portal and attacked the sad-eyed man. The same hands that had been wreaking havoc with his telekinesis were now rendered mute as he struggled to protect his face and neck.

His response to the attack was beyond panicked. As if Delva had looked inside him and seen one of his greatest fears and made it manifest itself, here in this little adobe house. The crows blotted out the light with a cacophony of squawks and cackles.

"Parker!" the man yelled suddenly.

Who is Parker? Maggie wondered, looking around and seeing no one else with him.

"Don't do it!" he yelled. "Don't! You won't make it!" But his shouts were muted, as if they were being warped by the beating wings of the crows.

Delva laughed. "He can't hear you. I've seen to that."

The man was glowing a brighter beige in the face of the attack, as the birds came on and on, in undulating waves, pecking him all over as he flailed at them, doing all he could to protect himself.

He pivoted and began to cast shattered pieces of furniture, candle holders, chair legs and bookshelves in all directions. It was no use. Finally, one of the crows bit him in the face, just below one of his eyes. Screaming, he stumbled backwards and nearly fell. Instead, he slammed into the wall and knocked one of the crucifixes loose.

It began to fall to the ground but the man caught it just in time with the invisible force. He brought it to him, and a globe of light erupted with such power around him that it was nearly blinding. In a wave of terrified squawks, the crows disintegrated in midair.

The room grew momentarily quiet as the battle turned.

But, incredibly, the sad-eyed man was still concerned about something else. "Parker! Stop!"

No, not something, Maggie thought. *Someone.*

He flung the crucifix back to its spot on the wall across the room, and running past Delva, the man violently knocked Güero sideways and then fled out the front door.

Delva looked at Güero. "We have time now," she said,

desperation in her voice. "Grab the girl and flee. Get to the house outside Tijuana. Misha, do you have the ointments?"

But Misha did not reply. Instead, she was pinned against the wall, gurgling blood.

With all the commotion, no one had noticed that a piece of the furniture the sad-eyed man had flung across the room, a shattered dining chair leg, had impaled Misha just below the heart.

Anguish came over Delva's shocked face. "Sister! No!"

"What do we do now?" Güero asked.

Delva did not answer for a moment. Instead, she crouched, like an animal, her wrinkled fists balled up in front of her as her eyes burned with anger. "Get the girl out of here and go where I told you. Wait for me there. I will join you . . . after I avenge my sisters."

Then, screaming with rage, she ran out the front door.

Chapter Thirty

FATHER SOLTERA SIGHED MOURNFULLY. Incredibly, impossibly, after everything, he was going to fail. So close. He was so close. Her room was just down the hall and to the left. As he slid down the wall, completely spent, it occurred to him that maybe this was the price for his sins. Perhaps this was the hand of God, pressing down on him with the weight of his transgressions, like Job seated in refrain, like David fleeing Absalom. And his despair was so deep that it threatened to obliterate him.

He went completely weightless, like how the moment of death is always described. When you become light as air and the world goes sideways, and suddenly you're up above, looking down on yourself, on the shell of what you used to be.

But no. That was not what was happening here at all.

What . . .?

It was Michiko.

She had picked him up in her arms and was carrying him the rest of the way. "My turn," she said, looking down on him with a tender smile.

"You're back," he said weakly.

"I would never leave you for long, *tomodachi*," she replied.

Tears began to form in his eyes and roll down his cheeks in a baptism of relief as his chest shuddered with sobs of relief. Slowly, quietly, they made their way. The hall was empty. No one was around. Not even the light seemed to move. When they passed by the check-in desk, he could see Jessica and Carlos, like he usually did. But now, they were frozen in place: Jessica on the phone, Carlos in the corner, the pages of the file he was flipping through caught in an unmoving blur. It was as if time and space had come to a halt.

"Am I dying?" he asked Michiko.

The question seemed to impact her. Michiko trembled with emotion as a look of stunned sorrow came over her face. Then, without answering him, she pressed on through the door of Gabriella's room.

He felt the somberness of the place again; the dim lights, the solitary bed. How many times had he been to this room, lonely and conflicted, desperate and so very afraid? Too many times to count. He hadn't meant to hurt anyone. All he ever wanted to do in this life was to help people. To guide them to God and a greater sense of purpose in their lives. To show them how feeding a homeless child on a cold day was more rewarding than any annual raise ever could be. Or how listening to someone on the suicide hotline, letting them talk as they eased their pain, would send *you* home with a better appreciation of the complexities of life. He wanted to show as many people as he could that, really, when you think about it? We're all priests. Each of us with our own confessional—the coffee shop, the office water cooler, the sidelines of a soccer game—where we can listen, witness and inspire.

Yes, he'd gotten sidetracked. But not by lust. At least not initially. No. The lust came after the shame of Joaquin Murietta and those he had murdered. That same shame had pried open the door to doubt. About his faith and about his place in that faith. Until the Holy Spirit was paralyzed enough within him for his defenses to drop . . . and for Gabriella to walk into church that day. Father Soltera could see it now, how lost he was by that point. And when you're lost? You seek. Sometimes in the wrong places. Or with the wrong person. Or in the wrong way. And when she had come into his life, he had looked at her . . . and simply been unable to look away.

He glanced over to her bedside; there was the quilt her mother had sown, right there at her feet. He was happy to be here and not be so confused and tortured for once. It felt good to come in this time with a pure heart, and a true purpose.

The machines beeped and forced air into Gabriella's lungs as her coma-ravaged body laid frail and waiting. He could somehow see her, far away, on that island, reaching out to him.

Reaching. Desperate to be free. Desperate to come home.

To her mother's loving arms, and gallons of *soupa de pollo*, and healing. Oh, so much healing. She'd be fine. He knew she would. If he could just finish his task.

"Closer . . ." he whispered. Michiko brought him nearer, one step at a time, until at last Gabriella was finally within reach.

Then, easily, hopefully, Father Soltera reached out, touched her hand and uttered one last prayer. It was good to just love somebody for what they were. *Father, please bless her. She is a good person.* Good to love them for what they could become. *Please help her reclaim her life.* Not for what they meant to you or could give to you. *Restore her health and help her chase her dreams.* No. But for what they could someday mean or give to others. *Help her be a light in this world.*

"She will be," Michiko whispered to him. "She will have a life, *tomodachi*, and she will always remember the priest who believed enough in her to sacrifice everything. She will. I promise."

He nodded weakly, with a faint smile, then stayed just long enough to see Gabriella's eyes open and look around. First, with confusion. Then, awe. Until, at last, she looked his way . . . and saw him, too.

They shared that one, last moment together.

Deep eyes of appreciation that looked both ways.

Slow blinks, to say goodbye, for voices too weak to speak.

The world turned and the universe tipped as the monitors blinked.

A hush fell over the room as an angel wept.

Father Bernardino Soltera closed his eyes and slipped into bliss.

———

THE BLACK-VEILED NURSE was staring at him. "Well?"

Hector gritted his teeth. "I won't do it."

She nodded like a patient professor. "So. For him, you will let all these men around you die a torturous death?"

Hector hesitated.

"I mean," she continued with a small wave of her hand, "look at them."

He didn't want to, but he did. To his right, one of the inmates was actually trying to strangle himself, his fingers having gone white at the knuckles for the effort, his face flushed with the blood being squeezed into it.

Hector looked to the ground.

"Still . . . no?" she asked.

He nodded.

"Really? Well then, I guess it's time that we finally meet face-to-face," she said with resignation in her voice. She levitated across the floor to him with blinding speed, grabbed his chin with one hand, and lifted her veil with the other.

Her face greeted him again. All four of her horrible eyes were staring at him intensely and the large gash that was her mouth was open wide, revealing rows of piranha-like teeth that glistened with saliva as she stuck her long, sharp tongue into the air and waved it at him. "Want a kiss?" she said.

He shook his head vigorously as the buzzing in the room spiked again, so high and loud that it pierced the blue shield in his ears. He tried to cup his hands over them but it was too late. Somehow, a piece of her had gotten inside his skull, like a sonic leech, attached to his brain and was now . . . sucking.

"Ahhhh!" Hector screamed, dropping to his knees.

"Gray?" he cried out. "Help me!"

"Aww, isn't that sweet? Still calling for help? We've barely even begun."

The room began to fade, the sound of screaming guards and prisoners, all in agony, coming from every direction. How long could he last, vulnerable like this, in such a place? Surely, not long at all. He looked over at Curtis, still pinned to the table. He was shouting to Hector, but Hector couldn't hear a word.

"He's saying you should do it, little pup," The Black-Veiled Nurse said as she stood over him. "So?"

From a corner in his mind, he heard The Gray Man. *Hold on, Hector. I have to help elsewhere right now. I'm coming as quickly as I can. But try to do this on your own. Once I intervene, the battle will only multiply, and she will call on even more evil.*

"What are you talking about? I can't do this. I'm not ready! She's way too strong."

Yes. You can. And remember, her strength is her weakness. She's far too arrogant, Hector. That will be your edge.

The Black-Veiled Nurse cocked her head to one side. "Curious," she said. "What was that? You kinda drifted away on me there, boy."

"N-nothing," Hector stammered.

"So? Are you ready to take care of Curtis?" she pressed.

Again, Hector shook his head. "No," he barely managed to get out. "I won't do it."

She nodded, but that horrible face tremored with a bit of frustration this time. "Fine," she said curtly.

His brain seemed to lurch against the inside of his skull as nausea overtook him. His mind became a pliable, porous thing. And the thoughts he had were not under his control anymore.

Yesssss, The Black-Veiled Nurse whispered into his mind.

Just give in, boy. Do the deed. You can't beat me. I mean, seriously? You? Someone who doesn't even know his own power, much less how to wield it.

"Get out of my head. Leave me alone!" he cried, trying to channel the blue from his hands to his head, knowing that there must be some way to do it but not having the slightest idea how. Why? Why had The Gray Man left him like this? Alone. Doomed.

Because you are a tool, like all the rest who are 'saved' by that side. A cog. A nut. A bolt. My side has been winning for millennia and will continue to do so. Do you wanna know why?

"No. No, I don't. Stop it. Please!" He was squeezing his head so hard now that he was sure it was going to pop.

Oh. I insist. Really. You should know, she murmured. *Because you all love sin. You really do. Even the so-called best of you at least love the* thought *of it. But. Do. You. Know . . . What you aaaall forget? Like, every damn time?*

He shook his head as he gasped for air.

She leaned close to him, clicked her piranha teeth rapidly and said with a laugh, *The* cost *of it.*

The room went red. He began to spin to another time. Another place. But . . . where? The past? No. The future? Not even close. He was in the present . . . but it was someone else's present.

Darkness, then harsh fluorescent light.

He heard the motorized sound of the wheelchair before he saw her, coming down the waxed-linoleum hall of a hospital somewhere, avoiding medical carts along a wall as a man in a white shirt and cotton pants cheered her on.

No.

"Marisol," Hector whispered. "Oh my God. It's Marisol."

And it was. Or what was left of her. After what he'd done to her.

The woman he once knew and loved was gaunt. She'd easily lost thirty pounds. There was a gouge in her throat from the bullet he'd shot through it, and both her head and her body leaned sideways in the chair, her legs so skinny that they seemed like poles, the knees collapsed together and her ankles twisted awkwardly. Only her hand, on the motorized steering bar, moved.

Paralyzed. She was paralyzed, apparently from the neck down. A paraplegic, with only limited use of one limb. Her left arm was lying limp against her side, her left hand curled up in the bird's nest of her lap.

"Noooo," Hector moaned, collapsing to his knees and doubling over. He told his eyes to close. The Black-Veiled Nurse told them to stay open.

Do you see your handiwork, boy? she said. *All because, what? Because she . . . loved . . . another man?* And the word "loved" came out warped and garbled, overlapped with curse words in foreign tongues that came out of the air from all around, as if she'd come into his mind with a motley crew of evil spirits.

The wheelchair buzzed down the hall as the man encouraged Marisol on, telling her how good she was doing, praising her for trying so hard. It was obvious now that he was some sort of physical therapist.

But when Hector saw her passionless, destitute eyes as she stared at the man like he was an idiot, as if she didn't care what he said, or how well she was or was not doing, as if she didn't care anymore, about anything . . . that was all it took.

He broke. Not in an emotional way or even so much a psychological way. No. In a spiritual way. His entire soul began to crater, from the center outward, like a porcelain shell that he had always known was there, just beneath his skin. He'd felt it resonate when he was lost in a meandering patch of prose or, yes, most certainly whenever Marisol touched him. When she would mindlessly run her fingers over his arm while they lay on the couch and watched a movie together, or when she would stand near him while he was lost in thought.

"Marisol?" he whispered with anguish. "What have I done?"

Incredibly, the wheelchair stopped in its tracks and Marisol's head tilted in his direction. He was on his knees close by, his body translucent, but she saw him. Her eyes widened with recognition . . . then horror . . . then rage.

Her physical therapist followed her gaze to where Hector was, but evidently seeing nothing, he instantly looked concerned. "Marisol?"

Hector had looked in those eyes and told Marisol that she was his bae. Then his love. Then the love of his life. He had told her that he would always protect her . . . that someday, always someday . . . he would marry her, and they would have babies together. Those eyes had looked right back at him with something like adoration once and said the same things. He could still remember how she would hold his hand, gently but firmly, whenever they were together, and how she would laugh sometimes, so hard at his jokes, that she'd snort. Most of all, most painfully of all, he could remember how he would kiss her on the forehead, and how she would lean into that kiss, every, single, time. But the way she was looking at him now was absent any love whatsoever.

Again, her physical therapist chimed in, this time quizzically. "Marisol, what's wrong? What do you see?"

Her answer was spoken electronically, through a voice box, and she struggled mightily just to get out two solitary words. But Hector's soul shattered completely beneath their weight.

"A monster," she said.

Chapter Thirty-One

PARKER SIGHED. It was now, or never. *Cover me!* he said to Napoleon, and then, for the first time in his life, he made a decision based on blind, irrational faith. Moving completely out of cover, he charged towards the house.

The guy with the Glock fired and two bullets whizzed past Parker's head, forcing shards of glass from the Range Rover to erupt in all directions. Parker dropped and rolled as a flurry of bullets chased him along the ground. But none, thankfully, found their target. That wasn't possible, either, and Parker knew it. The space between the car and the house, from point-blank range, was too big for all those bullets to miss. Rolling to one knee, he looked up and instantly saw the reason why.

The bullets that had been fired at him were netted in blue light, the force of their trajectory burning white-hot at the edges as their course was bent and turned off-target. The guy with the Glock now had the same stunned look on his fact that his friends had moments earlier.

Beyond him, Napoleon stood on the porch of the house, his hand outstretched, his fingers curled as he crumpled the blue net against the bullets and they fell to the ground. He turned as an old woman in a black robe shot out of the house and attacked him from behind. They struggled. A loud, crackling sound erupted through the air. A shockwave of heat rolled across the patio and out across the front of the house before Napoleon and the old woman disappeared through some sort of vortex that had opened across from the porch.

"What the hell was that!?" Melon shouted. With his body pinned against the Escalade and his head down, he hadn't seen anything but had obviously heard it.

I dunno, Parker thought, *but I hope that hell had nothing to do with it.*

Earlier, Parker had felt Napoleon's presence. Now, he felt his absence.

Parker was on his own again. The guy with the Glock lunged, tackled him in the chest and knocked him backwards. They grappled on the ground for a moment, each struggling for position. Parker took two vicious punches to his ribs and one to his chin. The world went hazy for a moment before he delivered a few shots of his own, both to his opponent's head. Incredibly, Parker found himself pinned to the ground, his opponent sitting on his chest, his hands wrapped around Parker's throat in a devastating choke hold.

Then the world became a series of freeze-frame events . . .

First, Melon, evidently out of ammo and separated from his backpack near the delivery truck, was yelling as he tried to get to Big Boy's gun. The two goons that had outflanked him were advancing on him relentlessly. It was only a matter of time before they killed him.

Then, defying all logic, the goons stopped in their tracks and quit firing at Melon.

Napoleon! Parker thought.

But no. It was Güero, in the doorway of the house. "Slaughter the girls! I want no evidence," he screamed. He swiftly ducked back into the house.

Parker was stunned. The goons slowly turned and took aim

at the delivery truck that held all the women. Parker's heart sank.

As the guns erupted into the air, Melon—tough, smart-assed Melon—screamed "No!" at the top of his lungs, the desperation in his voice confirming the hopelessness of anyone being able to stop what was about to take place.

He was wrong.

The Gray Angel came from the west and he came up from the sands. And when he came, the earth shook and the light from the sun seemed to bend beneath the weight of some unseen horizon. Parker didn't bother to tell himself that he was seeing things this time because, really, what was the point? He'd accepted Napoleon being back, hadn't he? Still, he found himself beyond stunned, past shocked, and somewhere in the neighborhood of incredulous by what The Gray Angel did next.

Countless bullets, tens if not hundreds, screamed their way through the air towards the truck full of screaming women, none of whom had any idea that death was coming. There was no way on earth anything could save them but for the simple fact that, for a brief moment in time, this place was anywhere *but* earth.

A cascade of iridescent slivers broke out at blinding speed across the air, intercepting the bullets at various points in their paths. It was so far beyond any level of comprehension that it almost numbed the mind. The slivers flashed black when struck, as if they were swallowing the bullets and teleporting them to some far-off corner of the universe. But it was the sound that got Parker the most; each sliver opened like tearing tinfoil before it crunched shut, absorbing the kinetic energy of each bullet and leaving behind a momentary blur of gray.

It was obvious that not everyone could see The Gray Angel. Parker could. And probably one of the goons, too, who'd gone hysterical and was now shouting *"Dios mio!"* over and over as he dropped to his knees. But no one else seemed to be dialed in.

The other goons, either standing or down with injuries, were baffled at what was happening, as was Melon.

What was happening was a miracle, on full display.

Whatever.

To Parker, it was an opening. At last.

Cars were barreling in from the distance, probably from a nearby safe house. Three Chevy Suburbans down one road, another Cadillac Escalade from the main highway. The Gray Angel waved his hand at the larger caravan, sending all three of the Suburbans airborne like so many toy Hot Wheels Parker had played with as a child.

But it appeared that the effort of this move, and of tele-porting away all the bullets, was taking a toll; The Gray Angel was beginning to fade away. There was something in the way he looked at Parker that said time was running out. For everyone.

Parker moved instantly to take out the guy with the Glock.

Using a classic Krav Maga move, he positioned his legs wisely to gain the as much leverage as possible, thrust his hips upward, then rolled to one side, flipping his opponent off him at a forty-five-degree angle. Then, with tenacity, Parker reversed their positions entirely. He wasted no time in putting an end to things. Instead of a classic, school-yard pin intended to punch someone repeatedly in the face, Parker kept his own head down tight to the ground and to the side of his opponent's right shoul-der, forcing him flat, pinning him hard. And in rapid succession Parker came up, shot an open hand into his opponent's trachea, sat up further and struck him hard in the stomach, before he pivoted back a few feet and punched him as hard as he could, directly in the groin. Incapacitated in so many ways, the guy with the Glock was done for.

Parker continued his advance.

The two goons who'd been shooting at the delivery truck had emptied their guns and were now retreating to the house. The Gray Angel tried to wave his hand at them, too, but his face looked pained and exhausted. He glanced at Parker one last time and then he was gone. But Parker knew that look all too well. It was the look that the fallen give to those who are left behind to finish the fight.

And Parker was going to finish this fight.

The goons made it through the doorway of the house and were just turning to slam the door behind them when Parker planted his boot directly in the middle of it, the wood cracking beneath the force as the door flew backwards and caught one of the goons in the face, shattering his nose. He screamed and tried to take a swing, but Parker grabbed his gun and twisted it upwards, cracking him in the chin and knocking him out cold.

"Look out!" a girl screamed from his left. Parker barely had a second to glimpse that way; he saw a blond girl tied to a wooden post. The Kincaid woman. It had to be. She was in an adjacent room where there was another girl, partially naked, tied to an altar. That had to be the minor. Crazy, sick bastards. If they had killed her? He was going to lose it, for sure.

The second goon was bearing down on him, but he was too slow and too close. Parker deflected the gun barrel away. A spray of bullets cut loose and exploded into the wall beside them. Pivoting, Parker shot his right fist out directly into the man's face, grabbed him by the collar and punched him three times in his right ear. He was out cold before Parker dropped him to the ground.

"Get him!" a man with a deep voice yelled. When Parker saw him, he didn't need the fine clothes and manicured look to tell him who he was. Parker had seen his file photo and knew his target completely. It was Güero-freaking-Martinez. In the flesh. And within reach.

Another man, bigger and more of a bodyguard-looking type, came at Parker from the right, lowering his handgun to fire in the process. Parker dropped to the ground and did a foot sweep to take him down. The bodyguard fell, getting one shot off into the ceiling before the back of his head hit the ground. Dazed, he tried to sit up. Parker gave him a solid elbow to the face. He rolled over and looked at Güero for the briefest of seconds before he jumped up and fled out the front door, Güero cursing at him the entire way.

Parker turned to face Güero, who had already raised his hands over his head in full surrender. "I'm not resisting," he said solemnly.

"So," Parker said. "You're the famous Güero Martinez, huh?"

Güero looked at him defiantly. "What's it to you?"

Parker shrugged. "Not much. I just wanted to meet, face-to-face, the pussy who sent his thugs to hurt my girl."

"You're girl?" Güero said disdainfully. "Who the hell are you?"

Parker gritted his teeth and replied. "I'm Detective Parker."

The name registered in Güero's eyes immediately. Slowly, his face began to melt with defeat. Then, quietly, over his head, Parker noticed that the fingers of Güero's hands came together and he slowly began turning the rings on them inward, towards his palms.

Parker smiled.

Good. A surrender would've been no fun at all.

———

MAGGIE KINCAID STOOD and watched in awe at the symphony of destruction that the army guy who had charged into the house was unleashing. His moves were smooth, confident and polished. She was happy he had arrived.

But it wasn't like she really needed him.

Luisa started to come around, forced awake by all the noise and chaos. As Güero and the army guy stood and faced each other, there was only one other guy left in the room: Eenie the Perv. Still hiding behind the altar like a little bitch, he was now coming around it, slowly, his hand shaking as he tried to free his gun, which was stuck in his jacket. He cursed, tugging and pulling on it. But that's not what mattered to Maggie. What mattered was that he was so focused on the army guy that he'd completely forgotten about her . . . and was now backing up towards her.

She stood tall and waited . . . waited . . . waited.

As he grew closer, she moved her hands up the wooden post as far as she could, pressed her forearms against the wood, and like a poor man's lumberjack, she spur-clawed a few feet up it. Then a few more. Without actual spurs, it wasn't easy. But adrenaline helped her dig her right foot into a natural indentation that she realized would give her some much-needed leverage. He was finally within reach. It was now or never.

She was on him like a crab. Leaping up with all her strength, she reached out with her legs and pulled Eenie in by his shoulders, swiftly and violently yanking him backwards into her and trapping his head between her thighs. He reached back to grab at her, but she pulled her head and face up and away from his hands. His weight had jammed her ribs against the post painfully, but Maggie couldn't have cared less. With one leg on either side of his head, she began to squeeze. Hard and then even harder. Hopelessly scissored between her thighs, he struggled to get away, but she pulled him back.

She was losing her grip. *C'mon, c'mon. Get him down and finish him.*

As if he'd heard her and was actually granting her request, Eenie dropped to his knees in a last-ditch effort to escape. In so doing, he'd given her all the leverage she needed to choke him out completely.

He desperately clawed at her legs, then reached up to punch her in the stomach. But punching backwards wasn't nearly as effective, and she barely felt it. Finally, he began to grab for his gun again, but it was too late for that.

She looked down over his forehead and into Eenie's panic-filled eyes. "Probably not how you fantasized it, is it?" she sneered.

Using her thighs to squeeze at his ears with all her might, his eyes bulged in their sockets as his face flushed red from all the pressure. He gasped, clawed weakly at her a few more times, and then finally, as he fell backwards, lifeless, she rode him down and landed on her feet.

Looking up, she saw that the army guy had his handgun trained on Güero, who had his arms raised in surrender.

But then, Maggie watched as Güero began turning the rings on his fingers in, just like he had that day before he'd viciously attacked Felix at the warehouse.

His surrender was a ruse.

———

PARKER LOWERED his gun and snapped it back into his holster, causing a look of surprise and then a smile to come across Güero's face.

"Maggie!" the girl on the altar cried out, forcing them both to look her way. "Maggie?"

"I'm here, Luisa," the blond woman replied, officially confirming that she was Kincaid.

Okay. I've got both my hostages in place. Just one last—

Güero screamed and charged him like a bull. Parker was only able to partially pivot out of the way and throw a glancing blow at his cheek before Güero wrapped his arms around Parker's waist, picked him up and violently slammed him backwards against the wall, forcing the air to rush out of his lungs and his ribs to groan in protest.

Immediately, Parker sensed something was very, very wrong. Not only the speed of Güero's attack but the force of it as well was beyond the ability of a man of his size.

Güero grunted, held Parker strong in his grip and began to smash him repeatedly against the wall, like a bull that had completely pinned the matador.

Reaching up, Parker boxed his ears. Nothing. He karate

chopped the back of Güero's neck with three successive strikes. Nothing. With each blow, Güero grunted louder and continued to squeeze the air out of Parker's lungs more tightly.

At one point, Parker was able to wrench Güero's neck so that he could see his face, and what he saw there completely terrified him. Güero's eyes were not human anymore, but rather large, glistening black orbs that filled his entire sockets.

Parker's heart sank. *Shit!*

It wasn't that he'd completely underestimated his opponent. No. That wouldn't be fair. How on heaven and earth was he ever to expect that his opponent would be . . . this.

The battle was swiftly going south, and the Kincaid woman seemed to sense it. "No!" she screamed. "Someone! Help!"

Güero sneered at him. "Still so sure of yourself, Detective?" And this only made things worse, because his voice had become garbled and thick. Parker tried to look away from the darkness in his eyes, because there was something about them . . . something that was calling to the dark void within himself, that had been coiled up for years in the corner of his soul.

Desperate, Parker went to his fail-safe move. With a vigor born of the simple will to survive, he grabbed Güero Martinez by the sides of his head and blessed him with a Glasgow kiss. Then another. And another. And another. Each headbutt crashing into more of Güero's face. First his nose, then the teeth in his mouth, then one of his cheekbones. Normally, Parker would look for his opponent's eyes to begin rolling back in his head, to register the process of losing consciousness. But this was not possible with a man with no pupils. Still, slowly, Güero began to blink, and each blink took longer and longer to complete.

Suddenly, his grip began to loosen, allowing Parker to pull air into his begging lungs. With that air, Parker unleashed a flurry of punches across Güero's face, head and neck, forcing him to relent. Finally Güero let go, stumbled backwards twenty feet and fell down.

Relief and joy came with a second chance. But some second chances only last exactly that long: a second.

Parker stared in dismay as Güero looked up, his face a bloody mess, and smiled. In his hand was one of Parker's stun grenades, which he'd somehow pulled from Parker's utility belt. Without even hesitating, he popped the pin, tossed it across the floor and . . .

"*No!*" Parker screamed.

The explosion that followed concussed the room in its entirety. A violent *woosh* of air sent Parker crashing into a table, which crumpled beneath him. He'd been here before, in the company of a stun grenade, countless times, but usually seconds after the explosion. It was non-lethal and used only to shock and disorient your opponent, so that you could overtake him. To this end, Güero had succeeded. Parker was down, his ears ringing and his vision blurry.

But at such close proximity, Güero had done the same thing to himself. On the ground and looking to be in a world of hurt, he instead seemed to draw again on whatever dark power was in him. Grimacing, he yelled, punched the floor and got to one knee.

Parker struggled to do the same, but he was having a much harder time fixing his bearings. Save for the ringing in a person's ears, the effects of the grenade were meant to be short-lived. He just needed a few minutes. Blinking, he rolled to one side, trying to get into a position to defend himself on the ground when Güero attacked. But he needn't have bothered.

Incredibly, evidently thinking that Parker was pretty much done for, Güero stood and began making his way towards little Luisa.

Kincaid was screaming her protests as Luisa's eyes grew huge in the face of her uncle, who was stumbling towards her with a face twisted in rage. Reaching the alter, he began to cut away the ropes that bound her to it. Luisa tried to fight him, but her struggles were weak. She seemed to be drugged or something. Sobbing, she cried out again as Güero ruthlessly pulled her off the altar and down to the ground. Then, he began to drag her by her hair.

Drag her away.

Parker blinked. Hard.

As Luisa kicked and cried and screamed for help.

Just like that day . . .

With . . .

Big sun. Massive desert. Small lives.

Waheeb.

Something in Parker's mind exploded.

No. Not again.

Not ever again.

As Güero dragged her in a confused fashion—first towards the back of the house before realizing there was no door there, then towards the front door—the cobwebs in Parker's head vaporized beneath the coursing vividness of his memories.

Luisa's hands were reaching, grasping, for the doorframe, for a crack in the wood floor, for anything to stop her progress . . .

Just like Waheeb's hands had grabbed at sand and stone and rocks that day.

"Someone help me!" Luisa screamed.

Helpless. Hopeless.

Like Waheeb had screamed. "Mr. Parker! Mr. Parker, please help!"

But this time Parker wasn't pinned down behind a boulder by heavy enemy fire.

This time he wasn't helpless in the face of yet another meaningless death . . .

"Let me go!" Luisa yelled through her tears as Güero pushed on.

. . . or at the mercy of people who lived for death.

No.

Not this time.

Parker got to one knee, stood with the surge of a massive

adrenaline rush and advanced towards the wall adjacent to the front door. Getting a running start, he launched himself up against it with one leg, pushed off as hard as he could, then spun in midair towards Güero and delivered a crushing punch directly to his left temple.

It was a punch that carried the weight of years of pain, anguish, horror and guilt.

A punch for Waheeb.

A punch that could even stop a bull.

Releasing his grip on Luisa, Güero's face went slack and he crumpled to the ground.

Melon came crashing through the door with a gun in each hand, his right arm bleeding and his face drenched in sweat.

"All clear?" Parker said.

"They're all down outside," Melon replied. "Here?"

Parker looked down at Güero and nodded. "All clear."

———

MAGGIE WAS FLOODED with relief as she watched the army guy spin Güero over and frisk him. Then he zip-tied Güero's hands behind him.

The other guy who had rushed in had a grin on his face. "We got his ass?" he asked.

"Yep," the army guy said.

Calmly, with a weary smile on his face, the army guy walked over, looked down at Eenie and then to Maggie. He was wearing desert camouflage pants and a beige shirt with camouflage sleeves. His face was rugged, with a chiseled jaw partially hidden behind about three days of stubble and his blue eyes were piercing. His hair was cut tight to his head and there was a small mole on his right ear lobe. He was easily taller than her, about six foot two, with broad shoulders that stretched his shirt tightly across his chest. To many women he would've been a hunk of a man, but to Maggie he was just someone in the way of her getting to Luisa.

"What the hell are you looking at? Cut me loose!" she said.

Looking stunned, he pulled a large knife from a sheath tied to his thigh. It glimmered in the light. "Pull your hands out of the way," he ordered.

She complied, feeling the blade as he worked it between the ropes. It took a few passes, but the ropes finally gave way and her wrists screamed with relief at being unbound at last.

Standing slowly, she looked around. Her bag was gone, of course, and with it her Eskrima sticks. Even with these army guys here, she wasn't going to be left vulnerable anymore. Not for one single minute. She jumped up and grabbed a mural from the wall, shook the fabric loose and snapped the wooden stick evenly over her knee. Then she ran over to Luisa and helped her up off the floor.

"Maggie?" Luisa said. "What's happened?"

"Shhh," Maggie said, hugging her tightly. "You're safe now."

"You're both safe now," the handsome army guy said.

She looked to him. "What's your name again?"

"Parker," he said flatly. Motioning his thumb over his shoulder, he said, "That's Melon."

"You guys alone?"

"Yep," Parker replied.

Incredulously, Maggie asked, "No one else?"

"Nope."

Great. Already Johnny Smolder and now he was going to be a man of few words, too? Maggie rolled her eyes. "Do you wanna tell me what's next?"

He squinted at her and her broken stick with a mild look of surprise and a smirk. "I'm guessing that you're Maggie Kincaid?"

She was surprised. "Yeah. How'd you know that?"

"Your Facebook post."

It worked. She smiled. "Is the military in on this?""

"Nope."

She looked him up and down. "Well. You look military."

"Private contractor, Ms. Kincaid."

"But—"

He looked at her intently. "Let's just leave it at that for now, okay?"

She wanted to argue, but her relief finally overcame her. "Sure," she said. "And thank you. For coming to help us, I mean."

Parker shrugged and looked around again. "Don't thank me yet. We still gotta get out of this shit hole."

Maggie nodded. "And the sooner the better."

Chapter Thirty-Two

PAIN WAS a promise of nothing if not more of the same. Trapped in the two words that Marisol had just said to him like an animal in a cage, Hector realized that he'd done a foolish thing challenging The Black-Veiled Nurse. She was far too powerful and far too . . . vicious. Even this agony? She was just toying with him. Like a cat with a ball of yarn.

He stumbled backwards, seeking a corner of his mind where he could escape everything, but it was his mind that would not leave him alone. There was Hymie again, shaking his hand and laughing, just two homies on the streets, chasing skirts and tricking out their rides. Hymie's smile, so bright, that same mouth squeezed tight, not that many years later, in the morgue.

Then there was the little gangster from four streets over that Hector had ordered to be killed, and the one girl outside Grand Central Nightclub, who'd given herself to him more out of fear than anything else. That was a "yes," for sure. He hadn't raped her. But was a "yes" when you can still see a "no" in someone's eyes, still a "yes"? Eyes couldn't speak, could they?

Yeah. They could.

David Fonseca's eyes had spoken, too. Standing there in that supply room of The Mayan, backed up against those palettes of potatoes, that frying pan over his head in a pathetic, last-ditch effort to defend himself. His eyes had said plenty. They'd said "no," too. No to losing whatever dreams he still had for his life. No to all the goodbyes he wasn't getting a chance to say to the people he loved. No to dying so young. Hector had shot him in the head anyway.

The blue inside him began to glow like a bulb, swinging back and forth in the distance. He had this power, so much power, with absolutely no idea how to use it.

Stop. Grab a hold of something. Grab a hold, he told himself. But . . . nothing.

More images of violence: stabbings, shootings, bodies, spot-lights from police helicopters circling, circling. Sirens. A life lived against a backdrop of red and blue flashing lights. All those tragic ends, like in the stories he read. Except he was the one who had written these ones, wasn't he? He was the author of the horrors in his little corner of the world. For a time, at least. There were those before him who'd had the job, and now Burro was out there doing it. Each of them simply scribblers of doom.

The blue kept swaying, calling, beckoning to him. But he'd backed himself into this corner of fear, as far away from The Black-Veiled Nurse as he could get, as she squirmed around there in his mind . . . seeking him.

Suddenly, it occurred to Hector how to get to the blue. How to get out of here.

He had to let go, one stubborn finger at a time, of the past. But how? He'd just been thinking of stories and authors, hadn't he? Yes. Jamming himself into the fetal position, still clutching at his ears and with his eyes squeezed shut, Hector wondered why his mind had turned to such thoughts. Then he remembered The Gray Man. What had he said back at Twin Towers? He'd said that to Hector, prose was his version of . . .

Prayers.

As if sensing his realization, The Black-Veiled Nurse began to scramble through his head faster, like a maggot hungrily feeding on a piece of meat. If she found him this time, he would be lost forever. He was running out of time. He needed to find the right words . . .

And the words came, clear as day, causing the blue light to glow bright. Brighter. Then brightest.

It was Hemingway. From *The Garden of Eden*. "When you start to live outside yourself, it's all dangerous."

It was time, at last, to live outside himself. To be dangerous enough to change.

The sweet bliss of abandoned truths, written large in a heart that never wanted to be so dark, sprang up inside Hector Villarosa. Words broke the bars of the cage. Words became the yarn that entangled the cat that was after him. And as the blue exploded, he was back on the floor of his cell block, with The Black-Veiled Nurse screaming with rage. "You pathetic little pig!"

He scrambled to get away from her on his hands and knees as she pulled out a long black whip with sharp barbs and began to snap it at him. It missed twice, then caught him on the left calf. His entire leg screamed with agony as he fell forwards onto his face.

"Stop!" he begged.

"What? Stop?" she mocked him. "No. I don't think so. I think you're the dumbest human I've ever encountered. All the others broke way earlier than this. But you? You think you're something special, don't you? Fine. I think we should go spend a little time with Hymie now."

"No!" Hector screamed.

"Yes. It's hot there, but he'll love a visit from his precious cousin."

Hector shook his head vigorously, stood weakly and called on the blue.

Evidently sensing its powers, she lowered her chin and stared at him. Tossing the whip aside, and with a cunning look, she flicked out her hand, like a magician using sleight of hand to reveal a playing card. Except in her hand was a straight razor, gleaming under the overhead lights. Panicked, Hector looked to Curtis. He was only a few feet away from her, still pinned helplessly to the table.

Hector glanced at her nervously, then back to Curtis. An idea came to him. Holding up his left hand, he signaled for her to wait. He took a few deep breaths and tried to shut out the agony in his leg. Whatever was in that whip had left behind something in the wound that was searing his flesh.

"No, no, no. You got the wrong idea. Please. Don't hurt me anymore," he said to her. "I'm done. I'll do it." He looked over at his friend sadly. "I'm sorry, Curtis. No father. Barely a mother. No brothers or sisters. All I ever had was you, bro. But she's doing shit to my head, man. I can't take it anymore. I . . . can't take it no more."

The Black-Veiled Nurse smiled.

"Hector. What are you talking about?" Curtis said nervously, concern in his face.

Shaking his head and looking to the ground, Hector willed the blue into his right hand and spun it in his palm like a pitcher with a baseball.

If The Gray Man had only taught him better, if they'd only had more time to train, it might not have come to this.

Curtis looked at the orb in Hector's hand with disbelief, then evidently seeing something in Hector's eyes that he didn't like, he began to thrash around in panic. "Hector! What are you doing?"

"Quit wasting time!" The Black-Veiled Nurse said, lowering the blade.

Hector nodded, wound up his arm and threw the orb as hard as he could directly at Curtis' head. Seeing what was coming, Curtis screamed.

When the orb struck him, his head would be vaporized, plain and simple. It would be a painless, instantaneous death . . . *if* the orb struck him.

But The Gray Man had said that this whole thing wasn't that complicated, really.

You simply had to know your right . . .

. . . from your left.

To remember that sometimes a weakness could be a strength.

Just like in his cell, dozens of times before, just before reaching its intended target . . . the orb veered sharply to the left.

It was the worst throw of his life and the best throw of his life.

Frustration and stunned disbelief twisted the face of The Black-Veiled Nurse as the orb curved directly towards her chest, casting a blue glint off the straight razor as it went by, before exploding a hole in her large enough to see through.

All four of her eyes blinked erratically as her piranha-like teeth chattered against a gasp of pain. Her mouth opened, and orange blood began to dribble from her nose slits. She looked around, then dropped the razor. Finally, managing to fix her gaze on Hector with palpable disdain, she sneered at him.

"Arrogant until the end, huh?" he said.

She stumbled a bit, then swayed. "I'll see you in hell," she said.

Hector stared at her for a second, then said, "I really hope not."

Then she collapsed and her body vaporized.

Chapter Thirty-Three

AS PROMISED, Juan had done his job and watched everything that had gone down through his binoculars.

Well. Not everything.

"What the hell happened?" he asked Parker as he arrived in a caravan of four pickup trucks. Instantly, men in civilian clothes began swarming the property. "Why did they start trying to shoot the trucks and why were they shooting blanks?"

Parker chuckled. Juan hadn't seen The Gray Angel either. Only he had, and maybe Melon. Parker only had a brief moment alone with Melon when they first came out of the house, and he'd asked him, point blank, but Melon had blown him off with a shrug. Like maybe it was something they'd talk about another day. Or maybe never. Melon had never been religious and there was no reason to think he'd suddenly seen the light . . . even if he had.

The poor women held captive in the delivery truck were given bottled water and told that there was no time to waste, that they had to get everyone out of there as quickly as possible, and that meant one more ride in the back of the dark truck. But they were assured that they were safely in the hands of the authorities now, and that they'd each eventually be taken to their respective embassies and reunited with their families soon. The old hags and the other injured prisoners were treated, then zip-tied and piled into the back of one pickup truck, all the dead into the back of two others. The lone goat in the house was loaded back into the other delivery truck, which also had a cow, sheep and pigs in it. Parker shook his head. It was lunacy.

From there, the house, barn and all the cars were set on fire. It was a classic CIA cleanse job.

Both delivery trucks were then driven off by two of the men who'd come with Juan and the other pickups followed. No one tried to take Güero. They knew better.

Parker, Melon, Maggie and Luisa were in the bed of the final pickup now, having split off from the main group just after leaving the property. They were making a beeline for the border, with Juan behind the wheel and Güero stuffed in the extra cab behind the seats. During the five-hour drive, an escort car in front and behind them, they ate granola bars, drank water and made small talk.

Luisa's head was in Maggie's lap and she was sound asleep. One of the men who'd piled out of the trucks during the clean-up identified himself as a doctor. After checking Luisa's vitals and determining that she was in no imminent danger, he agreed to radio ahead to make sure she would get further medical attention and more tests as soon as they got to the border.

Now, at last, the US border in sight beneath the setting sun, they all seemed to relax. The small talk turned into thanks and congratulations. Then Melon had to open his mouth.

"Man. Don't you two make for a handsome couple?" he teased, looking over at Parker and Maggie.

An awkward silence followed as Maggie and Parker looked at each other, then laughed it off. Parker had, indeed, given Ms. Kincaid a good once over. She was beautiful, with coffee colored eyes that kind of made him nervous, but truth be told, it was the confidence with which she'd snapped that stick in half, back at that house, while actually looking for a fight that had made him take notice of her even more. But noticing was one thing, and well, Trudy was his everything.

"Nah," Parker said, making an ugly face.

Maggie raised her eyebrows in mock defensiveness. "Um. Excuse me?"

"I mean. You're beautiful and all, for a blond. But there's a redhead in Napa right now that owns my heart and always will," Parker said.

"Wow! There it is!" Melon chimed in. Then, waving his hand in front of him like an actor in a play, he said with dramatic flair, "Cupid's arrow doth strike both deep and true!"

Maggie squinted at Parker, looking a tad incredulous but not angry. "Well, Mr. Parker. You're not half bad yourself. But answer me one question, just for kicks."

"What's that?"

"What's your favorite book?"

Looking surprised by the question, Parker mulled it over for a moment, then replied, "Hmm. Ya know . . . I don't really read much."

Maggie smirked. "I figured as much. Never would've worked out anyway, then."

"Ohhhhhhh, daaamn. Snap!" Luisa said from out of nowhere, a big smile on her face, obviously not asleep anymore.

Melon roared with laughter, and Parker did too. Maggie joined them, and as she did, Parker noticed her look at Luisa before she let out a long sigh of relief.

———

WHEN THEY FINALLY CROSSED THE border, a posse of black Lincolns awaited along with US Border Control trucks and a few ambulances. Standing in front of one of the Lincolns, with her arms crossed, was a blond woman with cropped hair that Maggie had never seen before. The woman waited until everyone was unloaded before she walked over and spoke to Parker. "Where is he?" she said, with no other greeting.

Parker motioned his head to Melon, who roughly unpacked a bitching and moaning Güero from inside the extra cab.

"What the hell is this? I want my lawyer!" Güero spat.

"I'm sure you do," the woman said. "But I'd like to introduce myself first. I'm FBI Agent Olivia Clopton."

Güero wrinkled his face with disgust. "I don't give a shit who you—"

Clopton stepped forwards, closing the gap between them swiftly, and drove her knee directly into his groin. "Oops," she said. "I'm sorry, Mr. Martinez."

Collapsing to his knees, Güero began to curse. "You *puta*! No food. No water. Now police brutality. Keep adding it up, you dumb bitch! I'll be out of jail in no time."

Luisa clutched Maggie's hand in fear. Maggie squeezed her hand back but also shook her head to tell Luisa it was okay.

There was something about Agent Clopton, a cold sort of focus. Slowly, she crouched down in front of Güero and used her index finger to lift his chin as he gasped a little for air. "You want to add things up, Mr. Martinez? Why don't we do that? Right now, I have eleven women ready to testify against you. Two that will testify that you were there when they were boxed up like animals to be shipped across state lines, four that have run your little sex warehouses for the last three years, four more that you've raped, and one—" Her voice cracked ever so slightly. "One who lived a special kind of nightmare thanks to you. Do you wanna know why?"

Güero shook his head.

"Of course, you don't, you cowardly piece of shit. So, while you massage your balls down there, I'm gonna tell you anyway." She did. And as Maggie listened to the story of a young girl, kept in the dark, forced to count the number of hands on her to have any chance of knowing how many men were raping her at the same time, she shook her head. When Clopton was done, she sneered at Güero. "You made a big mistake with her, though, tough guy. Wanna know why? Her real name? It's Alejandra. And guess what? She's a US citizen."

Güero squinted at her in surprise.

"You grabbed her from Ecuador, from a little town where they eat taper and make bright clay pottery. She told me that, while giving me her statements. Multiple statements, actually. She was in that town, but she was *born* in the US. Her family moved here but then got freaked out by the American dream and moved right back. How's that for a twist? But a citizen is a citizen here, for life, unless they change their citizenship. Alejandra never did. So . . . what do you think the grand jury felt when they heard her testimony?"

It was twilight, and everything was still. They were in a dirt parking lot, away from the border crossing, the sound of all the cars and semitrucks from the nearby highway still loud enough to create a steady roar. Parker shifted his weight from one boot to the next as Melon leaned against the front of the pickup truck with Juan. Three other men, Maggie assumed they were FBI agents, stood nearby with a half dozen Border Patrol agents.

Güero shot his head up in defiance. "You can't prove shit—"

"Your men in the Long Beach port are flipping. The San Pedro men are gonna get word of that and start singing, too. We've got agents in San Francisco right now raiding two of your sex warehouses there, and funny thing is, the more we find? I think that eleven women is gonna turn to twenty, then fifty. Man, we might even crack a hundred. And then there's Luisa and Maggie here and how they'll testify to being kidnapped and brutalized. A pregnant kid and her social worker? Oh. Man. You are so done."

"You had no right to come across the border. My lawyer will eat you—"

"Your friends in Mexico don't want anything to do with you anymore. Strings are being pulled. Papers are being signed. As soon as we had you, for sure, it was over."

Güero looked around at them all and then dropped his eyes slowly to the ground.

"Ahhhh," Clopton said. "You see that, everyone? *That* is the look of defeat."

She stood and gave a quick nod at the men around her. They all immediately picked Güero up and whisked him off to one of the cars.

Clopton looked at Maggie. "You're Maggie Kincaid, I take it?"

Maggie nodded and cleared her throat. "I am."

"Hell of a job you did over there. Beyond commendable."

"Thank you," Maggie said.

Turning to look at Parker, Clopton said, "We'll talk more later, but you didn't do half bad yourself."

Parker smiled and shook his head. "Aw, shucks . . . I have my moments, I guess. And I couldn't have done it without my trusty sidekick here."

"Hey, man. Don't be starting with no sidekick bullshit," Melon said.

They all laughed.

Clopton looked at Parker. "Regardless? I'll give you this much," she said, a tiny smirk coming over her face. "You're fun to color with, Parker."

She walked to one of the Lincolns and got in. It drove away with the rest of the vehicles.

The ambulance technicians walked over.

"We should get Luisa to the hospital and checked out now," Maggie said to Parker.

He nodded. "Fair enough. Juan here is going to drive us into San Diego. I guess this is goodbye. But you work at Eden Hill Shelter, right?"

"Yeah," she said.

"I used to work right down the street at Hollenbeck Station. I know a lot of guys there who run into a lot of women who could use your help. I'll make sure they send them your way if they already aren't."

"That'd be great," Maggie said with a nod. Then she went with Luisa to the ambulance and they both hopped in.

She asked one of the EMTs, a black woman with a round, gentle face, if she could borrow her cell phone. Luisa wanted to call her mom, and Maggie desperately wanted to call Julie.

As the ambulance drove away, Maggie looked out the back window. The man named Parker and the man named Melon were hugging each other while Juan was motioning for them to get in the truck.

Chapter Thirty-Four

HECTOR HAD JUST FREED Curtis from the table when his friend gasped at something behind him. Hector knew who it was before he even turned around: The Gray Man.

Curtis had evidently reached his limit. Who could blame him, really? Falling to his knees in awe, he only managed one word. "What . . .?"

Hector was about to try and answer him when The Gray Man shook his head and looked at Curtis. "You will not remember any of this," he said sternly, "save one thing. Are you listening?"

His eyes wide and his jaw slack, Curtis nodded.

"He," The Gray Man said, pointing at Hector, "helped to save you today, but not only in the way you think. Right now, at this very minute, a million other people who have committed the sin of murder are getting a chance to repent. Do you understand?"

Curtis' face melted as his eyes glistened. Again, he nodded.

The Gray Man disagreed. "I'm not sure you do. So let me be clear. You, Curtis Ruvelcaba, are one of those million people he has given that chance to."

Hector had never, ever seen Curtis get emotional, but he

began to cry uncontrollably. Something must've happened to him. On the inside. Deep down.

"Now you understand." The Gray Man looked at all the chaos around them, stood firmly and moved his right hand in a semicircle, fingers splayed, from right to left, right to left, right to left. Reality stuttered and shuttered. Now it was Hector's turn to be slack-jawed.

Time was reversing. One jerky half-twist at a time, like ungreased gears, slowly, to the moment before the appearance of The Black-Veiled Nurse. Suddenly, Hector found himself trapped back in his cell.

Then, time resumed.

Outside, the other inmates were squawking and shouting normally as they formed into their chow lines for the cafeteria.

"So, what now?" Hector asked.

The Gray Man's image held as he looked at him. "Now, it's time for you to make a decision."

"A decision?"

"Yes. To go or to stay."

"You mean . . ."

"Here or the next life, yes, Hector."

Hector stared solemnly out of his cell at the stark prison life outside. Then, looking around his little cell, his eyes fell on his copy of *West with the Night*. He realized that he really would've liked to have finished that book.

"I dunno why, but this decision is harder than I thought it would be," he finally said.

"Why is that, do you think?"

"I dunno. There's still . . ."

"Still, what?"

After a second or two, Hector looked at him. "I'm not sure I'm done here. Does that make any sense?"

The Gray Man took a deep breath. "What do you mean? In what way?"

"Hey . . ." Hector said with a smile. "You're still trying to train me, aren't you?"

"No, not really." The Gray Man smiled back. "This decision is yours and yours alone, son. I'm just curious."

"Uh-huh. Okay. If you say so. But if I'm honest, something's holding me back."

The Gray Man crossed his arms and leaned casually against the bars. "And what do you think that is?"

Hector mulled the question over for a few moments. "When all the chaos and misery was breaking out in the cell block earlier? I looked around at everyone . . . and in the middle of all that madness? Man. I could see, Gray, like, really see. Past all the fake faces and macho attitudes. I saw a bunch of men, in pain, facing death and . . . I think I saw *into* them, too, ya know?"

"How so?" The Gray Man asked encouragingly.

"I think I saw who they were and what they are . . . yeah . . . but also how they got here. So much hurt and regret, for so many different reasons, eating them all up on the inside. So much resentment and pride, keeping them from healing or asking for help. And maybe I'm crazy, but I actually think I can help them. Probably not all of them. But some."

"The light shines brightest in the darkest places, Hector."

"I know that now. It's scary, but I know it. And, well, there's something else . . ."

"What's that?" The Gray Man asked. But the tone of his voice was like that of a math teacher who already knew where his pupil was headed in the equation.

"That image of Marisol that I saw, in the wheelchair? Was that real?"

The Gray Man nodded. "I'm afraid it was."

Sadness crushed his heart. Hector leaned his forehead against the bars. "I want to write to her. To say I'm sorry," he said. "She might throw the letter in the trash, and I wouldn't blame her. But I've gotta try, man, to make what I did right. Or at least to make it not so horribly wrong as it is now."

Hector was stunned to see The Gray Man look away suddenly, his lower lip trembling. Was he crying? Was that even possible?

"The thing is," Hector pushed on, now getting emotional himself, "I can't believe I did what I did, Gray. I just can't. And I can never forgive myself."

"You may, someday."

"If *she* forgives me? Maybe. Maybe then, right? And she may never. But I've got to *try*, right?"

Again, The Gray Man nodded.

"I'm sorry," Hector added, not really knowing why.

"Do not be sorry," The Gray Man replied in a soft voice. Looking at Hector intently, he sighed. "Incredible."

"What?"

"Now, I know why you are my final one, Hector. You, a hopeless, hapless murderer, are showing the true depth of humanity. The hidden, perhaps sometimes even denied, truth that each one of you can be a "one," of sorts. Because each one of you has sinned and yet each one of you still has the ability to help each other. And that's what you can do here with the other inmates. But there's also that question of . . ." The Gray Man's voice caught in his throat, before he finished. "Love."

"Yeah. Exactly," Hector said as his eyes filled with tears. "I love her so much, bro. I love her so much that I can't let go yet. Do you understand that? Can you possibly understand that?"

The Gray Man reached out and put a hand on Hector's shoulder. "Oh, yes," he said, solemnly. "I do. More than you could ever imagine."

Then, he gave Hector a hug, which was warm, like the distant heat from a thousand stars. "I have to go now, Hector."

"You do?"

"Yes. I'm out of time. And there's someone I've been waiting a long time to see. But before I go, I want you to have something."

Hector looked up as The Gray Man gently took both of his

hands in his own and held them firm. "You have time, Hector, for redemption. You will need help, some good reading, if you will. I'll even send you my favorite book. But in the meantime? You have chosen to stay in a place where many others need redemption as well. There will be good days here and bad days. And as for Marisol?"

"Y-y-yeah," Hector sobbed gently.

"You are correct. The gap between the two of you may be too wide to ever bridge, son. Sometimes it's simply never meant to be. Sometimes the divide we are meant to bridge is only within ourselves, and many times, when we cannot count on the forgiveness of those we have wronged? We must learn to accept what it means to truly forgive ourselves and let go. It's okay, Hector, to love . . . and to endure the pain of having a broken heart. Because good can still come of it, one day. It can. And do you want to know why?"

"Why?"

"Because, Hector . . ." The Gray Man paused, then put something in Hector's hands. "A broken heart is an open heart."

Then, he disappeared.

Blinking away the tears in his eyes, Hector looked down. Cradled in his fingers was a small yellow and orange flower. He recognized it immediately because a talented tagger in the heart of Boyle Heights had one year spray-painted dozens of them on freeway overpasses, large and bright, loud and colorful.

It was a marigold.

Epilogue

A WEEK LATER, Parker's cell phone rang. It was Maggie Kincaid, telling him that she'd had a dream of Father Soltera. In the dream he was with an elderly couple, standing in a meadow. The man with him was wearing a gray suit and had his arm around the waist of a woman who was holding, of all things, a *Peanuts* thermos.

After speaking to the man for a bit, Father Soltera nodded, then walked to where Maggie was standing, next to a tree at the edge of the meadow, her bare feet being tickled by the grass. He asked her to have Parker do something for him that was very important. Never mind that Parker had never paid much attention to dreams before, or that the request was unexpected. There was a time when Parker would've taken a call like this and either asked Maggie if she was off her meds or drunk, but that time was long gone.

As a detective he was also trained to hear the most important words in any person's statement. And in this case, he only needed to hear two.

Gray. Suit.

So, he dutifully took notes with a pen and paper, then canceled his plans to go to the gym and instead drove to St.

Francis Church in East Los Angeles, where he spoke briefly with a nice woman in the church office named Carol, telling her Maggie's message while leaving out the part about it being told to her in a dream . . . and by an angel, no less. It didn't matter. Strangely, Carol did not ask for any specifics.

"That sounds just like something he would want," she said, tearing up as she found the key to Father Soltera's office and led Parker there.

Once inside, he saw the home of a modest, well-read man. A loaf of bread was still on the counter in the kitchenette and a row of pill bottles were lined up on top of the microwave. "I haven't had the strength to clean up in here yet," Carol said, her voice drenched in sadness. Parker simply nodded. Jesus watched them from a large cross on the wall near the bookcase as they searched around until they found what Parker had come for. And then he left.

The two-hour drive to Corcoran State Prison went by in a daydreamy sort of haze. His Spotify playlist worked its way from song to song with each passing mile, and he was relieved that the task before him had taken his mind off something that had been the center of his thoughts since he'd gotten back from Mexico. A decision. A big one. Maybe the ultimate one.

It had finally stopped raining in Los Angeles. He'd left behind a city under sunshine, with temps in the mid-eighties. As he made his way through the central part of the state, though, the skies became hazy again. He'd never been to Corcoran State Prison before but there was no missing its ominous, lonely presence in the distance when he took Exit 14. A solitary road led to the entrance gates and a guard who checked his ID and let him in. After he parked, he grabbed the paper bag on the seat next to him that Carol had given him, feeling its contents within, and wondered how this was all going to go over. But, feeling Napoleon's approving presence nearby, he pressed on. Regardless, it felt like a good thing, what he was doing.

Once inside, it took thirty minutes for him to be vetted and searched by the guards, the contents of the bag checked and double-checked.

Finally, after another thirty minutes, Hector Villarosa was led into the room.

Their eyes met the way two acquaintances from opposite sides of the law often do: hard and suspicious at first. Parker was almost positive that Hector was remembering him in the driveway of that chop shop in the old neighborhood at the same time he was. Having been the only other time they'd met in person and having been a moment of shared passive aggressiveness, this moment now seemed awkward at best.

Hector lifted his chin at Parker. "What up?"

"I hope that's not sarcasm I hear," the guard who led him in, a large man with a black goatee, said. "We had to jump through hoops to get this visit done. Same-day, unannounced visits? They aren't a thing. But this guy's old station house threw enough weight his way to make it happen."

"Oh?" Parker said, looking at the guard.

"Yeah. We called there to check on you. Detectives Klink, Murillo and Campos, and your captain? They all vouched for you, though they had no idea why the hell you were here."

"It's good to have homies," Hector scoffed as he sat down on a metal deck chair at the small metal table opposite Parker.

"Yeah," Parker replied with a smile, thinking of the comic look of exasperation Klink could get when something caught him off guard, and Murillo's big smile. Hearing Campos' name was a surprise, though. *Back already? He must be on desk duty.* Campos and his Muttley-the-dog laugh. Cool. And the cap? The cap was the cap.

The guard gave Parker a serious look. "You got fifteen minutes, understand?"

Parker nodded, and the guard left.

"Well?" Hector said, almost defiantly. His prison garb made him look different than he did that day on Winston Street. Parker noticed he had a lot more tattoos than he remembered.

Hector looked around nervously, then leaned in and whispered, "Did you get his ass?"

"Yeah," Parker replied in his own whisper. "Güero is done for."

Hector's mouth curved downward and his eye brows shot up. "Daaaamnnnn."

Without missing a beat, Parker said, "He's with the Feds now."

"How . . . No. I don't wanna know. Just glad it worked out."

"Is that relief I hear in your voice?" Parker asked.

"Yeah. He was putting a lot of heat on me in here . . . and threatening people I still care about. Funny, though."

"What's that?"

"The Gray Man? He's gone now, by the way. But he told me before he left that things would work out."

"And?"

"I didn't believe him. Now I do."

Parker laughed, eying the bag next to him. "Yeah. Funny how that works."

"You said you've seen him, too?"

"The Gray Man? Yeah. A few times. Including down in Mexico."

Hector made no reply. Instead, he just cleared his throat, as if he were waiting for Parker to continue.

"So," Parker said, "what I'm about to share with you, I expect that you'll get. What you've seen, what I've seen, what we talked about on the phone and—"

"Yeah, yeah, man. I get it."

"Anyway, our gray friend? He put in a request, with a friend of a friend, to have something brought to you," Parker said, sliding the bag across the counter.

"What's this?" Hector said, surprise in his voice.

"Open it."

Hector opened the paper bag and tilted it sideways. Out of it slid an old blue Bible. "What . . .?"

"It used to belong to a priest who worked at St. Francis Church in your neighborhood. You ever go there?"

Hector scoffed. "I look like the kinda guy who ever went to church, man?"

"Yeah, well . . ." Parker sighed deeply. "The Gray Man wanted something told to you, too."

"What's that?"

"That this is his favorite book."

"Hmm. Okay. Great. But how's it gonna help me in here?"

"I dunno," Parker said with a shrug. "I'm guessing the answers are in the book."

Hector furrowed his brow. "You mean, you haven't read it either?"

"Me?" Parker said, shaking his head. "Nah."

Parker watched Hector open the Bible and flip through it. The way his hands cradled around the spine and his eyes combed over the words with a glint of eagerness revealed that Hector was no stranger to books. "Man," he whispered, "did you look in this?"

Parker shook his head.

"There are notes everywhere by this guy," Hector continued. "At the bottom of the pages . . . between the lines . . . in the margins. Where's this priest at? I mean, why didn't he bring it himself?"

"He's dead."

Hector looked at Parker with surprise. "Dead?"

"Yep. One of Güero's bodyguards got to him."

A mutual moment of silence passed between them as Hector obviously tried to process that he was holding a dead man's Bible sent by an angel. Parker was still pretty scared of The Gray Man, so truth be told, he was happy this little gift had been sent Hector's way instead of his.

Then, Hector suddenly looked at him funny. He blinked rapidly a few times, as if a memory had just washed over him. "You will need him, in the long run," he murmured.

331

"What?" Parker said, stunned.

"Nothing," Hector said softly. "Just something The Gray Man told me once." Leaning forwards, he looked at Parker seriously. "Fine. I'll read that book if you do."

Parker scoffed. "What?"

"Yeah. Who's to say it can't help you, too?" He shrugged. "And besides . . . it'll give us something to talk about when you come visit."

Parker was bemused. "Visit?"

"Yeah, man," Hector mumbled, "I got nothin' now. No gang. And after Hymie? No family. The Gray Man's gone. I mean, who else gonna visit me in here?"

Maybe it was the way he said it, the words desperate, the eyes sad, the face vacant. But somehow, someway, this hardened criminal reminded Parker yet again, for the briefest second, of Waheeb, crying for help in the desert, just before he was dragged away. It was as if, surely, Hector Villarosa was at risk of being dragged away now, too. By fate. By the darkness of this place. By the other side. If he was left all alone.

And Parker couldn't have that. "Deal," he said firmly, watching as Hector's face lit with surprise, then relief, before his emotions were quickly disguised by a stiff macho chin and confident nod.

"S'cool," Hector said.

"S'cool," Parker parroted.

Then Parker got up and left.

He was just out of the prison doors and headed down the steps to the parking lot when he saw Napoleon waiting for him. "Good job, rookie."

"Thanks."

"You heading home now to that girl of yours?" Napoleon teased gently.

Parker nodded. "Yep. She's still mad at me for what I did, but she loves me."

"God and his miracles," Napoleon said with a smile.

"And she's got me started on EMDR therapy, twice a week. And a PTSD group on Saturdays at the VA. So, I had to make those little concessions, too."

"So?"

"So . . . what?"

"What next?" Napoleon said as they began walking to Parker's car together.

A decision. A big one. Maybe the ultimate one. Parker thought a bit before he answered. "I'm gonna ask her to marry me, that's what."

Napoleon nodded. "Smart move."

"Yeah. Sure. If she doesn't laugh in my face."

"And after that?" Napoleon asked.

"Maybe a nice little honeymoon in Greece or something."

"Yeah. Well. My money's still on her laughing in your face, so don't get too far ahead of yourself, champ."

"Nice. That's real nice. Thanks for that. Way to boost my confidence."

"As if that was something that ever needed boosting. And I'm just kidding. Greece sounds nice. And what else are you thinking about?"

Parker sighed. "Going back to the station house, I guess. Maybe talk to the cap and try and get my badge back."

Napoleon smiled. "Smart move number two."

"Yeah?"

"You can never get past anything by running from it, Parker. I'm sure you know that by now."

"Yep. It's just . . ."

"Yeah, yeah. I know. The administrative hassle of administering to the administration and all that. Don't let the bastards grind you down, Parker. Remember that."

They walked on, before Parker finally worked up the courage to ask his own question. The one that had been fumbling around in his mind for a while now. Holding his breath, he said, "What about you? What's next for you?"

"Me? Oh. I plan on sticking around. Maybe helping you out with a few more cases."

Parker exhaled with relief and grinned. "Really?"

"Yeah. East LA is my little sector of the universe now. At least for a while. And, well, you're in homicide, Parker. And where you find murder? You'll always find evil."

They were quiet together as the sun began to set in the distance. Napoleon added, "It should be fun, rookie."

"Yeah," Parker said, "for sure. But . . . are you ever going to stop calling me rookie?"

"Nope."

They laughed as they got in the car and drove back to Los Angeles together.

The sky over them was all gray.

But not the least bit gloomy.

Also by Tony Faggioli

One In A Million (Book 1 of "The Fasano Trilogy")

A Million to One (Book 2 of "The Fasano Trilogy")

One Plus One (Book 3 of "The Fasano Trilogy")

The Snow Globe

Another One (Book 1 of The Parker Series)

One Way or Another (Book 2 of The Parker Series)

One Gray Day (Book 3 of The Parker Series)

———

VISIT HIS WEBSITE TO SIGN UP

FOR HIS NEWSLETTER AT:

https://tonyfaggioli.com

And be the first to know about new releases and special events!